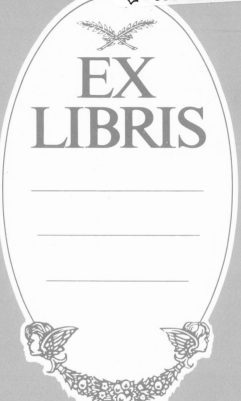

EX
LIBRIS

Romance
Treasury

THE ROMANCE TREASURY ASSOCIATION

NEW YORK · TORONTO · LONDON

These stories were originally published as follows:

IT BEGAN IN TE RANGI
Copyright © 1971 by Gloria Bevan
First published by Mills & Boon Limited in 1971

THE GENTLE FLAME
Copyright © 1971 by Katrina Britt
First published by Mills & Boon Limited in 1971

TO MY DEAR NIECE
Copyright © 1970 by Hilda Nickson
First published by Mills & Boon Limited in 1970

ROMANCE TREASURY is published by:
The Romance Treasury Association, Stratford, Ontario, Canada

Editorial Board: A. W. Boon, Judith Burgess, Ruth Palmour and
Janet Humphreys
Dust Jacket Art by: Muriel Hughes
Story Illustrations by: Muriel Hughes
Book Design by: Charles Kadin
Printed by: Kingsport Press Limited, Kingsport, Tennessee

ISBN 0-919860-20-6

Printed in U.S.A.   AO21

CONTENTS

IT BEGAN IN TE RANGI

IT BEGAN
IN TE RANGI

Gloria Bevan

"Mature person urgently needed to keep house for sheep farmer. Fond of children. Temporary," the advertisement said. Just what Maggie Sullivan needed to take her away from a disappointing love affair.

But she hadn't counted on John Dangerfield's refusal to hire her – simply because she wasn't middle-aged.

Then, as one domestic crisis after another occurred, Maggie found herself taking charge of the household. There really was no one else and the children adored her.

John Dangerfield was too involved with his farm and his neighbor, Ann, to appreciate Maggie's efforts – but you'd think he'd at least notice. Sadly, Maggie made preparations to run away a second time!

Dedication:
To my good friends Phyl and Alf Bush
and all their neighbors

CHAPTER ONE

Maggie glanced up from her table in the New Zealand back-country hotel. As she met the searching look of the tall man standing motionless in the doorway, she felt that disturbing sense of awareness. It was like coming alive again, after all this time! The next moment she told herself that she must be overtired from the long day's driving, to entertain such crazy thoughts.

She realized that the stranger's long strides were bringing him swiftly in the direction of her table. In a flutter of confusion she stubbed out her cigarette and picked up her coffee cup. If he imagined that merely because she chanced to be seated here alone, a solitary diner in the emptiness of the shadowy room—if he thought for one moment that her involuntary surprised glance could be taken as an invitation to seek her out—

"Pardon me." He paused at her side. She looked up, up, into strong, compelling features. A well-shaped mouth, a deep indentation in the firmly molded chin, eyes startlingly blue in a tanned face; the chilliest blue eyes she had ever encountered, dark hair and sideburns. Handsome as they come, she thought swiftly, with a cool stare that was deliberately impersonal. What then did he want of her?

A sudden grin transformed the bronzed features. It made him look, Maggie thought, all at once more human, less stern and forbidding.

"Strangers are pretty rare around these parts," he was saying in a deep, vibrant voice. "I guess you're the owner of the blue van out there in the yard?" He jerked a dark head toward the open door.

"Yes, I am, but—" An expression of alarm leaped into Maggie's wide dark eyes. "It's not—" The panicky thought tumbled through her mind. What if the van were damaged, out of order? Elderly and battered though it was, the van was her only means of transport. She just had to reach Te Rangi tonight. Why, if she didn't make an appearance within the next hour or so the Barrington woman with whom she had arranged the interview would conclude that Maggie wasn't coming. Someone else would obtain the housekeeping position. She had told Mrs. Barrington that she would be arriving late in the day, there was still time, barring accidents.

"Not to worry." The stranger's deep tones were soothing to Maggie's taut nerves. "Just that it's a bit in the way where it is. Wouldn't have troubled you except that I happen to have an appointment tonight back at the homestead—must zip away fairly soon." He straddled the chair opposite. Meeting that direct gaze, once again Maggie was aware of that odd lurch of the heart. "Give me the keys," he was saying, "and I'll shift her for you—run her out onto the main road. That way you'll be able to finish your coffee."

"It's all right, I don't want any more." Feeling suddenly flustered, Maggie gathered up her cigarettes, swung her suede purse over one shoulder and stood up.

"Sure?" He rose, towering above her. "I didn't want to barge in on you." Maggie detected an expression of genuine concern in his eyes. So he could be thoughtful, this stranger, as well as aloof. For some reason, though, he made her feel confused and uncertain. She had been so sure that these days nothing could shake her composure, yet now. . . .

They threaded their way together between the scattered circular tables covered with snowy damask cloths and set with gleaming silverware. At the counter a smiling young waitress took the money that Maggie handed to her. The girl nodded toward the tall man as though she knew him. "Good night!"

Then they moved out into the dusk and silence of the countryside lined with scattered farmhouses and small timber stores. Somber bush-covered hills were sharply outlined against the lemon afterglow of a spectacular sunset that shaded upward to merge into the clear washed blue above.

But Maggie was conscious only of the old van parked at an angle across the narrow metal driveway; an obstruction to any driver wishing to leave the parking area before herself. How could she have been so careless as to leave the van in such a position? Fortunately only one vehicle, a dust-coated Land Rover, was trapped by her thoughtlessness. And guess who that belonged to!

Her heart sank as she glanced around the trucks and cars now closely clustered behind her own vehicle. No doubt the drivers were at this moment enjoying themselves in the bar and would remain there for some time. It would be no easy matter to maneuver the old van out of the maze and onto the main road. Nevertheless she'd have to manage it, somehow.

The tall loose-limbed man at her side must have read her thoughts. "The keys?" His tones were soft yet peremptory as he extended a lean, tanned hand. "I'll move her out for you."

But some crazy urge of contrariness, something about him that affected her in the oddest way, made Maggie say quickly, defensively, "It's okay, I can do it!"

He was silent, but she was acutely conscious of his quizzical expression. She'd show him that she could turn the old van with as much expertise as anyone else. Heaven knows she'd had plenty of practice, and in trickier situations than this. Why, at some of the country horse shows and gymkhanas she'd attended, she had been forced to thread her way between horse floats and transporters to find a parking space for the van on steep and muddy hillsides. This was nothing.

But today something had happened to cloud her judgment. Put it down to the amused glint in the eyes of the watching stranger. Or nerves, from the long day's trip over unfamiliar roads. She swung the steering wheel too far, and only after considerable effort, succeeded in getting the van back to its original position. Then she tried again. This attempt to drive clear of old Studebakers and Chevrolets with dust-caked wheels finished in a wild swoop that barely avoided a collision with a gleaming late-model Ford, standing directly behind her.

Tense and nervous, her frenzied efforts to escape from the narrow confined space merely took her farther and farther from her goal. Confusion and self-consciousness merged into a helpless feeling of desperation. Now she was making frantic efforts to right the van before attempting a fresh effort to back around the cars in the rear. Bang! Crash! She knew only too well what the ominous thuds signified. She scarcely dared glance over her shoulder. When she did it was just as she had feared. Of course it was *his* Land Rover that she had struck. Angrily she reflected that even so, it would be her lighter vehicle that would have sustained the most damage. It was all his fault. If only he wouldn't stand there watching, waiting for her to make a mess of things. Why couldn't he *do* something? she thought distractedly, forgetting in her agitation that she had already refused his offer of assistance.

Climbing down from the van, she walked to the rear of her vehicle. *Oh no!* There was a deep dent in the van, and what was even worse, the collision had locked the bumper in the heavy front bar of the Land Rover. That she knew would be no easy matter to put right. At least, it wouldn't be easy for her.

"It's not too bad," the stranger bent to survey the damage. "Looks as though you got the worst of it, I'm afraid." He was eyeing the locked bumper bars, then he turned to face her. "Shall I—?"

She could have wept with anger and frustration. She turned her face aside, hoping that he hadn't noticed the hot color that was suffusing her cheeks or the dampness at her temples. "I'll wait here," she said in a muffled tone.

It appeared so simple a matter when he performed it, she reflected wryly, watching him disentangle the locked vehicles without apparent effort. A heave, a determined pull from those muscular arms and the job was done. Then he climbed up into the van and, in a few expert turns, had guided it clear of the vehicles parked haphazardly around it. Leaving the van on the road, he strolled back toward Maggie.

"Thanks." She tried to achieve a careless laugh. "It looked so simple to get out of that jam, until I had a go at it. I'll have to be careful in future," she said lightly, "not to tangle with any more Land Rovers." *Or their owners,* she vowed silently. "Well," she reached a hand toward the ignition, "I'll be on my way. I hope," she added with forced politeness, "that I haven't made you late for your appointment?"

He leaned an elbow on the window ledge and grinned engagingly across at her. "Maybe she'll wait—if I'm lucky!"

Maggie brushed the clinging tendrils of dark hair back from her forehead, then put the van into gear. She? Absurd to feel this odd little pang. As though it could possibly matter to her who he had an appointment with!

"Take care." He stood watching as she pulled away and followed the dusty shadowed roadway that cut through the small township. A few moments later an upward glance in the dust-smeared overhead mirror confirmed her suspicion; he was still standing motionless, watching her progress. No doubt, she reflected crossly, he was expecting at any moment to be called on once again to aid a clueless woman driver. Then she turned a bend in the road, and the watching figure was lost to sight.

Odd how he had moved her, first to awareness, then to interest and finally to a state of nervous tension where she had lost all her customary confidence and skill in driving. Maddening creature that he was. And yet there was something about him. It had been a long time since any man stirred her so. Two years, to be exact. She'd been so certain that she was finished for ever with all such foolishness.

Two years since the night when Colin, her fiancé (correction again: *had been* her fiancé), and Andrea, her best friend (correction again: *had been* her friend), had sought her out for the purpose of letting her know something that she should have guessed weeks earlier. Anyone but a complete idiot like herself would have realized from the beginning what was happening; would have correctly interpreted the warning signals that were so painfully obvious, afterward. For instance, there was Colin's sudden lack of interest in his and Maggie's approaching wedding; Andrea's odd silence whenever Maggie talked of her future with Colin. There were other pointers too, noted subconsciously in a corner of her mind but brushed aside as unimportant at the time. Like Andrea's state of wild excitement whenever Colin came to dine with the two girls in their small city apartment. And yet he had seemed happy enough with their engagement, until he met Andrea, and then. . . . As always at this point Maggie's clear objective thinking broke down. The old pain, the sense of hurt and humiliation, took over.

She had a sudden mental picture of Colin's florid, good-natured face. He had always been joking, laughing loudly. Now she wondered whether the jokes had served as a shield to hide his inner unease whenever he was with the two girls at the apartment.

Andrea, the Australian girl who had come to New Zealand on a working holiday. Dark, intense, and quite beautiful; keeping things to herself, things she should have confided to Maggie at the beginning, instead of letting her go on thinking, believing, planning, wearing on her finger the diamond solitaire that was in reality one big, glittering lie.

Once the position was made clear, events had followed swiftly. Unbeknown to her, Colin had been successful in gaining a position with a law firm in Australia. Within three weeks, he and Andrea were flying to Sydney. They planned to be married in Andrea's home town a few miles distant. Maggie didn't know how she could have borne it had the other two not left.

The winding road glimmered palely, a curl of ribbon lost amongst the dark mass of hills ahead. Long lines of softly waving toe-toes lined the shadowy highway; tall sentinels with feathery plumes, ghostly in the gathering blue dusk. Maggie switched on the headlights, her gaze fixed on the arc of light playing over the rough metal of the roadway, her thoughts far away.

No more engagement rings for her—ever. She had learned her lesson, had her fill of pain and misery. No sense in risking all that over again. Most difficult of all to bear had been the despairing feeling of being unwanted, thrust aside; the bruising blow to her self-esteem. Oh, she'd recovered, of course, managed to organize her life so that her time was fully taken up with other things. You could make yourself forget if you kept sufficiently active. Weekdays were taken care of by nine-to-five secretarial work in a law office. Early mornings, after-work hours and weekends were fully occupied with the care and training of Pete, her big bay gelding. What if grazing fees, feed bills, veterinary fees and show entry costs, not to mention the upkeep of the old van, made any savings from her generous pay almost impossible? Pete was worth every cent she spent on him. In a way, he was her link with home: a vast sheep station on the East Coast where she had grown up, the youngest child in a family of boys. Pete had been a brumbie brought down from the rugged Gisborne hill country and almost at once had shown promise of being an outstanding hunter. A great ungainly bay with powerful muscles, a coarse brown mane and a great heart, Maggie had loved him from the start. In the period she had spent in the city, her collection of show ribbons and silver trophies testified that Pete, despite increasing years, had lost nothing of his qualities of strength and endurance. He was still well known in equestrian circles as a brilliant jumper.

Nowadays the family was scattered, with the property long since sold. Her parents retired to town life in Gisborne. Anyway, you could look after yourself at 20. Or could you?

She could of course have enjoyed quite a different type of life, for there was never any shortage of alert, up-and-coming young businessmen eager to escort the small dark girl with the huge brown eyes and a trick of *really* listening. Maggie liked them well enough too, for a time.

She had managed to cope fairly well with her life, or so she had imagined, until the day when her employer had unwittingly shocked her once more into feeling. Out of the blue had come news that elderly Mr. Standish had decided to take a junior partner into his law firm. "You might be interested to know," he told Maggie as he paused at her desk one morning, "that I've found the right man for the job. He's been over in Sydney for a couple of years, but he's eager to return to Hamilton. Heard that I was on the lookout for a junior partner and phoned me from Sydney last night. Local chap actually. Name of Ames. Colin Ames. You might—" He broke off, an expression of embarrassment clouding his keen gray eyes in a thin lined face. Too late. A hazy recollection niggled at the back of his precise lawyer's mind. Maggie could almost see his thoughts ticking over.

Evidently the girl had forgotten all about that old trouble. She hadn't turned a hair. Water under the bridge now, probably. She might look small and rather childish, younger than her years. But one thing, you could always depend on Maggie not to let you down.

On the following morning he had reason to alter his opinion. Maggie, after a sleepless night of worry and indecision, faced him across the wide office desk. "I'm sorry, Mr. Standish, but I just can't stay on here. It's because of—well, personal reasons. Would a week's notice suit?"

Her employer was accustomed to sizing up situations. Now his shrewd perceptive glance took in Maggie's unaccustomed pallor, the dark smudges beneath her brown eyes. He hadn't realized the affair had been so deep. The next moment he knew that he should have anticipated this. He was annoyed with himself. Must be getting old to have overlooked that old romance between Maggie and his prospective junior partner. What had happened? He remembered now. Engagement broken at the last moment. Ames went off to marry her friend. Silly young fool! He had half a mind to tell him so too when he arrived. Place wouldn't be the same without her.

Before he could settle on the most effective line of persuasion, however, Maggie cut in. "It's no use asking me to stay on, Mr. Standish." She knew her employer was an astute speaker. She had no wish to parry the endless arguments she sensed he was about to put forward in favor of her changing her mind. "It's all arranged," she rushed on breathlessly. "I—I've taken another position, you see." Avoiding her employer's surprised expression, she sought wildly for inspiration and on impulse clutched at the first idea that presented itself. "In the country! I—I thought it would be a change. I'm sorry the notice is so short, but—"

"I see." For once the elderly man was nonplussed. He

had recollected Maggie's undivided interest in the show jumper that she kept in some suburban paddock, ten miles out of town. Got up at the ungodly hour of five every morning, winter and summer, she had told him once, to attend to the care and training of her mount. It came to him that any girl who arose at that hour and returned at night after a day's work to tend her horse must really enjoy country life. He sighed and making the best of a bad situation, wished her luck in her new venture.

When she reached the apartment that evening, Maggie had no appetite for her meal. Seated at the small table, she stared distastefully at the boiled egg and slice of buttered toast that she had prepared. In giving her notice today, she had burned her boats behind her, but she wasn't sorry. Being big-hearted, generous and understanding about a broken engagement was one thing; to be forced into a daily contact with an ex-fiancé was something else again. It might be cowardly on her part and probably proved a complete lack of self-confidence, but she couldn't help it. The prospect of having to see Colin and Andrea again put her in a panic state. Even were she to take another position in the town, it was inevitable that they would meet. The other two would be bound to look her up. She could imagine how it would be: Andrea, starry-eyed and sweetly considerate. Colin, his florid features redder still with embarrassment. "Must go and see Maggie," they'd have decided privately. "Have to do it sooner or later. Better get it over with."

No! She wouldn't sit here waiting to be pitied and condoned. *Poor Maggie.* She writhed inwardly as the sense of self-doubt returned once more to torment her. Damn Colin. And Andrea. Why did they have to come back here? Here, of all places. There were plenty of other towns, other law offices. Oh, damn everything!

Pushing aside the plate of untouched food, she mixed a mug of instant coffee and settled herself with the weekend newspaper. Turning to the classifieds, she ran her eyes down the long lists. No lack of opportunity there. Even in the suburbs there were plenty of positions that would suit her, now that factories were moving their offices out of town. But the suburban situations were too close to town.

Idly her gaze roamed over another column. It was headed Home and Farm Helpers. She hadn't really considered taking such a position, not seriously. It had merely been the first thought that had entered her head when she'd resigned today. Yet why not? The more she considered it, the more the idea appealed. No more grazing problems for Pete. No one to know anything of the past. It was an idea, at that. She studied the advertisements more carefully. It was a long list. Indeed, it seemed to Maggie that the back country of New Zealand was entirely peopled with farming households, all in desperate need of household assistance.

"Urgent need," ran one. "Unmarried mother welcomed," another. "Housekeeper, sober habits, live in."

Directly below was an item that held her attention. Unfortunately the first line of the insertion was missing. Maggie remembered now having torn away the page to wrap garbage in it. Still, even with what remained it seemed—interesting. She scanned the black print a second time.

"Urgently needed to keep house for sheep-farmer. Fond of children. Temporary. Three months. Sole charge. Excellent wages. Child no objection. Start immediately. Phone Te Rangi 165."

Child no objection. Well, she had no child, but Pete was every bit as dependent on her. Hadn't she tended him from the time when he'd been a wild young colt? There wasn't the slightest question that wherever she went, Pete would go too. Te Rangi, the advertiser had declared. But where was that? Maggie had considered herself to be fairly conversant, even if only by name, with most of the country districts. But this name was unknown to her. After a search she found an old automobile map of the country, but could find no trace of Te Rangi. Perhaps, though, that was all to the good. The farming district was apparently sufficiently remote even for her wishes. She could surely cope with the housekeeping part of the job. After all, she'd done it often enough at home in the past. Fond of children? Certainly she was attached to her brothers' families, if that meant anything. She didn't really know many other children.

There was something about that "urgently needed" that appealed to her. At least, she reflected forlornly, she would be indispensable to *someone*; even if the "someone" happened to be three unknown children living in the middle of nowhere with their sheep-farming father.

She stared with unseeing eyes at the busy street below, twisting a strand of long dark hair restlessly around and around her finger. As she hesitated, a tiny voice echoed in her mind, a voice that urged her on. "Why don't you? Give it a try! What have you to lose, Maggie?" Then, shrewdly: "They'd never find you there, Colin and Andrea, when they came looking for you. No one in this town need know your address. You could simply disappear for three months. Then at the end of the period you could make some other arrangement. Besides, think of all the money you'd be able to save." But she knew she wasn't thinking of the financial aspect just now.

From out of her childhood another voice whispered, the voice of a much-loved aunt, merry and kind-hearted, who had been in the habit of proffering scraps of advice to an impressionable small girl. "Never say no to life, dear!"

Okay, Aunt Myra, I'll take your advice! Impulsively Maggie picked up the telephone and requested the operator to put her through to the Te Rangi number. Evidently the place was some distance away. Well, that was what she wanted, wasn't it?

After making her snap decision, it was with a sense of letdown that she heard the voice of the operator. "Sorry, I can't get through to your number. I'll call you back."

Maggie sat waiting by the telephone. When the bell shrilled in her ear she jumped nervously. "Hello! Hello!"

A blurring of sounds that she thought were muffled laughter reached her. I must be connected with a party line, she thought confusedly. She said, raising her voice slightly. "About the position advertised in the *Herald*. You wanted a housekeeper—"

"No, we don't," a girl's childish voice cut in. Maggie could hear the giggling plainly now, followed by the sound of a scuffle. The next moment a woman's voice came through clearly. "Mrs. Barrington speaking. Was it about the position here?"

"Yes!" Maggie had to shout to make herself heard. "My name's Sullivan, Margaret Sullivan—"

Once again the line spluttered and the woman's voice faded away. Presently Maggie caught the words, "—you do understand—quite isolated."

"Yes, yes," she cried. "It doesn't matter—"

Another interference on the line. Then: "Very pleased to see you. We'll meet you if you get the bus to the nearest town. That's Panua—"

"No, no," Maggie found herself screaming back, "I have my own car. I can't come until Friday though, I'm afraid. How far away are you?"

In spite of the interference on the line the unknown woman must have caught her message, for all at once her voice came through, clearly audible. "If you're coming from Hamilton, it's the best part of a day's trip by car. We're at Te Rangi, five miles on from Panua. Do you know it at all?"

"No," Maggie called back, "but I'll find it."

"Good. We'll be expecting you, then. Just take the first road to the right when you go over the summit of the big hill after you leave Panua. You can't miss it. The road ends at Te Rangi. Amberley, the station's called. Friday, you said?"

"I'll be late—" The next moment Maggie realized that the line was dead. She could only hope that the unknown farmer's wife at the other end of the wire had caught the words.

Thoughtfully she replaced the telephone receiver. There, it was done! She was committed. Surprisingly, now that the decision had been taken she felt her spirits lift. She was running away, no doubt about that, but at least it was her own decision. She didn't *have* to wait here in the apartment for Colin and Andrea to call and make their stupid polite conversation, while all the time. . . .

Forget it, she scolded herself. Think of Mrs. Barrington, so desperately in need of household help. Probably she isn't well. Maybe she has just returned home after a spell in hospital. Or there's a new little Barrington in the house, and she needs someone to help with the baby. Hold on, Mrs. B.! Help is at hand! All I need to do now is to give notice of the apartment rental, finalize grazing arrangements at the paddock, and I'm away.

When she studied the map spread out on the small table, she discovered Panua almost at once. There it was in the smallest of print. Evidently it was a farming district situated on a long arm of a west coast harbor. Te Rangi, where the sheep station was, must be too small a place to merit mention on the map. Not that she cared how remote it was.

The following few days were filled with the preparations entailed by her departure. "Just as well you're moving Pete out of his paddock," the owner of the suburban property told her when she gave notice, "I've just sold all these sections to a local building firm."

Maggie breathed a sigh of relief. For once the all-too-familiar words failed to fill her with apprehension. She was free at last of the ever-recurring problem of finding fresh pastures for Pete within easy driving distance from town. It was a problem that had become increasingly pressing with the passing months. The city spread its boundaries farther and farther out, encroaching on lush green farmlands, bulldozing forest trees and running streams, until the landscape was flat and uninteresting.

It was an easy matter to arrange transport for Pete to the new district. A load of racehorses was being taken to a meeting farther north on the weekend; the driver of the big transporter offered to pick up Maggie's horse on the same trip, dropping him off at Te Rangi. "A one-horse town if ever there was one!" He grinned at his own joke. For a moment Maggie hesitated, struck by a dismaying thought. By this mode of transport, Pete would arrive at the sheep station a day later than herself. What if she wasn't hired? She brushed the unwelcome possibility aside. The unknown Mrs. Barrington had seemed so anxious for Maggie to come, almost as though the inquiry had been the single response to the advertisement. Yes, she assured the driver of the horse transport, the arrangement would suit perfectly.

She was later in leaving on her trip than she had anticipated. The sun was high in a cloud-filled sky when at last she swept along the wide smooth highway with its center strip of brightly flowering shrubs. She sped over the graceful arc of the bridge spanning the sparkling blue waters of Auckland harbor, then followed the main northern highway. Presently, at the foot of the Brynderwyn range, she branched off on a side road.

The winding metalled highway took her past sunny farmlands. Behind the homesteads, orchards were pink drifts of peach and nectarine blossom. Timber loading-ramps rose from the roadside; the vast green paddocks on either side were dotted with sheep and tiny lambs. Hedges of tall bamboo lined the deep ditches, and arum lilies grew wild in the long grass. Ahead of her the mountains were blue in the distance, purple where long cloud shadows slanted over the bush-clad slopes. She met little traffic on the country road. A silver milk tanker, covered vans with their loads of kumeras dug from the sandy soil of the north, cars and trucks, and once a farmer driving a red tractor. Soon, through a gap in sheep-threaded hills, she glimpsed a strip of beaten silver that was a long arm of the harbor and knew that she was well on the way to her destination.

It was late afternoon when she swept into the tiny township of Panua with its clean wide main street lined with old-fashioned stores. The scattered houses were painted in bright pastel colors, the sweeping green lawns studded with flowering trees and blossoming shrubs. Magnolias with their wine-colored cups and heady perfume, a profusion of camellias, and strange bird-like blossoms in blazing blue, violet and tangerine provided a riot of color.

Still seething with annoyance after her humiliating experience with the old van and *him*, Maggie began regretting her stop at Panua. She wouldn't think of him any more! *She wouldn't!* Concentrating on the road, she turned up the slopes of a bush-covered hill, dropping to a lower gear for the steep climb. She could glimpse only a fragment of the winding track as she went on between high dark banks where tall tree ferns swished their long dust-coated fronds across the windows of the van. Fortunately, she reflected, there was little traffic on the road. Once a long transport trailer, tightly packed with sheep, roared past her, followed by a logging truck. And around a bend of the road, a sudden glare of headlights behind her made her hug the fern-encrusted bank as a Land Rover sped past to vanish among the dim curves ahead.

Lost in her thoughts, Maggie hadn't realized how far she had traveled from Panua until all at once she was in sight of the tree-covered summit. Hadn't Mrs. Barrington made mention of a track not far from the hilltop? The next moment the dark banks on either side fell away as she swept up to meet a triangle of night sky pricked by faint stars. Moving over the summit, she swung down a steep curve, almost missing the timber gateway that glimmered faintly through bushy trees crowding the entrance. Maggie stopped the van and went to peer at the faded lettering on the wide white gate. Amberley. She was here! Swinging the gate wide, she guided the van through the opening and returned to close the gate carefully behind her. Then, following twin tracks that curved faintly over the hillside, she came in sight of a rambling old timber homestead nestling amongst a shelterbelt of towering evergreens. Lights gleamed from the windows; a lantern illuminated the long front porch that ran the length of the dwelling.

Clattering over a cattlestop, she swept past the dim outlines of buildings: a woolshed, barns, garages. She pulled up on the red gravel driveway below the lighted veranda. As she stepped from the van she reflected that by now Mrs. Barrington must be wondering if her new help would arrive today, as arranged. Maggie hadn't realized how far away the district was, or how much her speed would be cut down by frequent pauses at one-way bridges and winding unfamiliar roads. Never mind, Mrs. B., you can relax. Your helping hand has arrived late, but here at last.

She went lightly up the wide steps, conscious of the sweetly-perfumed starry pink jasmine that festooned the veranda. She pushed a button at the side of the shabby doorway. That was the first thing that wasn't as she had expected, for it was clear that the bell had ceased to function. Probably the children in the house were to blame for that. She rapped loudly on the door and the next moment was aware of muffled voices followed by a burst of stifled laughter.

Peering through a waving pattern on the glass panel, she realized that someone was coming to answer the summons. A shadow moved against the glass. The door was flung open, and a man stood silhouetted against the light; a tall man with dark hair, sideburns and an appearance that was all too familiar. Shock and surprise all but bereft Maggie of her usual presence of mind. She heard herself say idiotically: "Mrs. Barrington?" The glint of astonishment in the blue eyes changed to an expression of amusement.

"I mean—" she stammered and stopped short, hating herself for her confusion. She had never suffered from self-consciousness in the past, even when called upon to interview distinguished lawyers from abroad. What was the matter with her tonight? He was regarding her in a very unnerving way, as though he too were utterly taken aback.

"Dangerfield's the name. John Dangerfield. Too bad she's not here just now—but come in. Come in!" He stood aside as Maggie stepped into the long, narrow hall. "I didn't expect to see you again so soon." He made a gesture for her to precede him along a passageway. "Car trouble, hmm? What's the problem this time? Run out of gas? Not to worry. I can let you have some. In here—" He reached past her to open a door, revealing a spacious, dimly-lighted lounge room. Maggie had a swift impression of heavy old-fashioned furniture and faded carpeting. "Take a seat."

As she dropped down to a linen-covered couch she was disconcertingly aware of his puzzled expression. He didn't appear to be expecting her. On the contrary. And where was Mrs. Barrington? Wait, hadn't he made some mention of having an appointment tonight with someone, a woman, at his home at about this time? He had changed from the workmanlike khaki drill clothes in which she had last seen him. His cream shirt, open at the throat, was crisply laundered, the tan walking shorts immaculate. He wore knee-length, light-colored socks, deerskin moccasins on his feet. She would hazard a guess that the damp waves of his dark hair indicated a hurriedly taken shower. Could it be, her lips lifted at the thought, that it was Maggie Sullivan with whom he had an appointment, even though he might be unaware of the fact?

The thought made her decide to get the explanations over with as quickly as possible. "It's not the car this time. It's just—" She broke off, glancing up at him, a shadow of perplexity in the huge dark eyes. "This *is* Amberley station, isn't it?"

"Sure is." He was regarding her intently.

"But," she bit her lip, "I thought that Mrs. Barrington—"

His puzzled expression cleared. "Oh, you know her?"

"No, no, not really!" Oh dear, she thought, this is getting more and more involved. "Look," she leaned forward and two long dark braids swung around her small face, "I'd better explain. We seem to have got our wires crossed somehow. You see, I'm looking for a housekeeping job. You know? Looking after children, and all that, in the country. I called Mrs. Barrington a week ago about one I'd seen advertised in the *Herald*. She—" she stumbled and caught herself. He might as well know the truth. "You see, I arranged an interview with her here today and she said—well," Maggie finished in a rush of words, "I thought—I mean, I sort of hoped that the job was as good as mine."

He didn't answer directly. He fished a packet of cigarettes from a shirt pocket, offered it to her, and bent close to flick the lighter. Too close, Maggie found to her dismay. He was definitely distracting; whether he intended her to feel that way or not, the effect was the same.

Sitting down once again, he inhaled, studying her, still with that maddening expression of amusement. "Let me get this straight, Miss—"

"Margaret," she put in. "Margaret Sullivan. My friends," she added, "call me Maggie."

"I get it, Miss Sullivan. Well, I guess I owe you an apology. Problem is, things have been happening around here since that ad went in the paper last week. Mrs. B. took off in a bit of a rush unfortunately, or she could have put you in the picture about all this. She stayed only a couple of weeks herself. She did say something about someone coming up here tonight to see me about the job, but—well, I didn't connect it with you. If I'd known about you earlier," he said regretfully, "I'd have tried getting in touch with you. Not that it would have made any difference. Saved you a trip up here, that's all."

She caught him up sharply. "You don't need anyone here then, after all?"

"Not *need* anyone?" He turned that incredulous stare toward her. "You've got to be joking. You know, Miss Sullivan, I just can't tell you—" He broke off. After a moment he added, as if speaking to himself, "And not a single reply to the ad."

Maggie however had caught the muttered words. "Well," she pointed out cheerfully, "there's me!"

He turned away, stubbing the ash from his cigarette in a heavy glass ashtray that was already overflowing onto a low table. "That's right." There was a faint ironic smile at the corners of the firm mouth. "There's you. I guess I'll have to give it to you straight. You see, Miss Sullivan, you're not exactly—well, what we were looking for. Mrs. B. did say something about someone coming tonight about the job, but I didn't quite expect—" He ran a harassed hand over thick black hair. "Look, did you really study that ad of mine?"

Her wide ingenuous smile met his quizzical gaze. "Of

course I did! At least—" All at once she remembered. That missing portion of the advertisement that was torn away before she could read it. At the time she hadn't considered it important, but right at this moment she'd have given a lot to know what was printed in those first two lines.

"Hold on!" He leaped to his long length and strode toward an untidy pile of newspapers that cascaded over the end of a buffet. "Could be it's still around. Hey, it is!" Triumphantly he opened the page in question. She followed the gesture of his hand to a column headed Home Farm Helpers.

Swiftly her gaze ran down the list of insertions until she found the one she sought. Heavens! No wonder he had been so surprised to see her here. Middle-aged woman wanted, it said. Experienced. Sensible. *Able to drive car an advantage.*

All the same, she wasn't beaten yet. Not by a long way.

He needed her help desperately. Once glance around the untended room proved it. Fragments of earth and crumbs were scattered over the unswept carpet; the curtains could do with a vigorous shaking to dislodge the dust. She suspected that the sticky pink object adhering to a chair arm was a half-finished sucker. Yet he appeared determined not to give her a chance to prove herself. What was the matter with her, she wondered, that he had taken such an instant and unreasoning dislike to her? Well, not quite instant. She remembered that first involuntary, intent glance, then wrenched her thoughts away.

"The way things are around here at the moment," he was saying, "it would be a bit too much to expect anyone as young as you to take it on. Not fair to you. Three kids, and all the household chores thrown in. If Mrs. B. had stuck it out, things would have been a whole lot different. You'd have had plenty to do in giving her a hand, seeing to the kids' correspondence lessons, all that stuff. But hang it all, if *she* couldn't make a go of it. . . ."

So that was it, Maggie reflected. The older woman had given up the job in despair; run out on them. It must have been the children who had made Mrs. Barrington's position intolerable. Or the man facing her with his stern implacable look?

"Sorry, Miss Sullivan, but the idea's out." He made an expressive downward gesture with his hands. "You can see how it is?"

"No, I can't," Maggie returned with spirit, wishing that she had arranged her dark hair in any other way rather than these silly childish-looking braids. An upswept topknot would have been much more dignified in the circumstances. "If it's household experience you're thinking about," she said brightly, "don't give it another thought—"

He glanced up with interest, and she thought: Good. At least he's prepared to listen to me. That's a start.

"You've been doing something in the domestic line?"

She would have liked to say that she happened to be a qualified teacher of home economics in a girls' high school, or maybe a cooking demonstrator employed by a firm marketing stoves. Even a home helper in the city would have served, but it was no use; the habit of truth was too strong. Besides, she had a suspicion that she would need to be very convincing indeed not to be caught out by those all-observant eyes.

So she tossed the stupid braid with its confining elastic over her shoulder and looked him straight in the eye. "Actually," she said lightly, "I've been working in an office," adding quickly, "but I can cook and look after children, if that's all you need."

"You can?" He raised a skeptical black brow.

"Well, it's not my fault that I'm a bit young," she pointed out reasonably. "I can't *help* not being middle-aged, can I?"

"Oh, don't think I'm complaining, Miss Sullivan—Look, you seem dead keen on getting this particular job—"

"Oh, I am! I am!" Maggie cried impulsively. "If you only knew what it means to me—"

He shot her one of his piercing looks. "I still don't understand. What made you pick on this place, miles from anywhere?"

"But that's just what I liked about it!" To her chagrin she felt the hot color creeping up her cheeks. "You see, I live in Hamilton and this was the farthest away."

"Running away, Miss Sullivan?"

He had caught her neatly. "You—could put it that way." This seemed to be the day, Maggie thought bitterly, when she spilled out her innermost thoughts to a complete stranger, but what did it matter? After tonight she would never see him again. Nervously she loosened the silk scarf at her throat which had all at once become uncomfortably constricting. She heard her own voice say huskily: "It was just that Colin . . . we were engaged, you see . . . and then, at the last moment, he married someone else . . . my best friend—"

"There's no need to let me in on your private affairs," he broke in briskly. "It's just too bad that—"

"You mean that I'm too young. But it won't matter. The thing is you need someone to help, and I've come for the job. What difference does it make how old I am? Why," she hurried on, warming to her subject, "lots and lots of ads for household help say they have no objection to unmarried mothers—" She stopped short in some confusion. What was she saying? "And anyway," she rushed on, "you did say in the *Herald* that you had no objection to a child—"

His dark head jerked upward. "You mean—"

"Oh yes," Maggie said, "I meant to tell you before, but you didn't give me a chance. You see, I've got Pete. I've had to bring him along too," she went on with feeling, for the man seated opposite her was looking stern and withdrawn once again. Perhaps he didn't want Pete here on the station either. After all, she was well aware that farmers had objections to horses grazing on their property, chomping up precious pasture lands. "He doesn't eat much," she said pleadingly. As he made no answer but continued to regard her in that queer, thoughtful silence, she went on: "And he's no trouble at all. Honestly, you wouldn't know he was around. Intelligent too. You can tell just by looking at him. He's got that alert-looking face. He understands every word I say. I'd have brought him along with me today," she ran on, "but there happened to be a truck coming through here tomorrow. I thought that would be near enough." As she took in the harsh lines of his face, her voice faltered. "I know it sounds silly, but I just couldn't bear to leave him behind. He's one of the family. Besides, he'd miss me so much and I thought that you . . . wouldn't mind." His tight-lipped silence was making her feel more and more nervous. She rushed on in a flurry of words. "I couldn't leave him. He keeps losing his shoes all the time, even brand-new ones, and running off when you try to feed him. You know? Just for the fun of it. Of course I know that he's only teasing, but strangers don't understand—"

"What the devil," he broke in roughly, "are you talking about?"

She stared back at him with astonished brown eyes. "I told you. My horse—Pete."

"You told me." The stern lines of the deeply-tanned face relaxed and he broke into laughter. Maggie found herself laughing with him, but deep down she was thinking: Surely now he won't mind my coming. It seemed, however, that she was mistaken.

"I'm sorry," he was saying regretfully, "but it has to be 'no' to both of you."

She was too disappointed to care that from behind the

folds of the long velvet curtains at the window came a peal of muffled laughter. The next moment her companion strode toward the picture windows and jerked the curtains aside, revealing three shamefaced-looking children. A plain thin little girl of about nine, a freckle-faced boy a year or so younger, and a smaller boy with a mop of curly fair hair and an angelic face.

The man's expression was thunderous. "Out, all of you! Back to bed—fast! Do you hear? And don't let me ever catch any of you at that trick again!"

"We won't, Danger! We won't!"

The children in their night attire scuttled wildly toward the door, obviously relieved that the presence of the strange girl had saved them from a more painful retribution.

"Kids!" He sounded exasperated. "My sister's family," he explained. "Chris and her husband are geologists. They get around the world quite a bit. This time they're off for a stint in New Guinea, but they wanted the kids to stay here with me and finish the school year by correspondence. Mrs. B. offered to keep house for me while they were here. She's known Chris since she was a kid. It was Mrs. B. who taught Chris to ride—they're both crazy about horses." He sighed and looked away. "Seemed a great idea at the time, but the minute the others took off—well, Mrs. B.'s health isn't the best. She's not young. I guess she isn't used to kids. Never had any herself. Thing is," his voice was grim, "the kids are staying put here until Chris and Bob get back at Christmas, no matter what!" His considering glance rested on Maggie's small eager face. "Trouble is when Mrs. B. decided to call it a day she put that ad in the paper for someone else, but I didn't expect—"

"A helpless twit like me," Maggie couldn't resist putting in.

"I was going to say," he went on, disregarding her interruption, "to get any replies to the ad. You don't, up here in no man's land."

Yet he still wouldn't consider her for the position. He was quite determined on that point. The chilly look in the blue eyes seemed almost, incredible as it seemed, as though he were steeling himself against her. Or was it that he really was concerned more with her welfare than his own convenience? She said quietly, "You won't consider me for the job, then?"

"Afraid not, Miss Sullivan." Rising from his chair, he crossed the room and opened the doors of a large cocktail cabinet that stood in a corner. He spoke over his shoulder. "But that's no reason why you shouldn't join me in a drink. What'll you have? Gin? Sherry? It's a local brew, but not too bad."

"Thank you." She accepted the wineglass he extended toward her.

"Sorry," he dropped into the depths of the big wing chair opposite, "but it's out of the question. Not to worry, though. There are loads of farmers all over the country who would jump at the offer."

"But not you?"

The moment the words were out she regretted them. What could have possessed her to make such a personal remark?

"That's right," he agreed, and she glanced away from the mocking light in his eyes.

Maggie took a sip of wine, her gaze roving over the big room. The funny thing was that he really needed her. One only had to glance around the place to see how much it lacked a woman's care. The torn curtains, a half-eaten crust lying beneath the buffet. And those children . . . in that one lightning glimpse she had taken in the little boys' grubby hands and feet, the girl's uncombed hair and torn nightgown.

A thought crossed her mind and impulsively she leaned toward him, the words tumbling from her lips.

"If it's—I mean, my being here with just you and the children . . . what I'm trying to say is," she stumbled wildly on, "that if that's what's troubling you—" Catching a glint of laughter in his eyes, her voice trailed unhappily away. All right then, she thought hotly. Be amused! I don't care! Aloud she murmured: "I only thought. . . ."

"There's no need to concern yourself on that score, Miss Sullivan," the cool tones struck a chill in her heart, "seeing that the position isn't likely to arise." A sudden unexpected smile transformed the stern lines of the dark face. "Unfortunately."

"I see." She set down her wineglass on a low table at her side and turned to gather up jacket and purse. "I won't take up any more of your time, then." Rising to her feet, she glanced up at him. "Here's hoping," she said in a low voice, "that you have better luck with your ad next time. Someone who's at least 55. Someone who won't—" But she couldn't sustain that mocking gaze. The stinging words she had been about to fling at him died in her throat. She turned away. "Well, I guess. . . ."

"Just a minute." He was at her side, a look of concern flickering in his eyes. "You just can't take off like that! Where would you go, anyway, at night, on these roads? Nearest place that you could sleep is at least 100 miles farther on over the hills. With all this room here going begging—"

Oh, he could afford to be pleasant to her now, she thought crossly, so long as he wasn't forced to put up with her company or her cooking for three long months. She brought her mind back to the deep tones.

"Where did you set out from?"

"Where? Oh, Hamilton." It seemed ages ago, instead of just this morning.

"Wow!" he whistled softly. "That's a hell of a long trip to be turned down flat at the end of it! You'd better stay here for the night. Believe me," his engaging grin was difficult to resist, "I know this country. Deep gorges, one-way bridges and all the rest of it. No city lighting on these roads. It's fairly rugged territory, whether you go on over the hills or take the route back by Panua. No place for driving at night if you don't know every inch of the road. Garages are miles away. If you strike a bit of trouble with the car you've had it. Why not get a good night's rest here and carry on in the morning?"

Maggie hesitated. Weary and disappointed, with a dreary sense of let-down, she had no heart to continue along the winding hill track. Neither did she wish to take the endless miles back until she could find suitable accommodation for the night. She had noticed that there was none in the old hotel at Panua. All the same she had no intention of spending the night in *his* home, not after the way he had flatly refused even to consider her offer of household assistance. Thank heaven she had no need to depend on him for a night's lodging. The way she felt at the moment, still smarting with humiliation, it would be intolerable to be beholden to him for hospitality.

"Maybe you're right," she murmured, "about stopping. It's kind of you to ask me, but—"

"Right! I'll go and collect your gear from the van." He was halfway to the doorway when she ran after him, laying a hand on his bronzed, muscular arm. Once again that inexplicable magic flashed between them.

Maggie pulled herself together. "Don't bother. I've the inside fitted up like a trailer for sleeping, so I'm quite comfortable." And independent of you, she congratulated herself.

He nodded gravely. "If you insist."

They strolled side by side along the long passage. When they reached the door he stood watching her as she went down the steps and opened the door of the van.

"Good night, Miss Sullivan."

She turned. "Good night." On an afterthought she

flung over her shoulder. "I don't suppose you mind my being parked here for the night?" He deserved it, she told herself, the way he had treated her tonight. But after all, he had the last word.

"Not at all, Miss Sullivan," he returned pleasantly. "You stay right where you are. You couldn't have chosen a better spot. Right under my bedroom window where I can keep an eye on you."

Lips pressed firmly together, Maggie pretended she hadn't heard. Closing the door of the van, she sat on the bunk bed and began to take the elastics from her braided hair. The shining dark mass cascaded over her shoulders. Absently she picked up a comb and ran it through the long strands. Of all the infuriating men she had ever met. She couldn't understand him at all. So clearly in need of her services, yet refusing to consider her for the position, simply because she happened to be under 50 years old. It wasn't fair!

Presently she stripped off her jacket, dress and underwear and climbed into short cotton pyjamas. In the narrow bunk she lay still, hands crossed behind her dark hair, as she went back over the events of the day.

Maybe it was just as well that she wasn't staying on at Amberley, she mused, for her own piece of mind. It might be better if he did find his widow lady or his middle-aged housekeeper or whoever he wanted in the way of domestic help. There was something about him, something forceful and compelling that was definitely disturbing. He was undeniably good-looking in a tough suntanned sort of way. And that ridiculous name of Danger. Danger!

Her last thought before sleep finally overtook her was an uncharitable wish that he would have even more pressing problems with his ready-made family. Like measles. She only hoped that the three children would catch the infection together. No, better still, that they would go down with the complaint at three weekly intervals. He'd be forced to nurse each one, single-handed.

It seemed only a few minutes before she was awakened abruptly, conscious of a strange sensation. Something was rocking the van from side to side. Half confused with sleep, she leaped to the floor and reached for the light switch. The next moment the vehicle lurched violently. Plates and dishes came tumbling around her from a high shelf above. She made for the door, but before she could reach it something heavy struck her forehead. The world splintered into rippling ribbons of light, then dissolved into black nothingness as she felt herself falling down . . . down . . . down. . . .

CHAPTER TWO

When she first opened her eyes Maggie couldn't seem to focus her gaze properly on her surroundings. Gradually, it came to her that she was lying in a single bed in a big high-ceilinged room. The furnishings consisted of the bare essentials—dressing chest, closet, a fluffy cream sheepskin rug lying on the polished floorboards.

She raised her head from the pillow and stared at herself in a wall mirror; eyes dazed and dark-rimmed, face pale. In bewilderment she put a hand to the wide band of adhesive plaster running across her forehead. Where? How?

All at once memory came flooding back, bringing with it the thought of the van. She had been asleep, then the earthquake—that was it! She had been struck by something falling in the van during the quake. But how had she got *here*?

Memory supplied an answer to that query too, not very satisfactorily. If that "Danger" man had brought her in here . . . worse, if she were stuck here in his home. . . . The thought made her throw back the checked woollen rug; but before she could leap to the floor, the room spun around dizzily, and she sank back on the pillow. She'd get over this silly weakness in a moment or two, and then. . . .

A tap on the door interrupted her musing. As if conjured up from her apprehensive imaginings, he stood in the opening. His expression was concerned, almost anxious, although why her stupid accident should affect him she couldn't imagine.

"Hello! You're awake." He stood at the bedside, looking down at her. "How're you feeling?"

"I'm all right, Mr. . . ." she floundered. "Mr.—"

"Danger's near enough."

"It was—an earthquake, wasn't it?" she inquired shakily.

"That's right. Wasn't much of a jolt, actually." He sat himself at the end of the bed. "It's too bad that you copped that stuff falling from a shelf in the van."

Gingerly she put a hand to her forehead. "It's cut, isn't it?"

He nodded. "Doc happened to be over this way, so I had him over to stitch it up. What a shame the crockery landed on you."

"What—was it?"

He grinned. "Big black stewpan, actually."

Maggie stifled an insane desire to giggle. To think that it had been her heavy old saucepan, a legacy from her home in the country, that had knocked her out. She brought her mind back to the deep tones.

"Caught you on the forehead and knocked you out cold. Not to worry, though. Doc says you'll be okay in a couple of days—with rest, that is."

"With rest!" Maggie's brown eyes flew wide open. "But I can't stay here!"

"Why not?" He grinned across at her. "Seems to me you haven't much choice. Doc's orders. He said to tell you that otherwise he won't be responsible for the consequences."

"But that's ridiculous! I'm quite all right now. There's not a thing the matter with me." She glanced wildly around her. Then, meeting his formidable stare, her voice faltered. "At least I can get up—"

"Can you?"

"But of course. Look, if you don't believe me—" Impulsively she made a swift movement toward the edge of the bed. Immediately a wave of a dark sea rose to surge around her. As from a distance she was aware of his voice.

"Right! You showed me." His look was merciless. "Two days' rest and a try at getting up tomorrow . . . maybe. Depends how you're feeling. You know something," he observed unfeelingly, "you're lucky; could have collected a bad concussion out of that knock, but it turned out to be only slight—"

"How—do you know?"

He shrugged broad shoulders. "Doc said to check on how you were getting along, had me shine a flashlight in your eyes every hour just in case. You're in luck, though. Pupils weren't enlarged at all. Doc said to tell you he'd be back this way in a day or two. He'll look in on you, see how you're getting along."

"I see." Maggie leaned back, black hair spilling over the pillow, her thoughts in wild confusion.

It had been him then who had checked on her progress. Who else was there to keep the vigil through the long broken night except that disturbing Danger himself? The awful part of it all was that her obligations toward him were increasing at an alarming rate. To *him*, of all men! She supposed she should be grateful for his care. She would be too, had it been anyone else. But to be forced to stay on as an extra burden on him, knowing his definite views on the subject of having her here at all. . . . Close on that thought came another, even more disquieting. He must have carried her in here from the van. Before she could stop to think the words slipped out. "Then it was you who brought me in here?"

"That's right," he returned coolly. "No trouble." He waved aside her thanks. "Kids weren't one bit put out about the quake—took it all as a big joke—but I thought I'd better see how you were."

"And that was—" Puzzled, she consulted the gold watch on her slim wrist, but it had stopped. Her gaze moved toward the uncurtained window touched with a sheet of flame. "Is that really the sunset?"

She stared up at him, eyes enormous in a wan face. "It *couldn't* be!"

He nodded. "You've been out of it ever since last night."

Another disturbing thought crossed her mind. The van, her only means of escape from this intolerable situation. "The quake didn't do any damage to the van?" she inquired anxiously.

He shook a dark head. "Not a thing. She's okay, except for the flat tire. I'll get one of the men to change that today."

"Flat tire?" Maggie's mobile face, which mirrored every passing thought, now registered unmistakable dismay.

"Would have happened anyway," he was saying, "slow puncture, I'd say. You were lucky to make it this far."

Lucky! To be stuck for days; a trespasser on the reluctant hospitality of a man who hadn't wanted her in the first place and had told her so in no uncertain terms.

There was something else that she should know, something that niggled at the back of her mind, but she couldn't seem to pin it down.

"Well, I'll be all right soon anyway," she murmured inadequately. Her gaze roved the room in search of her suitcase. She wouldn't be surprised if he hadn't deliberately left it in the van, out of her reach.

"No, you don't!" The amused twinkle in his eyes confirmed her suspicion. "You stay right where you are until tomorrow. Doc's orders. Remember?"

"He didn't know how I'd feel about staying *here*!" The words were out before she could stop them.

A little ashamed of her outburst, she avoided meeting his gaze, afraid of his steely merciless stare. When she did look up he appeared not to mind in the least. In some odd fashion, she found his amused indifference even more annoying.

"Forget it," he was saying, "just concentrate on getting better."

So that you can get rid of me quicker! But this time she bit back the quick retort that rose to her lips.

"Oh, I almost forgot to tell you," he was saying, "your horse turned up in the transporter an hour ago. Ugly brute, isn't he?"

Ugly! Pete! Indignation made her voice emerge in a squeak. "I think he's perfect!" Immediately she belied the loyal statement by adding, "Anyway, you can't tell how good a horse is just by looking at him. You'd never believe what a marvelous jumper Pete is. He can take just about any hurdle. He never ever refuses, and he's a perfect build for a hunter. You just wait," she cried warmly, "until—"

"I'll do that." His tone was that of one soothing a fractious invalid. "Meanwhile, I've put him up in the hill paddock with the others."

"Thank you." Maggie was getting awfully weary of having to be indebted to him. Thank you, thank you . . . it seemed that her obligations toward this stranger were endless. And just what did he mean by "meanwhile?" The minute she was on her feet she'd be away from here. He needn't think that he had to put up with her a moment longer than she could help.

He stood up. "Anyone you'd like me to get in touch with? I could call through from here."

She shook her head.

"I'll be getting along, then. Send the kids packing if they come in here and worry you. I'll send Phil in with a bit to eat; might make you feel a whole lot better. Take it easy and don't worry. See you!"

That smile again. It did things to her, making her forget all the edged remarks that she should be hurling back at him. Before she could gather her wits together, he had gone.

Lying back on the pillows, she reviewed the situation. It was humiliating to find herself in his debt on so many counts; her van, her horse, even herself, and until tomorrow, there didn't seem to be anything that she could do about it.

A loud rapping on the door brought her back to the present. A moment later a child stood in the opening. Maggie had a confused recollection of a thin little girl in the lounge on the night of her arrival.

"Danger said you had to eat this." As the small arms lifted a tray precariously toward her, Maggie leaned forward to take it, surprised to find that once again the blackness hovered before her eyes. Swiftly she recovered herself this time.

"That's nice of you, Phil." She smiled down into the childish face with its clear, gray eyes and wispy brown hair. Maggie made a mental vow that the first thing she'd do on getting out of bed would be to comb those tangled strands and arrange them in neat braids. "Phyllis? Is that it?"

"I wish it was!" The gray eyes clouded, and the small girl's lips set in a mutinous line. With an angry gesture she tossed the tangle of brown hair back over her shoulders. "Instead of silly old Philippa!"

Maggie took a spoonful of steaming soup from the pottery bowl. Evidently blended from a variety of nourishing ingredients, it was rich and satisfying. She wondered who had prepared it.

"Oh, I don't know," she said easily, "I rather like it. Philippa, I mean. Doesn't it mean something about being fond of horses?"

"That's what Mom's always telling me!" The childish face puckered. "That's why I *hate* it!"

Hurriedly Maggie sought to retrieve her mistake. "Oh well," she offered placatingly, "Phil's good enough for me. This is wonderful soup you've brought me."

"Ann always makes super soup," the child said indifferently. As she swung herself up onto the bed, Maggie couldn't help but notice the outgrown red cotton dress crumpled and unironed, with buttons missing at the neckline.

"She brought it over yesterday," Phil said. "She told us there'd be enough left for tonight. There was too, until you woke up. But Danger said you could have his share."

"Oh, he did?" All Maggie's enjoyment in the nourishing liquid died away. The child *would* tell her that after she had consumed his supper.

"I won't let on to Ann that you had it instead," Phil confided. "She'd be mad. She's always bringing things for Danger to eat. Before us kids came to stay, he was all by himself. Only sometimes Mrs. Wahonga used to come and cook dinner for him. She's come back to cook for us tonight. She wouldn't stay while old Barry was here," adding in a low intense tone, "*she* didn't like her either!"

Maggie thought it wise to change the subject. "Do you like the meals Mrs. Wahonga makes for you?"

The child considered. "Mmm, only I don't like fish all the time. Look out, here comes Mark. He always jumps on beds!" The warning, however, came a little late. The small boy was already rushing across the room. With the help of the bedcovers he pulled himself up and threw himself beside Maggie. From beneath a mop of curly golden hair ingenuous blue eyes regarded her curiously. "You got a sore head? Does it hurt?" And in the same breath: "Do you want to see Poss?"

Maggie smiled into the sunburned little face that was smudged with earth stains. "Love to. Where is he?"

"I'll show you!" In a second he had lowered himself backward, dropped to the sheepskin rug below and was running out of the room on plump tanned legs. He was back in a few moments, followed by a small furry animal who came bounding after him. Maggie couldn't help smiling as she took in the pointed little face, thick dark fur, bushy tail and alert black eyes. Evidently the baby opossum was part of the family. She stroked the thick dark fur of the animal the small boy had thrust up into her arms. "I had one of these for a pet once."

"Really?" Phil gazed at her with interest. "What did you call him?"

"Just what you call this one. Poss—Oh, he's gone!" For the tiny animal had wriggled free of her grasp and fled through the open doorway. "Hello, who's this?"

A boy stood shyly just within the opening, a thin freckled lad with a hesitant smile and unruly brown hair.

"Oh, that's just Ian," his sister said carelessly. "He wants to show you his model plane."

Maggie leaned forward. "May I see it?"

Shyly Ian withdrew a light balsa wood model airplane from behind his back. Maggie knew, from her brothers when they were all children, the hours of infinite care and concentration that had gone into the assembling of the tiny airplane. She examined it carefully. "Why, it's a beauty!"

"Don't let him get it!" Ian swooped down to snatch the model a split second before a grimy, chubby hand reached toward it.

"Mark always breaks up Ian's planes," Phil remarked carelessly. She eyed her brother. "Serves you right, letting him see it."

"How was I to know the little horror was in here?"

While the two older children continued to argue loudly, the small boy snuggled up beside Maggie. "You got hurted in the quake, didn't you? Can I feel your sore where you got hurted?" Maggie dodged a small exploratory hand stretching toward the bandage on her forehead. "I wasn't scared in the quake," he boasted.

"How could you be?" his sister demanded scathingly. "You were asleep all the time. Anyway, it was only a tiny earthquake."

"It wasn't!" shrieked Mark. "It wasn't *so*! It knocked down all the jampots on the shelf in the kitchen!" he cried triumphantly.

"It would take just a teensie-weensie push to knock them down. Danger said," Phil said to Maggie, "that it was a big pot that fell on your head."

Maggie wished that she had acquired her injury in some more dramatic fashion. But—a pot! The heavy old stewpan had served on many a camping trip to cook generous quantities of food that would last for a weekend.

"Well, anyway," she murmured, "I wasn't hurt much. I'm going to get up soon."

"You can't!" Ian told her off handedly. "Danger said."

"Oh, he did, did he?" Maggie felt a surge of annoyance. Danger again. If she stayed here for a few hours longer it would be because she was forced by this stupid giddiness, not because of anything to do with his orders.

"He said we had to look after you," Phil said with importance. "I was going to make pancakes for supper, but I don't need to now 'cause Mrs. Wahonga's come back."

In spite of herself Maggie was curious. "Does she live here?"

The children burst into giggles.

"No, no," Phil explained after a moment, "she lives in a tiny hut down the track with her boy Hone. She makes flax baskets and sells them. She used to cook Danger's supper every night before we came to stay—"

"But when Mrs. Barrington came," Ian put in, "she didn't come any more."

"Oh well," Maggie murmured mildly, "I suppose there was no need—"

"Mrs. B. wanted her to come," Phil said, "but Mrs. Wahonga wouldn't! *She* didn't like her either! Here's Mrs. Wahonga now."

A bare brown foot in a green rubber thong was pushing open the door. A moment later Maggie caught sight of a beaming Maori face with smooth copper skin and white teeth. Mrs. Wahonga was a big woman; tall and plump, with a graceful carriage, a relaxed good-natured expression, and lustrous dark eyes. Her long waving black hair was tied back in a ponytail.

"*Aue*, what's this?" She set down a basin of steaming hot water on the bureau and turned toward Maggie with a beaming smile. "Too bad you got hurt in the quake last night." The sympathetic dark eyes rested on the bandage across Maggie's forehead. "Soon be better, though. You just rest, take it easy."

Everyone expected her to rest, Maggie thought with some irritation, when all she wanted to do was escape from here as quickly as possible.

Gently but firmly a plump hand propelled Mark from the bed. "Scram, you kids! Miss Sullivan wants a bit of peace—" Reluctantly the children moved toward the door.

The smiling woman waited while Maggie washed her hands and face, then Mrs. Wahonga handed her a fluffy clean towel. "That better, eh?"

"Much better," Maggie agreed.

Soon deft hands were making the bed with freshly laundered sheets. Then, picking up a hairbrush, Mrs. Wahonga began to run it over the long dark strands. Maggie felt like a child again as gentle hands pulled the hair back from her pale face, securing it at the back with an elastic band.

"I'll bring you some supper," she said, "that's what you need now."

"But I thought I'd had it," Maggie protested.

"Oh, that bit of soup was nothing!" Mrs. Wahonga shrugged a plump shoulder. "I'm going to cook some fish, just caught today. My boy Hone he goes out in the boat and gets plenty. Pretty good, eh?"

"But I couldn't possibly—"

"Course you could!" A graceful brown hand waved her remonstrations aside. "Then you get better quick, *ehoa*?"

Mentally Maggie agreed that Mrs. Wahonga, in her musical liting tones, had a point there. She would, she thought, do anything, eat any amount of food, if only it would hasten her recovery.

"All right, then," she smiled her pixie smile, "if it will get me out of bed sooner." Pleating the bedspread with restless fingers, she was scarcely aware of speaking her thoughts aloud. "I don't want to be a burden here, any longer than I can help. I know that Danger—" Her voice trailed unhappily away.

Mrs. Wahonga picked up the towel, a twinkle in her dark eyes. "Danger, he got a shock when you walked in here, eh?"

"Well, yes, he did rather." Maggie refrained from explaining that she hadn't exactly entered the room under her own steam, so to speak. But there was no need to go into details. "It wasn't that he wanted—" She stopped short, biting her lip. "I mean, it was just because of the quake—"

Mrs. Wahonga nodded, the basin held effortlessly beneath a rounded arm.

"He didn't want you around, eh? Because of that other one? His Cathy. That the trouble?"

Maggie sat up straight. "But I thought he wasn't—" All at once she realized that her interest could be construed by the Maori woman as something warmer. "Married . . . or anything . . ." she finished lamely.

"Danger? Married? No fear! Guess he learned his lesson about all that." Mrs. Wahonga gave her deep, rich chuckle. "I'd like to have seen his face when you walked into the house. Must have given him one big shock, you here—again."

Maggie stared up at her bewilderment. "But I've never been here before!"

The expressive dark eyes studied her curiously. "He didn't tell you, then?"

"Tell me what?"

Mrs. Wahonga shrugged a shoulder under a brilliantly patterned shift. "Guess if I don't let you in on it someone else soon will. Just—" her eyes rested consideringly on Maggie's big dark ones in a small face with the clean line of a small square jaw—"you so like that other one that he nearly married. I reckon he never got over that, Danger," she went on in her pleasant musical tones. "Two years ago now, but he never take a fancy to any other girl since then, not a real fancy. You so like. Just for a minute, when I walked in here tonight in the dim light, you had me fooled. I thought to myself, I thought, It's his Cathy. She's come back."

Maggie could scarcely contain her curiosity. "Was he—fond of her?"

"Fond of her? He just thought there was no one like her! When a man don't fall in love until he's 30, then he falls hard. Cathy—an announcer on television she was then—she came up here to stay on her brother's farm, just for a month she said, while she got over a sickness. Nervous breakdown, that's what it was, she said. But in the end she stayed for three months. She and Danger, they were always together. Folks around these parts were getting all set for a "tin-canning." They thought there'd be a wedding any day and there'd be a mistress up at Amberley at last. Then—"

As she paused Maggie leaned forward expectantly. "What happened?" she prompted.

Mrs. Wahonga shrugged. "You tell me! One day they were out riding together, happy as could be. The next Cathy had left the district." She spread her hands in an expressive gesture. "Nobody know if they have one big bust-up, or what. All we know is that she never come back. Anyway, a sheep station no place for a girl like her. She's an actress now, with a big part in a play at a theater in London. I saw her picture in a newspaper just the other day. Danger," she paused thoughtfully, "he different since then . . . sort of quiet. He don't laugh so much as he used to. More'n two years ago now, since Cathy left, but I don't think he'd forget." A broad smile broke across the brown face, showing perfect teeth. "Not much chance of forgetting his Cathy with you right here, *ehoa*?"

Maggie made no comment, and the lilting tones flowed on. "Danger, he go to dances sometimes, parties too, but he don't ever stay for long. Guess he don't care for girls any more."

Especially, Maggie thought to herself, ones that bring back painful memories of "his Cathy."

"Oh well," Mrs. Wahonga turned toward the door, her tones philosophical, "he get along all right by himself. He got his work. He *tangata whenua*," explaining, as she caught Maggie's puzzled expression, "he man of the land. Maybe he forget, one of these days."

And maybe he won't. Maggie disagreed silently. Not when he can't stand the sight of me around the place.

She brought her mind back to the woman's placid tones. "I gotta get that fish on cooking, before the men come in."

With her erect, graceful carriage, she moved from the room, leaving Maggie a prey to conflicting emotions.

A number of things were clicking into place, things that had puzzled her during her interview with Danger. Could it have only been last evening? Her chance resemblance to "his Cathy" must be quite arresting. It wasn't her fault, but it did make a lot of matters clear; such as Danger's inexplicable refusal even to consider her as an applicant for the position of a housekeeper in his home.

So was that it? He was still deeply in love with someone else, someone who didn't care. He must be, or he wouldn't have been so insistent about sending her packing as soon as was decently possible.

She was still pondering the matter when Mrs. Wa-

honga returned, carrying a tray. Delectable piping hot
schnapper fillets, garnished with a sprig of parsley and a
slice of lemon, lay on a hot plate.

"It looks delicious." Maggie found that, in spite of the
soup, she was still hungry enough to enjoy the appetizing
food.

The stout woman beamed happily. "You like fish?
Good. Hone, he get it way beyond the breakers. Plenty of
schnapper on this coast. Toheroas too, down on the
beach. You like toheroas?"

Maggie shook her head. "I don't know. I've never had
the chance to taste them."

Mrs. Wahonga grinned broadly. "You will. It's the
season now for catching them. There's plenty in the sand
down at the Gap. Eat up now. When you get outside then
you feel better! I've got to see to supper before the men
come in."

Maggie needed no further encouragement. The freshly
fried smoking hot fillets were a delight, as was the crusty
home-made bread lavishly spread with yellow butter. A
cup of tea from a brown pottery teapot completed the
meal.

Presently Mrs. Wahonga returned to collect the tray.
"I'll keep the kids away until tomorrow. Just you yell if
you want anything." The kindly brown face bent over her
as Mrs. Wahonga straightened the covers. "Tomorrow
you be fine, *ehoa*! Sleep well!" With a parting smile she
moved away, walking noiselessly in her rubber thongs,
and closing the door softly behind her.

A little later Maggie caught the distant murmur of
masculine voices, the rattle of crockery, an echo of a
musical Maori laugh, but she was only vaguely aware of
the sounds. She was busy thinking over what the Maori.
woman had told her. What had that other girl been like,
really? An actress, Mrs. Wahonga had said. She must
have possessed some special quality of attractiveness to

capture his heart, a man like that; to make him care so much that even now, after all this time, even to see someone resembling "his Cathy" cut deeply. She wondered who had been to blame for the break in the love affair, but that was something she would never know. Better to forget all about it. Trouble was, she told herself ruefully, Danger wasn't an easy man to forget; even for her, and she scarcely knew him. Something else occurred to her. Wasn't it generally acknowledged that a man tended to remain faithful to a particular type of girl, at least as appearances were concerned? So, the thought came unbidden: what an opportunity presented itself for revenge on John Dangerfield for his hurtful treatment of her last night. She wouldn't be surprised if, given half a chance, she could make him fall in love with her, just a little. What a chance that would be to even the score. Supposing it was her turn to have the upper hand; dependent on his generosity for medical care, and attention? What if their positions were reversed and she could take her revenge on him for all the humiliation she'd been forced to endure at his hands? *That* would teach him a lesson for advertising for domestic help. Then, merely, because of selfish personal reasons, refusing the single applicant.

But could she? Wouldn't there be an element of risk? Come on, Maggie, admit that it would be playing with fire. There's no disputing the disturbing effect he's had on you from the first moment you set eyes on his lean frame. Deep down, an inner sense warned her that it was a game at which two could play. She couldn't afford to be a loser a second time, knowing now the high cost of failure.

Love . . . and Danger. The words linked themselves in her mind with a curious insistence. It was a challenge that excited her beyond all reason. The next moment she brought herself up sharply, aghast at the direction of her thoughts. She wasn't staying on here. In a day or two she'd be leaving Amberley station, never to see Danger again. Besides, honesty compelled her to admit that any feeling she aroused in him appeared more like insufferably patronizing amusement than the stirring of a deathless passion. A tape rolled back and a deep no-nonsense voice echoed in her mind. "No need to concern yourself on that score, Miss Sullivan. The position isn't likely to arise."

It couldn't happen, of course. It was way beyond the realms of possibility, but wouldn't it be satisfying if it could! She fell asleep on the thought.

CHAPTER THREE

As she struggled through mists of sleep, Maggie was vaguely aware of someone calling her name. Then in the pre-dawn stillness she caught a sibilant whisper. "Miss Sullivan, Miss Sullivan, are you awake?"

Dimly she perceived a small figure in a white night-gown standing in the doorway; caught the urgent whisper. "Can I stay here with you?"

"Philippa! Is that you?"

"*Please* let me stay." The childish pleading voice was choked with tears.

"Of course you can. Hop in with me. What's the trouble?" Maggie asked as the small girl snuggled under the sheet beside her. "Nightmare?"

Philippa didn't answer. She was shivering, but whether from chill or night terrors, Maggie could not tell.

"Tell me." Maggie was still half asleep herself. "Then you can forget all about it and go back to sleep. What was it about, the nightmare? Something chasing you?"

"Mmm . . . it was awful. You won't laugh if I tell you?"

"Cross my heart and hope to die."

"It was the same dream I always have," Philippa whispered. "The Saint. He was coming straight for me with his teeth bared and that cruel mean look in his eyes . . . you know, all the whites showing. And he jumped, he jumped at me and I—couldn't get my legs to move, I just couldn't!"

"It was only a dream," Maggie soothed the distraught child, "something you ate for supper, I expect."

When Maggie awoke again Philippa had disappeared. But whether she had fled back to her own room ashamed of her nighttime fears, or because she was in dread of the teasing remarks of her older brother, Maggie had no way of knowing.

The room was flooded with sunlight. She could hear masculine voices and snatches of laughter somewhere near at hand. Moving carefully, she dropped her feet to the floor, relieved to find she felt no unpleasant reaction. She was better at last! She moved toward the window and leaning her elbows on the sill, took in the view. Clear high hills, dotted with grazing sheep, soared up into a sky of pulsating blue. In the valleys, dark native bush ran up the steep slopes. Well, she'd arrived at the sheep station in the back country at last, even if her stay here was only on a very temporary basis.

As she stood watching, a tall rangy figure emerged from the stables, Danger! He threw a sheepskin saddle-blanket over a restive roan horse tethered to a fence post. He bent to adjust the girth, then leaped lightly up into the saddle. A moment later he was joined by two young men astride their sturdy stock ponies, and soon the three cantered over the hillside and were lost to sight.

So the boss of Amberley together with his farm helpers had begun their day's work on the station while she had so disgracefully slept in.

A knock at the door made her spring back into bed, but it was only Ian, his tousled brown hair more unruly than ever. "Danger said not to wake you. He said to tell you he's gone over to the back paddocks to tighten the fence wires down by the macrocarpa trees. If you want him I can go over with a message."

Want him. Maggie's lips tightened. "There's something I do want to know, though, Ian. About the van, is it—"

"It's okay to drive, Danger said. He got Gavin to change the tire. Danger mended the broken shelf too, so you'd never know it had been smashed."

Danger again! All the same it was a relief to know that

the vehicle was once again mobile. Now all she need do was get herself in the same condition. She brought her mind back to the small boy facing her. "Is there anything you want me to do for you, Miss Sullivan?" he was asking politely.

"There is, you know. I'd like my suitcase out of the van." If that Danger man imagined that he could keep her a prisoner here, he'd soon discover that he was mistaken.

"I'll fetch it." He was gone before she could say more.

Presently Maggie flicked the catches of her cheap fiber suitcase, slipped into a gaily flowered housecoat and went in search of the bathroom. She found it at the end of the long passage; a huge old room with gleaming modern fixtures. Soon she was turning the silver taps beneath the shower, washing away all the weariness and upset of the last few days.

When she was dressed, in a crisp creamy open-weave shirt hanging loosely over tan shorts, her long dark hair tied back with a brown ribbon, she felt she could face anything, even this maddening predicament. As soon as Danger returned she would make it clear that she was now quite recovered and could leave at once. But in her heart she knew that he would insist on her waiting to see the doctor. In a way, she mused uneasily, she supposed she did owe Danger that much. Come to think of it, a doctor living in this remote area would be forced to make long and arduous journeys to visit his patients. She could scarcely leave Amberley station before his second visit, seeing that he was taking the trouble to check on her progress. Besides, Danger had promised . . . it always reverted to that.

When Maggie entered the sunny dining room with its high ceiling and dark paneling, she found the children at breakfast, noisily squabbling over a free gift that had tumbled from the packet of cornflakes.

It took quite a time to clear up after the meal. Mark had tipped a mug of milk over the table and onto the floor. At last, however, Maggie left the two older children to deal with the breakfast dishes while she wiped the black and white floor tiles and ran a duster over the heavy old kauri table and chairs.

In the kitchen, she discovered to her delight a huge white freezer stocked with frozen foods. At least, she reflected thankfully, as she took out crisp green lettuce, tomatoes, bread and cooked meats, that would take care of lunch.

The children, enthusiastically armed with dusters, broom and mop, offered to help with the household chores. Maggie was surprised at how soon the untidy room was set in order.

"You wouldn't think that Danger gave Mark a bath last night, would you?" Philippa observed, as Maggie, damp washcloth in hand, deftly removed the remains of breakfast from around Mark's mouth, then dried the puckered face.

"There!" Maggie released the squirming child. "Now you can go. What are you going to do today, anyway?"

Wide blue eyes turned trustingly toward her. "I'm gonna build my boat. It's going to be a big boat." He paused impressively. "The biggest boat in the world, with sails 'n everything. An' when I finish making it I'm going to sail way, way over the sea—"

Maggie picked up a comb and after wetting it, ran it through the silkily fair hair. "Just you?"

"Me and Poss. We're going to go way away until we find my mommy, and then we're going to bring her back here—"

"Don't take any notice of him!" Philippa had wandered into the room. "He's always talking about going to find Mom and telling fibs. Last week he was going to fly away in his own plane." Her young voice was scathing. "As if he could."

"Fat lot you know about it!", Mark flung himself toward her, his chubby face scarlet with indignation. "Dumb Dumb."

"*Don't* call me that!"

His sister aimed a blow at him, but with the agility of long practice Mark leaped nimbly aside, then fled. Maggie caught the flick of a furry dark tail as a tiny animal went scampering through the door after him.

"You can't believe a thing the little horror says," Philippa observed idly. She laid down a sheet of drawing paper on the table and went to the kitchen for a small jar of water. Soon, head bent and tongue protruding in intense concentration, she was sketching in bold watercolors: a line of pines on a windswept hillside, scudding clouds in an expanse of blue sky.

Pausing at the table a little later, Maggie was surprised at the vividness of the simple scene. The sketch possessed a quality of life and movement that even the garish colors couldn't hide. She studied it carefully. "It's the hill outside the window, the nearest one, isn't it?"

Philippa looked up at her in surprise. "How did you know?"

"Easy. Anyone would recognize it. Have you any other sketches around that you've done?"

"Lots and lots. Come on, I'll show you!" Sliding down from the chair, Philippa led the way to her bedroom. Oblivious of the chaotic surroundings of clothing and half-eaten apples, she ran to open a drawer. A sheaf of papers fluttered to the mat beneath. As she stooped to gather them up, Maggie caught glimpses of a variety of sketches. A fashion model standing, legs akimbo, in a modern stance; sheepdogs held by their long chains and peering from a line of kennels, an unmistakable portrait of Poss. There was no doubt in Maggie's mind that the child possessed considerable talent. Placing a sheaf of sketches on the bed, she riffled through them. "No horses?" she inquired smilingly.

She was unprepared for the small girl's reaction. "No!" she cried. "I'll never draw them or ride them, and I won't exercise that hateful Saint either. I don't care what Mommy says when she comes back. I hate him. He knows I do and he hates me too. I know he does! I can tell by the way he looks at me. Look at this!" She flicked up the hem of her dress, exposing a discolored bruise on her thigh. "That's what he did to me the day when Barry forced me to brush him down. He nipped me, just because of that. I'll never, never go near him again," she vowed. "You wouldn't either if—" Suddenly she stopped short, gazing up at Maggie with anxious eyes. "You don't like horses, do you?"

Maggie hesitated. "Never mind about horses . . . show me some more of your pictures. Do you know," she smiled, "I wouldn't be surprised if you turned into one of those lucky folk who are born being able to do something really well, something they love doing."

Philippa's thin face flushed with pleasure. "You're not just saying it?"

Maggie shook her head. "I bet your mother would say just the same—"

"Oh, Mom—" all the excitement in Philippa's face died away, "she just wants me to paint horses."

To draw the child's thoughts from the direction in which they were drifting, Maggie said with a smile: "Where's your hairbrush? If you bring it to me," she said winningly, aware of Philippa's suspicious glance, "I'll braid your hair for you. I know what long hair's like."

"All right, then." Slowly Philippa turned away and moving toward the cluttered dressing chest, picked up a brush and comb. "I'm glad old Barry's gone," she confided as she perched herself on the bed, while Maggie ran a brush down the tangled strands. "Always going on about the Saint, wanting me to ride him or groom him, or something!"

"The Saint?" Something niggled at the back of Maggie's mind. She carefully withdrew a grass seed that was embedded in the brown hair. "You don't mean that big white thoroughbred who wins all the trophies at shows and gymkhanas all over the country?"

The small girl nodded carelessly. "That's him."

"Then your mother," Maggie said incredulously, "must be Chris Erickson, the famous show-jumper! I'm always reading about her and the Saint in the newspapers and pony club magazines. He must be a wonder horse."

"He's not," Philippa retorted, "he's awful! He knows I'm scared stiff of him."

"Why bother, then?" Maggie said lightly, drawing the wispy thin hair back from the child's face. "You don't have to like horses, do you?"

"You do when you have Chris Erickson for your mother," Philippa said sullenly. "Mommy says that after a while I'll get used to him and I'll like him." All at once the childish lower lip quivered. "She sold my little pony, my Dandy, just because she thought that he was getting too fat. He wasn't! Ponies are always fat. She thinks I'm going to get fond of the Saint instead, but I won't. I don't care what they say!"

"Who are they?" Maggie queried gently, trying to stem the wild flow of words.

"Barry! Mommy told her that she had to make me ride her horse while she was away. I wouldn't, and that's why she left. I'm glad she did too!"

"I see," Maggie said, but she didn't quite. There was no reason, she mused, why Philippa should be forced to follow in the footsteps of her famous mother. Surely it was courting disaster to insist on a small highly-strung girl riding a horse such as the Saint. Maggie remembered seeing him once, pictured fleetingly on a television country show. The Saint was being decorated with the wide violet satin ribbon of Champion Hack. Nervous and high-spirited, with flaring nostrils and a wild eye, he appeared no mount for a beginner or a nervous rider.

"Does you brother Ian like riding?" Maggie inquired thoughtfully.

"Oh yes, but it's all right for him," the light childish tones quivered, "he's still got his pony. He's got Pancho. Lucky thing!"

"Did you have an accident once, when you were riding?" Maggie wondered if that might explain the child's terror of the big white show jumper.

Philippa shook her head. "No, but I will. I know I will, if ever I get up on him. He'd just love to buck me over his head and then jump on me. I know he would! Sometimes I have this nightmare—"

The question Maggie wanted to ask could wait no longer.

"How about your uncle? Does he insist that you do what your mother wants about the Saint?"

"Danger?" Philippa's expression cleared. "Oh, he doesn't worry. He just says to please myself. I wish my dad. . . ." As the childish tones lapsed into silence Maggie guessed that the girl's parents were in agreement on the subject of her riding prowess.

Phillipa swung around to face Maggie. "I bet you wouldn't make me ride him!"

Taken in surprise by the remark, Maggie hesitated, debating whether or not to confess that she too was an enthusiastic horsewoman. After being Philippa's confidante it didn't seem quite the time to make the truth known. Anyway, she was leaving here so soon. She said at last, "Not if you don't want to."

"That's good," Philippa said with satisfaction, " 'cause Danger said you might be staying here to look after us kids. He isn't sure yet, but—"

"He said that?" Maggie stood motionless, the brush

suspended in her hand. Well, if he wasn't sure, *she* was! She'd never, never stay on his station now, not for any money. Not even if he implored her to change her mind.

She began brushing the brown hair so vigorously that Philippa put a hand to her head. "Ow! You hurt."

"Sorry," Maggie said, "but I was thinking of something else." Gathering together the wispy strands, she tied them back with a ribbon. "There! Now I can see your face."

"Gee, thanks, Miss Sullivan."

As Philippa left the room to resume her painting, Maggie stood lost in thought. It was absurd of her to allow herself to be worked up about that man. She forced herself to concentrate on the matter in hand. Presently, with bed neatly made up with a primrose chenille spread, books stacked in a bookcase, paintbrushes and pencils thrust in a jar, and floor cleared and swept, order was partially restored to the dishevelled room.

In the boys' room things were almost as chaotic, although here the endless models of airplanes were mounted on high shelves well out of the reach of predatory fingers.

The two boys followed her from room to room, Mark sucking his thumb and clutching a reluctant Poss in his arms.

Maggie was turning down the cover of Mark's bed when a thought struck her. She turned to the older boy. "Does Danger usually come home for lunch?"

"Sometimes," Ian said carelessly. On an afterthought he added: "That's right, he is coming back today. He doesn't work far from the house ever since Barry went away. Today he said he'd be back 'cause he wanted to check on you."

Whatever that meant, Maggie thought irritably. She gave the pillow a vindictive shake. Well, he needn't bother. There was no reason for him to worry about her any longer. She could look after herself. And the family too, if need be.

To Maggie the morning flew by on wings; a frenzied glance toward the cuckoo clock made her hurry into the kitchen. For all she knew, Danger might make an appearance at any moment. She was determined to have everything ready on his arrival at the house, if only to prove what a treasure of a housekeeper he had lost through his own stupid prejudices.

Scones? She was practised in making them, and if only she could understand the controls of the stove— The boys followed her into the kitchen, watching as she experimented with the various switches. At length Ian dragged a stool forward. "There's a book about it up on the shelf." Thankfully Maggie took it and began to study the diagrams.

She found it a simple matter now to heat the oven, so while the temperature was rising, she mixed the ingredients. As the oven signal flashed, she slid the tray into the oven. Then minutes later she took out the batch of scones; not the feathery golden-topped beauties she had envisaged but scones with hard brown tops, edible, but only just. Well, there was no time left in which to whip up a second batch.

"Whee!" Ian cried appreciatively as Maggie set down the plate on a yellow checked tablecloth, "crusty scones. Just the way I like them. Danger likes them hard on top too!"

Mark, safely imprisoned in his high chair, banged imperiously on the tray. "Here he comes! Here's Danger!"

Maggie flew to the window. She was just in time to glimpse a rider on a roan horse canter down a steep grassy hillside. A few minutes later she was surprised to hear a car nearing the house, then the sound of brakes at the front entrance. There was an echo of men's voices in the hall, then Danger was strolling toward her. He was accompanied by a short stocky man with grizzled gray hair and a lined kindly face. Deeply tanned and wearing a cotton shirt and shorts, he carried a doctor's bag in his hand.

Danger's glance went immediately to Maggie. "Here's your patient, Doc. Miss Sullivan, this is Doc Smith."

While Danger went to wash, Maggie gazed into the weathered face. Guiltily she remembered his order . . . rest for two days. "I felt so well," she said a trifle self-consciously, "that I had to get up. It seemed such a waste of time lying there in bed." Her incurable habit of truth made her add: "With so much to do out here."

The doctor smiled. "All the same, I'd just like to make sure." His brief examination confirmed Maggie's own diagnosis.

"You see," Maggie said triumphantly, "I'm quite all right. Well enough to be mobile again."

"Hold on a minute!" The doctor's stubby hand was raised in protest. "No need to rush things. Give it another couple of days before you hit the trail, just to be on the safe side." He grinned teasingly. "What's wrong with staying on here a bit longer? Kids getting too much for you? Danger been neglecting you?"

"Oh no, no!" Maggie said hastily, "nothing like that!" She was nervously aware that Danger had entered the room in time to catch the doctor's words. "It's just that I—well, I'm really just a stranger here." She avoided Danger's glance. "And I've got to return to town."

The doctor, however, refused to be swayed by her plea. "Couple of days won't hurt . . . no sense in rushing these things." He fixed her with a stern hazel eye. "Promise?"

"All right, then," Maggie agreed reluctantly, "I suppose so."

"Right, that's settled, then." Soon the doctor was chatting with her, recounting some of his experiences in the wide remote area where he was the only available doctor.

"You will stay for lunch?" Heavens, Maggie thought the next moment, she was acting as though it were her place to invite guests to Amberley station. Involuntarily she glanced toward Danger. Of course he was eyeing her at the same moment, a hint of amusement lifting the corners of the firm mouth.

" 'Course he will," Danger answered for the older man. "Why d'you think he pulled in here at the stroke of 12?"

The family seated themselves around the table. Maggie, lifting the massive old silver teapot, tried to tell herself that the flush burning in her cheeks was because of the unexpectedness of her housewifely duties. It had nothing, but nothing to do with the ironical glint in Danger's eyes whenever she chanced to meet his glance.

Immediately following the meal, the doctor made his farewells. The children followed Maggie as she went with him to the veranda, watching as he climbed into his dusty old Chevrolet. With a parting salute, he took the winding driveway below.

For a few moments she stood looking out over the vast green solitude, conscious of a feeling of light, space, and air.

"Come on," she looked up, surprised to find Danger at her side, "and have a look around the place."

She hesitated, annoyed with herself at the inexplicable sense of panic his words had sparked in her. All this time at Amberley, and she hadn't even glimpsed a portion of the station, and yet. . . . She heard herself murmur: "The dishes—"

"Sling 'em in the sink. They'll keep. Phil and Ian can do them later. Come on, kids," he raised his voice, "no lessons today." To Maggie he said: "Wait here. I'll fetch the car." He was back in a few minutes at the foot of the steps, seated at the wheel of a gray Chrysler. "Into the back seat, you kids."

The children needed no second bidding. In a moment

they were tumbling into the car. Danger held open the passenger door for Maggie, then once more seated himself behind the wheel. As she watched the strong and sensitive hands shift a gear lever, Maggie had a sudden thought. "Able to drive car an advantage." She stole a surreptitious glance toward the controls, making a mental vow that during the journey she would familiarize herself with the car. She wouldn't be stuck, supposing he did ask her to drive the children somewhere. After all she was staying here for two more days.

They swept past a line of kennels, empty now, and moved on alongside two cabins, where men's socks were flung over a fence to dry. Fleeces were tacked to frames to dry out. "That's where Mike and Gavin live," Philippa explained. "Mike's going to teach me to play his guitar one of these days."

But Maggie's attention was caught by a rusty old car, the paint flaking in unsightly patches, the twin curved fins of surfboards rising from the hood. "Does it really go?"

"Sure it does!" Danger flung the decrepit vehicle a careless glance. "I have a beach buggy myself. They're just the thing for whizzing along the beach at low tide and collecting toheroas. Ever tried them?"

She shook her head with an odd sense of regret. If she'd been staying on. . . .

They ran past the stables and garage, the sheep pens, the shearing shed with its mellow red timbers. Then they were passing through a wide gate that was almost concealed by overhanging tree branches, taking a narrow winding path that led over sheep-dotted hills and down to native bush below.

But how much more attractive was this leafy green world at close quarters instead of from her bedroom window. A cluster of cabbage trees fluttered their stiff green fans in the light breeze, and great fronds of black-veined pungas glistened in the gentle spring sunshine. The air, spiced with the clean earthy smell of the bush, was incredibly clear. As they swept between an avenue of overhanging tree ferns, Maggie could have laughed aloud from sheer enjoyment. It just went to show what effect a knock on the head could have on you, she told herself. It made you so glad to be well again that nothing else mattered, not even being forced into the company of a man you simply couldn't stand; one who obviously felt exactly the same way about you.

They sped up a white curving track threading a high hill. At the summit Danger brought the car to a stop. Immediately the children were scrambling out. The two older ones ran down the steep slopes, laughing, falling and picking themselves up again. Mark exuberantly tumbled over and over down the grassy terraces that 100 years earlier had been dug by Maori warriors as fortifications in tribal battles.

"You can get an idea of the boundaries from up here." Danger shaded his eyes against the sun's glare as it emerged from behind the clouds.

"An idea!" Maggie leaned forward, taking in the vast scene. On the hilltop the breeze was strong, and she pushed away the dark strands veiling her eyes. All around her rose cleared high hills where seven-barred sheep fences swept upward to meet the horizon. The sheen of water gleamed from scattered dug-outs; directly below was a cleared grassy patch evidently used as an airstrip. In the dips of hills where tea-tree and native bush had been left to conserve the land, great boles of forest giants—kauri, totara, feathery rimu, reached for the sky. Beneath, the lighter green of tree-ferns starred the somber background, their drooping fronds lifting lazily in the breeze.

Maggie was conscious of a sense of remoteness, of something wild and free that she had once known and lost. She never realized how much she'd missed it, until now. She had forgotten what air could be like, far from city boundaries. Clear and fragrant, almost slightly intoxicating, on a day like this. It made her think all manner of wild things, like being able to remain at Amberley. She could have too, if only Danger hadn't been so—so difficult. Why couldn't he have treated her with fairness? Her soft lips tightened. That was all she asked, just ordinary fairness. But no, he had to thrust her aside simply because of some personal thing, darn him.

"All yours?" She was unaware of the wistfulness that tinged her tones.

"It's fairly extensive," he agreed. "Best part of 10,000 acres. A lot of it's in bush down in the gullies, but I've brought in 7,000 acres for grazing; run sheep and beef cattle. 10,000 acres of hill country around here wouldn't have meant much a few years ago when the whole place was covered in scrub. It took crop dusting to change the picture." He broke off. "Hello, here's Dusty now." As he spoke, a light aircraft swooped low over their heads and rose dangerously close to the steep slopes. The next moment the pilot released a load of fertilizer, and the fine dust settled over the clear ground. Then he was off, skimming the peaks as he returned for another load.

"What does it mean, the name Te Rangi?" she asked idly.

"Now that," Danger told her, "was something you should have asked Mrs. Wahonga about. For one thing, she could supply the right Maori pronunciation. The full name's—wait for it—*taepaepaetanga o te-rangi*—"

"Goodness! Whatever does all that add up to?"

"The place," Danger interpreted, "where the sun hangs down to the horizon. They were pretty lyrical, those old-time Maoris, when it came to naming a district."

"I can see what you mean." Her roving gaze was sweeping the hillsides. "I was looking for Pete."

"He's over there, down in the valley. The brood mares

are out with their foals in a back paddock. There's only a small bunch of them over here."

"Where?" Maggie followed the direction in which he was gazing.

"There, under the gumtrees, beside the Saint—" With an arm thrown carelessly around her shoulders, he leaned close, pointing a brown finger toward a cleft in the hills. "See him?"

But Maggie couldn't seem to focus for the stupid thud-thud of her heart. He was so near that she could see the tiny white marks fanning out from the deeply tanned skin at the corners of his eyes. Breathlessly she attempted to drag herself back to sanity, trying to concentrate her attention on the horses in the distant paddock. The white thoroughbred was obviously the Saint and the big bay was Pete.

"Make the most of it, Pete boy," she tried to speak lightly. "All that gorgeous fresh grass and oodles of space and company; it's all too good to last."

"Is it?" Very gently he lifted a hand to smooth back a long dark strand of hair that was blowing across her eyes.

Deliberately Maggie kept her gaze fixed on the paddock below, but all the time she knew that he was regarding her speculatively. To cover her confusion she said jerkily, "The children said that you were clearing some land?"

"That's right. We'll go and take a look." Putting two fingers to his lips, he gave a piercing whistle that made the children come pelting up the hillside, flushed and breath-less.

"On your way, kids!" They clambered in, then Danger slammed the door and turned the ignition. Soon they were swinging down a curving track, descending to the filtered sunshine of a bush-filled gully, then speeding up another slope. Now Maggie noticed that opposite, the hillside had been cleared of native bush, and the fallen tea-tree lay in cut heaps piled on the slopes, the branches dried out to a dark blackish tint.

Danger braked to a stop on the slope. "Got a chap in to bulldoze it all down. Now all I need to do is push it into the gully."

"All?" Maggie raised a teasing face. "Oh well, that's better than burning it off, even if it is a lot of work getting rid of it."

He grinned toward her. "How come you know so much about it? I thought you were a city girl?"

"Not always." Impulsively the words rose to her lips. "I only wish—" She broke off just in time to stop herself from voicing her thoughts—that I were staying here, and Pete too. It would all be perfect, except for the disturbing man at her side.

Even without turning she was aware of his quick inter-rogative glance. "What do you wish, Maggie?"

Please move away, she thought. She couldn't seem to reason clearly. All she could think of was his near-ness, the faint aroma of tobacco, and the fragrance of aftershave lotion. If only he'd stop looking at her. "Nothing," she said faintly. "Skip it."

Mark's shriek of "I can see Gavin and Mike!" brought her sharply back to the present. She stared toward the two horsemen far in the distance who were patrolling the long boundary fences in the valley below.

They moved over a bridge make from long stringy black ponga logs into a gully and swept into the damp greenness of a bush track, where the silvery notes of a tui echoed from high above in the leafy foliage.

As they drove over the hills Maggie could see the sheep: mothers with lambs, and occasionally a black one that made Mark call out with excitement.

Then they were in sight of the homestead, passing the mellow red shearing shed, the corral, the line of sheep-dog kennels, garages and sheds. As the car arrived to brake at the wide entrance, the children scrambled out and rushed up the steps.

"Thank you." Maggie turned to follow them into the house while Danger went to park the car.

In the lounge room she sat on a low seat by the window, watching Danger as he, with long easy strides, mounted the steps two at a time. It was all very well for him to be so cheerful and lighthearted, she thought crossly. He wasn't dependent on someone else for the carefree freedom of his life here. She sighed. Well, she'd have to have it out with him sooner or later, and the sooner the better. She swung around as he entered the room, turning a small diffident face toward him.

"There's something I wanted to ask you about—"

"Go ahead." He fished in his shirt pocket and extended a cigarette packet, lighted one for her, one for himself, then stood eyeing her. That compelling gaze he seemed to keep especially for her, and which she found so difficult to meet was upon her again.

"Just what did you mean," Maggie said in a low voice, "when you told the children that I might be staying?" She studied the glowing tip of her cigarette.

"Just what I said. Well, Maggie," he murmured softly, "it's up to you."

Maggie! "But I thought. . . ." Nervously she twisted a strand of hair around her fingers. "You said—"

"I've changed my mind," he returned calmly.

"Oh, I see." A sudden wild hope flared in her mind, filling her with excitement. She turned away, fearful that he might read the triumph in her expression. So he was about to apologize to her at last for his mistaken assessment of her capabilities. No doubt he would explain that he had judged her too harshly, and too soon. He now realized her undoubted ability to cope with children *and* household chores, despite her youthful appearance.

She waited . . . and waited. At length, in the growing

silence she realized that he hadn't the slightest intention of explaining, much less apologizing—ever. There was nothing but the bald, take-it-or-leave-it statement: "It's up to you!"

"What . . . made you change your mind . . . about me?" The words came unbidden to her lips.

He was as tall and erect and remote as ever as he looked at her. "Let's just say," he bent to flick the ash from his cigarette, "that I guess I owe you something at that."

The indignant thoughts chased one another through her mind. He was offering her employment merely because of the accident that had befallen her while on his property. Compensation for damages sustained. Wasn't that the legal jargon? Oh, he was hateful! Hateful! Anger surged through her, overriding every other emotion. She was deadly sick of always being on the receiving end of his charity. This time it would be her turn to call the tune. She drew a deep breath, schooling her voice to calmness. But in spite of herself, it emerged with a betraying tremor. "That's funny, because I've changed my mind about the job here. I've decided that it wouldn't suit me after all. So I guess that makes us about even."

He shrugged. "As you wish." His eyes were chips of blue ice. For a moment she was aware of a queer ill feeling that came perilously close to regret, but pride prevented her from retracting the words. A snatch of melody sung in soft Maori syllables gave her the cue she needed. "I can hear Mrs. Wahonga . . . I must see her . . . about supper. . . . Excuse me." She fled toward the door before he could notice the telltale color that was flooding her cheeks.

In her haste to escape she narrowly avoided colliding with the Maori woman. Mrs. Wahonga held up a plump detaining hand. "Hello, Miss Sullivan." The great dark eyes studied Maggie with frank appraisal. "You know something? You not so like that other one, not now I can see you properly. Cathy, she so much taller, you only little. It was seeing you all of a sudden like, same sort of face, same big brown eyes, that gave me such a turn."

Maggie flashed her pixie grin. "Sorry, Mrs. Wahonga."

But the woman continued to regard her consideringly. "You different too," she conceded candidly. "That other one, she liked herself a lot, she did."

"Oh well," Maggie perched lightly on the kitchen table, "I guess actresses are like that, wouldn't you say?"

"Don't ask me! I never knew anyone in that game, 'cept Cathy. Now don't you go bothering your head about supper. I'll put the chops on to cook right away!" She turned toward the giant refrigerator in a corner of the room. "You look a whole lot better today. Not so white-looking. Soon be well again, eh, *ehoa*?"

"I'm well now," Maggie said. "At least, I feel fine, but the doctor made me promise to stay here for two more days." She wondered at the deep sigh that escaped her at the thought of leaving. What was there to attract her, apart from the wild freedom of her surroundings? A kindly talkative woman, three perfectly ordinary children, and disturbing John Dangerfield himself.

Seated with the others at the table that evening with shafts of flame from a glorious sunset lighting the windows, Maggie found the meal delicious. Mutton from the farm, roasted kimera, fresh green salad, followed by luscious boysenberries topped with ice cream.

"No trouble," the woman disclaimed the chorus of compliments on her cooking ability. "I must get back home now and cook for my boy."

Gavin, young, fair, fresh-faced, eyed her teasingly. "You should have had an extra meal with us—"

"You could easily have managed it," his friend Mike, thin and dark, spoke in his quiet voice.

"That's what you think," Mrs. Wahonga countered. "I'm off now." She hesitated, looking toward Danger. "You all going down to the beach tomorrow?"

"All of us," Danger said.

Mrs. Wahonga turned to Maggie. "You're in for a great day. It's good fun getting toheroas." She gave her rich chuckle. "Good eating too."

"I'm looking forward to it," Maggie smiled back. "If I'm lucky I might be able to take some back to town with me. Do you think—"

Her voice was drowned in a flood of surprised cries as the children stared at her, wide-eyed.

There was a wild howl from Mark. "Don't go, Sullivan! Don't go!" His high chair lurched at a precarious angle as he leaned forward to clutch Maggie in a compulsive grasp. The tears splashed onto her arm. "I won't let you go! I won't, I won't!"

"Now you've done it." Danger, catching her eye, grinned ruefully.

Your fault. But she said the words under her breath. Aloud she heard herself calling through the uproar. "But I have to leave!"

"*Why* do you?" Philippa shrilled. "I thought you were staying here to look after us. You said you liked it here. Why can't you stay?" Then, pleadingly, "I *wish* you could."

"Me too," Ian put in his quiet boyish tones. "You make great scones, all brown and crusty."

"Don't you like us?" Philippa regarded Maggie anxiously. "We'll help. We'll be awfully good. We'll do the dishes every night if you'll stay, won't we, Ian?"

Her brother nodded. "Why can't you, Miss Sullivan?"

Maggie felt a pang in her heart. How to explain to these pleading, bewildered children that it was their uncle who made the decisions around here; he'd certainly made it plain enough that he didn't want her at Amberley station, not one little bit.

"It has nothing to do with you children," she said at last.

A chorus of eager young voices cut her short. "Then why—"

"I just can't," she said lamely.

Ian's freckled face turned toward her, eyes clear and candid. "But Miss Sullivan, couldn't you—"

"That's enough!" Danger cut in sharply. "Finish your supper, all of you." And to Mark: "Take it easy, chap. No need for all that roaring. You'll get looked after all right. Mrs. Wahonga."

"Don't *want* Mrs. Wahonga!" Mark banged his spoon imperiously on the tray of his high chair. "Want Sullivan! Want Sullivan!" As the child's howls increased in volume, Danger stood and carried the small boy away. Mark was still shrieking and sobbing.

"Seems you have quite an admirer," Danger said dryly to Maggie when he returned to the head of the big table.

Which is more than I could say for you. Maggie couldn't quite summon up the necessary courage to say the words aloud. She was annoyed with Danger for shutting Mark away in the bedroom. Loud sobbing could be heard, punctuated by a pause, then banging that sounded like a small foot aiming vigorous kicks against the closed door.

"Well, anyway," Gavin said with a grin to Maggie, "you'll have quite a day tomorrow. Probably be a big crowd, though you don't notice it down on the beach, it's so vast. People come from miles away, even as far as Auckland."

"But only the locals know just where to find the biggest and best toheroas," put in Mike, with a knowing wink in Maggie's direction.

"But we'll show you where to go, Miss Sullivan," the two chorused in unison.

"Nothing but the best for Miss Sullivan, eh, Danger?" Mike added.

But the boys' employer appeared to have lost interest in that annoying trouble-maker who had forced herself into his home. "Tide'll be dead low around midday," he remarked. "Quite a good arrangement for the weekend." His cool gaze shifted to Maggie. "It would help if you'd take the kids down in the car."

"The car?" Taken by surprise, she stared at him blankly.

"It's all because of the quota," Mike explained. "They're awfully strict, the beach inspectors are, about taking toheroas since some greedy people grabbed more than their share, last year. Now there are only two weekends during the whole year allowed for digging. And then you're only supposed to take ten each, and only three gatherers to a car. That's when it comes in handy to take along some extra collectors, like the kids—"

"Thanks very much," Ian said sarcastically.

"No offense, pal."

"Ten toheroas per person per day, perhaps," Gavin put in.

But Maggie was scarcely aware of the teasing voices. Still smarting with humiliation after her interview with Danger, she was feverishly trying to memorize the position of the gears in the big Chrysler. "Able to drive a car," his advertisement had stipulated. This time she was determined not to fail him.

"How far away is the toheroas beach?" she inquired.

"No distance at all." Danger answered laconically. "A few miles over to the Gap, then once you hit the beach, about five miles along the sandhills should do it."

"Only we don't tell that to city scroungers," Mike confided.

"Only to special folk. Ones we really go for," his friend added, turning a sunburned face toward Maggie.

Danger didn't say anything at all. But then he

wouldn't, Maggie though angrily. Catch the boss of Amberley joining in any complimentary remarks concerning Maggie Sullivan!

All at once she became aware that the loud cries from Mark's bedroom had died away. "Shall I go fetch Mark now?" she appealed to Danger. "He seems to have quietened down."

"I'll get him." He returned a few moments later carrying a chastened Mark, who in silence resumed his cold meal, with only an occasional gulping sob.

The tear-stained babyish face and swollen eyelids went to Maggie's heart, and she felt a sudden misgiving. These children really needed her, and she was deserting them, leaving them in the care of a neighbor and a man who was inexperienced in family life: a man who was forced to neglect his duties on a vast station in order to work close to the homestead. How could she? Yet how could she remain knowing that Danger's offer of employment had been made only from a sense of obligation?

Afterward, without being told, Philippa and Ian cleared away the dinner dishes and began to wash them. For once, Maggie noticed, there was no ensuing squabble.

She went up the hall, noticing a light under the door of the small room that Danger used as an office.

Later when Maggie was in the bathroom, preparing Mark for bed, the telephone rang and she went to answer it. A girl's voice answered, a girl who was obviously taken aback by Maggie's polite "Hello!"

"I'm sorry," the stranger shouted, confused. "I think I've dialed the wrong number. That's not Mr. Dangerfield's place, is it?"

"Yes," Maggie replied softly, "that's right."

"But—I—" At last the unknown caller appeared to recover herself. "Is he there? Danger, I mean? Would you tell him please that it's Ann—"

"Just hold the line and I'll get him."

When she opened the door of the small room off the passage, she saw that it was almost filled by a huge old-fashioned desk, littered with papers and account books. The look of concentration that lingered as Maggie entered the room vanished as he absorbed her message.

"Right, I'll take it," and went to the telephone. As Maggie kneeled beside the child in the big bath, she caught the murmur of Danger's deep voice. A few moments later a dark head appeared around the corner of the door. She glanced over her shoulder inquiringly.

"Must go out. If anyone wants me I'll be over at Ann's place. Ian knows the number. Okay?"

Maggie nodded, "That's all right." As she continued washing Mark she reflected that this Ann must be awfully important to Danger to make him forget everything else and dash out the moment she called. She remembered now that Ann was the girl who was in the habit of sending over home-baked goodies for the master of Amberley. Hadn't she supplied the soup, intended for Danger and consumed by herself? Oh well, if Ann were all that wrapped up in him and he was so obviously in love with the girl, she would soon be in a position to make him soup every night of the week without fear of some strange girl benefiting from it. Only for some reason, the thought gave her small satisfaction. Absently she scrubbed Mark's small slippery back until an outraged "You've done that" brought her abruptly back to the present.

In spite of a recent concussion, followed by a long day filled with unaccustomed activity, she hadn't felt a bit weary—until now. She saw the children to bed, mended a torn dress belonging to Philippa, then decided to call it a day. She refused to admit that the house, without Danger, seemed strangely lifeless and curiously empty.

CHAPTER FOUR

"Reckon you can sort out the gears?" Danger leaned a bronzed elbow on the window ledge of the car as he bent inquiringly towards Maggie.

"Oh, yes." Perched high on a mound of cushions for height behind the wheel, she nodded with what she hoped was an air of careless confidence. "What I don't know, though, is how to get down to the beach."

"We'll show you," the children chorused from the rear seat. But Danger silenced them with a lift of his hand. "You'll be okay, Maggie. Just follow me in the beach buggy. The boys have taken off already in their jalopy, but we'll meet up with them down at the Gap." His glance moved toward a battered old vehicle that was lurching along the curving hill track toward the main road.

A few moments later Danger appeared at the wheel of his beach buggy: a decrepit vehicle with heavy-duty tires, tattered upholstery and paintwork badly corroded by the onslaught of salt water and sea winds.

Maggie put the car in gear and turned toward the children with their gaily colored beach pails. "You've forgotten to bring your shovels."

"No, we haven't!" They all spoke at once. "You're not allowed to have shovels. You just have to use your fingers in the sand."

"Oh!" At that moment Danger, with a grin in Maggie's direction, took off, and she followed a short distance behind.

"Faster! Faster!" shouted Mark, bouncing up and down in the seat, but Maggie was determined to keep a safe distance from the other car. Golly, she thought, she couldn't afford to take any chances with the expensive Chrysler; especially in view of Danger's already low opinion of her driving ability. Galling though it was in her present mood of resentment toward him, she had no choice but to obey his orders.

Above, the sun played hide and seek with the clouds. A top-dressing plane, silver against gray cottonwool shapes, skimmed the hills, leaving in its wake a rising cloud of fertilizer dust.

Danger waited at the second gate, closing it after Maggie had driven through; then both cars were out on the main highway. She found that after her first uncertain fumbling with the gears she was rapidly gaining confidence and could occasionally glance around toward isolated farmhouses, each built on a rise and surrounded by cleared green hills with their grazing sheep. Then they were running through a small clean township turning into a side road, to speed past a dairy factory and a fish canning industry. Soon the beach buggy was pulling up beside the fast-flowing waters of a wide tidal river. As Maggie drew alongside she could see no sign of a ferry, or of any human habitation. There was nothing but arum lilies growing wild among the long grasses that rippled in the wind and the high hills rising on the opposite side.

"Here it comes!" Mark shouted as a barge swept around a curve of the river. In a few moments both cars were being transported to the bank on the other side.

Then they were driving along pleasant country roads bordered by farmlands. The route took them over a series of green hills, and at last, they were in sight of the sea.

Maggie, following the beach buggy across a narrow rough track between towering flax-covered cliffs, caught the low murmur of the surf. Then she swung the car onto a grassy headland where picnickers were grouped beneath bright beach umbrellas.

"Follow me!" Danger threw back over his shoulder, and for once she was content to do just that. Skirting the scattered picnic parties and taking care to avoid the children who ran amongst parked vehicles, she backed the Chrysler into a narrow space between the beach buggy and a long stock transporter.

The children climbed out at once, to rush away over the long grass, while Maggie found herself strolling at Danger's side as they moved toward the crowd ahead.

"I suppose you know just about everyone here," she said, to break the uncomfortable silence and the odd disturbing feeling that overtook her whenever she found herself alone with him.

"Just about."

Indeed, before long they were surrounded by farmers and residents of the backblocks area. There was, however, one familiar figure. Maggie found herself looking up into a lined tanned face.

"You feeling all right now?" Doc Smith inquired, and Maggie smilingly assented.

As they made their way through the groups, she could see smoke rising in the clear air from a barbecue at the cliff edge. A short distance away a beach house was overflowing with a constant steam of picnickers who were crowding the open doorway.

"Danger!" A tall, well-built girl rose from her seat on the grass and came hurrying toward them. "I thought you were never coming! I—" On catching sight of Maggie, she stopped short.

"Hi, Ann," Danger said in his laconic way. "This is Miss Sullivan."

"Oh—" Just in time Maggie stopped herself from blurting, "The girl who sent over the soup!" For of course this was Ann, who according to Mrs. Wahonga, "looked after" the bachelor of Amberley. She was also the girl at whose summons he had rushed away without a moment's hesitation. Danger, who never appeared to hurry himself for anyone else.

While the other two chatted, Maggie covertly studied

the other girl: tall and strong-looking, with weathered skin and short fair hair bleached by the sun. She had a direct manner of speech, Maggie mused, as the other two strolled along at her side. Their conversation, though, was all of stock and farming problems. As they went on Maggie reflected crossly that for all the notice the other two were taking of her, she might just as well not be here at all.

"Wait a minute, Ann! Danger!" Maggie looked toward a tall, sensitive-looking young man with fair hair and beard who was threading his way through the mob in their direction.

As the thin young figure reached them, Ann suddenly realized that she and Danger weren't alone. She turned toward Maggie. "My brother Tony, this is Miss Sullivan."

She met his openly appreciative glance. "Maggie."

"Nice to meet you, Maggie," he stood at her side, "Danger didn't tell me—"

"None of your business."

As they sat on the lush green grass it seemed that Tony's gaze was riveted on her face. Strange, the thought ran through her mind, that he and Ann are so alike, yet she seems so exceptionally strong and he so thin, almost delicate.

Tony's smiling glance divined her thoughts. "Don't say it! We happen to be twins, Ann and I, but I guess there was a mix-up somewhere along the line in the muscle department. Staying up at Amberley, Maggie?"

She nodded. "That's right." In the brief pause she realized that the other girl's gaze was frankly curious. So Danger had told Ann nothing regarding his temporary housekeeper. She wondered why, and then decided that probably she didn't signify in his life. She wasn't sufficiently important to mention to his girlfriend—if Ann was his girlfriend. Certainly the other girl had been hanging on every word. And there was no doubt, she thought with curious reluctance, that they would be a perfect complement for each other. A girl so tall and well-built would be perfectly matched by John Dangerfield's lean height. Besides, didn't they belong to the same free, outdoor world? Not like her. She plucked at the long grass at her feet. "Just until tomorrow."

All at once she flinched from explanations regarding the humiliating circumstances of her enforced stay at Amberley, dependent on Danger's generosity. He was doing nothing to help her out, she thought vindictively, merely eyeing her with that amused lift to his lips, saying nothing at all.

She threw caution to the winds. "Danger—well, he didn't really expect me. It was all a mistake—"

"A mistake!" Tony stared across at her incredulously. Maggie wondered why he wasn't sun-tanned, like everyone else she had met in the district. "Some guys sure have all the luck!"

But now, having started, Maggie had a wild impulse to force Danger to be aware of her. She'd make him notice her!

"Yes," she said, "I came to Te Rangi after a housekeeping job—"

Tony's disbelieving tone was subtly flattering. "Not *you*."

"Well, why not?" Maggie tossed back her long black hair which was blowing around her shoulders in the fresh sea breeze.

"Nothing, nothing . . . but any girl who looks like that—"

"Like me, like this?" Ruefully she glanced down at shabby blue jeans and worn sneakers. "Wear your oldest clothes," Philippa had advised. "Anyway," she smiled, "you don't look like a farmer to me."

"That figures," Tony said. "because I'm not, actually. Just thought I'd give it a go. But you—"

"Unfortunately," Danger broke in, "we couldn't come to terms. The job wasn't suitable."

Suitable to whom? Maggie thought hotly, but this time she thought better of the frank disclosure. Instead she murmured: "So I'm going back to town tomorrow."

"Pity." The fair man sent her a warmly significant look.

"Yes, I—" Looking up, she met Danger's glance; ensnared in that brilliant blue gaze she couldn't seem to drag her eyes away. Wildly she clutched at her spinning senses. "So I thought I'd have a day out at the Gap," she said rapidly, "get some toheroas to take back with me, if I'm lucky."

"So here you are!" Gavin and Mike paused beside Maggie. "Hey, what d'you know?" Mike said. "The girls are cooking toheroa fritters up in the cottage—loads of them. Be ready in a couple of minutes, they said. Boy, I can hardly wait."

"Well, if you'll excuse me." Maggie, her thoughts in a turmoil, watched Danger saunter toward the men standing around the smoking barbecue.

"Come and have a look around." She realized Gavin was talking to her. Together the group moved away, threading their way between parked cars and Land Rovers. From the hill paddock adjoining the area, black steers crowded the boundary fence, their great dark eyes staring curiously toward the picnic, on the other side of the barbed wire.

She paused at the cliff edge, glancing down over tall spears of flax in bloom to the misty ocean-blue of the sea far below. Beyond an expanse of sand, white-crested breakers rolled in from the Tasman to splinter on the shore in a shower of spray. A swift look aroun assured her that the children had joined a family group seated beneath a beach umbrella on the grass. She would need to keep a careful watch on Mark with this sheer unprotected drop so nearby.

As the party strolled on around the headland, Maggie met many members of the small friendly community. Soon she had lost all count of names and faces, but what did it matter? After today she would never meet any of them again. To her surprise Tony too seemed a stranger to many of the groups. As they made their way toward a white timber cottage overlooking the sea, she said inquiringly. "Don't tell me that you're a visitor here too?"

Ann answered for her brother. "He is, you know—in a way."

"In a way's right," Tony smiled. "Oh, I was born here in Te Rangi," he explained in his light tones, "but that's about how far I went in the sheep-farming caper. Been away at boarding school in town for years, then on to 'Varsity. Architecture's my line," a shadow crossed the green eyes so resembling his sister's, "or I thought it was!" He tried to laugh. "Failed my final exams, so I guess that means another year of hard study." His expression sobered. "That is, unless I give it up to return to the farm."

"You don't have to," Ann put in quickly. "It's not," she confided with sisterly candor to Maggie, "as if he'd be any use. I can manage fine on my own. Tony knows that."

"Do I?" he appealed to Maggie. "That's what *she* says. Oh, it was okay while Dad was around, but since he died Ann seems to have this idea that she can carry on a man's job, do the whole thing single-handed. Guess it's time I did something about it."

"Phooey!" Ann turned toward Maggie with a smile that revealed large white teeth. "He's being self-sacrificing. He's always wanted to be an architect. Just because he didn't quite make the exams this year, he's using it as an excuse to help me. But it's only a tryout, just for the summer holidays. If he wants to carry on after that, okay, but it would be a darn shame to drop his studies at this stage; just another year and he'd be through for good."

"Do you think you'd like sheep-farming?" Maggie asked Tony.

He sent her a quizzical grin. "Like mucking around in sheep pens and shearing sheds? What do *you* think? Oh, it's okay for Ann. She's never happier than out on a horse rounding up sheep or stray cattle. She simply won't hear of selling and coming to town."

"But it's not as if I need him. Not really!" Ann's voice warmed. "Not with Danger just over the hill if I need advice in a hurry. Like the other night, when one of the pedigree Romneys looked like passing out, he came over like a shot, just in time to do a life-saving act. Besides," a small secret smile played around the wide mouth, "I mightn't always be on my own here."

Maggie's heart gave a queer little lurch. Danger and Ann? Well, why not? What could be more suitable?

Apparently, however, Tony put a different construction on the words. "You mean, hire a manager?" he grinned cheerfully. "That would cost us a packet."

Ann said, still with an air of suppressed excitement, "I didn't say a manager."

Grinning, her brother lifted Ann's work-stained tanned hand, large and capable, with the palm roughened and crisscrossed with cuts.

"He'll need to be a tough sheep-farming guy himself—"

"Don't worry," once again the secret smile played around the wide mouth, "he is. I might give you a surprise one of these days."

"You're putting us on," Tony said laughingly. "Not that I wouldn't be the first to wish you luck, Sis. I mean, that would solve everything."

Maggie had the odd conviction that Ann and Danger's wedding wouldn't solve anything at all, at least not so far as she was concerned. She couldn't understand the feeling of desolation that flooded her, like a cold hand clutching her heart.

"Everybody in for lunch!" a woman's voice called from the white cottage, and various groups began to converge toward the small building at the cliff edge.

Inside Maggie found that the wide picture windows of the living room overlooked the incredible blue of the ocean. From a small adjoining kitchen came the appetizing aroma of coffee. On a side table two electric frypans were piled high with delectable golden-brown fritters. On the great solidly built kauri table were plates of scotch eggs, barbecued steaks, chops and sausages, hams, scones and thick slices of homemade bread mixed with stone-ground flour. Never had Maggie seen such an array of home-prepared goodies. There were cans of beer for the men, soft drinks for the children, plus a variety of wines distilled from locally grown grapes. All around was a spirit of warm friendliness that reached out to include the strange girl whom Danger had brought with him.

All through the picnic Tony didn't leave her side, plying her with food and chiding her on her lack of appetite. At least, she thought resentfully, someone found her sufficiently attractive to seek her out. Danger hadn't even bothered to stay and escort her to the cottage. It was almost, ridiculous though it seemed, as if he were avoiding her. She turned animatedly toward Tony, who appeared only too delighted to listen attentively, as she rattled off the first thoughts that entered her head.

"Not a bad way," he remarked a little later, "to fill in time while we're waiting for the tide to go out."

Maggie nodded, but her eyes were fixed on a man, tall and lean-hipped, who was weaving his way through the crowd. Of course he was heading for Ann. Why not? Weren't they old friends? Friends, or— With an effort she wrenched her thoughts away and tried to concentrate on Tony's pleasant conversation.

Afterward willing hands made short work of the dishes piled high in the kitchen sink. Soon everyone was spilling into cars, trucks, and Land Rovers. In a few moments the mass of vehicles swerved from the headland into the rutted track that led down to the ocean beach below.

Maggie waited with the children in the car until Danger in the beach buggy, accompanied by two other men gave her a signal to start. He went ahead, glancing over his shoulder to Maggie as she revved up the engine and moved over the grass. On the steep boulder-strewn track the road engaged all her attention, but once on the sand she had only to follow the tracks of the beach buggy in the gleaming wet surface. Now she could take in the endless sandhills where marram grass retained a precarious hold; the rugged cliffs high above with their yellow clay banks. Ahead, the beach stretched away in an inmensity of sand; the vehicles that had preceded her already blurred with haze in the distance.

A check in the overhead mirror showed a jalopy a short distance away, with Gavin at the wheel.

At last the beach buggy pulled up and Maggie drew to a stop alongside. Danger was holding the door open for her. For a moment she stood still, looking around her. She was intrigued by the men and women, old and young, who were already kneeling on the wet sand as they thrust their hands down in search of the shellfish. Plastic pails made splashes of color along the shoreline. All at once she realized that Danger was eyeing her with his maddening look of amusement. "You'll be just as keen as the rest, once you get started."

She laughed up at him. All at once the day seemed to swing into focus: the sparkle on the sea more glittering, everything suddenly novel and exciting. "Show me!"

"I will! I will!" Mark circled excitedly on the sand as he rushed from place to place. "Here! No, here!"

But Danger's glance was on the sand. "See that bit of a bubble? Might be worth trying. Come on, Maggie, let's give it a go." Together they knelt on the wet surface, thrusting hands deeper and deeper while the sea water rushed to fill the sandy opening.

"Oh," Maggie cried disappointedly as she caught sight of a flash of disappearing white shell, "he's getting away!"

"That's what he thinks!"

Maggie made a further effort to catch the shellfish and somehow, somehow found herself clutching Danger's hand. Immediately everything fled from her mind except the masculine magnetism against which she struggled in vain.

"He—escaped," she said huskily, standing up. He was still kneeling on the sand, with a laughing, quizzical expression. "Do you mind?"

"Not—really." But the words stuck in her throat, and hurriedly she began to dig in a fresh spot, bending low so that he couldn't see how shaken she was. She scarcely realized she was digging feverishly with no quarry in sight, until all at once a tiny shellfish appeared in her hand.

"Throw him back," Danger advised matter-of-factly, "he's far too small for regulations—or a meal."

As the shellfish scuttled deep into the sand, she realized that Tony was at her side.

"Bad luck," he commiserated. "You could always return next year when he's bigger, or stay at Te Rangi and wait—"

She scarcely heard him. She was watching Ann approach them, hearing Danger's voice as he turned away. "Want a hand?"

They moved away together along a beach that had all at once become vast and strangely lonely, in spite of the other groups scattered along the coastline. She must have been crazy to have imagined the fleeting physical contact with Danger to have meant something more than the trivial task they were engaged in. Something like falling in love.

Maggie found to her surprise that the toheroas were more elusive than she had anticipated. May of the spots where she and Tony dug yielded nothing. When she did catch a fleeting glimpse of a white shell, it vanished into the wet sand immediately. Or perhaps she was too inexperienced to know how to grip the smooth shell before it burrowed away.

The children were having more success as they wandered from place to place. Even Mark had captured a baby toheroa which he clutched in a chubby hand, refusing to obey the older children's orders and return the tiny creature to the sand.

Tony, glancing down at the small boy's belligerent, screwed-up face, smiled tolerantly. "Determined little cuss, isn't he?"

"Is he ever!" Maggie agreed. "Even when he's cross and miserable like that somehow he gets around you." She peered into Tony's yellow plastic pail. "How many have you found anyway?"

He shrugged thin shoulders under a cotton shirt.

"None—yet. I'm depending on you to help me."

They strolled along the sand while the children ran ahead. With an effort, Maggie wrenched her thoughts from Ann and Danger, whom she could see in the distance. She tried to concentrate on the matter in hand. She couldn't help but notice that wherever there were Maori diggers the toheroas were plucked from the sand without difficulty. Judging by the speedy way in which they obtained their quota, the relaxed Maoris appeared to know far more of the ways of the shellfish than anyone else. Maggie decided to dig in the vicinity of a happy Maori party, and almost immediately both she and Tony managed to capture their quota of shellfish with no difficulty at all.

The golden afternoon slid away, and Maggie was surprised to find that the tide was on the turn. People were collecting picnic gear as they strolled back in the direction of the vehicles parked below the tide mark.

Maggie walking with Tony as they made their way toward the beach buggy, was suddenly aware of a note of urgency in the light banter. "Look, it's goodbye, isn't it? Just like that? One day together and then—" He spread thin hands in an eloquent gesture.

A shadow fell across Maggie's face. How could she have forgotten that she was leaving here tomorrow? *Tomorrow!* The wild remoteness of the ocean must have bewitched her into forgetting. Or didn't she wish to remember?

Tony, however, misinterpreted her silence. "You feel that way too? Well, it doesn't have to be. I'll keep in touch . . . call you tonight."

"Look what I have!" Mark clambered into the car, turning to thrust a sand-encrusted hand clutching an extremely small toheroa toward Maggie. "It's a big one, isn't it?" he demanded.

She smiled. "Compared with you, maybe."

"Phil says it's too little, and it isn't. It isn't so. It's *big*!"

The two older children, reaching the car at that moment, hotly debated the point. In the loud argument that ensued, Tony was forced to raise his voice. "Don't forget, Maggie. Tonight. 'Bye!"

He went to his car while Maggie climbed behind the wheel of the Chrysler.

On the return journey over the sand she drove carefully, remembering Danger's instructions to keep the car below the tide mark. Although there was room she knew better than to offer the walkers a lift, realizing that the people on foot were part of the toheroa-gathering plan. Indeed, it seemed that the outing was planned with the precision of a military operation.

"Hey, Miss Sullivan," Ian said suddenly, "can you cook toheroas?"

"Heavens," she thought, "I don't even know how to get them out of their shells."

"It doesn't matter," Phil said carelessly. The children must have perceived her hesitation. "Danger'll show you."

"Bags I do the mincing," Ian called out.

"You did it last time!" protested his sister.

Maggie was thinking with relief that if she had only to deal with minced shellfish, it would be a simple matter to make them into fritters.

Indeed when at dinner she served the fritters, she felt a justifiable sense of pride in her achievement. As the meal progressed, however, she had to admit that Danger took her culinary skills very much for granted. Perhaps, she thought forlornly, Ann had spoiled him in that direction. The appreciative comments of the two farm helpers, however, made up for their employer's preoccupied silence and lack of appreciation.

Later she passed Danger, engaged on the telephone in a long conversation with a stock buyer, and went out to inspect the van. She couldn't think why she had neglected to look it over before this. Now she noticed the newly erected shelf. Broken crockery and glass had been cleared away. The utensils were neatly replaced above the bunk bed with its gray Army blankets. Apparently everything was in readiness for her departure, except herself. Odd how she felt so reluctant to leave. It must be the children who were playing on her heartstrings. The children. . . . All at once she realized that it was long past Mark's bedtime. Closing the van door behind her, she went to find him. Could he have put himself to bed? Surely not. Yet, come to think of it, she remembered his fair head drooping listlessly over his high chair during dinner. He had looked quite exhausted. A swift search through the children's bedrooms, however, brought no sign of him. Maggie wandered out into the deepening twilight.

Mike was seated on the step of his hut, his dark head bent over his guitar, work-roughened hands plucking idly at the strings. Gavin lounged beside him. He took the cigarette from his mouth and glanced toward Maggie. "Coming to the concert?"

She smiled and shook her head. "Sorry. I've lost something—Mark, actually. It's long past his bedtime and he's vanished, conveniently, I expect. You haven't seen him around, have you?"

"Not a hair or hide." Mike resumed his playing. The plaintive notes followed Maggie as she went into the stables, peered into the great dim cave of the shearing shed, the shadowy garages, then returned to take a path leading around the side of the house.

The two men were still seated in the doorway of the open hut when she returned a little later, a worried frown creasing her forehead.

The pluck-plucking stopped abruptly as Mike glanced up. "No sign of the little one?"

Maggie shook her head. "I can't think where he could be." She glanced perplexedly around her. "And it's getting awfully dark."

Gavin came to stand beside her. "The other kids don't know where he is?"

"The last they saw of him was at dinner."

"He'll be around. Having fun watching us looking for him, I bet. Come on, Mike, let's go and collect him." And to Maggie: "You can relax, Miss Sullivan. We'll have him back safe and sound within a minute or so." He grinned cheerfully. "We know lots of hiding places that you don't."

As Maggie watched them stride away into the gloom, a little of the anxious ache niggling at the back of her mind died away. Absurd to feel concern about Mark, here in his own home, and yet— She couldn't seem to banish the terrifying pictures conjured up by her too-vivid imagination. The waterholes for one; a small child could tumble into one with fatal results. The high hills . . . in the vastness of the station Mark could lose himself once he was beyond the first gate. Most worrying of all was the thought that he had been in her care. If only she'd put him to bed earlier!

The men's return a little later did nothing to allay her anxiety.

"Nowhere else to look," Gavin said, puzzled. "Oh well, he'll show up at any moment. He'd better put in an appearance before Danger finds out he's missing."

"Who's missing?"

The deep voice made Maggie glance behind her. How long had he been standing there, his cigarette a red glow in the gathering darkness?

"It's just—Mark," she said slowly.

"He's taken off," Gavin put in, "at his bedtime. Wouldn't you know?"

But Danger's eyes were fixed on Maggie's anxious face. "You should have told me."

Anger flared along her nerves. Of course he would have found the child right away. No problem. Wasn't it typical of him? Yet at the same time she couldn't help but feel a sense of thankfulness. For all his annoying ways, she had to admit that there was something definitely reassuring about him. He did get things done.

"Wait here. I'll go and have a look—" He spun on his heel. "Gavin, you take a look down the road. You never know what ideas the kid gets into his head. Mike, search over in the horse paddock, will you? Maggie, you go up to the house . . . we'll get him back in no time."

Slowly she made her way toward the lighted lounge. The television was switched on, but she couldn't concentrate on the screen in the empty room. At last she stood on the veranda, leaning over the rail and peering into the darkness.

A moment later Danger came striding toward the lighted house, alone. As he stood looking up at her, she caught the glint of his eyes in the light of the overhead lantern. "No luck yet. I suppose you checked in the van?"

"Oh yes, yes! I was in there just a while ago. I can't help thinking," the words spilled from her lips, "it's silly, but I just can't forget about the waterholes—"

"It's okay," his voice softened. "I've checked all the near ones. Not that Mark'd be likely to take a header into one, not after the tongue-lashing I gave him when he first arrived here."

Maggie let out her breath on a long sigh of relief. "Well, that's something. You—you don't think," she faltered, "that anything's happened to him?"

"Mark? Not on your life! He'll be along any minute, proud as Punch at getting the better of everyone."

But two hours later, despite the searching of the two older children, Maggie, Danger and the men, there was still no sign of a small chubby child. As the minutes dragged by, Maggie blamed herself. If only she'd been more careful. If only . . . regrets, recriminations.

Another hour went fruitlessly past before Maggie, waiting at the window of the lounge, caught sight of Danger approaching the doorway. He carried a small boy in his arms.

"Safe and sound," he said. "Better get him to bed."

"Oh, thank heaven!" Maggie said on a long breath of relief. "I'll take him now—wherever did you find him?"

"Asleep in the van." His voice was grim.

"The van!" Maggie cried incredulously. "But I looked there first of all!"

He grinned. "Bet you didn't look *under* the bunk bed. He was well hidden by the covers. It was just a lucky chance that I happened on him."

Mark, still half-asleep, smiled angelically. "I'll have a word with him about all this in the morning," Danger said.

Hurriedly Maggie took the child into her arms. "Just a quick wash, and I'll pop him into bed."

Mark clung to her as she carried him to the bathroom, a subdued Mark who seemed strangely listless. Perhaps, she thought, he was still half-asleep. It wasn't until she was pulling the sheet up over the small pajamaed figure that it struck her that Mark's eyes were glazed. And surely that high flush burning on the babyish cheeks was something more than sleep. Putting a hand to the child's forehead, she was horrified to feel the heat there. He was feverish, no doubt of it. He must be ill, she thought, or he wouldn't have slept all this time in the van while we were calling his name. She watched him swallow a crushed aspirin uncomplainingly.

"What made you hide out there in the van, Mark?" she asked gently. "Why did you do it?"

Sleepily the glazed blue eyes opened; the childish sounds were suddenly clear and indignant. "*Wasn't* hiding! I was going away with you."

"Oh, Mark!" She bent to drop a kiss on the small, flushed cheek, her long dark hair falling around her face. The next moment, she felt rather than saw someone else in the room. Turning swiftly, she realized that Danger had been a silent witness of the little scene. How long had he been there, watching—and listening? He came to her side, looking down at the small boy who already was breathing softly, with closed eyes.

"I think he's feverish," Maggie whispered. "I've given

him an aspirin. That should bring his temperature down, unless—" She stopped short, struck by a sudden horrifying thought. "Wouldn't it be awful if he was getting something?"

"Could be. And if he is," Danger said quietly, "maybe you'd better think about changing your mind."

"About leaving here tomorrow, you mean?"

He didn't answer, but merely continued to regard her with that cool inquiring look. (Well, it's up to you, Miss Sullivan.) But it wasn't Danger whom she must think of just now. All that mattered was the welfare of a three-year-old boy whose outward aggressiveness, she realized now, served to conceal an inner insecurity; a deep longing for his absent mother, or for someone who could take her place.

"All right then," she said slowly, "I'll stay."

Glancing at him, she was just in time to surprise a triumphant gleam that flickered in his eyes. Hastily she amended: "But just until you manage to find someone else."

He had the last word after all. What was even more annoying, his soft whisper had the effect of making her forget all those good resolutions about not allowing him to affect her.

"*If* I find someone else!"

CHAPTER FIVE

Maggie woke early on the following day, to a morning of pale eggshell-blue skies and high winds. For a few minutes she lay still, thinking, remembering. She couldn't understand why she felt so happy that once again fate had detained her at the vast sheep station. A country girl at heart, despite all those dreary years spent seated at an office desk? She hoped though that Mark wasn't suffering from some serious complaint. The thought made her spring from the bed, and slipping into a short filmy house coat of palest pink she hurried along the hall. On the way she met Ian, tousle-headed and obviously on his way to the bathroom shower.

"How's Mark feeling today?" she asked quickly.

"Dunno!" Swinging a towel in his hand, he blinked sleep-rimmed eyes. "He's still asleep in there—" His voice quickened to a note of alarm. "Heh! You're not going to *wake* him, are you? Can't we have a few minutes more in peace?"

Maggie laughed and went along to the room shared by both boys. One glance at Mark's heavy-lidded eyes and flushed cheeks told her that he was far from well. His forehead, when she put a hand out to touch him, was still burning hot.

He shifted restlessly in the bed. "I'm hot. Can I have a drink of water?"

"I'll get it for you. Don't throw off the blankets, Mark. You'll have to stay in bed today, I'm afraid."

Even this dreaded fate, however, awakened little interest in the sick child.

"You haven't a headache, have you?"

"Nope." The fair head turned listlessly toward her, and

Maggie bent to catch the muttered words. "I wanted to go with you."

"Well, I'm not going away now," she said cheerfully. "I'm going to stay right here and look after you. And that means," she added, "that you have to stay in bed until you're better."

"You're not going! Great!" The glazed blue eyes showed a spark of interest. Then as he flung himself sideways Maggie caught sight of clusters of pink spots that were dotted along the plump arm. Measles! The complaint she had so lightheartedly wished on the children just to spite Danger. Somehow the wish had backfired. She was struck with nursing Mark back to health herself. And Ian slept in the same room as the sick child. Wildly she wondered if the two older children had been inoculated against the infection. Perhaps they had already caught the germ.

Mark too had noticed the spots on his body. "I've got marks," he muttered in a puzzled tone, "here, and here, and here. Lots of marks!"

"Yes, I know you have. It looks like measles to me."

"Measles!" A look of pride spread over the flushed small face. "I bet Philippa and Ian haven't had them."

"Give them time," Maggie thought gloomily. Wildly she made calculations in her mind. Three children, at three-weekly intervals, each one ill for at least two weeks. . . . She was conscious of a wild urge toward hysteria. How amused Danger would be if he guessed how her malevolent wish had rebounded, keeping her a prisoner here for weeks to come.

During breakfast she found that her misgivings regarding the two older children were well founded, for neither had had measles. Nor had they been inoculated against infection. "Betcha we get them at Christmas," Philippa said glumly, then she brightened. "But I don't care, so long as you're not going away!" She beamed happily at Maggie.

Ian gave a loud cheer, inquiring in the same breath when Maggie intended making more of those super crusty scones. There was no mistaking the pleased surprise with which Mike and Gavin reacted to the news of Maggie's altered plans.

"Gee, that's great!" Mike's narrow face wore a delighted grin.

"They're having a dance at Mataroa next week," his friend suggested eagerly. Overcome with sudden shyness, he looked to his plate of poached eggs on toast and murmured uneasily, "That is, if you'd be interested?"

Maggie smiled. "I might be." Her thoughts were with Danger, who had added nothing to the general atmosphere of excitement. But of course he wouldn't. Why should he pretend feelings he didn't possess? He was pushing back his chair, his expression abstracted. "You'll have to excuse me, folks. Have to get cracking on that fencing job down in the far hill paddock." His gaze went to Ian and Philippa. "Better get to those school assignments today, kids. Dishes, then correspondence work. Right?"

Maggie stifled a pang of disappointment. What had she expected of him? A speech of welcome? "Wait—" she appealed to Danger as he was moving with his long easy stride toward the door. "What about Mark?"

He eyed her coolly. "Better give Doc Smith a call and have him come up to the house. He mightn't be able to make it today, though, depends on where he happens to be. Got his number? It's on the phone pad. Just as well to be on the safe side." He was as polite and impersonal as if she were no more than a strange girl who had come knocking at his door in response to an ad. Well, she pulled herself up short, wasn't she?

"I'll come back at lunchtime and check. 'Bye." He was gone, striding up the long passage. A few moments later Maggie, watching through the open window, saw him vault a low fence and go whistling over the grass toward the horse paddock, a bridle jingling over his arm. It was odd how lifeless the place seemed without him. She jerked herself back to reality. With Philippa and Ian engaged in what was practically a hand-to-hand battle over doing the breakfast dishes, Mark yelling from his bedroom, Gavin and Mark arguing over the scores in a recent football match, the screen door banging. Lifeless? Quiet? She must be crazy!

Throughout the morning as she performed the household chores, punctuated by frequent attempts to get through to the doctor and endless visits to Mark's room, the thought persisted. Danger. He might have shown, or pretended to show, some slight appreciation of her decision to stay here to help. Distant as ever, at least so far as Maggie Sullivan was concerned. There seemed no way of cracking that cool composure. For no one could have regarded his reaction to her altered decision as exactly enthusiastic. Could it be—once again the thought plagued her, and she stared unseeingly over the soaring green hills. It was her ridiculous likeness to that other girl, "his Cathy," that put him so much on the defensive. Was it possible that, cool and aloof, he was nevertheless resisting just such an attraction? Was he making certain that there was no possibility of his being hurt or rejected a second time? That was, if he *had* been hurt or rejected. If only she knew the truth of it all. Close on that thought came the other. Supposing, just supposing that were the truth, wouldn't it be the easiest thing in the world to make him fall in love with *her*. Oh, not desperately, not fathoms deep or anything like that, but just sufficiently to make him wish to please rather than antagonize her. She really was getting awfully tired of always being the one placed in the wrong . . . inept, foolish, inexperienced. What a triumph it would be were their positions reversed. In spite of herself she sighed. Wouldn't it be wonderful if that could happen. But of course, there was Ann. She must have been carried away by flights of fancy to have lost sight of the other girl in Danger's life.

The sudden croaking notes of a cuckoo clock recalled her to the present. Heavens, the morning was rushing by. All at once she remembered her employer's instructions regarding the children's correspondence lessons. Of course they might have settled themselves down already at the old table in the dining room. They *might*. Certainly both were old enough not to need reminding of so important a matter, but from what she already knew of the pair she thought it most unlikely.

"We forgot," Philippa and Ian cried in unison, when Maggie found them at last. They were seated on the floor in a corner of Philippa's room, deep in a game of Monopoly. "Okay," reluctantly they dragged themselves away from the enticing piles of mock banknotes, "we'll get started."

"Why not take your work out to the table on the veranda?" Maggie suggested. "I'll have to set the lunch on the table in the dining room later." She paused. "Don't you have to listen to the radio for lessons too?"

Phillippa nodded carelessly. "Broadcast to schools and all that? That's not till later. Come on, Ian, back to the salt mines—" Grumbling resignedly, they looked for the green canvas mailbags that brought the school assignments to be completed within a certain period.

With the older children occupied and Mark sleeping, Maggie hoped to get a clear run through the morning chores, maybe even put through a load of washing in the machine before lunch, but the ringing of the telephone halted her.

"That you, Maggie?" Tony's light friendly tones echoed in her ear.

"Yes, that's me." She had forgotten all about his promise to get in touch with her before she left Amberley.

"I was afraid you'd have taken off already," he was

saying on a note of warmth and relief. "Tried to get through to you half a dozen times last night, but there seemed to be no one around. Look, I have to see you some place. Do you realize that I haven't even got your address—"

"But I'm not going."

"You're not?" She caught the note of delighted sur-prise in his voice.

"I've changed my mind. Or rather," she laughed, "I've had it changed for me. Last night," she explained wryly, "Mark came down with measles. Sure you still want to see me?"

"I'm immune, and even if I weren't it would be worth the risk. Listen, there's a dance on in the next village to-night. I though maybe we—"

But Maggie cut in. "Sorry, but I can't make it."

His laughing tone challenged her. "What's the trouble? Is Danger such a slave-driver that you can't even escape for one night? I don't believe it."

"No, no, no!" For some reason she was reluctant to discuss her employer with anyone. "It's just Mark. He's a pretty sick little boy. I think I'd better stick around here. Once the doctor arrives, I can find out just how bad he is. I'll feel differently then."

"Okay, Nurse Sullivan. How about giving me a tinkle when things quieten down a bit? Let me in on what's hap-pening over there?"

"I'll do that—" She broke off. "Sorry, I must run. It's Dr. Smith, I hope, I hope."

The doctor, by some fortuitous chance when Maggie phoned him, had called at the homestead after making other calls in the district. He ran a professional eye over her. "You're looking much better."

Maggie laughed. "Feeling it too. Maybe it's just as well, with Mark down with measles—at least, that's what it looks like to me."

"Let's take a look at the young man."

Of course her suspicions were only too true. As she had expected, the doctor gave orders for Mark to stay in bed until the spots had disappeared. "Anyway," his eyes twinkled in a lined, weathered face, "I doubt it you'd be able to keep him there any longer." He gave Maggie a few simple instructions on the care of her patient, plenty of liquid, light diet, no chills, then bent toward his bag. "I'll leave you some pills to take the temperature down—Danger's darned lucky to have you here to lend a hand."

Somehow Maggie felt she could confide in this man with the wise, kindly face. "I really only came after a housekeeping position, but," she hurried on breathlessly, "Danger didn't seem to think I was quite—well, suitable. Then I was hit in the quake. When I was all ready to go, this morning, Mark came out in spots, so—"

"So?" The wise experienced gaze went to Maggie's averted face.

"So then I said that I'd stay, for a while. What else could I do?"

"You sound as though you've changed your mind about the job here."

"Oh no! I love it at Amberley." The words came of their own volition. "It's just that Danger—he thought I wouldn't be suitable." Meeting the doctor's quizzical glance she added hesitantly, "He seemed to think that I was too young ... or something."

"Too young? Or too much like someone else?" the doctor suggested shrewdly. He bent a grizzled head and picked up his bag. "You know all about that, of course?"

"You mean, my similarity to that other girl? I did hear something about it," Maggie admitted, "from Mrs. Wahonga. She had quite a shock when she first saw me." She longed to question him further, but she knew his lips would be sealed. Had he not imagined that Danger had already brought up "his Cathy" the doctor would not have mentioned it.

"I can imagine." He was regarding her with his kindly gaze. They strolled up the hall, and at the front entrance he paused. "Well, goodbye again, Miss Sullivan. You're doing a great job up here at Amberley. Keep up the good work." With a friendly lift of his hand, he went down the steps and into his car. Maggie watched him speed down the curving path.

In the ensuing week, if Tony hadn't made a nightly phone call, all thought of him would have fled from her mind. There were more pressing matters to engage her attention. For even though Mark's attack of measles proved a mild one, Maggie found that a fretful and convalescent child was a more trying patient than a feverishly ill one. Bored and irritable, he demanded ceaseless attention. By the end of the fifth day, Maggie in desperation threw caution to the winds and made no protest when the older children climbed up on Mark's bed and helped to amuse the irritable prisoner.

As the days went by she had to admit that Danger was proving a wonderful help as far as entertaining Mark was concerned. The small boy slept during the afternoons. In the evenings, Danger spent a lot of time with the small patient, reading aloud the comic strips that delighted Mark. Once the ridiculous supposition crossed Maggie's mind that perhaps in amusing Mark, Danger was spared the necessity of being thrown into her company. She pushed away the small pang of hurt. He need not have bothered. She had other things to do once the evening meal was cleared away. There were the lunches to prepare for the two young farm helpers who were clearing a patch of scrub far from the homestead. She had to make certain that the two older children were bathed and in bed at a reasonable hour, Mark's endless wants had to be attended to, and inevitably there were odds and ends of ironing to be done. If Danger imagined that she spent her evenings seated in the lounge watching television and awaiting the doubtful pleasure of his company. . . . All the same, she thought wistfully, it wouldn't hurt him to be just a little more—companionable. He might have spent an evening with her just once. He might, but he didn't. If he wasn't closeted with Mark, he was shut in the small room off the hall he termed his office. Maggie could see a line of light under the door when she went to bed and wondered how late he sat over the account books. On two occasions during the week he had left his desk to get out the Chrysler, a brief "you can reach me at Ann's place if you want me," tossed over his shoulder to Maggie. It seemed, she thought forlornly, that Ann had merely to summon him and he rushed to her side, just like that, whereas with her. . . .

Yet at the end of the week when he did enter the lounge where she was curled up on the sofa she felt a curious sense of constraint.

Sinking into a deep wing chair opposite, he offered her a cigarette and rose to hold the lighter toward her. "Feeling the strain?"

"No." She jerked upright, squaring her shoulders, hoping that the subdued lighting would serve to conceal the smudges of fatigue around her eyes.

"Bad luck, old Mark catching measles."

She laughed. "Bad luck for whom? You, Mark, me?" She couldn't resist the light remark that nevertheless hid a barb.

But of course he refused to be trapped so easily. "Mark, for one. I've got to hand it to you, Miss—"

So it was "Miss Sullivan" again. A spurt of hurt lent an edge to her tone. "Why do you call me that?" she broke in. "Isn't it a bit silly saying Miss Sullivan all the time, instead of just Maggie?"

"Well, just Maggie, you've done a great job of nursing. Mark's pretty well recovered and you know exactly what that means." The corners of the firm mouth twitched. "All we need to do now," he drew on his cigarette, "is wait for the others to succumb—"

"Could be three weeks from now," Maggie agreed, "and then it might only be Phil—"

"Or Ian—"

"And that would be another three weeks—"

She couldn't restrain the laughter that bubbled to her lips, and surprisingly, he laughed with her. It was almost as though they were a long-married couple discussing *their* family in *their* home. The absurd thought made her avoid his smiling glance.

"I have an idea." He was eyeing her speculatively. "How about taking a day off tomorrow?"

For a second her face brightened in anticipation, then quickly fell. "Oh, but I couldn't. There's Mark—"

"Forget Mark! I've fixed it all up with Mrs. Wahonga. She's coming over first thing in the morning. I'm taking you for a ride over the hills. We'll return the other way, along the beach. Must get you out of the house somehow."

"I'd love that!" She was pleased and surprised, touched by his unexpected thoughtfulness. To be free of the confining duties in the sickroom, to be out and away, giving Pete his head as she rode over the sandhills. . . . Her eyes were alight with pleasure. The boss was actually taking time off work to entertain her. He was noticing her—at last.

"It's in the line of duty." He was watching her narrowly. "Ann's just called to say she's had a bit of bad luck. Some of their steers have escaped from the paddock and taken off into the bush on the hills. If someone doesn't round them up soon, they'll get so far inland we'll never catch up with them. She's enough on her plate already without spending a day looking for them. We could give her a hand."

All Maggie's new-found happiness drained away. Ann.

So that was the real idea behind the offer to take her riding. Oh, she might have known! He wasn't thinking of her one little bit. It was Ann who filled his mind to the exclusion of anyone else. She made an effort to hide her sense of disappointment. "She's all on her own on the farm?" Mentally she answered her own question. She's not really on her own, not with Danger helping her every spare moment he has; and hated herself for the uncharitable thought. She brought her mind back to Danger's voice.

"Oh, she's got a young chap there, but he's only learning the game too."

"Couldn't Tony help?" she asked, for something to say.

"*Tony*! On a horse? Rounding up cattle? Riding hell for leather through heavy bush on steep hillsides? Can you see him? I can't. Oh, he means well enough—" to Maggie the faint praise was more damning than outright criticism, "but he's just not cut out for that sort of life."

Some devil of contrariness urged her to argue. "Well, I think it's pretty marvelous of him, giving up a 'Varsity career to come home and take over the family property."

"Giving up?" The thick dark brows rose in an ironic glance. "Somehow I had the idea that 'Varsity had given him up."

"He can try again!" Maggie flashed back. "I think it's to his credit if he does have another go at the exams. Far more praiseworthy than those students who just fly through with no effort at all—" She caught herself as something Ian had said to her shot through her mind. "Uncle Danger was a whiz at 'Varsity. Cleaned up lots of sporting trophies and simply took exams in his stride. It's awful having an uncle like that," Ian had complained bitterly to Maggie. "Bad enough him being in the first 15 Rugby team right through but a Rhodes Scholar as well! And Mom and Dad expect me to live up to *that*."

Luckily, Maggie consoled herself, she wasn't expected to know anything of his scholastic career.

"Tony sure has a champion over this way," he observed coldly. "I had no idea that you two knew each other so well."

"I don't know him well," Maggie returned with spirit. "At least—" She stopped short, remembering the nightly telephone calls from the farm over the hills. Tony would inquire how things were going with her, ask about Mark's progress, make plans for a meeting once Maggie was free of her sickroom duties, but that was all. Nothing, surely, to cause Danger to regard her like that. For his sardonic look, the one she disliked most of all, was back on his lean dark face. Whatever had she and Tony's harmless friendship to do with him, for goodness' sake?

She was glad when Philippa and Ian, rushed into the room in order to watch television. Further conversation was out of the question. Although Maggie watched the screen too, she was unaware of the flickering scenes. She was reflecting that whatever she did seemed to displease him, even her choice of friends.

CHAPTER SIX

Maggie could scarcely wait for the ride over the hills. It must be the thought of taking Pete out again that was making her look forward to the outing with this keen sense of anticipation. Was it only two weeks since she had arrived here?

She was up early, slipping into a black sweater and slacks. Then she went up the passage and out into the pearly gray stillness of the morning. The men had already ridden over the paddocks and wouldn't be in for breakfast for a while yet. No one was in sight as she went over the long grass, wet with dew and cool to the touch of her bare feet. As she had expected, the horses were already penned in the corral. Danger's big roan stallion was pacing restlessly along the tea-tree barricade. As she came nearer a low whinny caught at her ears. The next moment Pete emerged from the shelter of a towering macrocarpa and trotted toward her. All through the past week she had been too confined to the house to visit him in his valley paddock. Now she noticed that his bay coat had acquired a silky gloss. He'd put on weight too, but what could you expect with all that lush spring grass?

Affectionately patting Pete's sturdy neck, it was a few moments before she realized she wasn't alone. She moved with a smile toward Philippa, who, wearing neat shortie-pajamas, leaned on the sliprails at her side.

The small girl's sharp features wore a puzzled expression as her gaze moved from Maggie to the ungainly-looking bay to whom she was crooning endearments. "Whose horse is that?" Philippa demanded suspiciously.

"Mine." There was a ring of pride in Maggie's tones. "I brought him up here with me, or rather he arrived the next day by horse transport. I've scarcely set eyes on him

since. Poor Pete, to him it must seem like forever."
Pulling a carrot from her pocket. she offered it to the
horse. "He's sort of old," she murmured with the reluctance to which she invariably admitted to Pete's years,
"but you'd never guess it. Honestly, I've had him since he
was young and he jumps just as well now as then—well,
almost. He won three red ribbons at the last gymkhana I
took him to. He can take a four-foot jump, no trouble."
Her smile faded as she took in the small resentful face,
the twisted unchildlike curve of the thin lips. "Why,
what's wrong?"

"You never told me!" Philippa blurted out accusingly.
"I thought you didn't care about riding. You tried to fool
me, didn't you? But you can't any more. You thought you
could butter me up. I know." Her lips puckered and tears
blurred the angry high voice. "You're just like the others,
only *they* didn't pretend. *I hate you!*" Philippa turned and
ran toward the house, wispy hair flying around her thin
shoulders. The next moment she paused, looking up at a
rider who was cantering down a slope. "Danger!
Danger!" She rushed to meet him, and Maggie was uneasily aware of the two talking together. A few moments
later Phil ran inside. Danger left his mount to graze and
came striding toward her.

"That's done it," he observed with his tantalizing grin.
"Poor old Phil thinks you've put one over on her.
Catching you and Pete out in that big love scene was just
too much for her—"

"I know." Maggie's voice was low. "I suppose I should
have told her about Pete before, but I . . . kept off the subject of horses. I thought," she finished a trifle incoherently, "that if she liked me enough it wouldn't matter
when she did find out." She hesitated, wondering how
best to frame her inquiry. "She—seems to have this thing
about the horse her mother left her to ride. I'd say that
she was scared stiff of mounting him, or even going near

to groom him. Tell me," she raised clear brown eyes, "is he really so dangerous?"

"Oh, that—" He grinned down at her. "Don't give it another thought. The kid's got some bee in her bonnet about the Saint—can't say that I blame her altogether. Chris must have been out of her mind to expect a nervous rider like Phil to handle a highly-strung mount like that. Guess now it's a deadlock between the kid and her mother. Chris can't seem to get it into her head that a daughter of hers isn't all wrapped up in the idea of being a top rider."

"Maybe Phil wasn't nervous before. Evidently she didn't feel that way about her little pony she was so fond of."

Danger nodded. For once, it seemed, they were in agreement. "It didn't help any, getting rid of the pony. Then Mrs. B. made things a thousand times worse; pushing the idea and forcing Phil to groom the Saint, who promptly nipped her on the leg for her trouble. Anyway, what does it matter?" His glance rested on Maggie, small and slim, a long piece of grass in her smooth, white, office-work hand. "If Mrs. B. spent the entire time she was here fighting to hold her end up and lost, what the hell could you do?"

These were fighting words, and Maggie's blood rose to the challenge. She'd show him. Old Barry, as Phil termed her unfortunate predecessor, by trying to force a timid and terrified small girl into liking a mount in which she hadn't the slightest confidence, had lost the child's trust. With her it would be different. She'd take things quietly, gently, gain Philippa's confidence first, and then. . . .

Something in the set line of her lips must have betrayed her thoughts, for she realized he was watching her with that maddening, amused, condescending glint in his eyes. "A sheer impossibility, wouldn't you say?" His voice was careless.

All at once she felt she had to prove to him that he couldn't answer for her in that infuriating autocratic manner of his. "Not really," her voice matched his for coolness. For once, she realized with satisfaction, she had gained his attention.

"What d'you mean?"

"Oh, I don't know." She made it sound nonchalant. "I wouldn't mind betting you that I could get around Phil. I mean," her pixie smile flashed out, "given time and a free hand."

"It's all yours, Miss Sullivan. If you can get Phil friendly with the Saint, you're not just a much-needed housekeeper, you're a real miracle-worker." The flicker of amusement in his blue eyes set alight the fuse of her indignation.

"Well, why not?" she demanded. "She likes me. At least," she amended, "she did, and she might again. And if I could just give her some confidence in herself, maybe get her started on Pete—" But she knew by his quizzical look, and the lift of his lips, that he didn't believe her. He never did believe in anything she could do, she thought hotly. That was the trouble, he had no faith in her—ever. But he'd have to change his opinion about her, one of these days.

"I could," she repeated stubbornly. His grin drove her on so she added recklessly. "You'll see!"

"Will I?" Oh, he was infuriating, looking at her with the indulgent glance of one listening patiently to a prattling child. But she'd show him . . . just let him wait. She flung around to stare up at him, dark eyes enormous and sparkling with anger, "You don't believe me, do you?"

Still he continued to regard her with his lazy smile. "Let's just say that I believe you could give it a try!"

"Oh!" She turned away in exasperation, and they went in silence toward the house.

Mrs. Wahonga was strolling in at the gate. "Hello!" she greeted them with her broad smile. "You out bright and early, Miss Sullivan?"

"Maggie," she corrected smilingly.

The brown eyes beamed at her. "That's better, *ehoa*. Maggie."

"I'll carry that for you." Danger took a long newspaper parcel from the woman's arms. "Is this the breakfast menu for today?"

"You guessed it, Danger. My boy Hone, he go out at the bay yesterday with a *kon-tiki*. Come in with a big haul. Lots of schnapper and kahawai."

Strolling up the steps beside her, Maggie asked her curiously. "*Kon-tiki*? What sort of a line is that?"

Mrs. Wahonga gave her rich chuckle. "The best, in the breakers. You get Danger to show you how it works one of these days."

"That's a promise," he said, and left them to wash up while Maggie went to the kitchen with Mrs. Wahonga.

But later as she went to the corral with Danger, she forgot everything else: the feeling of antagonism that Danger's careless words had sparked, and Philippa's changed attitude. She slipped the bit into Pete's mouth, and throwing over his back the fluffy white sheepskin and saddle, bent to tighten the girth.

At her side, Danger was saddling his big roan stallion. Then they were out in the open, through a gate, and cantering up the narrow tracks that threaded the steep cleared hillsides. They flashed past the short mowed grass of the airstrip and took another slope. Maggie's cheeks were flushed and her eyes bright. Pete, of course, was no match for the powerful stallion, but he kept up well. Presently they drew rein as the horses entered a gully filled with native bush. The air was heavy with the fresh, pungent smell of damp ferns and moss. Dried leaves crunched beneath the horses' hooves as they moved on through the green gloom, lightened at intervals by sunlight filtering through the leafy branches high above of giant totara, kauri, rimu. Then they were in the sunlight once again. Maggie thought she could go on forever like this, with the fresh breeze tossing her hair and the roar of distant surf in her ears.

At the summit they pulled in their mounts and paused to gaze at the turbulent sea far below. Beyond a line of sandhills was an expanse of shimmering molten silver. The horizon was veiled in haze. "There's a track down through the bush," Danger told Maggie as he urged his horse forward. "I bulldozed a road through last summer, but the bush has grown a heck of a lot since then. Time I had another chance at it. I'll go ahead and clear away the creepers. Take it easy with Pete. It's fairly steep."

The overgrown track was certainly precipitous, Maggie thought a little later, as her mount picked his way carefully down the twisting slope. At times great fern-encrusted ponga logs lay across the path, blocking the way, but the horses were sure-footed. Danger always rode ahead, pausing to pull aside a hanging rope of black supplejack trailing from a tree high overhead, or to lift a curtain of thorny creeper, as Maggie made her way beneath. Then they were out in the sunshine once more, surrounded by massive sandhills. As the horses' hooves sank into the dry white sand, Danger called back: "Better make for the hard, down by the water."

She leaned forward in the saddle as Pete scrambled up a sandhill and made his way down the opposite side. Then they were moving over shimmering wet shoreline still littered with fragments of foam left by the last great breaker. As they rode along the shore, Maggie's spirits rose on a wave of enjoyment. She felt one with this wild untamed world where seagulls dipped and soared above the waves. There was nothing in sight but an immense sweep of lonely beach. Slackening their pace, they let the horses splash along the water's edge. Maggie laughed as an unexpectedly large wave crashed around her, drenching her with sea water, and causing her sweater to cling wetly around her slim figure.

Danger, soaked too, laughed with her. "We may as well take them right in now."

"Why not?" Maggie cried, as together they urged their mounts in over the breakers. Soon she was crouching low over Pete's neck as he swam beneath her. Maggie laughed aloud in sheer exhilaration as tide and current carried the horses into the shore.

A magic day, she found herself thinking, full of life and movement. The high wind that sent the waves crashing in a shower of foam on the wet sands ruffled the marram grass growing along the sandhills and bowled the frail wheels of spinifex over and over at the water's edge.

In the warm sunshine her sweater and slacks dried out as they moved along at the edge of the surf. They had traveled some distance along the shore when Danger turned his mount. "Here's where we head up into the bush again," he told Maggie. As she urged Pete over the sand drifts she glimpsed high hills clothed in dense native bush ahead.

Riding in single file along a winding bush track, Danger drew rein at a small clearing and waited while Maggie rode alongside. He was gazing out over a gully and following his glance, she drew in her breath sharply at the sight that met her eyes. Against a somber, dark background of native bush, kowhai trees with their delicate green foliage and blossoms of clear bright yellow, filled the gully with a splash of gold. She said wonderingly. "You didn't tell me."

"Kept it for a surprise!" he grinned. All at once, for no reason at all, she felt her heart turn over.

"I've never seen anything so lovely," Maggie said softly.

"Nor me." Danger's eyes rested on her flushed face; as she met his unfathomable look a feeling of excitement welled up in her. The kowhai-filled gully shimmered in a golden haze, and she could scarcely see the scene for the trembling sensation that assailed her. What had come over her? To feel like this about Danger, of all men.

"Don't look at me—like that." For an endless agonized second she wondered if she had spoken the words aloud. Then his voice jerked her back to relief and reality.

"That's Ann's place over there—" He was pointing with his whip. "See the homestead? You can just catch a glimpse of it through the trees."

She forced her eyes toward the sprawling timber homestead that glimmered faintly through a shelterbelt of tall blue gums. Schooling her voice to a light conversational note, she said; "How far does it extend—her land?"

"Far enough." He made a sweeping gesture covering the surrounding hills. "With all this bush on the place it's the devil's own job to round up the cattle if they happen to get away. We'll take a look around here for a start. See where the track starts?"

She nodded, pulling on the reins, but somehow a little of the day's golden luster had dimmed. Why had he not spoken of "Ann and Tony's place," instead of just "Ann's?" She was fast becoming a champion of Tony's rights, she reflected wryly, and thought how delighted he would be if he knew.

They had been riding for some time along a twisting track in the unfamiliar green gloom of heavy native bush when Danger, riding ahead, gave a call. "There's one!" He urged his mount onto a narrow track on the steep tea-tree-crowded incline. Maggie, following, suddenly caught a moving flash of black a short distance ahead. "Look out!" Danger cautioned, "he's coming up." The next moment a steer, with Danger in swift pursuit, crashed through the undergrowth and fled past Maggie on the narrow track.

Another steer followed, and another, until soon the missing cattle were all accounted for and being driven back through the bush in the direction of the cleared hillside paddocks.

When they sighted the homestead, Danger dismounted to open a wide taranaki gate, waiting while Maggie guided the steers through the opening. Then he pulled the wire loop over the post and gave his heart-stopping smile. "Ann'll sure be relieved to have that lot back in the home paddocks. Like to call in and give her the good news?"

"If you like." She had no particular desire to meet Ann today. On the contrary, she was becoming awfully tired of hearing her name on Danger's lips. She had no doubt though, that Tony would be delighted by her surprise visit. Anyway, how could she refuse?

Together they took a winding path that led over the paddock toward an old colonial-style house with a wide veranda running the length of the dwelling. Danger tethered the horses in a grassy paddock nearby. He and Maggie strolled in at a small gate and crossed the sweep of green lawn.

"Maggie!" Tony emerged from the stables, harness dangling from his hand. Surprise and pleasure mingled in his expression. "You came!"

He seemed unable to believe his eyes. Heaven knows, she reflected ruefully, conscious of windswept hair and crumpled clothing, she couldn't be much to look at at the moment.

"Ann anywhere about?" Danger was asking.

"Over there in the shed." Although Tony waved a thin hand in the direction of the outbuildings a short distance away, his eager look remained riveted on Maggie's small flushed face. "She said something about getting out the tractor."

"That's good enough for me. I'll find her." With a careless nod Danger strode down the path to the shed.

Tony led Maggie through the house and onto a wide

patio that had evidently been a recent addition to the old home. Black cane chairs were scattered over the polished timbers and a low table was set in the center of the cool open porch.

"Take a seat." He tossed down a scarlet cushion and Maggie dropped to the floor. "What'll you have? Tea, coffee, juice? Or something stronger? Just say the word."

"Juice sounds wonderful. We've been out riding for hours. I've never been so thirsty."

"Right! Juice it is!" He bent to turn the switch of a radio, flooding the room with soft background music, then went into the kitchen.

Left alone, Maggie's glance went to the student note pads and architectural textbooks that were scattered over the floor. Idly she reflected that Tony must be still thinking of a career along those lines. Well, good luck to him. Her gaze lifted to the vista of rolling hills outside. If Danger didn't locate Ann in the shed he would search for her, she knew he would. She mustn't allow herself to forget, even for a moment, that Ann was his girl.

She wrenched her thoughts away as Tony returned, carrying a tray in his arms. Ice tinkled in tall glasses. Sitting down beside her, he handed her the cool grapefruit juice. "You know, I'm surprised that you're sticking it out at Amberley, measles or no—"

She wrinkled up her nose. "Why, do you still think I don't look the type?"

"You look good to me, Maggie. It's just—oh well, if I'd taken a guess I'd have said you were a city girl."

"That's funny," she teased, "I thought at first that you were a city type too."

She realized he was eyeing her closely, the pale green eyes thoughtful. "But you, you really like it up here?"

She nodded. "I love the country, especially at this time of the year when the new lambs are frisking about all over the place, and the kowhai's out on the hills." Reflectively she stirred the ice in her drink. "I was brought up on an isolated sheep station on the East Coast. I guess that accounts for it." She smiled across at him. "Kowhai in the blood, I mean."

Tony sent her a wry grin. "You can have it! Kowai gold and all. Give me the city sidewalks, a nightclub or two, some friends to drop in every now and again, and I'm happy. It beats me how you—"

Maggie finished her drink, then laughingly said "That's just me, I guess. Anyway, it's a change from office work. The kids seem to like me. At least—" All at once she remembered Philippa's stormy peaked features. But she could recapture the child's confidence, of course she could. She just *had* to make good that rash, unconsidered promise she'd flung at Danger. With a start she brought her attention back to the fair, bearded young face. What was Tony saying? Something about arranging a barbecue. "We're having one, one night soon. I could zoom over to Amberley and collect you. What do you say?"

"All right," she said, "just give me a call first."

He raised light eyebrows. "That's about as far as I ever get with you,' he murmured moodily, "a talk on the phone. That's why—" He stopped short as Danger and Ann entered the room together.

The other girl was wearing jodhpurs. Her white schoolgirl-type blouse was open at the throat. Rolled-up sleeves revealed the well-developed muscles of her arms. Tall, strong, vital—once again the thought passed reluctantly through Maggie's mind that they made an arresting pair: the lithe sinewy sheep-farmer, and the tanned girl with cropped hair bleached by the sun during long hours spent in the open air.

"I hope Tony's been looking after you," Ann smiled at

Maggie. Throwing a switch across a chair, she turned to the man at her side. "How about you, Danger?"

"Beer for me, thanks."

"I'll fetch it."

She was back in a few minutes with the drinks, settling herself in a low chair by Danger's side. The two fell into a discussion regarding the recovery of the missing steers, then went on to arrange for the docking of the lambs in a week's time. Maggie was only half aware of Tony's voice as she caught snatches of the other conversation. She gathered that Danger would be available to help Ann with her farm duties whenever she needed him. She had only to ask. Clearly there wasn't anything that he wasn't anxious and willing to do to help the other girl. How very different from his attitude to Maggie Sullivan.

Gray cottonwool clouds were rolling in over the hills when at last the party headed for the house paddock where the horses were tethered. Tony gave Maggie a leg up as she vaulted into the saddle. "When am I going to see you again?" he whispered. "Before the barbecue, I mean. It's my turn to come and see you. When?"

Maggie smiled into the pale eyes. "One of these days," she murmured vaguely.

"Or nights. I might just drop in on you one of these evenings. Just say which one—"

"I don't know." She was confused, uncertain as to whether her position as housekeeper at Amberley gave her the right to invite guests to the house—Danger's house.

But wouldn't you know, she told herself scornfully a moment later, that Danger would overhear the softly spoken words. Swinging lightly up into the saddle, he turned his restive mount. "Any time," he said easily, "and that goes for Ann too. She knows that."

Maggie's gay smile faded. With Danger, it always came back to Ann.

They moved away amidst a chorus of farewells. Danger, riding ahead, held open a white gate for Maggie where "Manaia" was printed in black painted letters. Presently they took the winding white metalled track that encircled the hillside. At the foot of the slope they pulled their mounts to a walk as they entered a bush-filled gully with its soft subdued light sparked with patches of sunshine.

It was a pattern endlessly repeated on the return ride to Amberley, Maggie found. Cleared green hills ended steeply in ponga-filled gullies. Always on the rise the wind met them, blowing cool and fresh on their faces.

At length they caught sight of the homestead, peaceful and sheltered among tall trees. While Maggie urged her mount forward, Danger paused to close a taranaki gate behind him. She turned a flushed face over her shoulder. "Race you to the boundary fence!" she cried impulsively. It was a wild and stupid gesture, she knew, for what match was Pete against the powerful thoroughbred stallion? On the flat stretch of grassland ahead Danger would beat her hands down, and that would be one more triumph for him. She had asked for it.

The thoughts flew through her mind, then everything else was forgotten. She was off, urging her mount forward, enjoying the exhilaration of flying along as Pete raced ahead with his long easy stride.

"Come on, Pete," she whispered, leaning low, "show him what you can do!" Hair streaming behind her in a dark cloud, she was aware of the sound of hoofs behind her. Above their pounding she could hear Danger shouting: "Maggie! Maggie!" The wind carried the rest of his call away. Something loomed ahead, a great fallen log, unnoticed before in her blind rush. But no matter, Pete had taken higher jumps than this with ease. She was only half aware of Danger's shout as she leaned low over the flying man. The big horse gathered himself for the upward leap. There was a split second where she glimpsed a second log, dangerously wide, lying below; then she felt the horse twist beneath her. Hills and sky blurred in a crazy pattern; she caught the dull thud of hooves striking wood as she was thrown clear.

Maggie had the oddest feeling of not wanting to move. She was perfectly, rapturously comfortable where she was, yet for some inexplicable reason she must stir herself to action. Dazedly she wondered whether it was the feeling of the strong arm encircling her shoulders that gave her this feeling of deep content. Or maybe it had something to do with the muscular shoulder she was leaning against.

As her eyes flickered open she found herself staring directly into Danger's face. Only, she reflected, still in that state of dreamy content, it didn't seem like him. Not with that drawn look of anxiety, an expression in his eyes that was so near to a caress that it made no difference.

"Maggie! Maggie darling!" How different her funny little nonsense name sounded said like that, tender with feeling. Danger's cool remote tones were ragged with anxiety over her, she marveled idly, making her name sound like an endearment all the same.

Only she must have dreamed the endearment part of it all, she thought drowsily. When she opened her eyes once more he was shouting: "Wake up, Maggie! Wake up!" She stirred in his arms and struggled into a sitting position on the grass, then wished she had stayed where she was. When she did manage to focus her gaze, he was practically yelling at her, his eyes aflame with exasperation and anger.

"You fool! You crazy little fool! Didn't you hear me calling you not to risk it? Couldn't you see," he demanded in a hard, angry tone, "that the thing was a mile wide?" For one electric moment she thought he was about to shake her.

Dazedly she shook her head.

"Hell, I thought you were never coming out of it!" He let out his breath on a long sigh of relief.

"Was that what happened?" Maggie stared around her. "I remember that Pete—" A terrible fear ran along her nerves, and her eyes widened in apprehension. "He fell too! I know he did! He's not . . . not. . . ." She couldn't put the dreaded thought into words.

"He's okay." Danger jerked his dark head toward a cluster of leafy puriri trees a short distance away. "He was up on his feet again a lot quicker than you were."

"Thank heaven for that!" She could see now that Pete was grazing quietly. Slowly she stood up. "No bones broken at any rate." She smiled shakily.

"I made certain of that." His voice was grim.

"You did?" She digested the information with mixed feelings. No doubt he had done what he would have done for any rider who had taken a fall. All the same, she wished. . . . To hide her embarrassment she asked quickly, "How long was I out for?"

"Five minutes or so. One moment you were sailing over the top, then when Pete caught sight of the second log he tried to twist around and boom! You were down. I thought you were never going to come out of it."

Maggie pulled at a long grass stalk and nibbled it thoughtfully. "I just can't understand how a silly little fall like that could have put me out."

"Can't you?" He rose to his full height and stood looking down at her. "Once you've had a bad dose of concussion it doesn't take much to make you go out like a light." His tone was as cool and impersonal as ever.

Maggie sighed. Here we go again, she thought, back to square one. She was "just Maggie" again: hurting herself, causing him concern and inconvenience, being a nuisance to him, as usual. She *must* have imagined that "darling!"

CHAPTER SEVEN

Maggie assured Danger that evening that she was now perfectly well, thank you, with no aftereffects from the fall. Honestly, there wasn't the slightest need to worry about her. The master of Amberley listened politely and completely ignored her protestations. The next morning Mrs. Wahonga came strolling up the driveway, her wavy black hair in a ponytail, pleasant face creased in a beaming smile as she caught sight of Maggie on the veranda above.

"You unlucky with accidents, eh, Maggie?"

She laughed. "Am I ever!" *Unluckier than you know, Mrs. Wahonga, trapping myself here with Danger as a boss.*

All morning as she worked through the chores while the older children sat over their correspondence lessons, Maggie could hear the woman's musical voice as she softly sang the age-old chants of her ancestors. When the lunch dishes were cleared away Mrs. Wahonga seated herself on the sun-splashed veranda floorboards, her flexible fingers busy weaving a basket from long strips of green flax.

The children grouped themselves around her plump figure while the small possum scampered around their feet. "Please, show me how to make them," Philippa begged wistfully. Mark, pushing belligerently on sturdy tanned legs past his sister, shouted, "Me too! Me too!"

"All right, *ehoa*! Don't rush me. We'll have to get some more flax from the bush first."

"There's plenty down in the gully." Philippa cried eagerly. "Come on, we'll show you."

"That's an idea," Maggie put in. "Maybe if there's

enough, you'll show me how to weave kits too. I used to know once, ages ago, but I've forgotten."

Philippa threw a baleful look. "*I* thought of it first!"

Maggie decided to ignore the girl's ill humor as the children ran down the steps. Mrs. Wahonga, carrying Mark in her arms, rose to follow them. They crossed the yard, passed through a gate, a paddock, a second gate and moved down the slopes of a grassy hill. In the gully below Maggie caught the soft murmur of a running stream. On reaching the bush-fringed banks, they came in sight of thickly clustered flax bushes with their dramatic tall black stems and tassels of burnt-orange. Miraculously producing a knife from her capacious pocket, the Maori woman cut the flax, and soon they were returning to the house with armfuls of the long green spears.

Back on the veranda, under Mrs. Wahonga's direction, the long leaves were torn into narrow strips. Patiently guided by deft brown fingers, they all began to weave the flax. Even Ian was making an attempt at a basket and Mark, not to be left out, pushed the flax in and out with tiny fingers, his face set in an expression of intense concentration. Mrs. Wahonga, singing softly in her native tongue, paused to offer instruction when needed.

Maggie's fingers moved with increasing confidence as her kit began to take shape, but all the time her thoughts wandered. As she watched Mrs. Wahonga leaning back against the veranda rail as she worked, she found herself envying her relaxed and philosophical attitude. But then—she glanced up to meet Philippa's sullen stare—the Maori woman didn't have her problems to contend with. She hadn't intended to deceive the child, her troubled thoughts ran on, not really. It just hadn't seemed important, when she'd first arrived here, to mention her interest in riding. For at that time, she hadn't expected to be staying at Amberley for more than a few days. Now unfortunately the damage was done; there was no doubt the small girl regarded Maggie as both a liar and a cheat. For since the moment when Philippa had discovered that Pete belonged to Maggie, the child had been coldly polite, but that was all. Who ever would have imagined, Maggie mused, that she would be concerned over a strange child's opinion of her? Come to that, who would have dreamed—her painstaking fingers fell motionless as she stared unseeingly at the flax base—that she would allow any man to fill her thoughts to such an extent? A man already deeply involved with another girl. *And you'd best not let yourself forget it, Maggie Sullivan!* She wrenched her thoughts from drifting any farther.

By the end of the afternoon Maggie felt a sense of pride in her achievement. Even though her flax kit might bulge in unexpected directions, it nevertheless fulfilled its purpose as a light, strong, flexible basket, and wasn't at all bad for a first attempt. Well, not quite a first attempt. It was rare for Europeans to be skilled in the art, but kindly Maori neighbors had once taught her how, although she had long since forgotten it.

As she glanced idly through a week-old newspaper, Maggie perceived a way of recapturing Philippa's friendship. She ran her eyes over the advertisement, taking in the details of the children's art contest that was being organized by a city firm. The subject could be any New Zealand scene, the work to be executed in paints, crayons or pastels, but it must reach the judges in ten days' time. Maggie clipped the advertisement, then went in search of Philippa.

She found her lying on her bed, curled up with a book. The small girl's look of surprise changed to a mutinous stare as Maggie closed the door behind her. "Look," she held out the clipping, "here's something just in your line. A painting competition for children of your age, with money prizes and all. It's an old paper, but you've still got time to send in an entry. Anyway," Maggie went on persuasively, "there's that sketch you were doing the other day, the one of pine trees on a hilltop." She seated herself on the bed at Philippa's side. "What do you say?"

The girl sent her a cold, scornful look. "All those town kids . . . I wouldn't have a chance!" But in spite of herself she held out a hand for the clipping. The thin braids fell around her peaked face as she perused the advertisement. "I couldn't. . . ." The high childish tones were uncertain.

"Of course you could!" Maggie argued. "You could at least try. Why not?" She pressed her advantage. "I thought that last watercolor you did was super."

Philippa considered the matter, gray eyes thoughtful. "I might do another one, a better one—if I have time," she added loftily.

"That's the idea!" It was a small triumph, Maggie told herself, but she had succeeded in capturing the child's interest. "Have any paper?" she asked. "Good thick stuff, I mean?"

Philippa nodded, excitement lighting her gray eyes. "And I've got something else too! Some super new paints that Uncle Danger gave me for my birthday, just before you came!"

"Well then," Maggie urged, "what are we waiting for?" She moved away, thankful that Philippa's acceptance of the painting contest was a move in the right direction. At the door she paused, arrested by the high childish tones. "But I won't have any horses in my picture!"

"No horses," Maggie agreed, and turned away to hide her smile. She left the room before the conversation turned to more personal channels and she lost the slight victory she had gained.

That evening after the children were in bed and Mrs. Wahonga returned to her own cottage to tender to the

needs of "my boy Hone," Maggie sat alone in the subdued light of the lounge. As was his custom in the
evenings, Danger had entered the room for only a few
minutes in order to view the daily news items flashed
across the television. She couldn't help thinking that he
looked quite distractingly good-looking: freshly-
showered, wearing a crisp dark gold shirt and fawn
slacks. His eyes held a warmth of expression that made it
seem all the more strange that he appeared almost to
avoid being with her. Yet the way he looked at her at
times, almost she could imagine . . . with a start she realized where her random thoughts were leading.
Remember, Maggie, she scolded herself, that you're
employed here as a temporary housekeeper, nothing
more. So far as she was concerned, Danger was no more
than her employer, or was he? She wouldn't mind
betting, though, that if it were Ann who happened to be
here at the house tonight he would forget all about those
stuffy old account books of his.

As if in answer to the thought, the doorbell at the front
entrance shrilled through the room. Maggie leaped to her
feet. Danger too had caught the sound, and they went up
the long hall together.

"Hi, Danger, how are you? Hello, Maggie."

She recognized Tony's light pleasant tones. In the dim
glow of the overhead lantern she caught a glimpse of Ann
and a heavily-built young man with wide shoulders and a
countryman's shy smile.

In the lounge Ann sat down on a low seat, the light
forming a halo of her short fair hair. To Maggie the other
girl appeared unfamiliar out of the work clothes in which
she was accustomed to seeing her. Maggie couldn't help
thinking that Ann's yellow linen dress was at least an inch
too long, and the sleeveless armholes exposed those too-
muscular upper arms. But a sheep-farmer's wife needs
well-developed muscles, she reminded herself; someone

who's capable of lending a hand around the farm should the need arise.

"We thought we'd drop in. It seemed a long time—too long," Tony added softly to Maggie. "Seems a year at least since I saw you."

"Yesterday?" She laughed and turned to find Ann at her side. "Oh, Maggie, I almost forgot—" Ann smiled, showing prominent teeth. "This is Jim—Jim Blakey. He's got a run over the range, but he manages to make it over to see us once in a while. When he gets lonesome, I guess. So we brought him with us. Jim, Maggie."

With old-fashioned courtesy the big man stooped over her, extending a huge, work-calloused hand. Maggie rather liked this quiet young man with the steady gray eyes. She said smilingly, "Are you really all alone on your farm?"

He gave her a shy grin. "Sure am."

"But you do get lonesome sometimes?" she queried gently. The next moment she regretted the light words, for it was clear that this personal question had the effect of putting him in an agony of embarrassment.

"I—don't mind." She had to strain to catch the muttered words.

"Don't waste any sympathy on him— Thanks, pal," Tony accepted the drink Danger was offering him, then sat at Maggie's feet. "He doesn't have to be on his own. All he needs to do is find some nice girl and ask her to marry him. Thing is, he's too darned shy to ask anyone—"

Beads of perspiration gathered on his weather-roughened forehead as the young farmer made an effort to control his obvious embarrassment. "I—I—"

"Oh, leave him alone, Tony!" Ann seated herself on a chair, swinging a bare tanned leg. A plain girl, Maggie reflected, nose too large, hair in need of shaping and thinning. Yet there was about her something honest and direct and likable. The sort of girl who would be a wonderful mate for such a man as Danger. *She* would understand exactly what he was talking about when he discussed farming details with her. The thought was somehow depressing. She pulled her wandering thoughts together, and turned to find Tony at her side. There was no mistaking the warm expression alight in his pale eyes.

"Something odd's been happening to me lately," he was saying under cover of the laughter and talk echoing around them, "I can't seem to fight the feeling. It's you, Maggie. Ever since that day up at the Gap when I first met you, I can't seem to get you out of my mind—"

She smiled at him over the rim of her glass. "You haven't enough to do over at your place—"

"Not enough to do!" he repeated incredulously. "If you only knew—"

"Well then, maybe you have Jim's problem. Evidently there are so few girls living around the district that when someone new comes along, wow! They can have themselves a ball."

He shook his fair head. "You have me all wrong, Maggie. Can't you see what I'm getting at? I—" He broke off as Gavin and Mark, freshly shaven and wearing cool white shirts and linen shorts, strolled into the room.

Mike carried his guitar. "Hi, folks!" Seating himself on the floor, he plucked idly at the strings. "I've been putting in some practice," he went on. "A little number specially for you, Maggie."

"A Maori love song," Gavin put in, "not one of the well-known ones, though. Hope you haven't come across it before, Maggie."

"How could she?" Ann inquired bluntly.

"Don't forget," Danger said, "that Maggie's a city girl. Or was," he added smilingly.

She threw him a swift surprised glance. He was regarding her with that faint hint of amusement in his glance that affected her, like making her want to retaliate in some way. A flare of anger surged through her. What right had he to label her like . . . stock in a supermarket, when actually he knew nothing about her. Ann too, seated on the arm of Danger's chair, leaned close in an attitude of unconscious intimacy. They were laughing at her, both of them.

The plaintive notes plucked from the guitar strings fell across her turbulent musing, and she recognized the Maori melody—a love song, one that she had sung many times on a concert platform in another part of the country. She was aware of the English translation as well as being conversant with the Maori lyric; understanding as did few Europeans the significance of the action dance that accompanied the song. An ancient race having no written language had passed on through the generations their customs and culture in chants and lilting melodies that could shake the heart.

How little they really knew of her, any of them. Why, right up to the time when she had left the East Coast, Maori farming neighbors and their families had been her friends. She had even joined the members of a local Maori concert party; replaced one who had fallen ill on the eve of a tour planned throughout the district. She wore a traditional flax costume woven in conventional patterns of red, white and black, a small jade image swinging from her slender neck. She had enjoyed being a part of the moving feats of swaying skirts as they performed their action dances, the beat sustained by the twirling poi on its long string. The small flax balls had long been lost, but she would never forget the plaintive melodies or the rhythmic movements.

"Actually," she thrust up her small square chin and looked Danger right in the eye, "I happen to know that song quite well."

She realized with wicked satisfaction that he was regarding her in some surprise, his dark head with the black sideburns bent attentively in her direction. "You do?"

"That's right." Her quick smile flashed. "My Maori friends on the East Coast taught it to me, ages ago. They showed me how to do the action dance too."

The look of astonishment that crossed Danger's face was such an unexpected victory that it went to her head. Without stopping to think, she had kicked off her slippers. Rising to her feet, she stood for a moment motionless, with arms extended. Then, dark eyes lighted with a glimmer of mischief, a half smile curving her lips, she danced with quivering wrists and swaying hips to the movements of the song. Her voice, low yet clear, took up the melody in the soft Maori syllables. In her short-short dress of scrolled tan and white pattern, tanned skin and long dark hair falling around her face, she could have been a Maori maiden herself, so fluid and effortless were her rhythmic movements.

As the last plunk-plunk of the guitar died away she paused, flushed and smiling, conscious of the enthusiastic applause that was echoing around her.

"That was great!" Tony cried, moving toward her and clapping loudly. "More! More!"

But her eyes had flown to Danger. For a long moment he held her gaze in an unreadable look. Was he surprised? she wondered. Or appreciative, or disapproving, or what? She couldn't tell.

"Good for you, Maggie. I bet," he added in his off-handed way, "that you haven't a clue as to what the words mean."

And that, Mr. John Know-it-all-Dangerfield, she thought triumphantly, is just where you're wrong! Aloud she said quickly, "Oh, but I do! My Maori friends—"

"Well then—" His bright gaze challenged her. As Mike's work-roughened fingers plucked at the strings, once again Maggie fell into the swaying movements of the action dance. The poignant words of the age-old love song came unhesitatingly to her lips as in her own tongue she took up the haunting melody.

"I shall not again
    give you my hand
For you may turn the other way
    and secretly jeer at me.

When I look at you
    you turn your face away
But in your heart, dear
    I know you . . . love . . . me."

As the lilting notes died away, some impulse she couldn't define made her avoid Danger's glance. Breathlessly she waved aside the chorus of pleas for her to continue with her impromtu entertainment. Someone set a record spinning on the turn-table, and the next moment the insistent beat of rock music pulsed through the room. As Danger rose and began to push back the carpet, exposing smooth polished floorboards, Tony caught Maggie's hands in a firm glasp and drew her to her feet. Then they were moving to the rich, glorious tones of John Rowles, the New Zealand singer, Maggie's short dress flying around her.

All at once excitement shot through her, for Danger was striding purposefully in her direction. Taking her in strong arms, he bore her away into the vibrant beat. For a second she was aware of Tony's look of open-mouthed astonishment; then she forgot him, forgot everything else in the world in a sense of heady elation. She couldn't tell how long the dance lasted. She only knew they were moments snatched out of time. Knew too that she was strangely shaken, aware of Danger's closeness, the faint smell of tobacco and shaving lotion, the strength of his arms around her.

Suddenly it was over. Danger left her to speak with Ann. No doubt, Maggie mused uncharitably, they had some pressing farming problem to discuss that couldn't wait. Jealousy was a failing that she had always prided herself on being free of, until now. She could scarcely take in Tony's conversation, for her gaze kept straying toward Danger, his dark head bent attentively toward Ann. She was glad when making coffee gave her an excuse to leave the room.

Tony followed her into the kitchen, helping her to arrange the pottery mugs on a tray. "You see, I'm quite domesticated." He grinned. "It's a matter of necessity when you're used to 'batching' in town."

The phone was ringing in the hall as she passed carrying a tray. Danger came to answer the call. "Sorry," she couldn't help but hear as he spoke into the mouthpiece, "but I'm afraid you're too late. The position's been filled." Replacing the receiver, he saw Maggie. "Let me carry that—" He took the tray from her and went to the lounge where they sipped coffee and listened to the latest overseas recordings that Tony had brought with him.

It was late when at last Ann started for the door. "Well, I guess it's an early start in the morning."

Maggie went with Danger to see the others off. While the group gathered in a small knot on the moon-flooded veranda, Tony snatched her hand. "Maggie! What are you doing on the weekend?"

She smiled her pixie smile. "I told you, I'm a working girl. Remember?"

"But damn it all," his whisper was urgent, "Danger must let you off the chain sometimes! Oh, hell—" He broke off on an exasperated breath as Danger himself came over. "See you again, Tony!" he said, and the younger man had no course but to turn away, sending Maggie a wry backward look.

Jim, standing at the back of the group, moved forward to extend his hand toward Danger. "Thanks a lot!"

Maggie realized that she had all but forgotten the big man. Poor Jim, he was a type of man who was fated to be overlooked.

Tony's last glance as he went reluctantly down the steps was for Maggie, but she was saying goodbye to the others and didn't notice. Ann seated herself behind the wheel of the big car, the engine revved up, and a moment later the vehicle swung down the winding drive.

Maggie leaned over the veranda rail, watching until the winking red light vanished around a bend in the curving pathway.

Beneath her, the sweeping lawns were flooded with silver. A full moon, riding high in the sky, made the scene almost as bright as day. It was very still. Somewhere in the dark hills around them a sheep coughed, the mournful notes of an owl echoed close by. More-pork . . . more-pork.

She was very conscious of Danger, smoking silently at her side. In an effort to combat a growing sense of dangerous intimacy she rushed into speech, giving voice to a question that had niggled at the back of her mind all through the evening.

"That phone call, that one you took tonight—I was going up the hall and couldn't help overhearing. It was someone else applying for the housekeeping position here, wasn't it?" Without waiting for an answer, she rushed nervously on. "Why did you tell them that the position was filled?"

He didn't answer for a moment, so she turned to see his dark strong profile. Then he tossed his cigarette into the bushes and swung around to face her. "Well, isn't it?"

"I—had the idea," Maggie's voice was very low, "that I was only here until—well, until someone else turned up to do the job."

"You want to stay, though, don't you?" He put a hand under her small square chin, tilting her face upward until she was forced to meet his inexorable look. "Don't you?"

Before she could guess his intention he had caught her close. She could see his eyes, dark and brilliant, then his kiss blotted out everything as a dizzying sense of rapture swept her senses. It took her some moments to realize that she was clinging to him.

His low vibrant voice did things to her heart. "Still want to get away?"

She could scarcely speak for the tumult of her senses. A pulse beat in her throat. "I—" The spell was shattered as she became aware of a frantic childish voice. "Maggie! Maggie!" She drew herself free as a small pajamaed figure rushed through the open doorway and hurled himself into her arms. "I couldn't find you anywhere! I thought you'd gone away and were never coming back!" Mark was still choking back sobs as Danger picked the small boy up and took him back to bed.

And now it was Maggie who was awake. Still aflame with a kiss that sent her senses spinning, she tried to control her whirling thoughts. A light kiss, no harm done. *No harm!* Be honest, Maggie. You know quite well that nothing will ever be the same again here at Amberley, not for you. And I can't leave . . . the children . . . they depend on me. At least Mark does; and he's little, helpless and needs me quite desperately.

Besides, how am I ever going to leave if Danger puts every other applicant for the position off by telling them that he's already suited? *He's* suited. He doesn't act as though he is, avoiding me, shutting himself away in his office each evening, yet emerging the moment that Ann enters the house.

It was a kiss of expediency, she told herself; of course that was all it was. A selfish way for Danger to have her remain here. The awful thing was, she pummelled her pillow helplessly, that she knew she didn't want to leave here, ever. Deep down where it mattered, she knew that the children were not the real reason why she didn't just cut her losses and run. At last she faced the truth. She was in love with John Dangerfield, deeply and hopelessly. But he regarded her as little more than a not-too-capable employee. If only she could banish him from her mind, but try as she would she could think of nothing but his strength and tenderness, the ironic gleam in the blue eyes; eyes that could soften and darken at the most unexpected moments, the curving sensitive lips. . . . A longing that was half pleasure, half pain surged over her. She mustn't think of his kiss.

With a deep sigh she made a determined effort to return her senses back to reality. So long as he didn't guess her feelings for him maybe she'd be able to survive the next few weeks; somehow, until the time came for the children's parents to return. But she knew that really she had no choice but to stay. Being with him, hearing the deep tones, meeting his amused glance was a bittersweet anguish against which she had no defense. Only she must never again allow herself to be too near him. She might be "just Maggie," but she couldn't take his light lovemaking. With her it must be for real or not at all; there wasn't much doubt, she mused forlornly, as to which category she belonged. He was in love with someone else, someone more suitable in every way to be the wife of a busy sheep-farmer. With Ann he was at ease, talkative, relaxed, whereas with her. . . . With a stab of pain she remembered his amused grin: "Oh yes, there's *you*, Miss Sullivan." Besides, *she* didn't happen to remind him of someone whom he much preferred to forget.

If she'd realized what was happening she might have done something about it. Her heart told her that she had known all along, but wouldn't allow herself to admit the truth. Now she must endure the exquisite torment of being with Danger, preparing his meals, caring for his home; knowing all the time that it meant exactly nothing.

A fool in love. A long-drawn sigh escaped her lips as her mouth curved in a sad little droop in the darkness. To think to even a score, she had actually thought to make him fall in love with her.

CHAPTER EIGHT

Maggie took tea for morning break out to the men working in the drafting pens. Danger's curt "thanks a lot, Maggie," as he took the steaming pot from her hands, was quite impersonal. Clearly in his book the scene on the moonlit veranda last night had been a trifling incident, already forgotten. As she wandered back to the homestead, Maggie paused beside the sheepdog kennels on the slope leading to the woolshed. Inevitably her eyes strayed to the pens where a tall figure in a dark sweat shirt moved amongst the milling sheep. Lean, burned, curiously remote; what was it about him that stirred her so? She sighed to herself that she should be thankful that to Danger, his kiss had been a light and meaningless gesture. If only she could feel the same way.

During the following few days he was involved with seasonal work on the station, so busy that she scarcely saw him, except at a late evening meal. Long before she was awake, he had saddled Red to ride over the vast grazing paddocks, picking out the fat lambs, and sorting the hoggets that later would be ear-tagged.

"Tell you what, kids," he said to the children, "seeing that this is the last weekend of the toheroa season, I'll give the men a day off. We'll go and collect toheroas at the Gap. How about you, Maggie?" As he swung around to face her, his brilliant smile made her heart contract. "You could do with a spell away from the house. Come on now, admit that you're fed up with kids and housework."

But not with you, Danger, never with you. The crazy words sprang to her lips, but she forced them back, murmuring instead: "I love it down on the beach."

"It's a date then. Get your pails ready, kids. Right now I must get cracking to finish ear-tagging the ewes."

He went whistling down the side of the house. Maggie, as she cleared away the dinner dishes, was looking forward to the outing tomorrow. On the vast immensity of the lonely shore, perhaps even her own heartache would seem dwarfed. Besides, Danger would be with them. A pang shot through her. And Ann, she reminded herself bleakly.

However Saturday brought an urgent telephone message from the other girl. Maggie, answering the ring, caught the worried note in Ann's direct tones. "Listen, Maggie, Danger's not around, is he?"

"No, but he'll be back soon," she said.

"Good. Have a problem and he's the only one I know who can help me. He's so darn good about everything. Just as knowledgeable as any vet when it comes to trouble with the sheep. And boy, have I got trouble! Three Romneys down with some sickness I've never seen before, but Danger'll know how to cope. Could you ask him to get in touch with me the minute he comes in?"

Over a heavy heart Maggie promised that she would, even though she was certain that there would be no day spent on the beach tomorrow, not now.

Of course she was right, she told herself as she passed on the message to Danger. Striding to the telephone, he immediately put through a call to Ann. From the adjoining lounge Maggie caught the deep voice. Yes, he too had that trouble, but not to worry. He'd be over in the morning and bring the stuff with him. As luck would have it, he had plenty of vaccine left after treating an attack suffered by some of his own Romneys, the year before. He'd stay over there with Ann after giving the treatment, to see how things went.

Maggie made an effort to crush her sense of disappointment. It was absurd to feel this childish feeling of letdown over cancellation of a day at the beach, and yet. . . .

"Sorry about tomorrow, Maggie." Danger had entered the lounge and came to stand at her side. "But this happens to be a priority job."

"It's all right." At least, she thought forlornly, avoiding his gaze, he hadn't forgotten about his promise.

"Can't we go?" Philippa glanced up from the book she was reading; Maggie saw her own disappointment mirrored in the girl's drooping lips and anxious eyes. "But you said—"

"Couldn't *I* take the children?" Maggie offered impulsively, aware that the younger girl had put aside her resentment and was looking hopefully toward Maggie.

Danger eyed her with his bright, searching look. "It's an idea! Reckon you could handle the beach buggy?"

"Why not?" She smiled into his lean tanned face. That was one of the disadvantages of being so small. No one, and especially Danger, ever believed you were capable of doing anything. "It'll be a good chance," she added, trying to infuse a note of enthusiasm into her voice, "to get some more toheroas."

"Last chance," he put in.

Only it won't be the same without you. With a sigh she brought her thoughts back to the present.

"Tide's dead low at three in the afternoon," Danger was saying. "All you have to do is be sure to take the buggy down on the wet sand. For pete's sake, steer well clear of those freshwater streams. They're dynamite! I don't know how many cars we've had to pull out of there, stuck in the sand. Some of them had had it before we could get there with the Land Rover—Hey, I nearly forgot—" All at once his voice changed to a cool and distant note. "Young Tony sent you a message. Said he'd be coming over here tomorrow night to see you." She was aware that he was watching her narrowly. What did he expect her to do, she wondered crossly. Appear overcome with excitement? Blush? "He wants you to call him back."

"Thanks." Apparently it was quite in order for him to be as friendly as he pleased with Ann, but Maggie Sullivan wasn't to show the slightest interest in Ann's brother. She'd half a mind to show him . . . at least she wouldn't give him the satisfaction of guessing her feelings. "I'll put a call through to him later." Her tone was carefully noncommittal.

In the morning, however, all thoughts of Tony fled from her mind. She attempted to fill the cookie tins with home baking and produce a large fruit cake as an answer to the country-sharpened appetites of both men and children.

The work was hampered by Mark. Under the mistaken impression that he was helping, he cheerfully rolled out biscuit dough until it was an unappetizing shade of gray; managing at the same time to plaster both himself and the floor with the mixture. Cleaning up the mess, Maggie reflected ruefully that being so busy kept her from dwelling on Danger—or did it? The truth was that she seemed only fully alive when he was close at hand, within sight and sound. The planned excursion today was simply a chore, part of her duties here, whereas had he been with her. . . . Oh, what was the use? In misery and frustration she banged the cutter furiously on the sheet of rolled dough.

She had just thrust the tray in the oven when she looked through the window to see Danger backing the beach buggy out of the shed. A little later he was showing her how to work the gears. "It's simple, actually. Low here, this is top, down for second, over thisaway for rear. Nothing to it! You can't hurt the old bus no matter what you do. If you want the brake—" He stopped short with a sideways glance. "You're not listening!"

"I am! I am!" Maggie protested hastily, in an agony of apprehension that he might have caught her eyes fixed on his tanned profile. Her mind had been on him rather than on driving, and she had been neatly caught out. If at this moment he asked her to take the wheel she couldn't. She just couldn't. She hadn't heard a word of what he'd been telling her.

"You take over now and give it a go." To her horror he swung wide the heavy old door and leaping to the ground, stood watching. No doubt, she thought in confusion, he was just waiting to criticize her. Guessing, she took a chance on the gears and pressing a foot to the accelerator, shot off with a wild lurch that made him jump swiftly to one side. Where in heaven's name was the next gear, she wondered in panic. Luck was with her, however, and after that it was easy. She moved a short distance along the driveway, to stop with a jerk.

Danger came running up to her. "You'll manage! Just take it easy on the steep grade up to the cliff. Put her into low if you feel like it. She has loads of power. You'll be okay," he said unfeelingly, and turned to pick up his wide-brimmed sunhat from the grass. "I'd better get over to Ann's place and see to those Romneys. She'll be waiting—toheroa fritters for tea. Right?"

"Don't bet on it," Maggie said, stepping lightly down from the high, tattered seat. "The cook doesn't ususally hunt for food. She just has to cook it."

"Ah-ha," Danger said smugly, "but this cook happens to be someone rather special. Picked her myself!"

With a teasing grin, he swung on his heel and strode away, leaving Maggie staring after him, a prey to conflicting emotions. *He'd* picked her! Why, she was the last person he would have chosen to have in his employ. He'd made no secret of that. The words of the Maori melody he was whistling caught at her heart with a pain she could scarcely bear.

> When I look at you
>> You turn your face away
> But in your heart, dear,
>> I know you love me.

I know you love me. If only, if only it were the truth!

A little later, however, she had to admit to a sense of satisfaction as she drove the beach buggy along roads that were still more or less unfamiliar. The two older children, riotously happy, were in the back seat; Mark was at her side. When the barge had ferried them over the river to the main road, Maggie found that many others had taken this last opportunity to seek the shellfish from the sands. Ahead, the stream of traffic comprised trucks, jeeps, Land Rovers and Trekka, interspersed with clean and shiny cars, obviously coming from other parts of the country.

When they reached the steep rough track between the flax-covered hills, Maggie could see no crown on the grassy clifftop. A swift glance toward the beach cottage showed her that the door was closed. Today she did not head for the cliff, but continued along the boulder-strewn track as she joined in a stream of vehicles moving toward the misty, violet-blue of the ocean below.

Presently the road petered out in a path between the sandhills. Mindful of Danger's warning, Maggie guided the beach buggy along the damp surface, taking care to avoid the trickle of water from freshwater streams coming from the hills that had proved so treacherous to strangers. Vehicles, dwarfed to tiny proportions by the limitless shoreline, were dotted along the misty expanse of the beach. Maggie could discern groups of toheroaseekers bent low as they thrust hands deep into the wet sand in search of the shellfish. Plastic pails made gay splashes of red, blue and saffron on the long stretch of sand; high rugged cliffs of yellow sandstone rose sheer above the sandhills.

Moving a few miles along the coastline, she at last reached the area where she had stopped with Danger on the previous excursion. Maggie braked, and the children tumbled wildly out of the car. Nearby a group of Maori men and women were collecting white-shelled toheroas in swift succession. It was a good omen, Maggie thought, knowing the inborn skill of a race whose ancestors had depended for their staple food on the bounty they could wrest from bush and sea. Maggie, however, was not so lucky. A tiny bubble in the sand led her to dig on the spot, but the toheroas she found were so small that she threw them back in the water-filled depression, where they immediately burrowed out of sight. The children were more fortunate, and offered to find enough shellfish for Maggie to collect her quota, but she was determined to dig the elusive toheroas for herself. At last as she dug deep in a fresh patch of shining wet sand, she withdrew a large white shell, then another, and another. Engrossed in her task of placing the last shellfish in her scarlet pail she did not look up as a car moved slowly along the sand nearby.

"Maggie!" A man's shout made her glance upward. Crouched on the wet sand, she pushed aside the long black hair blowing across her face in the salt-laden breeze. She found herself looking into Colin's round, smiling face and almost lost her balance. He was wearing dark sunglasses, but otherwise he looked just the same. Only why didn't she feel excited about seeing him again? It was an effort to infuse a note of warmth into her tones.

"Where did you come from?" she asked in amazement.

"That's what I'm asking you." He leaped from a late-model burnished maroon car and hurried toward her. "I just couldn't believe it was you! If you only knew the trouble I've had, asking everyone in Hamilton where you were, trying to find out what had happened to you, where you were—"

"Me?" Maggie said dazedly, brushing a sandy hand across her eyes. This was a different Colin from the one she remembered. He was animated, excited, with a look in his eyes she hadn't seen since, since. . . .

"Let's get away from this mob," he suggested eagerly, "and I'll tell you all about it. Gee, if you only knew—" He broke off, his gaze running over her, tanned and attractive in mimosa-colored shorts, yellow silk shirt whipping around her slim figure in the breeze, bare feet. "I guess it's my lucky day!" he cried jubilantly. "Come on, Maggie," he caught her hand, "let's go! We'll take a stroll along the beach." His glance went to the children who were regarding him with frankly curious eyes. "It's a darn sight too crowed around here for my taste."

Maggie hesitated. "But your toheroas. You haven't—"

"Damn the toheroas! It's *you* I want to see. Don't you understand, Maggie? It's always been you, only," his voice dropped to a low, unsteady note, "I was too much of a fool to know it."

She snatched her fingers from his eager grasp and inclined her head meaningfully toward the children. "We'll have to take them along with us."

"What do you mean?" Colin's full florid face wore an expression of bewilderment. "Can't you see I'm doing my darnedest to get rid of them?"

"But we can't," Maggie protested. "I mean, *I* can't! I'm looking after them, or supposed to be."

"What!" He stared at her, his eyes behind the dark sunglasses incredulous. Really, Maggie found herself thinking irrelevantly, he was a round sort of person;

round eyes, full face. There was no doubt that he had gained quite a lot of weight during the years he'd been away in Australia. Incredible to think that once, 100 light years away, she had imagined herself in love with this short pompous man with his astonished stare.

She couldn't help bursting into laughter at his aghast expression. "It's simple really," she explained, "I took a job up-country. I thought it would be a change from office work."

"You?" His amazed look was scarcely complimentary to her capabilities, she thought.

"I don't see what's so earth-shattering about it," she said, nettled. "I've always loved the country, and I can cook—" She stopped short, belatedly remembering the quickly prepared pre-cooked dishes she had produced at the apartment when Colin had dined there with her and Andrea. "When I want to," she added.

"But where is this place you're working? Who with? What's the woman's name?"

She waved a hand vaguely in the direction of the surrounding hills. "A sheep station . . . up there." Somehow she was reluctant to acquaint Colin with the fact that there was no other woman at Amberley station. She told herself that the situation was so complicated she couldn't be bothered explaining it all. But she knew that she wouldn't discuss Danger with Colin, especially in his obviously emotional state of mind. Why was he searching for her? Hadn't his and Andrea's marriage worked out?

She called to the children. "Put the pails in the beach buggy. We're going for a walk along the beach." And when they came running back to her: "Colin, this is Ian, and that's Philippa—and Mark."

Shyly the three acknowledged the introduction. The next minute they were capering far ahead of Maggie and Colin, chasing one another along the gleaming sand, pausing at the edge of the breakers to pick up strings of beaded wet seaweed, and examine a starfish stranded by the outgoing tide.

As she strolled along beside the water, Maggie was struck by a thought. She turned an anxious face to Colin. "Andrea—" His face had taken on a withdrawn expression, and she felt a prick of apprehension. "I never heard from her again after the—the wedding. She's—all right . . . isn't she?"

He shook his dark head. "That's one of the reasons why I wanted to catch up with you, to let you know. She was killed, Maggie." His voice was low and strained. "It happened in a car crash three months ago."

"Killed? But that's horrible! Were you driving?"

The full lips were set in a downward curve. "She was with—someone else at the time. Things didn't work out so well after we left here," she had to strain to catch his low tone above the roar of the surf. "It wasn't all Andrea's fault. It didn't take long for both of us to—well, I think we both knew that we'd made a mistake. One thing: she was killed instantly, a head-on collision. She never knew what happened."

"I see," Maggie said slowly. So the whirlwind romance had blown itself out. Poor Andrea . . . impossible to imagine Andrea not alive. She had always been so vital and full of fun, so outgoing. Now Colin had returned to New Zealand, seeking his old love, and she—why, she couldn't care less about him! Almost guiltily she brought her mind back to his low confidential voice.

"So then, just when I'd decided to start again and return to Hamilton, I was lucky enough to hear about this partnership available in your office. Believe me, I couldn't get back fast enough. Took the first plane I could from Sydney and went hotfoot to your apartment in Hamilton. I couldn't believe it when no one had any clue as to where you'd taken off to. I asked everyone. Why, even your boss didn't know where you were. Said if he did he'd be sending for you; that he hadn't had a satisfactory typist since you left. Heck, didn't you even leave an address with the Post Office to have your mail sent on?"

Maggie shook her head. "I didn't know where I was going. I was . . . moving around a good bit. Anyway, there wasn't anyone to care particularly—"

"Well, there is now!" Colin caught her hand, and this time she couldn't free herself from the warm pressure of his clasp. "Now that I've found you again, do you think I'm ever going to let you go? Not on your life! I've missed you, Maggie," his voice was low and tender, "more than you'll ever know. Now that things are sorted out and we're together, everything's going to be different. For a start you can tell that farm woman you're working for just where she can take her mother's helper job. You'll have to make it plain to her that you've had enough of it. You're leaving with a week's notice. Tell her she'll have to cope with her brats on her own—or find someone else." Before she could protest he was running on, his voice eager, excited. "No problem. Your old job's waiting for you back in Hamilton—not that you'll be there for long," his smile was meaningful. "That is, if I have any say in the matter. I have—other plans for you, for us, Maggie. Together we can travel, have ourselves a ball—"

"But I'm not leaving here," Maggie broke in, stemming the headlong rush of words, "not for a month or two anyway." She succeeded in wrenching her hand free. "I just can't opt out of my job."

He stared at her, a puzzled frown lining his smooth forehead. "Why not?"

Flustered, she sought wildly for sound reasons, but her mind had gone blank. "They—seem to like my funny crusty scones," she offered inadequately. At Colin's incredulous look she added hastily: "Besides, I promised

Danger—" The name slipped out before she could stop to think.

"*Who* did you say?"

"I mean," she ran on hurriedly, "that I said I'd stay here for two more months. They were in a bit of a hole, actually, when I happened along. It wouldn't be fair to let them down."

"Forget it! There are loads of women all over the country wanting housekeeping jobs. They call them home-helpers or some such thing, don't they?" His voice was indifferent.

"But they won't come way up here to these remote districts," Maggie assured him. "They just won't!" Warming to her subject, she added: "There's nowhere for them to go in their spare time, you see. They get stuck on the farm and they hate it."

He sent her a sceptical look. "You seem to be making out all right."

"Oh, you mean the beach buggy? That was so that I could come and collect some toheroas for dinner. I make them into fritters—"

"I know all about toheroas," Colin broke in irritably. "What I don't get is why the heck you seem to think you have to stay in this godforsaken hole looking after these brats as though it were some sort of sacred trust."

"We are not brats!" Mark, running back at that moment, had caught Colin's words. Planting his tanned feet squarely in front of Colin, he placed small hands on his hips and shouted aggressively, "You're not going to take Maggie away. I won't let you! See!"

In spite of himself, Colin's full lips broke into a reluctant smile as he eyed the small belligerent figure. "Okay, chum," he said soothingly, "I won't *take* her away." In a low tone he added for Maggie's benefit, "but I'll do my best to persuade her to come with me, all the same."

He must, however, have reckoned without the keenness of Mark's hearing. "She won't go! She won't!" Mark's roars of protest drew startled glances from nearby parties of toheroa-gatherers. "She's going to stay with us, aren't you, Maggie? Forever, 'never, 'never, so there!"

"Oh come off it, young feller. You're not the only male who wants her around. Come along, I'll take you over to the others." Colin swooped down on the struggling, scarlet-faced boy and endeavored to seat him on his shoulder. Mark, with a furious kick of his bare foot, sent the horn-rimmed glasses spinning to the sand. Then, leaping down, he hurriedly picked himself up and ran away.

"Little devil!" Colin bent to retrieve his sunglasses and set them carefully in place—a trifle unsuccessfully. Maggie tried to suppress a smile. Colin was so neat, so pompous and self-opinionated. Why had she never realized it before? Now, out of the past she remembered more than one occasion when her own high spirits had been dampened by Colin's silent disapproval. Imagine his trying to win Mark over by giving him a ride on his shoulder.

He swung around toward Maggie, his voice sharpening. "What's so funny?"

Hastily she straightened her twitching lips. "Nothing, nothing. It's just that Mark's so little. Did you ever see anything so brave, defying you—"

"Brave! Damned little nuisance, I'd call him. They seem to think they own you, these kids. It's time you showed them where to get off."

"Oh well, it's only for a few weeks." Maggie couldn't help feeling a little sorry for Colin. He was so obviously out of his element in this vast stretch of beach with uninhibited children: plus an ex-fiancée who had taken off into the blue and plainly wasn't prepared to go along with his plans.

"What that kid needs is a good belting." Colin was

glowering after Mark's small figure in a red bathing suit. "His father should see to it!"

"He can't," Maggie spoke without thought, "he's away."

"Away? What sort of a set-up is this you're mixed up with?" Plainly Colin's law-trained mind was already probing into the discrepancies in Maggie's vague account of her life at Amberley.

"Oh, just temporarily," she said airily, "and anyway, Mark isn't usually as bad as this. It's just that he's fond of me. You know?" Her great brown eyes twinkled at him. "You could call it male jealousy!"

But clearly Colin was in no mood for banter. "I'd call it plain bad temper. Oh, why are we wasting time worrying about kids? I can't get over it yet," his expression softened as he gazed at her, "running into you like this, after I'd just about exhausted every way of finding you. I guess it's my lucky day," he said softly.

"Well," Maggie said briskly, "it isn't mine, that's for sure. I had to dig for ages to find my quota of ten toheroas. Just look at my nails—" She extended a work-stained hand, the nails chipped and broken. "I often wonder if it's worth all this—getting shellfish, I mean."

Colin sent her hands a swift uncaring glance. "I wasn't meaning that," he said pointedly. "Don't you see what I'm trying to get through to you, Maggie? All this time, ever since I got back to New Zealand, I've been looking for you. And now—Damn! Not again!" He broke off, staring with an angry frustrated glance at Philippa and Ian, who were wandering in their direction. Bless them, Maggie thought, they'll never know how glad I am to see them right now!

"Look," Colin entreated a few minutes later as the children strolled down to the edge of the breakers, "can't we get rid of them somehow? There's something I must say, something pretty important . . . don't you understand?"

The trouble was, Maggie reflected, that she understood only too well. If Colin imagined that he had only to meet up with her again to pick up the pieces of a shattered love-affair; if he only knew how much her feelings for him had changed. She'd have to make the situation plain to him before he left her today, otherwise he might track her down. Somehow she couldn't endure the thought of Colin arriving at Amberley, discussing her with Danger. "All right then," she said, "let's go back to the car. We can keep an eye on the children from there."

Colin's plump face cleared. "Now you're talking!" There was a note of relief in his voice.

Calling to the children, they retraced their steps. As they seated themselves in the luxuriously upholstered car, Colin thrust his head out of the window. "Go and find some toheroas—or something!"

"We're not allowed to get any more," Ian answered in his polite boyish tones.

"Well, get something else, then. Shells, seaweed, anything. So long," he added in a low tone, "as you get the hell out of here!"

"He means he wants us to scram," Philippa explained, quite without rancor, in her high, carrying treble. "He doesn't want us around." Maggie giggled uncontrollably as groups kneeling on the wet sand turned curiously toward Colin with his self-conscious, reddened face.

"Let's get out of here," he muttered angrily, turning the ignition. "We're going along the beach," he shouted to the three on the beach. "You kids had better come along too."

Mark eyed him suspiciously. "Do we have to walk?"

"That's the idea."

"Why do we have to walk," the small boy argued, "when there's lots of room for us inside the car?"

In reply, Colin angrily started the car. The next moment the vehicle was moving along the moist sand. Maggie, glancing back over her shoulder, waved encouragement to the small figures trudging along in their wake. To Colin she said: "Don't go too far up the beach," for they were heading toward the high cliffs.

His black look told her that he would brook no advice in his present mood of resentment.

"I mean," Maggie chose her words carefully, "it's such a gorgeous car. You don't want to get stuck in the soft stuff—"

"I know what I'm doing!" He spun the wheel with an angry jerk.

Oh well, I did warn him, Maggie thought. Aloud she murmured, "So long as you don't tangle in one of the streams—look out, there's one right ahead!"

But her warning came too late. Already the wheels were sinking in the soft sand. Collin, swearing softly under his breath, revved the accelerator again and again, but in vain.

"It's no use," Maggie said, "you'll just have to find someone to pull you out." She glanced along the sand, but at this particular spot the beach was deserted. Except for the groups they had left, the main body of picnickers was gathered at the far end of the stretch. Of course there was the beach buggy. Maggie wondered whether it would have the necessary power to drag out the big, heavy car. They'd have to do something. All at once she realized the tide was coming in and over the flat expanse, sweeping in rapidly.

Colin was frantic now, as he tried in vain to make progress. The car remained motionless—worse, Maggie felt certain the wheels were gradually sinking deeper into the stream.

The next moment she became aware of the children. They were waving and calling. As they came nearer she realized what Ian was shouting. "It's okay! Here's Danger!"

Danger! But there was no time to think of anything else as the four-wheel-drive vehicle approached them. A dark head was thrust from the open Land Rover. "Trouble?"

He caught sight of Maggie, seated beside the driver. Astonishment, and something else, mingled in Danger's face as his eyes met hers. Almost, she thought in confusion, he looked hurt . . . disappointed in her . . . but how could that be? She must have imagined that fleeting expression in the blue stare. He was leaping out of the Land Rover, coming to stand at the side of the stranded vehicle.

"Friend of yours, Maggie?" He sounded so pleasant, so polite, and yet—and yet—

"It's Colin," she said faintly, "Mr. Dangerfield—" she shrank from stating that he happened to be her employer. She tried out her brightest smile. "I hope you've a tow rope with you?"

"Never without it," Danger said cheerfully. "Not to worry. We'll have you out before you know it."

Maneuvering the Land Rover until it was directly behind the maroon car, he attached the heavy tow rope with deft movements. Then while the wheels of the car skidded free, the vehicle was dragged out of the stream and up onto firm sand.

"Thanks a lot!" Colin watched while the rope was disengaged and stowed away in the Land Rover.

"We get used to this up this way," Danger said. "I just came down to see if everything was okay down here. Get the toheroas, Maggie?"

"Oh yes, yes!" She was confused and uneasy.

"Right! I'll pick them up, take the kids back with me. Jump in, all of you!" At once the three climbed obediently into the Land Rover.

"So long." Danger lifted a lean bronzed hand in a gesture of farewell.

"Thanks again!" Colin called after the departing vehicle. He turned to Maggie. "Thank the lord for that!"

"You mean the tow?"

"And taking those damned kids off our hands." He flung her a triumphant glance. "Chap must have seen that they were getting in the way."

"I suppose." Maggie prayed that Colin's supposition wasn't correct. Wildly she searched her memory. That first night when she had met Danger, she had confided to him that she had been engaged to Colin but that he had married her best friend instead. Of course Danger would remember. He never forgot anything, especially anything concerning herself that she preferred him to put from his mind. That was why he had left her and Colin alone today. Her heart took a sickening plunge. He thought—what else could he think in the circumstances—that she was still in love with Colin, a married man, and he with her.

"So—at last!" Colin guided the car up the track and braked to a stop in the shadow of the rugged clay cliff above. Switching off the ignition he turned to Maggie, lifting a long strand of her dark hair with unsteady fingers. "You know how I feel about you, you must—" Suddenly he was ragged with emotion. "I love you, Maggie. I always have . . . your hair, your funny little square chin, the way you laugh. I've waited so long—for this!" Before she could protest he caught her close, so close that she could do nothing but remain in his arms, tense and rigid, while he caressed her arms, her neck. Then she felt the pressure of his lips on hers, his warm breath on her face. It seemed an age before she could wrench herself free. Tossing back her tousled hair she took a deep breath. But why, oh, why did it have to be at that particular moment that another vehicle swept past them? A Land Rover with a lean brown man at the wheel, a man who had to have witnessed the little scene. There was no smile for Maggie now as he glanced toward her flushed face. "Forgot to collect the toheroas." He swung in the direction of the beach buggy standing farther along the sand.

"We'd be a darn sight more private in town," Colin muttered. "People turning up every five minutes."

Not people, Maggie thought over a sinking heart, only the one person in the world who mattered. Danger. Now he'd think—what would he think? That she was resuming an old affair with a man who was married to her friend? How could she possibly explain matters to him, especially when he had eyed her with that stern implacable glance? The blue sky blurred as a deep anguish surged through her. But what did it matter to Danger, she reminded herself despairingly, what she did with her life? It wasn't as though he had the slightest interest in her. All that mattered really was making Colin realize now, this minute, that things weren't as he expected them to be.

"It's no use," she said, gently repulsing him as he tried to take her once more in his arms.

His full lips drooped petulantly. "You used to like me to kiss you." He threw an arm around her shoulders, drawing her to him. "What do you mean," he asked softly, "it's no use?"

She twisted out of his grasp. "You know—you and me. It's over, Colin. Don't you see? For me, it is, anyway. I—just don't feel the same way about you any more. Oh, I know it must sound awful after—after everything, but—" she sought wildly in her mind for some way to soften the blow, "it's been so long."

"Only a couple of years."

"Well, anyway, too long for me. I guess," she said gently, "I couldn't have cared so much as I thought I did, or I wouldn't be feeling this way now."

For a moment he was silent, staring at her sullenly, then he said suspiciously, "There's someone else, isn't there? Someone you're wrapped up in here?"

The blindly aimed shaft came so close to the truth that Maggie caught her breath.

"No, no—"

But he brushed her words aside, his tone sharpening. "Now I get it! That farmer guy, the one in the Land Rover—I saw the way he looked at you. He took the kids away too, and he called you Maggie." Suddenly he was gripping her shoulders, his mouth twisted in an ugly line, his eyes dark and angry. "So that's the way it is. *It's his place you're on!* That's why you didn't want me around." His grasp tightened savagely. "Now I know why you didn't want anyone to know where you were, *or who you're with!*"

She was tugging frantically at his hands; those soft white hands that were suddenly so strong and unyielding. "You're hurting me!" she gasped. At last he loosened the cruel grip.

"You're hurt. What about me? All this time I've been thinking of you, imagining you as different, above all this sort of thing. All the time—I suppose," he said bitterly, "his wife would be the last one to know."

"Colin—"

"No wonder you wouldn't shift away from here, from him," he sneered. A note of self-pity crept into his hoarse voice. "You could have told me, though, instead of letting me go on and on, building up a pretty picture, thinking of you the way you used to be."

Maggie put her hands to her neck, bruised and sore where his fingers had marked the delicate flesh. "You have it all wrong," she said in a muffled tone. "You—never let me explain—"

"Explain what? Don't trouble telling me any more lies, Maggie. You're in love with the guy, and you know it."

Her cracked laugh was a poor attempt at lighthearted amusement, but it was the best she could do. "You must be crazy!" She was unaccountably angry with him.

"Am I?" He leaned back in the seat, studying her. Something in her expression must have given her away. To her intense mortification she could feel the hot, tell-tale pink creeping up her cheeks. She turned, but it was too late.

"Well, I guess it's your funeral if you get yourself into a mess—"

"I can look after myself," she said in a thick, unnatural voice that sounded strange even to her own ears. "Take me back to the beach buggy, will you? I'm late as it is!"

"Let him wait. I've waited a lot longer than that to see you again." Distractedly she twisted a strand of hair around and around her finger. "Please, Colin, just—take me back."

Reluctantly he put the car into gear and moved over the wet sand in the direction of the decrepit vehicle. He had barely reached it when she leaped out of the car. Once inside the beach buggy she could scarcely distinguish the gears for the mist that shimmered before her eyes. At last, after some fumbling, she moved away, catching a glimpse of Colin's set angry face as she swept past. Glancing over her shoulder as she drove between the sandhills, she saw that he was still sitting motionless, staring after her. Thank heaven, she mused, that her route took her far from the main highways. She couldn't endure the thought that he might follow her, find out where she was staying; perhaps even—she felt a sickness at the pit of her stomach—challenge Danger as to her status in his home. It was bad enough to have her employer thinking—Oh, why couldn't she forget him! There was no fun in living like this—so close to him in one sense, so far in another—no fun at all.

Oblivious of the passing scenery, she reached the homestead at last. Having put the beach buggy in the garage, her dragging footsteps took her inside and down the long hall.

At the end of the passage a full-length mirror gave back her reflection. She paused, staring in dismay. Could that be herself, that pale dishevelled-looking girl with the disfiguring red marks around her neck? Hastily she pulled up her collar to hide them as a tall masculine figure strode into view. Had he noticed the bruises, she wondered in panic. Impossible to tell from his chilly gaze. The thoughts tumbled wildly through her brain. He'd remember her offer to take the children up to the Gap today. No doubt he'd conclude that her meeting with Colin had been planned. How could you explain that it was an accident, that Colin was no longer a married man. It made no difference now to her own feelings anyway.

Slowly she turned to face him. "Danger—" As she looked up into the stern forbidding face her voice faltered. "About today—" she had to force herself to go on. "It was a real surprise to me, running into Colin. He—"

"No need for explanations, Maggie," he said gently, but something in the finality of his tones struck a chill in her heart. He remembers about Colin, she thought sadly, and he's thinking the worst of me—as usual.

"Oh, by the way," he was grave and unsmiling, "Tony rang again, says you didn't call him back today. Better put him out of his misery."

"No, I forgot, I'll do it now," she said contritely, uncaring, for what did it matter about Tony?

"Seems you're very popular around her, Maggie," he murmured grimly.

She could have wept. With everyone but you, her heart answered.

She summoned all her willpower. "I wanted to tell you—" There was so much she wanted to say, to explain, but how could she with Danger regarding her like that, so distant and withdrawn. The lines etched around his mouth were all at once stern and forbidding, his eyes when he turned toward her were chips of blue ice.

"Yes?"

She turned despairingly away. "Nothing." Oh, what was the use? What was the use of anything? They moved away together in a constrained and uneasy silence.

CHAPTER NINE

It was funny, Maggie told herself with an unconscious sigh, but when it came to affairs of the heart, lovers never arrived singly. Either one was lonely and neglected, or else they came two at a time, like Tony and Colin. But never the man you wanted. Fate wasn't all that generous. Trying desperately and ineffectually to forget Danger, she was finding it more and more difficult. Lean, burned, wildly exciting, and way beyond her dreams, he towered above everything else in her life. The thoughts beat endlessly like dark butterflies against the cage of her mind: How can I get over this feeling for him? How can I make him understand? Forget him, she told herself sternly, but she couldn't do that either.

Deliberately keeping herself endlessly occupied with household chores, she was indifferent to everything and everyone else. Tony's daily telephone calls barely registered with her, and Philippa's unconcealed air of resentment scarcely penetrated the fog of anguish in her mind. She had other more important problems, for which she could find no solution. How to endure the pain of being here with Danger; aware of the careful politeness in his tone, the icy disdain in his eyes. In the face of all that, what mattered a child's grudge?

Nevertheless, she felt a faint surprise when one morning Philippa approached her, a sheet of drawing paper dangling from her hand. "Please, Maggie, have you got a stamp?"

"Oh," Maggie turned from making a bed, "you did do the entry, then?"

The small girl stuck out her chin in a defiant gesture. "It's nothing." With an assumption of nonchalance laughable in one so young, she extended the picture.

"You can look at it if you like," she offered with vast condescension.

As she studied the sketch Maggie had to admit that the scene, crudely colored though it was, possessed some quality that held her. There was a freshness about it, an impression of clarity in the air; and yes, she marveled, the sky really was that incredible blue, up here in the hills. Nevertheless she had no wish to raise false hopes in the small artist. "It's worth sending," she murmured. "Look, I've got some cardboard and a big envelope that should fit it. I'll fix it up for you—"

"If you like." As the child turned away Maggie resisted an impulse to give the thin shoulders a sharp slap, but the next moment she forgot Philippa and the picture. She could hear Danger's step, his familiar whistling in the yard. As always her stupid heart began playing tricks with her.

Later in the day Ian wandered into the kitchen, and as Maggie expected, began talking of the agricultural show that they were all planning to attend on the weekend. It was an annual event held in a farming district 80 miles distant.

"It's fabulous!" He watched her take a batch of cookies from the oven. Then gingerly picking one p, he waited for it to cool a little. Maggie was spreading butter on a stack of sliced bread that she was making into sandwiches for a picnic lunch at the show grounds on the following day.

"Danger's going to drive the horse float with Pancho. You're taking us with you in the car. Mrs. Wahonga's coming too," he munched happily on a cookie, "with her boy."

Maggie nodded. She was thinking that to her the day at the show would be fraught with the bittersweet pleasure of being with Danger—that was, if he could bring himself to stay near her. Since the incident on the beach when he had come upon her in Colin's embrace, he had been noticeably cool and distant. Which was ridiculous, she mused, seeing that he hadn't the slightest romantic interest in her himself. It was really very strange. But then she and Danger never seemed to manage to understand each other. Even without understanding him, though, she loved him; no use denying it. No use thinking, hoping, longing either. She forced herself to concentrate on her present task.

"How many events are you entering in the Pony Ring tomorrow?"

"Only two. One over hurdles and Best Kept Pony."

"Best kept pony! You must be joking!"

He looked a trifle shamefaced at Maggie's incredulous expression and teasing smile.

"Well," he shifted uneasily beneath her gaze, "I know I don't groom and excercise him every day like you do Pete, but I'm going to give him a good brush down tonight. I can still enter him, can't I?"

"You haven't a hope," Maggie told him, "but I guess there's no harm in trying! Better get on with cleaning your gear too. How about your jodhpurs? Bring me your white shirt and tie. I'll give them a press."

"Okay . . . I'm leaving Pancho in the corral tonight all ready for the morning."

"Tell you what," Maggie offered. "I'll go down to the paddock with you later on if you like . . . help you give him a good brush down. We'll give him a wash first, to make his coat really shine and—" She broke off, aware of Philippa standing silently in the doorway, stroking the thick dark fur of the small possum she held in her arms. "Oh, Phil," a thought ran through Maggie's mind, and she smiled appealingly at the small girl, "I expect your horse could do with a spot of grooming too, even if he isn't going to the show tomorrow. How about if you come with us and give the Saint a rub down too?"

Philippa shrank back, a wary look entering the gray eyes. "No, I won't! I won't go near him! He hates me—"

"Not even if I hold him? You wouldn't mind just brushing him?"

"He wouldn't *let* me brush him. The minute I come just a teeny bit near him he rolls his eyes; all the white parts show. He knows I'm scared of him," she added, "I don't know how. He just—knows."

Maggie sighed and put the suggestion aside. Well, it had been worth a try. Perhaps if she could persuade the girl to ride Ian's placid pony she might gradually wean her from her obsession about horses in general, and the big white show jumper in particular. "I was wondering," she said gently, "if you'd like to enter one of the pony events at the show tomorrow? On Ian's pony, I mean."

"Aw, heck," the boy put in disgustedly, "she's not going to have Pancho. He doesn't want her riding him. She'd ruin him," he complained bitterly.

"I don't want your old pony anyhow. I only want my little Dandy." Philippa ran from the room with tear-filled eyes, slamming the door furiously behind her.

Maggie sighed as she cut through the pile of sandwiches. What a hope! She had been so confident in her powers of persuasion—the quick charm of manner that so often in the past gained her her own way, especially when it came to swaying masculine opinions. Yet with Philippa it seemed that nothing made the slightest difference. She was further away than ever from fulfilling her boast that she could make the child forget her fears and trepidations—her terrifying nightmares of the Saint. Time was going by fast, too fast. She was no nearer to her promise given so lightheartedly to Danger: that she could banish the child's fear of the famous show jumper.

Was it all mere wishful thinking? Like that other idea that she'd had in mind in those early days of her stay here. Had she really imagined that she could influence the master of Amberley, make him fall a little bit in love with her—just like that? She must have been out of her cotton-pickin' mind!

Fearful of sleeping in in the morning, Maggie awoke just as the first rose-and-gold shafts of sunrise spread across the eastern sky. Perched on a branch of a nearby macrocarpa tree, a tui was earlier still, his bell-like notes falling clear and pure into the stillness.

She went to the window to look out on an early morning scene that gave promise of a glorious day. There were sufficient fleecy white clouds to make the journey to Tamona not too hot, and a fresh breeze was blowing. If only things were different between Danger and herself. But in spite of everything, she couldn't help but sense a faint feeling of anticipation as she showered and slipped into an impeccably tailored pantsuit of gray-colored linen, swept back the long black hair and tied it with a matching chiffon scarf. A little thrill of pleasure shot through her as she met her reflection in the mirror. Her translucent dark-gold tan had appeared so gradually that she had been scarcely aware of it. Not that he would notice her, not the way he felt about her at the moment; with Ann in the party as well.

After that everything was a rush, getting the picnic hamper packed, slipping ice-cold bags in the cooler, placing the big fruit cake in a colored tin.

Philippa looked a different child when she was feeling happy, Maggie thought. The girl's gray eyes sparkled with anticipation. She wore daisy-splattered thongs on her narrow feet, and her gaily patterned floral shift was freshly laundered.

She scarcely recognized Ian in his neatly fitting jodhpurs, canary yellow pullover, and hard black riding hat. Only Mark was his usual chubby, endearingly aggressive small self, and Danger. . . . The dark blue of his stretch T-shirt pulled over corduroys made his eyes seem bluer than ever; a cool icy blue whenever he encouraged Maggie's direct look. She had to admit though that he was polite enough to her—in an impersonal, employer-to-housekeeper sort of way.

When everything was ready, Danger guided the horse float down to the corral. Fortunately, Maggie thought, Pancho appeared quite accustomed to road transport and stepped willingly up the landing and into the float. Down in the paddock Pete whinnied. Maggie knew a moment's regret that she had refused Danger's suggestion to take Pete in the double float and enter him in the hack events. But it was too late now. Anyway, she wouldn't have stood a chance against Ann who she knew was planning to enter a number of hurdle events with her bay thoroughbred Redwood.

"You okay?" With the float prepared, Danger came to stand beside the car, where Maggie sat behind the wheel, the wildly excited children in the back seat.

She nodded.

"We should make it in a couple of hours," Danger was saying. "Over the river, then on up the main road until you come to the turn-off—you'll see the signpost. Keep me in sight if you can. If you have any problems just pull in and wait for me to return and sort things out."

Taking in his strength and grace, the lines of the lean tanned face, she was thinking that she would wait forever, if it would do her any good. But of course it wouldn't.

"Okay?" With a start she realized he was staring at her with his old penetrating look. She dropped her gaze guiltily. "Yes, I know."

"Right! We're away, then!"

It was easy enough to keep Danger in sight as they went down the winding slope, through the gate and over the farm road that circled the sheep-threaded hills. Maggie caught up with him at the landing where a cluster of dust-smothered cars filled with adults and children waited for the arrival of the car ferry.

Once on the main road, however, it wasn't so easy. It seemed transporters, horse floats, jeeps, Land Rovers and cars were all bound in the same direction. Apparently everyone in the remote, scattered farming area was intent on attending the country show; no doubt a focal point for the outlying districts. Gradually, however, the traffic spread out, the miles dropped away. At last, following Danger's Land Rover, Maggie turned at a signpost and presently drove through a small township. Each side of the road was lined with bungalows painted in rainbow colors. Then the houses and country stores were left behind, and there was only the expanse of fenced paddocks with grazing cattle and sheep.

"I can hear a merry-go-round!" shouted Mark. Turning a corner Maggie came in sight of the showgrounds, a green expanse surrounded by tall evergreens. Cars, trucks and horse floats were milling around the entrance where a man in a white coat directed her with his flag toward a wide parking lot on the grass. Maggie drew in at the side of the Land Rover. Already Danger was letting down the flap door of the float and leading Pancho out onto the grass.

He helped Ian saddle the pony, then as the boy sprang up on his mount, gave the pony an affectionate slap. "Off you go, both of you! See what you can find out about the course." Maggie watched Ian put Pancho to a trot as he guided the pony up a grassy slope and rode toward an area where horses and riders milled about amongst the painted jumps and hurdles.

"His events aren't on until this afternoon," Danger remarked, "but he can get an idea of the course. Here, Philippa," fishing in his pocket he held out some change, "take these. Give yourself and Mark a ride on the merry-go-round, and anything else you fancy in the sideshow department. Just look after him, will you? Make sure you're back here in an hour. You have your watch?"

Philippa nodded, then the two children hurried away in the direction of the various sideshows.

"Come on," he looked at Maggie with a smile that made her heart flip, "you haven't seen anything yet!"

Together they strolled over the grassy paddock to a crowded area where a giant ferris wheel traced a moving pattern against the blue. Showmen waiting at the entrance of their tents were calling attention to the various sidshows. Here was all the fun of the fair, Maggie thought, and something else besides. Suddenly her heart was spinning as crazily as the bobbing, painted horse of the merry-go-round. If only it could always be like this, just she and Danger alone together, everything else forgotten.

She realized they had paused beside a shooting gallery. A line of contestants, with fierce concentration and narrowed eyes, took careful aim with their rifles at the endlessly moving belt of cardboard hares.

"Why don't you have a whirl?" Maggie urged. Laughing, she looked up at him; something in his deep brilliant gaze, something she couldn't define leaped between them.

"Want me to?"

For Maggie the sunlit scene was all at once touched with a new luster. She was pierced with a brittle happiness that was half pleasure, half pain. "Why not?" she heard herself say. "You might—win something."

"What I want," his voice was curiously low, "happens to be way out of reach. Still—" a smile touched the lips that today had forgotten to be stern; his gaze moved to the shelves above the shooting gallery, crowded with an assortment of cheap novelties. "Would you want one of those if I won it for you?"

"I don't know. Try me and see."

But in her heart she knew quite well that she would prize any trophy he chose to give to her. She wouldn't care what it was, even one of the garish plaster figures of an Indian, so long as it was from him. That was how silly she was today.

"You've asked for it," Danger said, and took her hand in his. It was something to do with the day, she told herself as he drew her to the open tent. A blue day, wild, free, cloud-fretted. A day of enchantment where flags fluttered their colors in the breeze. The creaking tune from the merry-go-round touched her with a poignancy she could scarcely bear.

"Stay with me," Danger was saying. "You could bring me luck!"

He tucked her arm through his, and in her bemused state of heady excitement, she was oblivious of the openly admiring stare of the young male tent attendant.

"Going to win a present for your girl?"

"That's the idea," Danger agreed, and Maggie's heart gave a wild leap, then settled again.

"Six shots for a dollar, sir. Here's your rifle."

As Danger leaned over the counter, Maggie felt that at last she was free to gaze at him without the risk of being observed, without his guessing. . . . As she watched he took careful aim, then bang! bang! bang! Three shots rang out in swift succession, puncturing the cardboard hares. The attendant was the only one of the party who failed to look pleased.

"You're taking all his profits," Maggie whispered.

"Your fault. I told you you'd bring me luck. Here we go again."

Maggie held her breath as three more shots rang out, flattening two out of the three moving cardboard shapes.

"Good for you! Give these to your girl, sir." The young man in charge of the shooting gallery reached to a shelf, selecting from amongst the jumble of tawdry ornaments and luridly colored pictures an ornate gilt alarm clock. "Just what you need for setting up house."

"There you are, Maggie. One thing," Danger added in a low tone, "it's not half as ghastly as the yellow glass vase. Or how about that lurid-looking plaster tiger on the top shelf."

"For me?" She glanced up in mock reproach as he handed her the alarm clock. "And I thought I was always so punctual in the mornings."

"No arguing, Maggie. You heard what the man said? I have to hand you over the spoils."

Such a tide of happiness swept her that for a moment she could scarcely see the gilt clock with its fat cupids for the stupid tears that trembled on her lashes. "Thanks, Danger."

"That's nothing. There's more to come, lots more. Wait for it. There. Interested?" He was placing in her arms a massive chocolate box decorated with a picture of garish red roses. "You can't say you don't want that."

"Lovely. The children—"

"The heck with the children. It's yours—and this. Don't say I didn't warn you!" The plaster tiger with its orange spots and ferocious expression joined the clock. A moment later it was followed by a yellow glass vase, so tall that Maggie just managed to peer over its rim. She balanced the motley collection of articles in her arms. "What'll I do with it all?"

"Hand 'em to me. We'll stow them in the car," Danger suggested promptly. She passed him the trophies, and they strolled away in the direction of the parking lot. Presently they moved past the pens where pedigree cattle and sheep stood in stalls in the long, covered enclosure. Then, once again, they were out among the casually dressed crowd, watching the giant ferris-wheel high overhead. In a moment, two small familiar faces flashed by. Philippa was shrieking with excitement; Mark subdued and rigid, was wide-eyed in terrified fascination. The giant wheel spun around, and Maggie, turning away, found herself looking into a fun mirror nearby. Danger's lean height was distorted beyond all recognition. "My," she teased him laughingly, "how you've grown!"

"Look who's talking." He pushed her to a twin mirror where her own reflection was widened out of all belief.

They strolled on among the throng, pausing to glance at a stall displaying tanned fleeces in vivid shades together with various articles made from the sheep's wool. "Around here they use lichens and vegetable dyes to get the colors," Danger told her. "Hey, here's someone you know."

"But I couldn't possibly know anyone away up here—"

"You do, you know."

He took her arm and at his touch, once again that frail fleeting happiness pierced her. Such little things . . . a kiss on a night of white brilliance . . . an hour among the crowd at a country show . . . but they would be all she would ever have. The colorful scene around her shimmered in a haze of unshed tears.

"Maggie!" She was aware of a familiar voice, rich and musical. Then she caught sight of Mrs. Wahonga. At first she found it hard to believe the sight before her eyes. A man was busy shearing a sheep; the Maori woman was picking up fragments of wool that littered the platform and knitting them into a garment. She glanced up from the work to wave a plump hand at Maggie. At her side two European women were engaged in the same task, but it was clear that they had only just begun while the Maori woman's sweater was growing every moment.

"Do you see what I see?" Maggie murmured wonderingly. "Mrs. Wahonga. She's actually using fencing wire to knit that garment."

"That's right," Danger said. "Number Eight. Used to be a common sight, I believe, 100 years ago; seems Mrs.

Wahonga's carrying on the tradition. Successfully, too, by the look of things. I'd put my money on her every time."

Maggie watched the shearer with bulging muscles and sweating features hold the sheep motionless in his grip. He continued to toss the shorn fleece down on the platform for the knitting contestants to pick up. "She's knitting a sweater straight from the fleece."

Danger nodded. "Haven't you ever come across Maori knitting? Kiwi Craft, they call it around here. It's quite something, making a garment from the actual fleece. She's way ahead of the others too. Trust Mrs. Wahonga. The secret's in her attitude, I guess. She's kept her cool. It would take more than a Kiwi Craft contest to throw her. Just take a look at the other two, will you?"

It was clear to Maggie that the European women had allowed their nerves to get the better of them; their faces were flushed and beaded with perspiration, their hands visibly trembling. How different was the comfortably relaxed air of the big Maori woman. Raising lustrous dark eyes from her flying needles, she tossed back her flowing ponytail, sent Maggie a beaming smile. She nodded in the direction of a tall, powerfully-built young man who stood watching the contestants from the forefront of the group gathered around the platform. "Hey, Maggie," she called proudly, "that my boy Hone!"

As the good-looking young man shyly took her hand, Maggie gazed at him in amazement. For some absurd reason she had imagined "my boy Hone," who seemed to need so much care from his mother, as a 12 year-old boy, not this pleasant-faced young man with his mother's wide and friendly smile.

Though her hands on the thick needles never wavered, Mrs. Wahonga's plump shoulders shook with silent laughter. "You think he just little, eh? Not any more." She bent her attention once more to the bulky garment swiftly taking shape beneath her skilful fingers.

"Keep it up, Mrs. Wahonga," Danger called and turned away. To Maggie he said teasingly: "A bit bigger than you thought, eh, *ehoa*?"

"A bit." She smiled into his face. As they strolled along the winding path it seemed to Maggie that it was an exciting, exhilarating day, full of life, movement and color. She wished it could go on forever. As it happened though, her feeling of elation lasted for exactly five minutes longer. They had paused to watch a tug o' war contest, where with straining muscles and encouragement from the roar of the crowd, each team pulled for two minutes on a huge rope. As one team pulled the other across the center line, Danger, glancing at his wrist watch, said suddenly: "Just have time to see Ann. She's due to go on in a minute or so in the F.E.I. Competition. Come on, let's see what's happening up on the hill!"

As she turned to go with him, Maggie's new-found happiness died away. He had merely been filling in time with her until Ann was riding in her event. To Danger that would of course be the main attraction of the day. She swallowed and tried to hide her sense of hurt. Together they climbed the grassy rise, watching the riders in their dark green hunting jackets urge their mounts over the combination of jumps.

"This is the final round—" the loudspeaker blared in the still air. "Ann Macklow on Redwood. Here she comes now!"

Over to the left on the long timber stands, the crowd was leaning forward expectantly. There was a sudden hush as the bay cantered toward the first hurdle, then gathered himself for the jump. Maggie, stealing a sideways peek, realized that Danger was watching horse and rider attentively. At a fast pace the hunter took each jump perfectly, sailing over with no apparent effort. As horse and rider came nearer Maggie caught a glimpse of Ann's face, set in concentration. She couldn't help but admire the other girl's perfect seat. It was as if she were molded into one with her mount. "No faults so far," Danger was saying, "fast too. Now for the last jump." Then Ann was up and over, the crowd was applauding, the announcer calling the winning time. Ann, saluting the judge, left the ring. The next moment she came cantering over the grass toward them.

"Congratulations! That was great." Danger's face was alight with interest. Watching him, Maggie thought: He never looked at me that way. Now I know he never will. But she crushed the ache in her heart and made herself say smilingly: "Congratulations, Ann."

"Thank you! Thank you!" The other girl was flushed, excited with her success. "Oh, Maggie, Tony's here. He's been looking all over for you. I'll go back and tell him where you are. See you soon!" With a wide smile and a flash of white teeth she cantered away, leaving Maggie staring disconsolately after her.

That's done it, she thought dispiritedly, and wasn't surprised to see that Danger's face was set and stern again. All the warmth and teasing and laughter of the morning was wiped away.

"Time we found the kids," he said. "How about if you collect them while I bring the lunch up here? We can have it under the trees. That is," icicles crackled in his tone, "if you don't want to have yours with Tony?"

"No." She turned away despondently. Why was it that things never worked out the way you wanted them to? Why did it have to be Tony who was anxious to be with her, but never, never Danger? Except of course when it happened to suit him.

She comforted herself bleakly a little later as she spread a tablecloth on the grass and began unpacking the picnic hamper. With the children all talking at once, and Ann giving a blow-by-blow description of her victory, Tony could scarcely become too personal. She couldn't, however, prevent him from staring at her in that absurd manner, following her every movement with his pale eyes; she sensed that was not lost on Danger. Quiet and withdrawn, he sat a little apart. Anyone would think, Maggie thought spiritedly, that it was he who was disappointed about Tony claiming her company.

Presently Jim strolled over to join the luncheon party; a smiling greeting for Maggie in his steady gray eyes. Big and quiet, there was something solid and trustworthy about him. She fleetingly thought that it was too bad that such an obviously worthwhile man was forced to lead a lonely existence on an outback farm. Of course Danger was unmarried too—She pulled herself up as the tea she was pouring overflowed onto the cloth. There she went again, thinking of Danger! Anyway, the parallel wasn't the same. Danger obviously had a future bride already picked out. Ann and Danger's marriage would please everyone, she thought drearily. Tony could return to his interrupted studies with no qualms of conscience about the sheep farm he and his sister had inherited. Danger would be perfectly capable of dealing with two farms, she was certain. Oh yes, Ann as mistress of Amberley would please everyone—except her.

Ann had gone to collect the prize money, leaving her mount tethered in the shade of the trees. When she returned she took her tea to sit beside Danger, where they immediately became deep in conversation. Maggie, spreading out the food she had prepared so carefully and attractively, found that somehow it had no appeal. But the children were doing justice to the picnic lunch; especially Ian, hot and irritable in his unaccustomed riding gear, and Mark, whose chubby face still bore evidence of pink candy floss.

Afterward Jim helped her clear away the remains of the picnic. Danger, handing around cigarettes, said with his laconic air, "You're on at one, Ian. Better get going."

They all moved toward the pony ring. Maggie watched

Ian join the line of small riders on their burnished ponies standing on the flat below. Even from a distance she could see the boy's pallor, and she realized that the event was more of an ordeal than he had let anyone know.

The starting signal was given; one by one, each rider went over the jumps. Ian was first on the list. As his mount cleared one after another of the hurdles, Maggie hoped that he would at least gain a place. She knew that it would make the boy's day. Today at least one of her wishes was granted, for Ian completed the course without a fault. Although the remainder of the competitors in the event followed, not one equalled Ian's record.

His face was beaming as a little later he was called to the center of the ring; the judge placed the red ribbon of first place around Pancho's broad neck.

Ian's face was still radiant as he came cantering over to receive a chorus of congratulations. Maggie knew that for one of the party the day was complete. Although he could scarcely expect to gain a place in the section of Best-Cared-For-Pony, that didn't matter now. He had what he wanted.

She couldn't say the same for herself, she thought, as the afternoon wore on. Danger had taken Ann to the large sheds where against a background of drafting pens and stockyards, the prize-winning stock was on display. "You wouldn't be interested in Hereford cattle?" He had half offered to include Maggie too, but she could scarcely admit to a knowledgeable interest in stock. Anyway, she was sure he had merely made the offer out of politeness (or a shortage of housekeepers in the country), she thought waspishly. So instead, she strolled around the exhibits with the children and Tony, who seemed determined not to let her out of his sight. She sensed that he was impatient with the children and wanted to get rid of them, but— Oh, she liked Tony well enough, but today she was in no mood for intimacy. Danger had spoilt her for any other man's company. Why not admit it? Nevertheless she made an effort to appear interested in the display of farm machinery he was pointing out to her.

"Actually," he was eyeing her closely, "I couldn't care less about all this. All I wanted was a chance to have you to myself—can't we do something about these kids?"

Maggie laughed. "It'll cost you two tickets on the hoop-la and a trip through the crazy house—"

"Cheap at the price. Philippa! Want to see some sideshows?"

She stared at him for a moment, then grasped the proffered opportunity. "I'd rather see the children's art display."

"Beat it then, and take Mark along too. Here's some money; might come in handy."

Philippa pocketed the coins with alacrity. "Mark won't go unless Maggie comes too."

"Oh, all right, then—" With a resigned shrug of his shoulders and an expressive glance toward Maggie, Tony went with them to the long open shed where sketches were pinned to the walls. Not that Tony could really complain of the children here, Maggie though amusedly, watching Philippa running ahead. The small girl was oblivious of everyone else as she ran from picture to picture. Even Mark appeared to find a measure of entertainment in the bold and colorful designs.

As they mingled with the crowd, Tony took Maggie's arm. "Why didn't you call me yesterday?" he whispered. "I waited all day, longest day of my life, honestly. I thought 'if she wants to come to the show with me she'll let me know.' What a day I put in. Will she? Won't she?"

"I'm sorry," Maggie's voice was abstracted. She was gazing at a boldly executed portrait of a buxom blonde of massive proportions and bulging muscles. The picture bore the simple title: Mommy. "I meant to get in touch with you, but I was busy and somehow," she turned on him her gay, pixie smile, "I forgot."

"Forgot! she says." Tony groaned. "That's almost as

bad as being out with some other guy. Not that there could be anyone else. That's what I kept telling myself all day yesterday—not in Te Rangi.''

Maggie felt a pang of the heart. So Tony too had already written off Danger when it came to possible husband-material, for anyone except Ann. With an effort she concentrated on the light tones.

"Come on, let's park the kids some place and have a bit of time to ourselves—"

But Maggie had caught sight of men standing near tall logs on a grassy area a short distance away. "Wood chopping!"

He sent the area a disinterested glance. "What of it? It's just the jigger-chop. They always have it at this sort of show. Why they want to wear themselves out bashing away at an old tree trunk gets me. Come on, Maggie—"

She scarcely heard him. She was glancing toward the men waiting near the logs. One tall rangy figure in white shirt and slacks appeared strangely familiar. "It's Danger!" she breathed excitedly. "I didn't know he was entering in it—"

"He wasn't," Tony murmured morosely. "Seems that some guy pulled out at the last minute. They persuaded Danger to take his place. He's an old hand at the game," he added carelessly, "so I suppose that's why they were so eager to get him.''

"Let's go and watch." Maggie called to the children.

"But, Maggie—" Tony caught her arm.

Ignoring his protests, she was already hurrying over the grass. Men in white, axes in hand, were already standing at the side of spaced logs, each of the same diameter. As she reached the watching crowd, an announcer called over the loudspeaker. She saw Danger stroll forward to stand beside a tall log. He tested the sharp blade.

"Go!" As the signal was given, Danger, with an easy swinging motion, plunged the singing blade deep in the log. The chips flew around him as the ax fell with swift precision, sunlight glinting on the flashing blade.

Maggie darted a swift glance at the other contestants. No doubt but Danger was already in the lead. Now he had cut a deep notch, ramming the end of the jigger so that it stood at right angles to the log. Leaping up onto the platform, he proceeded with rhythmic blows to cut another notch higher up, to run the jigger in again . . . and another. . . .

Maggie found herself standing in the front of the throng, beside Ann. She was scarcely aware that she was calling excitedly. "Hurry! Hurry!" A Maori man of magnificent physique, obviously an experienced bushman, was almost at the same stage of progress. What if he beats Danger, Maggie thought. They're chopping neck and neck! How could Danger be so calm, so unconcerned? Now he was on the last jigger, had cut almost through the bark-trimmed log. The crash! The log toppled to the grass below, and Danger leaped down lightly. Within two minutes the other three contestants had felled their logs. The announcer was addressing the crowd through his loudspeaker.

"—pleased to announce the winner of the jigger chop and Jubilee Challenge Trophy—John Dangerfield!"

They waited to see him presented with a gleaming silver trophy. As he turned aside, Ann ran forward, her plain features transfigured with excitement. "Now it's my turn to congratulate you, Danger. You've done it again!"

"Thanks, Ann." They strolled back in the direction of the family party. As they came nearer, Maggie saw Danger push the trophy toward Ann; heard him say carelessly, "Here, take care of this for me, will you? Cups are more in your line than mine." All at once Maggie was aware of him looking directly toward her.

"Congratulations." Somehow the word emerged in a croak.

"Thanks, Maggie." He stooped to pick up his blue T-shirt. Forturnately, she thought, he didn't appear to have noticed the unaccustomed huskiness of her tone. Or maybe he just wasn't interested. Why should he be? But as for her, loving him as she did, how could she help this desolate feeling? For Ann, a silver chalice—the real thing. And for herself? A cheap gold clock, and imitation gold at that.

The thought caused her to behave more kindly to Tony than she might otherwise have done. "You won't mind if I carry Maggie off for a while?" he was saying to Danger. "The kids will be okay?"

"We'll look after them." It was Ann who answered.

Maggie turned away. She wished she hadn't come here today. She wished— But you had to pretend, to look as though life wasn't getting the better of you. And Tony meant well, she couldn't deny that. He insisted on taking her to an afternoon tea stall, cool and shady under a green canvas awning. Looking at his animated expression, she told herself wryly that at least someone in the party was feeling happier for her being here.

She didn't see the others again until the end of the Grand Parade at the close of the day. Animals selected from the New Zealand stud-breeding industry were led into the main arena to form a great circle on the green.

There were champion red and white Hereford cattle, prize-winning ribbons draped around their sturdy necks, massive Shorthorn bulls, rings through their noses and led by proud owners, pedigree sheep, children with their calves, and entrants of the pony ring. They were followed by trotting sulkies and draft horses, then Arab stallions, mares and foals and champion hacks. The moving chain formed a great ring as they made a full circuit. Then it was over, the crowds were converging upon the gates. Horse floats and transporters began moving in the parking area; and tired children, clutching balloons and eating hot dogs, were propelled reluctantly to dust-coated cars.

"Enjoy it?" Danger stood at her side. Before she could do more than nod in reply, he had run on: "Better get away before the mob. Kids are waiting in the car."

She had a wild impulse to giggle at Tony's expression of open-mouthed surprise. "Wait a minute—" But before he could say more, Danger, with a curt nod, had shepherded her away.

"I'll keep in touch." Tony called after her, but she scarcely heard him. How could she think of anything or anyone else when she was alone with Danger in the crowd; pressed close to him, his warm touch on her arm as he guided her through the throng?

When Maggie walked into the kitchen, Mrs. Wahonga was already there. She threw Maggie her beaming smile. "You have a good time at the show, eh— What's this?" She broke off in pleased surprise as Ian flourished a scarlet prize ribbon before her eyes. "Look, Mrs. Wahonga! My first red one!"

"Good for you, boy!"

"How about you, Mrs. Wahonga?" Maggie asked quickly. "I bet you won that contest for knitting a pullover from the sheep's wool."

"Oh, that was nothing," but the pleasant face was smiling contentedly.

"Did you *really*?" Philippa had entered the room in time to hear the last words. "Where is it? The pullover? What did you do with it?"

"Oh, I give it to my boy Hone."

Maggie stared across at the Maori woman in amazement. "Do you mean to say you made that huge sweater? I mean it must have been a huge one, to fit Hone! It must have taken much more work than the ones the other women were making! Why ever did you make it for him?"

The woman looked puzzled. "He needs it. You know? When he goes out fishing at night, he gets cold."

Maggie gave up. "You really deserved to win that contest. What was the prize, anyway?"

"Look!" The big woman pointed with pride to the fluffy sheepskin slippers, resembling scarlet canoes, on her feet. The temperature was still high, but evidently Maggie thought, Mrs. Wahonga was determined to use her prize; no matter how uncomfortably hot the slippers might be.

"Oh, Maggie, I almost forgot—" She brought her mind back. "Some man, he keep calling you ever since I got home. Ring! Ring! Ring! I tell him you out, maybe won't be back until late, but he take no notice. You know what? I think he like you a lot, that Colin!"

"I see." Absently Maggie began to collect the children's jackets. As she moved, her thoughts were chaotic. Colin! Again! She had thought she'd made her point cruelly plain to him. But to telephone her here at Amberley! He must have done some swift detective work to discover her whereabouts. But of course it would be a simple matter to inquire on the beach after she had left him. Anyone living in the district would be aware of John Dangerfield's young housekeeper.

At the shrill ring of the telephone, her hand froze on the door handle. "If that's him I can't speak to him—"

But of course it was, and she did, for Mrs. Wahonga was holding out the receiver. There was nothing else Maggie could do.

She was only vaguely aware of what Colin was saying, confusedly conscious of Danger having entered the room. He couldn't help but overhear every word she said. Even in her bewildered state she couldn't mistake Colin's intention of coming here next weekend. "To say how sorry I am about the other day," he told her. "To put things right again."

Frantically she tried to dissuade him. "No, please! I mean, I won't be here!"

"Oh, come on, Maggie, you made up that story this minute."

"No, honestly—" she heard herself babbling into the receiver, "I promised . . . someone else." All at once she remembered the invitation that Tony was repeatedly pressing on her: that she come with him and Ann to their beach cottage on a weekend. It was an invitation that she had continually sidestepped under the excuse of not knowing whether or not she would be free of her household duties. For although Danger had urged her to arrange for Mrs. Wahonga to relieve her while she took a couple of days off, so far she hadn't done so. No need to inform her employer of the real reason why she stayed at Amberley. At last she came up with a satisfactory excuse that happened to be the truth—well, near enough anyway.

"It's some people who live around here," she heard herself saying. "They have a beach cottage around the bay. I said I'd go with them . . . I don't know whether it'll be on Saturday or Sunday, or maybe the weekend. Anyway, Colin—" a frantic glance behind her showed that Danger was bending to take off Mark's shoes. She couldn't get involved in an emotional argument right now. "I'll call you back," she said faintly. With that Colin had to be content.

"There you are, chum!" Mark scampered away. As Danger straightened, Maggie met his chilly blue gaze. If only she could make him understand! "That was Colin," she said nervously. "I told you. He—"

"I gathered that," he broke in dryly. "I thought we'd discussed that before, Maggie." She looked away from his bleak, impersonal stare. "Your personal life is your own affair—"

"But—"

"And as for weekend arrangements, you can count the time your own. Mrs. Wahonga can easily fill in for you. You're due for some time off anyway. Seeing you want to go over to the cottage for the weekend—"

"I don't want to go all that much, not really," she protested breathlessly. "It was just . . ." Her voice died away beneath his sardonic look. A look that she knew from experience meant one thing only. Once again she'd done the wrong thing, or so he imagined; had earned his silent contempt. Not that he was saying so, not aloud. He had no need to. His grave stare made his opinion of her devastatingly, hurtfully clear.

"Just that you're so much in demand, I take it?"

All at once she couldn't endure the twist of the mobile lips, the hard mocking tone. How dare he censure her? For that was what his look implied. He took it for granted that she was having an affair with a married man and leading Tony on into the bargain! He wouldn't allow her to explain. Well, let him think what he liked. It was unjust and terribly unfair. She wouldn't stand it another minute.

"Yes, I do want to go," she told him in a flurry of words. "Tony asked me over to the cottage with him and Ann, ages ago. Have you any objection to that?"

"None at all, Maggie—if that's what you want." He turned aside. "I'll fix it with Mrs. Wahonga to come for a couple of days . . . mind the kids."

Up to the last few moments, she hadn't had the slightest intention of leaving Amberley for a visit to the beach cottage owned by Tony and Ann. Neither of them meant a thing to her. She didn't care if she never saw them again. But she was committed. Now she must make the best of it.

"Thank you."

"Don't thank me." At the door he turned, hatefully polite. "It's all in the rules, Maggie. You deserve some time off . . . I guess I should have thought of it before. Easily fixed though, *now that you've made up your mind.*"

Whatever that meant, she thought furiously. Made up her mind concerning holiday time due to a household employee? More likely he meant "made up your mind about men friends." Her footsteps dragged as she went pensively to her own room. Why did everything have to be such a mess? Why couldn't she and Danger ever understand each other? How was it possible to love someone so desperately, and to hate him at the same time?

CHAPTER TEN

If Maggie wasn't looking forward to the visit to the beach cottage, she knew that Tony certainly would be. Twice during the week he called to chat with Maggie and to make arrangements for the visit. "Don't do a thing about food," he told her in his soft, light accents. "Ann'll bring along all the goodies. She's been on at me for weeks to come with her and tidy up the place." Over the wire she caught his scornful laugh. "She's got a hope."

"Why not? You could—"

"With you there? After all the effort and time I've spent persuading you to come with me? Not a chance! All I'm thinking of doing is getting you away from the others—"

The others? Maggie's heart missed a beat, and she was barely aware of the remainder of the conversation. Would Danger also be at the cottage? Seeing that Ann would be there wasn't it to be expected? She didn't want to put the question to Tony. She wished Danger would come—no, she didn't! It would be unbearable for her if he did. His tight-lipped silence was only endurable because he was out early in the morning to return only in time for a late dinner at night. But it would be different at the cottage; different and infinitely harder to bear his silent contempt, even if he was busy with Ann. With Danger you could never seem to conceal anything. Those keen blue eyes caught you every time. She must guard her telltale glance, hide the feelings she had for him at all costs. Being in love was something she could do nothing about, couldn't fight against. All she could do was try to discipline her voice, her glance, and definitely avoid his touch.

She was relieved that Danger was far from the homestead, patrolling the boundary fences on Red, when Tony called for her. He was driving the family car, his bearded young face bright with anticipation.

"Isn't Ann coming with us?" Maggie inquired as she got into the passenger seat. He closed the door after her.

He threw her an expressive glance. "Don't tell me you want her around today? Actually," he turned the ignition and threw the car into gear, swinging around on the wide gravel driveway, "she's coming later with Danger—much later, I hope!"

A sense of excitement stirred in her. So Danger was coming to the cottage after all. Not with her, not because of her, but coming nevertheless. It was awful to long for him so much, even in his unmistakable mood of disapproval toward her; even though he was obviously in love with someone else. As Tony opened a gate, she watched him with an abstracted gaze. Love . . . it did things to you, made you so—so helpless so that your whole universe was suddenly centered on just one man. A deep sigh escaped her: a man who in a few short weeks she would never see again. Funny how a kiss could change your life so that nothing was the same again, ever . . . and there was not one thing that you could do about it. With an effort she threw her heavy thoughts aside. Tony was singing lightly as they sped up the winding curves. "You sound happy."

"Can you blame me?" He threw her a smiling sideways glance. "Have you all to myself at last—on a day like this."

It was a wonderful day, Maggie admitted, glancing idly around her. Rinsed blue sky, clouds racing overhead in the breeze, air crystal clear.

Soon they were taking the car-ferry over the river crossing. Once on the opposite bank, they swept along pleasant white roads bordered by hilly, sheep-dotted paddocks with their seven-barred fences. Presently they turned into a side road, unfamiliar country for Maggie.

Leaning back, she watched the landscape slip by. Emerald paddocks, lush with spring grass, had dividing boundaries of great clumps of feathery toe-toe. Deep ditches lined with tall bamboo stretched on either side of the roadway; cream cans rested on timber stands at farm gateways. The wild peach trees growing along the route had shed their pink blossoms, but on the kowhai branches the last remnants of gold still lingered. Soon a sawmill appeared, and as they climbed a pine-covered slope, Maggie caught the tang of freshly-sawn timber. Then they descended, skirting mangrove swamps with their choked muddy streams, sweeping up a rise where the air was spiced with the sharp fragrance of tea-tree bushes covering the slope.

Up here in the hills there was only the sheep—and a tiny white church. As Maggie looked at the small building set high on a rise, she mused that it was probably made use of by all sects in the scattered district. She fell into a daydream. She and Danger were being married in a tiny white church atop a green hill, then woke up sharply with the wry thought of his horrified expression if aware of that particular technicolored fantasy.

"Bring your swimsuit with you?"

"Yes, of course." She jerked back to reality and the bearded young face at her side. They were moving over a narrow ridge, and she glanced down to the vast acres far below.

"Not long now," Tony remarked. "Look, you can see the sea."

Leaning forward, she discerned between a gap in the hills a line of blue on the horizon. "Do you use the place much?"

"Heck, no! When we were kids we thought it was the only place on earth. It's pretty quiet—a few cottages, lots of greenery about, good sheltered harbor. They say it's great for fishing—" he threw her a distasteful grin "—if you happen to go for that type of entertainment."

Maggie smiled. "I don't mind sampling the results."

"Oh, I'm with you there. It's a funny thing," he confided, "but I've never wanted to go near the place for years, until you came along—" He sent her a warm smile. "Only way I could think to get you out and away from Te Rangi for a while—" He broke off, then went on thoughtfully, "You sure stick close around home there. I mean, it's a day's work to have you leave the place. Anyone would think," he said lightly, "that you liked being on the job day and night."

"I suppose so." But there was no real amusement in Maggie's sad little smile.

"Tell me something. Don't you ever get fed up with being over at Amberley all the time?"

All at once Maggie didn't want to discuss her personal problems or her life at Te Rangi. "It's only temporary," she said stiffly.

To Tony her short answer went unnoticed. He shrugged thin shoulders, saying on a note of relief, "Thank the lord for that."

"Anyway," Maggie said, "you mightn't be staying long here yourself. If you decide that you're not cut out for sheep farming after all—"

He threw her a wry look.

"Maggie, you have it all wrong. I decided that when I was five years old, or maybe a shade earlier. I'm hoping that I won't have to change my mind about the farming lark. If things turn out right, and I think now that they will, there'll be no problem. With Ann married to a man who knows the work and loves it—what's the matter, Maggie? Getting fed up with the drive? Won't be long now."

"No, no," she returned hastily, "I love the drive." With an effort she pushed away the wave of misery that had swept over her. That was the worst of having an expressive open face that registered every passing emotion for all the world to see.

"That's okay, then. For a minute I thought you looked . . . sort of sad."

"You imagined it."

She'd have to do better than this at the cottage, she told herself. What if she gave herself away once again and Danger guessed . . . suspected. . . . The thought made her try out her gayest smile. She burst into animated chatter that she managed to sustain until they swept over a rise and came in sight of a wide blue bay. At the water's edge small neat holiday homes were painted in bright shades and surrounded by green trees, and colorful flowering shrubs. Fishing boats and pleasure craft skimmed the calm waters of the sheltered bay.

As they took the road that bordered the sea, Maggie noticed that the beach wasn't sandy, as she had expected, but was made up of small colored pebbles. Tony followed her gaze. "Rock hunter's paradise," he told her. "They say there are stones here that you don't come across anywhere else along the coast. Red jasper, green beryl and that glassy black stuff—onyx, isn't it? We used to spend hours collecting it when we were kids. That was before rock hunting got so popular. Now you never know who you'll run across up here in no-man's-land. Parties come up from town by chartered bus, hot on the trail of the colored stones. Here's our shack, last place on the point—"

On reaching the end of the headland he turned into a winding drive. A small timber dwelling on the rise was almost concealed by trees and great bushes of hibiscus and tropical plants. A wide veranda ran along the front of the beach house. As Tony put a key in the lock, Maggie glanced through the uncurtained French doors. She could glimpse a wide spacious lounge with a polished timber floor and comfortable worn chairs. Beyond, twin bedrooms were each fitted with bunk beds and a painted dressing chest.

The stale smell of a dwelling long unused met them as they went inside. Tony went from room to room, opening windows and flinging wide the French doors, letting in the fresh sweet smell of flower-scented air. "Tide's on the turn. It's now or never if you want a swim."

"Race you in." Maggie hurried into a bedroom, to emerge a few minutes later wearing a white swimsuit that formed such an arresting contrast with the golden tan of her skin.

Tony, in swim shorts, joined her almost immediately. She knew a moment's surprise when she took in his frail physique. He looked far too thin, almost delicate; and certainly in no fit state to take on the strenuous physical toil involved in the running of a large sheep station.

"Let's go!" He caught her hand, and they went down the dusty overgrown path. Then they were crossing the metal road, painful to Maggie's bare feet, running over a strip of long grass anding path that led steeply between high lupins to the water below.

On the pebbly shore, Maggie gingerly picked her way over the small strip that was all that remained of the beach at high tide.

After the first breathless shock, the water was a delight, clear and rippling with a breeze that tossed the tall trees along the shoreline. They struck out side by side. When Maggie paused, breathing hard, to cling to an anchored dinghy, she found Tony beside her. Although there were a handful of swimmers far along the shore, they appeared to have this part of the bay to themselves.

"Maggie—" He threw a wet arm around her shoulders, but she slipped from his grasp and laughing, headed for deeper water, long black hair streaming behind her.

"Come back! Or I'll come and get you."

She only laughed and went on, her clean strokes taking her swiftly through the water. When at length she paused to float idly on her back, she realized that Tony had turned and was swimming to shore. She turned to follow him. When she reached his side at last, she saw with a tinge of alarm that his thin face had a bluish tinge, and his teeth were chattering with chill.

"Think I'll—go in." Although he made an effort to hide his discomfort, Maggie realized that he was far from well. To spare his feelings she said quickly, "I've had enough too."

"Don't you want to sunbathe?"

"Not on these pebbles!"

"Okay, then," she caught the note of relief in his tone, "let's go inside."

While Tony went to the bunk room to dress, Maggie switched on the electric percolator. Even if Tony made no mention of his chill and exhaustion she would see that he had a hot drink right away. She was stirring coffee into pottery mugs that she'd found on a high shelf in the kitchenette. A car came into the driveway and braked at the side of the house. A few moments later Danger and Ann, their arms laden with cartons and cans of food-stuffs, entered the room.

"Hi, Maggie," Ann said cheerfully, "I see you found the coffee. Where's Tony?"

"In there—" She jerked her dark head toward the bunk room, all the time conscious of Danger's glance. Still wearing her dripping swimsuit, wet hair hanging around her face, she must look a mess. She didn't dare look up at him directly for fear of seeing that derisive look that was all he ever seemed to have for her these days. She tried to focus her thoughts. "He seemed—a bit cold."

Ann nodded. "He's always like that after a swim. Guess it's something to do with being so thin and all that. He can catch a chill in the water faster than anyone I ever met."

"Who says so?" Tony cried indignantly. He was pulling a sweater over his bare shoulders as he emerged through the curtained opening. His fair hair was sleekly combed, and a little color had come back to his pinched cheeks.

"I do," his sister returned mildly. "Remember that other time when you finished up with a dose of pneumonia?"

"Do you mind?" Tony pulled a face at her, then tossed his damp swimming trunks through the open window, where they landed neatly on top of a hibiscus bush. "Hello, Danger!—ah, do I see coffee?"

They pulled stools up to the counter room divider and sipped the hot liquid. Ann, laughing and animated, chatted gaily, and Tony appeared to have recovered his good spirits. Maggie was silent, avoiding Danger's glance, conscious all the time that he too was making little contribution to the conversation. Why had he come, she wondered crossly, if he only wanted to show his disapproval of his make-do, unsatisfactory housekeeper?

"We stopped next door on the way here," Ann was saying. "The Stenburgs are down for the weekend too, with their yacht, so I asked them all over for a barbecue tonight." She focused her green eyes on Maggie. "We've known them for ages, Wayne and Denise, they used to come down to the cottage when we were all kids. Now they're both married, but they still weekend at the beach. They're going out for a sail soon, anyone can come, they said. How about you, Maggie?"

Hesitatingly she stared into her mug. Was Danger going sailing, she wondered, and made up her mind that in that event, she wasn't. She couldn't bear that icy disapproving look in his eyes every time she glanced up to meet his bleak gaze. Tony, however, saved her the trouble of making a decision by saying promptly, "Not for Maggie and me, thanks. We're off for a hike around the bay. That's right, isn't it, Maggie?"

She nodded smilingly. "If you say so, boss," and was immediately conscious of Danger's penetrating angry stare. So he didn't approve of that idea, either. But then she thought indignantly, he didn't approve of anything she did. She wouldn't put it past him to have come here today with the sole intention of keeping an eye on her. Oh, it was quite in order for him and Ann to seek each other's company, but when it came to Maggie Sullivan that was something else again. Not that it would do him any good. She'd go for a long walk with Tony, the longer the better. He could scarcely join them. Even he could hardly do that.

"Count me out too," Danger was saying, "I'll give you a hand to clear the place outside if you like, Ann. Have a scythe about? And what about that beat-up old lawn-mower that used to be parked under the veranda—is it still around?"

Ann nodded happily, her green eyes shining with a sudden pleasure. "That would be marvelous!"

Maggie thought, an afternoon alone together, with herself and Tony out of the way. Why shouldn't Ann look delighted?

A little later as they sat around a picnic lunch, Maggie had to admit that Ann was a splendid cook. She remembered her own home-baked scones, with their customary all-but-burned tops that Danger and Ian protested they preferred. Once again she was reminded that for a sheep-farmer's wife in a remote district, Ann was the perfect choice.

Perversely, once she was with Tony, taking the dusty metal road that curved around the bay, she found herself wishing that she had remained at the beach house. She could have helped in clearing away weeds from the over-grown paths and garden. That way she would have been with him. Only, she reminded herself with a sick feeling of anguish, he didn't want her.

Tony seemed unaware of her disinterest as he pointed out various landmarks and told her of the owners of the various keelers, catamarans and tiny yachts with sails like vivid butterflies, that skimmed the tossing wavelets.

Absorbing little of what she saw, Maggie passed the neat cottages, each surrounded by a green lawn. Invariably a boat of some description was pulled up at the side of the dwelling. They moved onto a small wharf where the wind tore at Maggie's damp hair and whipped her short skirt around her legs. Then they leaped down onto the beach where the ebbing tide had exposed a shelf of rocks: their varied colors intensified and gleaming wetly. Strolling along the shore, they passed an occasional "rock-hound," but the searchers, intent on the rocks and pebbles, took little notice of the dark-haired girl and the fair, bearded young man at her side. Crayfish pots lay along the shore. When they reached a headland, fishermen were standing on the rocks casting their lines into deep water beneath. At any other time Maggie would have enjoyed it all immensely. A new place was always of interest to her, especially anywhere on the coast, but today her thoughts kept returning to Danger. Danger and Ann . . . she had to make a conscious effort in order to concentrate on what Tony was telling her.

It was no easier to bear, she found, when they returned to the cottage. For the sight of Ann and Danger, laughing and joking together as they worked, made Maggie more than ever aware of her own dull ache of misery: the hopeless longing for something unattainable. Better, she told herself, to keep busy. She offered to make a salad to accompany the barbecued steaks. Tony insisted on helping her. Soon he was finding tomatoes, washing crisp lettuce on leaves, opening a can of sliced beetroot.

"Thanks." She was barely conscious of him. Her mind was on the voices she could hear outside in the garden. The twilight was fading and a fat yellow moon was climbing over the dark sea when at last the other two, earth-stained and hot, came inside for a shower and a change of clothing.

Maggie watched Tony set up the barbecue grill. When all was ready, he picked up a bottle of methylated spirits, pouring a few drops over the charcoal. "This should start her off in a hurry. Got a match, Maggie?"

She passed him the box and turned away for a second. She saw it happen. The bottle slipped from his grasp, and overturned. As the liquid touched flame, a great sheet of fire rose. She saw Tony dart back with an expression of pain, heard his call. Then she was running into the house, snatching a cloth from a table and wrapping it around the blistered hands. "It's Tony—burned!" she gasped, as Danger came hurrying toward them.

In two strides he had reached a medicine cabinet. While Maggie threw water on the blaze, Danger swiftly smeared Tony's badly burned hands and chest with burn cream. "It's a job for a doctor, I'm afraid. I hope," Danger added under his breath, "that he's down at the beach this weekend."

"He is!" Ann cried as both men got in the car. The girls tumbled into the rear seat and slammed the door. "I saw him arrive when we were talking next door."

Already the car was tearing down the drive and speeding along the rough metal road. Maggie caught a glimpse of Tony's face, pale and drawn with pain. Then they were lurching into an entrance. Danger braked to a stop outside a small neat white cottage.

Just as Danger leaped from the car a woman came onto the veranda. "David around, Mrs. Trelawny? We have a burn case—Tony."

"I'm so sorry," the white-haired woman was sympathetic, "but he was called away to a maternity case at the hospital." She caught her breath as she took in the extent of Tony's injury. "Better get him over to the hospital. I think he needs some treatment. I'll tell you what—I'm on the way there myself. I'll take him right away."

"Wonderful!" Ann breathed on a note of relief. "I'll come with you."

"No need," Tony protested faintly, but Ann, not taking the slightest notice of her brother's words, went with the doctor's wife as she settled Tony in the front seat of the big comfortable car. As the vehicle sped down the drive Maggie caught Tony's face as he turned back, forcing a smile from swollen lips.

So where did it leave her, she wondered. It left her to share the long drive back alone with Danger, something she certainly hadn't bargained for on this trip; something that filled her with a trembling sense of awareness that was half dismay, half secret delight. After all, it had been taken out of her hands . . . poor Tony.

"Don't worry too much," Danger said. "He'll be right again in a day or two. Hell! I've just remembered that barbecue. Better zip back and tell the others it's all off. Hop in, Maggie!"

In spite of everything, she couldn't help but feel excitement in being here with him in the dusk, his strong dark profile outlined against the fading light.

In the end it was quite some time before they left the cottage. The friends next door, horrified at the news of the accident, insisted on Danger and Maggie sharing a drink with them. And afterward when they returned to the cottage, there was the food and drink to collect and the barbecue to put away. Maggie repacked the cardboard cartons with foodstuffs, while Danger went outside to collect garden tools and stow them away.

Last of all he picked up the telephone receiver. "We might be lucky enough to get some news by now," he told Maggie.

To their relief, they learned from the hospital that Tony had already arrived and was now feeling "comfortable." They could inquire again in the morning as he would be staying for at least two more days.

"Comfortable?" Maggie raised dark brows.

"Means they'll have given him an injection to deaden the pain," Danger replaced the receiver, "and that's something. He's in good hands now. Well, that's about it." He turned to latch a window, then taking the cartons from Maggie, waited for her to go out onto the veranda before he secured the French doors.

Out in the soft scented darkness, the stars that formed the Southern Cross blazed in a night sky. The pine-clad hills were a fretted outline against the sea. It could all have been so different, Maggie thought wistfully, if only . . . .

The night wrapped around them. Darkness, she knew, was her enemy—darkness and the enforced intimacy of the car. She stole a glimpse of his profile, outlined in the dim green glow of the dashboard. How stern he looked. Unconsciously she sighed. No doubt he was wishing it was Ann who was sharing the long drive with him back to Te Rangi.

Just when the silence was growing unbearable, he turned on the radio and music, soft and muted, beat around them. Maggie, who felt her gaze drawn inexorably to the man at her side, forced herself to look out of the window. There was nothing to be seen but the blurred shape of hills and, a faint glimmer of light from an isolated farmhouse among its shelterbelt of surrounding trees.

Trying in vain to control the fast beating of her heart, Maggie shrank away from him as far as she could in the small enclosed space. Lights glowed ahead, and she realized they were approaching a small township. That would be Dargaville. She remembered that after sunset the car ferry wouldn't be in service. Danger would be forced to take the long way home. Home? She brought herself up short. If only it were!

In silence they sped through the darkened streets and out onto the lonely country roads. They came in sight of Te Rangi, and soon Danger was pulling up at a farm gate. Maggie said quickly, "I'll open it for you if you like."

"It's okay." Lights glimmered from the old house as they sped up the rise toward Amberley. When they reached the garage, Danger switched off the engine. Resting a hand on the steering wheel, he swung toward her. Maggie faced his grave withdrawn look. "There's something I must tell you."

Her heart gave a wild leap, but the next moment her excitement subsided. What Danger had to say to her would be nothing to be excited about. "Yes?" she asked faintly.

"I had a long-distance call today from New Guinea, from Chris," he said, still in that deadly quiet, controlled tone. "Thing is, Maggie—"

She glanced up at him, eyes enormous in a pale face. "You mean they're coming home earlier than you expected?" She rushed on breathlessly. "That's what you're trying to tell me, isn't it?"

"That's about it," Danger drawled. "Next week, actually. Seems the job folded up all of a sudden. They want to get home, so—"

"So you want me to go?" Her voice was very low. "That's it, isn't it?" She was twisting a strand of hair around and around her finger.

"I didn't say that." Ice dripped in his tone. "You know you're welcome to stay on—"

"No, you didn't say it!" A wave of anguish engulfed her as bitter thoughts rushed through her mind. Oh, she knew well enough what he was trying to get through to her. She could understand only too well the words he didn't say. No doubt, she mused miserably, the news of his sister's early return to Amberley had fitted in with his plans very well. But that wasn't the real reason why he wanted her to leave. He was angry with her, angry and disapproving. Hadn't she sensed his cool contempt for her ever since that day at the Gap when he had caught her in Colin's embrace? That was when he suddenly changed toward her, became so cold and distant, his face set in those stern lines. Now he'd decided to let her go, just like that! How could he be so unfair?

The bitter injustice of his attitude, something in the closed dark face she loved, damn him, drove her past endurance. "I know you want to get rid of me," her voice was husky with emotion, "now that the others are coming back. It's not my fault," she rushed wildly on, her voice choked with tears, "that I happen to look . . . like that other girl . . . that one that you—"

"That's not true!" Even in the dim light she saw with a little shock of surprise that his eyes were blazing. "Who told you about that?" She felt his clutch on her bare arm in a swift and savage pressure.

"Someone . . . I forget . . . Mrs. Wahonga, I think. Does it matter?" Trembling, she realized that this time she had gone too far, but a desperate recklessness drove her on. She was leaving here anyway; he couldn't stand the sight of her, so what did it matter? What did anything matter any more? "Not a suitable person to have care of the children, that's what you're thinking, isn't it?" Before he could answer she flung at him: "When I happen to have friends, when anyone shows the slightest interest in me, like Tony . . . or Colin . . . you disapprove. Oh, you don't say so," she whispered, "but all the time, all the time. . . ." Her voice trailed despairingly away. With a gesture of hopelessness, she pushed the dark hair back from her forehead. "You just don't care how I—"

"*Don't care!*" Roughly he pulled her toward him. His kiss blotted out the world in one wild rapturous moment and sent the stars in the night sky tumbling wildly around her in a blaze of heady excitement. Only for a moment;

then she fell back as suddenly he released her. Dazed, shaken, trembling, she looked up to see his eyes, dark with an expression she couldn't read, but there was no mistaking the hateful satirical lift to the firmly cut lips.

"Why not?" he said on a breath. So he's shaken too, she thought in surprise, in spite of himself. She heard his voice through the tumult of her thoughts. "You let other men kiss you. Those—*friends* of yours."

There was no mistaking the ironic smile, and Maggie's heart plunged wildly. He was mocking her, as usual.

"Oh! You—" She felt the sting of tears behind her eyes, then a wave of anger such as she had never known was surging through her. "You don't know anything about me." She was fumbling with the door catch and then swung the door wide and leaped to the ground. "But you needn't worry!" She turned to fing the words over her shoulder. "You won't have me on your mind or your station much longer. I'll go just as soon as you like!" She was hurrying over the long grass.

"Maggie!" She could hear him calling. He sounded as domineering, as hatefully sure of himself, and of her, as ever. This time she was determined to ignore him. Let him call. She wouldn't take the slightest notice. "Come back here!"

"No!" She heard a car door slam and quickened her steps. Now she was running along the darkened pathway, but it was useless. Those long legs could easily outpace her, and she knew it.

Swiftly he caught up with her, stopping her headlong rush. "Maggie, don't feel that way—" He was so close she could have put up a hand to touch the lean dark face she loved—had loved. "Forgive me, Maggie. No hard feelings. Let's part friends."

She wanted none of it, especially not friendship, not with him.

"Leave me alone!" She flung herself around and darting swiftly beneath his detaining arm, rushed blindly up the steps and toward the open door. Another minute and she was inside the lighted hall, but she need not have hurried, she told herself. Danger hadn't followed her in after all. Deep down, in some tiny traitorous corner of her mind, she almost wished he had.

CHAPTER ELEVEN

Somehow Maggie managed to get through the long night. If the tears ran unheeded down her cheeks, what did it matter? But in the morning she knew that it did matter. Her image stared back from the mirror: heavy-lidded brown eyes burning in a colorless face. Whatever happened she mustn't let Danger see her like this. That was the one thing remaining from the wreckage of all the high-handed confidence with which she had begun this new life. Danger didn't suspect. . . . Don't let him guess, she prayed, and feverishly began to apply make-up that added a flush to her wan cheeks. But what if, at the breakfast table, her faintly clownish appearance betrayed her lavish use of make-up to the children's quick eyes and they drew Danger's attention to it. Well, she would just have to risk it, hoping that this would be one of the days when he left the homestead long before she was awake, not to return until dark. By then surely she'd be able to get a better grip on herself. Right now her hands were shaking so badly that she had difficulty in applying her lipstick.

When she reached the breakfast table she was relieved to find only the children there. She realized at once that Danger had already informed them that she would be leaving within a week, so that was one ordeal she needn't face. Funny though, she reflected forlornly, as the excited chatter echoed around her, how the news of their parents' arrival had filled their minds to the exclusion of everything else. It was as if she had already gone out of their lives. But what else could you expect, she asked herself over a deep sigh. She was only a fill-in, after all, and that went for Danger too. Someone to look after their comfort, someone perhaps to have a light love affair with, until the real love took over. Only Mark seemed to have a thought for her. He was staring at her, a spoon of breakfast cereal suspended near his mouth. Maggie could almost see the thoughts passing behind the wide, candid eyes. "When Mommy comes, aren't you coming back here, Maggie?"

She shook her head.

"Not—ever?"

"Not ever." She tried to push aside the surge of pain.

"Is that why you don't want your breakfast?"

"No, no, of course not." She managed a shaky laugh.

"I don't want you to go away!" Mark shrieked, banging wildly with his spoon and scattering cereal in all directions. "I won't let you!" The tears spurted from his eyes and between tears and laughter herself, Maggie gathered him close.

"You can't have everything, you know," Ian reminded him, when at last Maggie had managed to calm the small boy.

"That's right," Maggie agreed over a heavy heart, thankful that Mark's grief had served to divert her own lack of appetite from the children.

Suddenly she leaped to her feet. "I have to call and find out how Tony is this morning—"

"It's okay," Ian said quickly. "Danger called the hospital before you came out. They told him that Tony's much better. Danger said to be sure to let you know that Tony can have visitors this afternoon. Gee, I nearly forgot to tell you."

"Thank goodness he's all right." As she sank back in her chair, she reflected that her employer evidently believed her to be emotionally involved with Tony. Well, that was all right with her too. Let him think what he liked—so long as he didn't suspect the truth.

"Hey, Phil," she was vaguely aware of Ian's voice, "forgot to tell you something. There was a letter for you in the mailbag yesterday. I stuck it amongst all that junk on your dressing table—"

"A letter—for me!" Jumping down from the table, Philippa was already halfway to the door. When she reappeared even Maggie, fathoms deep in her own heartache, was conscious of the radiance of the small face.

Philippa glanced up from the typewritten sheet she held in her hand. "Guess what?" she breathed incredulously. "I've won it! I've really won it! The sketching contest, I mean. The judges say so in the letter."

"They must be blind," Ian said disgustedly, but his sister ignored him and held the letter toward Maggie. "You read it!" The childish voice was warm with an unaccustomed friendliness. "You made me enter it. If it hadn't been for you I wouldn't even have tried—"

Scarcely aware of what she was reading, Maggie scanned the printed lines. "They're enclosing a check, they say," she murmured. "It must be still in the envelope."

"What's a check?" Philippa looked puzzled.

"Money, you dope!" her brother informed her. "Give it to me if you don't want it."

Small fingers shaking with excitement, the girl drew a small printed slip from the envelope. "Ten dollars!" She stared down at it unbelievingly. "All of my own, to spend."

Ian made an attempt to snatch it. "Of all the greedy—"

But Philippa evaded his hand. Her gray eyes glowed as she turned back to Maggie. "I'll do something for you if you like. Something you wanted me to do awfully, before—"

Maggie brought her heavy thoughts back from a distance. "The only thing I wanted was for you to have a ride on the Saint," she murmured unthinkingly.

"That's it! That's what I mean! I don't mind doing it

now, just once, before you go. It's what you wanted, isn't it?" she asked anxiously.

Maggie nodded. Why was it, she wondered through the fog of misery clouding her senses, that things you wanted only came to you when you were no longer interested in them, when you had ceased caring whether you had them or not? She wrenched her mind back to the excited small girl at her side. "Are you quite sure you want to?"

"Uh-huh," Philippa pushed the wispy brown hair back from her small face. "Just once, so that I can tell Mommy that I did what she told me to."

"All right, then. We'll go down to the paddock just as soon as I've cleared away the dishes."

"I'll help you!" This was a new Philippa, eager, wildly excited and friendly, whom Maggie scarcely recognized as the sulking child of the past few weeks.

Presently Maggie, followed by the children, went to the harness shed. While Ian carried the saddle, she tossed sheepskin and bridle over her arm, then they went down to the grazing paddock.

As they came near, Pete glanced up. He turned his big ungainly head inquiringly, then gave an affectionate whinny. Before long Pete would be missing the company of his friends in the paddock, Maggie mused sadly, but not so much as she herself would miss— Stop it! she scolded herself. It's no use. It never was. Opening the gate, she strolled toward the perfectly proportioned white horse. The Saint eyed her warily for a moment, but he stood quietly as Maggie slipped a bridle in his mouth and saddled him. He stood motionless, flicking the flies away with his long, silky tail, as Maggie gave Philippa a leg-up to the high back. Even through her own spiritual turmoil, she noticed the look of nervous apprehension that tensed the child's face, the rigid grip of small hands on the reins. The Saint appeared so docile, and yet— For a fleeting moment she thought that perhaps Phil had been right about the thoroughbred. There was a mean look in those wild eyes and flaring nostrils. Or was she too imagining the danger? Certainly the horse appeared to be calm enough. Nevertheless— "I'll put him on a leading rein if you like," she offered.

"No, thank you," Philippa said through clenched teeth, "Mommy wouldn't like that. It wouldn't be the same. I'll have to ride him my own self."

Pushing away a faint twinge of apprehension, Maggie watched as the white horse with his high arched neck and dancing gait, moved up the grassy slope.

Philippa's triumphant tones floated back to them. "Look at me! I'm riding him!" she called over her shoulder. Her mount broke into a trot. Then it happened. Before Maggie's horrified gaze the horse stumbled and taking fright, reared high. A doll-like figure came flying through the air. Still rearing wildly, the white horse galloped away, tufts of earth flying up from his hoofs. The young rider lay still where she had fallen, a crumpled heap on the grass.

Running to kneel at her side, frantically Maggie looked down into the pallid face of the unconscious child. "Wake up! Phil! It's Maggie!" A flood of thankfulness poured through her as the eyelids fluttered open. Gradually the child's eyes focused. A small moan escaped the pale lips. "My arm. . . ." Only then did Maggie realize that Philippa's arm was lying beneath her. The small girl winced with pain as Maggie, with all the gentleness she could muster, lifted Philippa.

"Where am I?" The look of alarm that widened the gray eyes faded and an expression of relief took its place. "I rode him, didn't I, Maggie? I rode the Saint! I can tell Mommy! I wasn't scared, was I?"

"Not a bit," Maggie assured her. "Phil, do you think you can stand up? I'll help you."

Carefully the child stood, still rubbing her arm. "Wow, it hurts."

"Try not to bend it." As Maggie helped Philippa toward the gate, Ian held up a length of twisted wire. "This is what the Saint was caught in. It was hidden in the long grass, and he didn't see it. No wonder he reared!"

Slowly, the other two children unusually subdued, the little party returned to the house.

Although Maggie had dreaded the thought of Danger's arrival for the midday meal, she was conscious of an enormous sense of relief at the sight of his red tractor flashing down a hillside near the homestead. Not knowing whether or not to seek medical advice for Philippa, she had kept the child lying quietly on a couch in the living room, a stack of comic books at her side. "I won't have to do any school work today, will I?" Philippa begged.

Maggie kept her glance averted when Danger came striding into the room. She was thankful that the children saved her from having to tell him the news: all spoke at once as they rushed to tell him of Philippa's accident.

"You really made it up on the Saint?" he grinned down at Philippa. "Just in time too! Good for you!" He kneeled at her side. "What's all this about a sore arm? Let me have a look. Does it hurt when I move it like this?"

The small girl shook her head. "Not much."

"Or this?"

"Only a teeny-weeny bit."

"Not much wrong there." Maggie winced at the remoteness of his voice as he turned to her.

"I didn't know," she said in a muffled voice, "whether to phone and get Dr. Smith to call or not."

"Difficult to tell sometimes," he agreed still in that chilly, polite tone, "whether there's a break or not, but there's nothing to worry about. She'll be right— Oh, Maggie—"

She was probably in for a lecture regarding her carelessness in allowing Phil to get hurt today. The week the child's parents were due back wasn't exactly the ideal time for Phil to sustain an injury. She braced herself for the expected battle and hoped that he would put her distress appearance down to the accident of the morning.

"You did it! You actually did it!"

"Got her up on the Saint, you mean? It wasn't really my doing," she confessed in a low voice.

"Who, then?"

She raised her heavy glance. "It was Phil's own idea. I—had such a fright. I was afraid her arm might have been broken."

"No, nothing like that. I'll fix her a sling."

"You will tell Mommy, won't you," the child broke in anxiously, "that I did ride that horrible old Saint?"

"Sure thing. Better keep quiet for a couple of days, though, Phil. Park up on your bed for the rest of the day. Okay?" To Maggie he said: "Suppose the kids told you about Tony? Thought you'd like to know; might save you all the trouble of getting through to the hospital. It's difficult to get through on the exchange at times."

"Thank you." How could he look so set and stern? Surely she couldn't be all that forbidding, to make his expression change so when he looked at her.

"You'll be keen to get in to see him this afternoon."

"Yes. I—"

"Thought so. I'll be working over in the shed. The boys can come with us. They can nip back to keep an eye on Philippa now and again. Take the car. You can't miss the hospital. It's five miles along the main road past the beach. Quite a drive, but I guess you won't mind about that—"

She turned dispiritedly away. Was that what he imagined? That she was so crazy about Tony that she couldn't wait to see him again? Oh well, what did it matter what he thought?

"Lunch is ready." She forced her tone to a light note.

Making a pretense of eating, she was aware of Mark's curious gaze, but fortunately he made no comment on her lack of appetite. At last the interminable meal was over. It was going to be a long, almost unendurable week, yet still crazily, hopelessly, she couldn't bring herself to invent some excuse that would take her away from here at once, tonight. Mrs. Wahonga could easily take over for a few days until Danger's sister and her husband returned, but she knew she wouldn't, couldn't, tear herself away, even knowing how he felt about her.

The long drive to the country hospital was after all a respite. No need to pretend to be happy, to make a show of eating, to listen endlessly for his step.

Afterward she couldn't have given any details of the scenery that went sliding past the open windows. She took the lonely northern roads winding between vast paddocks with their boundaries of softly waving toe-toe.

It was impossible to miss the low white stucco building, built to the sun, and surrounded by flower beds and sweeping lawns. A friendly nurse led her down long shining floors to a sunny ward. At the last bed, Maggie caught a glimspe of Tony's sensitive young face. His hands were a mass of bandages, but he smiled at Maggie in delighted surprise. "You came all that way—Gee, Maggie, that's great." He threw her a teasing glance. "I never knew you cared— Come to think of it, you look awfully white under all that tan. Anyone would think—"

"Never mind about me." she cut in quickly. "It's you who matters." She glanced at the bandages on his chest. "Much pain?"

"Not too bad now. Stupid thing to do, though. I knew it was too good to last, having you all to myself. That was the worst part of it, mucking everything up . . . for us. . . ."

"Don't worry," she smiled. "There'll be another time. I'll be seeing you again before I go."

His pale eyes widened in surprise. "So soon? How come, Maggie?"

She shrugged her shoulders, turning her heavy eyes away from his curious glance. "Seems that Chris and her husband are coming back to Amberley sooner than they expected. At the end of the week, actually, so—"

"So that makes two of us, Maggie."

It was her turn to look astonished. A desolate feeling of dismay swept her. Did he mean, did he really mean that— Aloud she said: "You're going away too?"

"Guess so. I'll need to be back in town for 'Varsity next term."

"Then," she hazarded, "you've decided—"

He lifted a shoulder beneath blue-striped hospital pajamas. "Had it decided for me, this morning. One thing, burning myself to blazes last night did some good. It brought things to a head. I know now that wherever I happen to finish up, it won't be on a sheep station. That's for sure! Not now that Ann's getting married—"

Her heart plunged. "Married?" she whispered.

"Sure. They fixed it up at last. Thought he'd never get around to it."

She forced the words through stiff lips. "You mean, your sister Ann—"

He gave his light laugh. "You guessed it. Hurried things up at last with her sheep-farmer. Seems he was waiting for her when she left the hospital last night. They both came up here this morning to tell me the big news. Going to put the other station on the market and move over to our place."

But Maggie wasn't listening. Her thoughts were spinning wildly, and she was trying to understand. Last night Danger, after their return from the beach, had been shut away in his office. Shut away from her, she mused bitterly. This morning he had been working away from the homestead, she knew that.

"You mean—" She turned puzzled brown eyes toward him.

Tony grinned. "I'd give a lot to know who did the proposing. I mean, she must have had a hand in things, pushed him along in the right direction. Can you see old Jim getting up enough courage to—"

"Jim! Ann and *Jim* are getting married?" she asked in a strange, husky tone.

He glanced at her in surprise. "Who else? They have the big question settled at last; getting married right away. Beats me," he added aggrievedly, "what *you're* looking so happy about."

"Am I?" Hastily Maggie made an effort to compose her features, but she couldn't hide the crazy, unreasoning hope that had taken possession of her. All this time she had been imagining everything to be so different. How clear it was now. Danger's endless visits to the other sheep station and swift response to Ann's pleas for assistance, had been no more than the friendly gestures of a neighbor who was conscious of the plight of a girl struggling alone against almost insurmountable burdens. The next moment she came back to reality with a jerk. Not that Ann and Jim's marriage could make the slightest difference to her. Nothing that anyone else did could alter Danger's feeling toward one Maggie Sullivan, late of his employ. And she'd best not allow herself to forget it.

The sharp ring of a warning bell made Maggie realize that the brief visiting period was almost at an end. She stood up, smiling down at him. "I'd better be going—"

"It's a long trip," he agreed. "Nice of you to come all that way to see me, Maggie. Well," he sent her an oblique look, "I guess it's goodbye—and good luck!"

"Good luck?" She turned back to him, puzzled. "What do you mean?"

"You know. I guess," he went on in a low tone, "that I've known right from the start, only I tried to fool myself." His lips curved in a gentle smile. "I mightn't be too much on the ball when it comes to sheep-farming, Maggie, but I can see as well as the next man when a guy and a girl are falling in love. Now that you're talking of leaving Amberley I can't see Danger—"

A barb pierced her heart, but she tried to smile gaily. "You're wrong, you know!"

"Am I?"

The final bell shrilled through the long ward. With a sense of relief she lifted a hand in a gesture of farewell, then went to join the stream of visitors exiting.

On the long drive back to the homestead she could no longer keep a tight rein on her emotions. Often she glimpsed though a mist of unshed tears, the wide green farmlands burnished with gentle spring sunshine. Bad enough, difficult enough, to get through this endless week without Tony jumping to that ridiculous idea. She only hoped that she'd succeeded in laughing him out of his fantastic notion that Danger could be in love with her—with *her*! How little Tony really knew of the bitter score. Danger despised her. He couldn't care less that she was leaving Te Rangi forever. Nor, come to that, could anyone else at Amberley. Tony was already looking forward to resuming his studies in the city, having renounced all thought of her simply because of that crazy idea. He must be out of his tiny mind.

The children were so absorbed in plans for their parents' return that they seemed scarcely aware of Maggie's existence. She was merely someone to care for the day-to-day essentials of living, the ordinary dull things. When it came to love, only Mark was loath to lose her, and he was so young, he would soon forget.

No doubt about it, she had failed all along the line. Failed utterly with Danger. When it came to Philippa, the hollow victory of making good her challenge to the master of Amberley had ended only in disaster. Now Philippa would be more afraid than ever to mount the temperamental thoroughbred.

Thank heaven, she told herself bleakly, that a certain sense of familiarity with the long northern roads saved her from any wrong turnings. In this state of mind she found difficulty in concentrating on her driving. She could think of nothing except one man, a man whom she had to learn to forget—somehow.

She didn't hurry as she parked the car in the garage. There was all the time in the world—now. Slowly she went up the veranda steps and into the house, tossing her soft leather shoulder purse down on the table. It must have been the brightness of the late afternoon sunshine outside that had blinded her for a moment, so she hadn't noticed the man standing by the long velvet curtains. He turned suddenly to face her. Her brown eyes flew to meet his odd, unfathomable glance. If only she'd known that Danger was waiting for her here, she would never have come to this room.

"He's not worse, is he?"

"Tony?" She raised her heavy glance. "No, no." She produced a wavering smile. "He's better, ever so much. Very bright really."

"Then why've you been crying?"

"Crying?" But she couldn't meet that direct gaze. Swiftly she turned away, making for the door. "I'll—make some tea," she said almost incoherently.

"No, you won't, Maggie!" In a few swift strides he had blocked her way. Tall, lean, rangy, he gazed down at her. "You and I've got a bit of urgent business to fix up—"

"I can't think what!" She tried to sound ungracious, but it was difficult with Danger looking at her as if, as if there were no longer any misunderstandings between them. For some reason she couldn't understand, he seemed oddly stirred. His eyes were a dark blue, burning with a light she hadn't seen for a long, long time. What had happened? Why was he looking at her like that? And why was she suddenly trembling?

"After you took off today, I had a visitor. That Colin chap—"

"Colin!" She stared up at him, wide-eyed.

"That's right. We talked and he put me straight on a few matters. I put him in the picture over a few things too."

Her heart was beginning to beat suffocatingly.

"What—sort of things?"

"Oh, about you and me. Why didn't you tell me," he demanded in a low tone, "that Colin happened to be a free man? I got the impression all along that—well, skip it—"

"You didn't give me much chance," she protested faintly, trying to keep hold of her feelings which were rapidly flying out of control.

"If you were crying because you didn't want to leave here—if that's it, Maggie—"

The sudden heart-catching tenderness in his low voice caught her unaware, so that she forgot to lie and pretend. She acted like someone in a trance. She nodded.

"Just the place, Maggie?"

Still under the spell, she shook her head.

"The children, then?"

"No."

"Then," with a deep triumphant laugh he picked her up in his arms and carried her to the couch, "there's no problem! You're not leaving, you know." He held her close, cupping her small square chin in strong and sensitive hands. "You're staying right here with me, for keeps. How does that strike you?"

Flushed with happiness, secure in his arms, she laughed softly. "I can't imagine anything more wonderful."

"I can!" Gathering her close, his lips sought her own.

Pulse leaping, she found herself responding to that swift and urgent pressure. At last she drew herself free, her eyes dark pools of excitement. There was still something she had to know. "That other girl," she whispered, "the one who looked like me—"

"Cathy? Forget her," his voice was laced with tenderness. "There never was anything between Cathy and me, anything that mattered. Oh, she was a bit like you, I'll give you that. Had the same sort of face, that kind that goes to a man's head, but she wasn't *you*, my darling. They only made one of you," his tone deepened with pride, "and that happens to belong to me. I love you very much, Maggie. I have ever since that first night when you looked up at me from the hotel table. And if you think that I'm ever going to let you go again—" A heady excitement swept her as once again he took her in his arms. It was heaven, Maggie thought contentedly. It was coming home. It was wild excitement and deep content all at once. "Is this a proposal, Mr. Dangerfield?" she inquired laughingly a little later.

"What else, Miss Sullivan?" He was caressing her dark hair. Neither was aware of the noiseless opening of the door.

It was a few moments later that Mrs. Wahonga came into the room. With a beaming smile toward Maggie and Danger, she set down a tray with champagne and three stemmed goblets.

Maggie glanced up from the shelter of his arms. A glimmer of mischief in her dark eyes. "Now just how did she know? Maori mystique, would you say?"

"Poof!" Mrs. Wahonga disclaimed with her rich chuckle, watching Danger pop the cork, "didn't take no Maori mystique to work that one out! Right from that first day when you walked in here, I could tell what was going to happen. Anyone could see it! You two . . . just made for each other."

Tiny bubbles rose in the crystal as Danger raised his glass high. Pride and tenderness mingled in his deep tones. There was no doubt at all, Maggie thought happily, of how he *really* felt about her, not with that special look for her in his blue eyes. He said: "We'll drink to that!"

THE GENTLE FLAME

THE
GENTLE FLAME

Katrina Britt

Susie's wedding to an attractive Frenchman was over; her happiness was assured. Time for Vicki to relinquish her role as her sister's protector; time to leave the charms of southern France for her other responsibilities in London.

But Vicki was strangely reluctant to leave. Surely it couldn't be because of the arrogant Guy Ransart? A brilliant surgeon, his energies were directed toward his career and his associate, the elegant Dr. Janera Molineux. Besides, he'd made it plain that he thought of Vicki, if at all, only as the accident-prone sister of the bride!

"I can manage," she told him stiffly. "You don't have to concern yourself with me." But her heart gave the lie to her words.

CHAPTER ONE

Vicki deeply inhaled the clear, fresh mountain air through the open window of the Mini; fondly christened Sarah. Early the previous morning she had sailed from Southampton to a small Breton port. From there, she had driven up into the hills above Nice.

The sun had followed her all the way. Vicki loved the sun and Sarah seemed to do the same, for she purred along without once overheating under her hood. Unfortunately, the summer had gone, but Vicki was finding it warmer than she had expected. Her hands were moist when she stopped the car to check her whereabouts.

It was a relief to sink blissfully into the silence around her while she studied the map. A casual glance at her watch told her she had made good time, so she decided to stop in the next town to stretch her legs and have something to eat. According to the map, it lay only a kilometer or so ahead.

The silence, broken now by a distant tractor, was complete. It washed away the tension that had built up inside her during the journey. What utter bliss to sip a cool drink in the shade after being cooped up in the car. Not that she was complaining. The trip had been delightful.

She had meandered happily along past old *châteaux* surrounded by almond and olive groves, vineyards and orchards. In the distance, the hills, remote in their obscure, inexorable quality of light, looked down on valleys etched in shade.

The towns emitted the friendly atmosphere of small communities and were neat and charmingly reminiscent of a bygone age. Narrow streets, medieval and twisting, crept past old churches, schools and picturesque houses, to culminate in a *château* or old castle, dominating the town.

End of season meant no congested roads. Vicki had reveled in the scenery unhindered by traffic and a surfeit of tourists. She was beginning to love the homely quality beneath the veneer of strangeness one experiences in a foreign land. Susie must have experienced it, too, for she had described the countryside with a fervor of one being under its spell. Well, she would soon be with her again and, with this thought in mind, Vicki drove on.

The town was slumbering in the sun when Sarah slid into the tiny market square. It was like a stage setting with the sun pushing stiffly spread fingers of golden light through giant plane trees onto the cobblestones. Several elderly people sat around, their heads nodding forward blissfully; near a fountain, a young artist was painting on a portable easel. His subject was an old rustic asleep with his head leaning forward on his chest, his dog stretched at his feet.

It was pleasant to sit and have a cool drink at one of the small tables outside the café and watch a party of teenagers arrive on motorbikes. Their voices strident on the clear air, they converged on the café to fill up the tables and sip *sirop de menthe*.

The girls, tanned and vivacious, wore their long hair piled in chignons on their pretty heads, while the good-looking boys sported sproutings of beards or sideburns.

Vicki finished her drink and sauntered back to Sarah, sorry to see the end of her journey but eager to see her sister again. Susie would be glad to see her, she knew that. Pulling out of the square, she recalled her dismay when, months ago, her sister had announced her intention of going to France on a twelve months' teaching exchange. Although only two years older, Vicki had felt responsible for her since their mother had gone. The sisters had been the best of companions, doing everything together with the exception of dates.

What misgivings Vicki had on the day of her sister's departure had been swept away by Susie's enthusiasm. Both girls were heartwhole, with neither of them taking their dates seriously. But Vicki had wished then that her sister had a male to anchor her in London. Paris was an unknown quantity to a girl of Susie's inexperience. She had been gone only a couple of months when her letters became full of the manly charms of Robert Brissard.

A farmer, he had attended an agricultural exhibition in Paris where Susie had met him at a party. Within a week of their first meeting, they were engaged. Vicki was rocked, wondering what kind of man Susie had fallen in love with. That he was 20 years of age and a bachelor had calmed her down a little until a letter arrived, later, to say she was getting married in two weeks and could Vicki come over as soon as possible? It had been quite a week running around for a bridesmaid's dress and new outfits beside arranging for a period of leave from her job. In between, she had sent up a prayer of thankfulness that, at least, Susie was waiting until she arrived before taking the last irrevocable step.

Shaken, Vicki knew that her concern for her sister was still as deep as it was in the days when her whole life had focused upon her, when pandering to Susie's needs and wants was part of her own growing up. She had been 14, Susie 12, when their parents were divorced. They had been shattered, with Vicki's heart aching more for her adored father.

Ralph Kendon had been a test pilot, an attractive man of medium height with abundant fair hair and twinkling blue eyes. At least they had twinkled until the breakup of his marriage. Young though Vicki was, she had gathered that his job was responsible for the trouble between her parents.

Angela Kendon could no longer stand the strain of having a test pilot for a husband. The final blowup had come when a plane he had been testing dived into the Atlantic; he was missing, presumed drowned. Fortunately, he had been picked up by a trawler.

Ralph Kendon loved his wife and daughters, but he also loved his job. His dive into the Atlantic had been the last straw for his wife. She stated an ultimatum—either he gave up his job or she would leave him. When he had refused, she had kept her word and gone, leaving him with the two girls. She had taken a modeling job and, after the divorce, had married a wealthy industrialist and gone to live abroad.

The girls went from school to training college; Vicki to train as a secretary, Susie as a kindergarten teacher. Their holidays had been spent with their father and a housekeeper. Each time she was home, Vicki sensed her father's zest for living waning. He had aged considerably since his divorce. It occurred to her rather sadly that he had never really believed her mother would leave him.

He still carried on with his job while Vicki quivered over the risks he had sometimes deliberately taken. She had been 21 when he had crashed for the last time. Heartbroken, she had continued working at the air terminal as secretary to one of the executives, thus feeling that the last link with her father was unbroken.

Susie had fretted more over the loss of her mother. Not long after the divorce, Susie had contracted rheumatic fever, almost succumbing to it. With the idea that her mother's presence could contribute to Susie's recovery, Vicki had written several letters through the lawyer, pleading with her to come. In the end, she had replied to say she was expecting a baby, and the doctor had advised her against traveling any distance.

Susie had recuperated, with Vicki fussing over her like a hen with a chick. The bout of rheumatic fever had left a heart murmur, but as the years passed she did not appear to suffer any ill effects.

Now, Susie was to be married and Vicki hoped with all her heart that she would be happy in her choice. Their parents' divorce had not put Vicki in favor of connubial bliss, rather the reverse. Even so, Vicki was all for her sister getting married; she needed someone to take care of her.

If Vicki felt a little sad, it was only at the thought of the emptiness of her own life with Susie gone. During the trip, small incidents had warmed her heart: the kindly beam of a shepherd's smile when she had pulled up to allow his struggling flock of small, sturdy sheep to cross the road, Madame gaily waving the duster she was shaking outside her bedroom window when she passed. The growing warmth inside her was gradually melting away all the past burdens, and she was responding to the beauty of the world around her in a way she found incomprehensible.

She was shaken out of her thoughts by the increasing steepness of the road ahead, gradually narrowing until it resolved into a mere shelf of overhanging rock with a sheer drop into the ravine below. It was only at intervals now that there was room for another vehicle to pass. She drove gingerly around bends, to discover the muffled beating of the drum in her ears was actually her own heart threatening to knock a hole in her ribs.

Her hands, moist with sweat, clung to the steering wheel as she sent up a silent prayer that no car would suddenly confront her on the narrow stretch of road bordering on eternity.

One did. It roared around the corner without a warning. There was no room to pass; the shriek of two lots of brakes simultaneously applied was enough to pierce the eardrums. Instantly, a man leaped from the other car which had stopped inches from Sarah's nose and poured out a volley of French.

Dressed in a dark, business suit, he was six feet tall with

slightly dishevelled dark brown hair, and piercing blue eyes.

Thankful that she had taken French in her secretarial course, Vicki drew a deep breath and willed herself from shaking.

"*Pardon, monsieur*," she said in a low key. "We are both at fault, I think, since neither of us sounded a warning."

The man's keen gaze had already taken in the English license plate of her car. Dark brows elevated. "Is that so?" he said, this time in perfect English. The deep, cultured voice was controlled, but the blue eyes glittered so furiously with anger that, for two cents, Vicki was sure he would have pushed her and Sarah over the ravine. He wrenched open the car door. "Mademoiselle will please move over while I reverse the car onto a wider stretch of road."

Vicki, feeling that nothing could surprise her after finding herself still alive and in one piece, slid along her seat like a lamb to allow him to lower his long length behind the wheel. Then, eyes closed, hands clenched, she waited for something to run into them from behind. No one's luck could hold out that long.

Quaking inside, Vicki's resentment increased, as the Frenchman coolly and efficiently reversed Sarah. It was obvious he was deliberately prolonging the agony, since he could have easily moved his own car. At last he halted Sarah. Vicki opened her eyes to find her companion turning her way, his arm on the wheel, to study her intently.

When he spoke, the alien tones were trenchant, giving reproving emphasis to every word. "Are you not aware, *mademoiselle*, that this is a one-way road? No traffic is allowed to ascend because of the treacherous landslides on the ravine side, which happens to be the one you are driving on."

She looked at him blankly, only too conscious of his aloof indifference to her heightened color and embarrassment. Her brain, as she dwelt on what he had said, took in details of his appearance. He had all the charm of a well-bred Frenchman with a hint of ruthlessness in the set of the chiseled mouth and masculine nose. His hands were long, tapering, clever hands; well cared for, strong and flexible.

Vicki quivered, seeing the reason for moving her car which was in the path of traffic descending the hill. Naturally, he had given no warning of his approach, for the last thing he expected was to meet a foolish English girl defying the rules of convention by using a forbidden route.

She moistened dry lips, lowered her gaze to her lap and said contritely, "I apologize most humbly, *monsieur*. Had I kept my mind on my driving I could hardly have missed the one-way sign at the foot of the hill."

In the silence which followed she felt his enigmatic study of her profile: the luxuriant tawny hair, the lilting eyebrows above an adequate sweep of gold-tipped lashes, the nose small and clear-cut over a slender jawline and slim neck.

At last he said, in cool level tones, "I suggest you drive with more care in future especially when in a strange country. *Bonjour, mademoiselle*." And he went to his car.

When he passed her, he was staring ahead. Vicki exhaled anger via her lungs in a manner of an engine letting off steam. What a man! Granted, she had been at fault, and the mistake could easily have ended in tragedy. However, she was on unfamiliar ground and like many other drivers in a foreign country, was making her quota of mistakes.

The man had evidently been angry because of the delay. Vicki knew Frenchmen regarded their midday meal as being the most important one of the day. This man could have been rushing home to his. Crossly, she wished he would choke. Then, because she could never be angry for long, she smiled reminiscently. He really was very attractive, with enough years to make him interesting. She guessed him to be in his late 20's and wondered if he was married. It was more than likely. Married or not, she could imagine the female inhabitants of his locality had their eyes fixed permanently on stalks when he was around.

In the meantime, Sarah had completed the ascent with hardly a murmur. Rushing streams were glimpsed more frequently now between massive trunks of trees lining the road; the air was cooler and invigorating.

Mentally, Vicki ticked off the landmarks, stopping to inquire the way to the Jasseron farm when a slim boy clad in workman's overalls trundled by on a tractor.

"*Oui, mademoiselle,*" he said, with a white, shy grin. He knew it well. It was only a kilometer ahead.

It was around one o'clock when Vicki saw the farm Susie had described in her letters. There it lay, back from the road; red-roofed, blue-shuttered, its mellow stone walls hung with vines and creepers.

Vicki was drawing up at the gates when Susie bounded toward her, boisterously accompanied by a black and white dog. Through the car window, Vicki smilingly took in Susie's appearance; her tanned skin, the sun streaks heightening her fair hair, the happiness in her eyes and her fitness in the gay top and green slacks.

"Vicki!" she cried on a joyful note. "I can't believe you're here! You've made it in record time—or rather Sarah has. Good old Sarah!" She patted the hood affectionately before pushing down the exuberant dog. "Down, Gaston!" she laughed easily. "You'd better make his acquaintance or he'll never stop barking."

Vicki looked down into eloquent brown eyes brimming with life and friendship. She reached an arm through the car doorway, tickling the pointed ears and whispering endearments, while Susie fastened back the gates for her to drive into the courtyard.

Susie kissed her and proudly shot forth a slender hand on which gleamed a diamond ring.

"It's lovely," Vicki said fondly. "No need to ask if you're happy."

"Of course I'm happy. Who wouldn't be with a man like my Robert? Wait until you see him. You'll love him." They walked, arms linked affectionately, toward the farmhouse. "Madame Jasseron is waiting to meet you. I think I told you in a letter that I was staying here until we're married."

"You did." Vicki smiled into the small round face and sparkling eyes. "I'm awfully glad you're looking so well. If that's what love does for you, I'm all for it."

Happily she looked toward the doorway of the farmhouse where a woman now stood. She wore a blue striped shirt over dark slacks, was around 35 with a flexible, expressive face, mid-brown hair, and fresh skin.

She greeted Vicki warmly, inquiring if she had had a good trip and expressing her delight that she had arrived in time for *le déjeuner*. But first a glass of *sirop*.

The farmhouse was cool and inviting with the bittersweet smell, the aroma of baking bread blended with savory, delicious stew. The kitchen, large because of its importance, was furnished with a hutch of colorful crockery, a solid oak table and chairs, and an old-fashioned buffet. Gleaming copper pans decorated shelves with hams and bunches of onions suspended from the ceiling.

The *sirop* was disposed of with chuckles over Madame's teasing Susie over her wedding. Vicki went upstairs to wash before dinner, accompanied by Susie.

Her room, next to Susie's, was similarly furnished with a delightfully colored quilt on the bed. There was a bedside table, two comfortable chairs, an attractive tallboy in oak, a wardrobe, and a glass-topped dressing table containing a ewer and bowl. The ewer contained spring water, and tipping some into the bowl Vicki cupped it in her hands to bury her face in its softness. In between Susie's bright chatter, she gave news of friends back home until they went down to dinner.

Monsieur Jasseron, who at busy periods on the farm took a packed lunch with him and didn't return until the evening, came in to dinner to welcome the guest. A florid-faced man, thickset and jovial, he greeted her courteously, hoping she would enjoy her stay with them.

The table, laid simply with a gaily checked cloth and matching napkins, had a wine-glass and a dish of dainty curls of butter at each place. Golden brown, freshly baked bread cut into crisp chunks, along with a bottle of wine and a dish of fresh fruit, occupied the center of the table.

Monsieur poured out the wine while Madame, following the custom of serving her guests first, passed around her own special *hors d'oeuvres*. Meat came next, thick, tender slices of veal to be eaten with a special sauce. Vegetables were served when the meat had been eaten, followed by fresh fruit and cheese. The coffee at the end of the meal was ground then and there by Madame, who poured boiling water onto it before straining it into their cups.

Later, Monsieur carried in Vicki's luggage before going back to the fields. Susie helped her to unpack her cases in which wedding presents had been crammed between the clothes.

"I like your outfit, Vicki," she said, admiring her sister's slender figure clad in beautifully cut beige slacks and matching sweater top. "No one would believe you'd traveled in it."

Vicki shook out a sleeveless white jersey dress to find it uncreased and fresh after being packed in her case. "Yes," she answered. "Thank goodness for man-made fibres and synthetic yarns. It's comforting to know even the wool mixture ones can be washed out and drip-dried overnight. Which reminds me, what do I wear tonight when we dine with your beloved at the Château?"

Susie, dreamily admiring a pure silk hand-painted scarf, said, "Seeing that we're the only guests something like the outfit you're wearing will be okay."

Vicki stared. "Are you sure?"

Susie, tying on the scarf, surveyed her pretty reflection in the dressing table mirror. "Sure I'm sure. It's casual, but you make it look elegant. Besides, it tends to get very cold now here at night. I would take a coat too. You'll find slacks are easy to slip off later on." She smiled into the mirror. "This scarf is really lovely."

But Vicki had not heard her last remark; she was standing there with a shocked expression on her face. "Susie," she said sternly, "what kind of a place is this Château Brissard?"

Her look was too much for Susie, who collapsed on the bed in fits of laughter. "It's wine-making time, you innocent. We might be expected to help out."

"Help out?" Vicki lifted an arched brow.

Susie nodded, wiping her streaming eyes with the back of a hand.

"Tread the grapes, of course."

Vicki thoughtfully put a dress away in the sweet-smelling wardrobe.

"Do they still tread grapes? Surely it's all done by machinery today?"

Susie explained knowledgeably, "When the crop is a bumper one I suppose it's essential to use vats. I believe the smaller crops are used in presses." She hugged her knees, still wearing the scarf. "It's all so old-world and the people are so delicious. I simply love it here. Just imagine—in six and a half more days I shall be Madame Brissard, Robert's wife."

Vicki smiled indulgently. "That's how it should be." Sitting down beside her on the bed, she gazed into the small vital face fondly. "Glad you like the scarf. I bought it for you."

"You darling! Thank you, it's fabulous." She flung her arms around her sister's neck and hugged her. "It will be lovely to wear when the horrid *mistral* sweeps across the country."

Vicki's eyes were suddenly serious. "You are happy, aren't you, Sue? You're not saying this to impress me or anything like that?"

Susie was highly indignant. "Of course not, silly. Wait until you're in love. You'll wonder what's hit you. Oh, life's wonderful!" She flung her arms as if to embrace the whole world in her joy, collapsing across the bed with a sigh of pure happiness.

"You know what marrying a Frenchman means, don't you, darling? It means among other things that you'll be living in France most of the time. Sure you won't tire of the quiet and grow homesick?"

"Homesick with Robert?" Susie's voice hit a higher key at what she regarded as a ridiculous question. She sat up, her face softening at Vicki's serious one. "Don't look so scared, darling. I know what I'm doing. I'm not marrying for the sake of it or to get away from my job. I love Robert so much I couldn't face life without him now."

Her tone and subsequent flush told Vicki enough to put her mind at rest. However, there were still unknown facts which tended to bother her.

"What kind of family has he?" she asked carefully.

"Rather nice." The reply came without hesitation. "His father is very much like him, not so tall but the same easygoing temperament." She gave a small laugh. "I always thought the French were explosive, but Robert is like a lamb."

Some of them are, Vicki thought wryly, recalling the incident on the mountain road when blue eyes smouldered with anger and an arrogant profile swept past leaving a tantalizing memory. Thank goodness Susie had not chosen a man like that for her future husband. She brought herself back with an effort to the subject in hand.

"And the mother?"

Susie removed the scarf and was carefully smoothing it in folds. Vicki knew a swift uneasiness that Susie dispelled by showing a smile.

"Rather overpowering, I think," she now answered. "There isn't much of her, but she's strong and fit. Naturally, I have the feeling that she expects others to be the same. She likes telling me how hard a farmer's wife has to work. She appears to be tireless. You should have seen her helping to gather in the grapes. They were in her basket swifter than I could look at them."

Vicki placed a comforting arm about Susie's slim shoulders. There was little difference in their build. Both were of medium height, slender and small-boned. Yet Vicki always felt the taller. It came with mothering her sister over the years.

"Robert's mother has been gathering in grapes all her life, probably, whereas you are only a beginner. Don't try to do too much. By that I mean, trying to keep up with her in things she is more experienced in. Does she know you had a heart murmur?"

Susie's mouth set obstinately. "No. I don't think she would be pleased. I haven't even told Robert!"

Vicki said gently, "Don't you think you ought to?"

"I hadn't really thought about it. Well, you know how it is. I've been so busy. I've only packed in my job this week. Besides, I could have outgrown it. You've said so yourself."

Vicki agreed. "Yes, I did. Even so, we have no proof.

There's no point in taking risks. I think Robert should be told."

She was unprepared for the look of distress on her sister's face.

"Please, Vicki," she said cajolingly, "promise me you won't say anything about it yet. I love Robert so much I'm awfully afraid of something happening to prevent our marriage."

"What could happen, you silly little goose? You're suffering from the usual pre-wedding nerves. I promise, but I think it's wrong to keep it from your intended. He has a right to know."

"I'll get around to telling him," Susie said, adding rather belatedly, "After we're married."

CHAPTER TWO

"The actual picking is over." Susie waved a pearl-tipped hand toward the vineyards where a few pickers were clearing the last of the vines. Already the leaves were a fading, yellowish brown curling at the edges.

They were on their way to the Château Brissard in Sarah; Susie's wave of the hand had taken in vineyards reaching far away in the distance in never-ending patterns on the Brissard estate.

In a vague kind of way Vicki noticed the vastness of it. Her mind was on what Madame Brissard had told Susie about farmers' wives having to work hard. The estate looked prosperous enough; she hoped they would not expect too much from someone like Susie who had never had to do the hard tasks a farm entailed. Indeed, Vicki had spoiled her through the years.

Susie had cooked the dinner because she was first home in the evening, but Vicki had done all the chores keeping the apartment spick and span and doing the decorating. Susie might not be cut out for a farmer's wife, but the prospect held no terrors for her once she was married to her Robert. Vicki stole a glance at the quiet happiness on her face as she indicated the Château now visible among the vines.

A large water trough was set in the center of the courtyard with the evening sun reflecting on dozens of freshly washed bottles and crates nearby. Vicki braked at a large stone barn. Immediately a man appeared in the doorway; a pleasant, smiling man, rather tall with the tanned outdoor look usually accompanying an open-necked shirt and pants.

Susie ran to him, they kissed, and starry-eyed, she introduced them. "Robert, my sister Vicki. Vicki, Robert Brissard, my fiancé."

"Welcome to the Château Brissard, *mademoiselle*," he said in good English. His voice pleasantly cultured, his hand-clasp firm.

Vicki looked up into square-cut features topped by fair hair slightly waving into a widow's peak on his broad forehead. She liked his clean-cut freshness and the candid way his hazel eyes met hers when she returned his greeting. There could be no doubt about his love for Susie. His eyes caressed her when he looked down at her clinging to his arm.

Madame Brissard joined them. Robert said, "This is Maman—Maman, Mademoiselle Vicki Kendon."

Vicki saw an elderly, brown-haired woman with precise, defined features void of expression, a poker face with rather sallow skin, prominent cheekbones and dominant eyes. Were they a little calculating? She could not be sure and resolved to keep an open mind in no way influenced by what Susie had said about her mother-in-law to be.

She appeared to be a woman who had made the best of herself through the years. In the tailored shirtwaister top, her bust was firm and high, giving her a youthful look, and if her waist had broadened in favor of her hips the clever cut of her slacks concealed the fact charmingly.

"So you are Vicki," she said in English with a charming accent, her eyes roving swiftly over Vicki. "Like Susie, you have the delicate air."

"We might look delicate, but I can assure you we are two normally healthy girls," Vicki said firmly, keeping her fingers crossed for Susie.

Madame Brissard apparently looked on a woman merely as a man's helpmate, something amounting to a smaller carbon copy of himself. No wonder Susie was perturbed.

"I'm sure you are," Madame Brissard said. "You are

young and therefore strong. Come, tell me what you think of our wine."

She led the way to a door at the foot of the château leading to the cellars, and Vicki followed. When her eyes became accustomed to the dimness, she saw long stone-arched caverns lined with wooden casks and bottles of wine. Madame stopped at a rough-hewn table containing, among other items, sealing wax and labels, and filled two silver tasting bowls with sparkling red wine.

"*Eh bien?*" she asked when Vicki had sampled it.

"Delicious," Vicki answered, as indeed it was.

Madame smiled knowledgeably. "It has not quite matured. Now you shall try an older vintage to see the difference."

Again her bowl was filled, this time with wine from a bottle which was dusted before Madame drew the cork. It was smooth as silk and as heady as a drug to Vicki's inexperienced palate.

"It certainly has a kick," she said.

"But a nice kick, *non*? You do not drink much wine in England?"

"Not on the scale that you do here, but it is becoming more popular since people are taking more holidays abroad."

Madame shrugged. "To us wine is as essential as bread."

The Château Brissard was not palatial with a moat and drawbridge. To Vicki it resembled a large country rectory, outdated but full of old-world charm. Madame Brissard escorted her throughout with more than a little pride. The furniture was traditional; exquisitely designed to really give a lifetime of pleasure to more than one generation. The rooms were lofty with beautifully carved ceilings and doors while tall windows framed landscape views of charming countryside.

Susie and Robert were in the *salon* when they entered.

They looked so happy that Vicki felt a lump in her throat. Monsieur Brissard entered, and her heart warmed to him when he flung them an amused glance.

He was a trifle shorter than Robert, more thickset with his hair receding a little from his forehead. There were no depths in Monsieur Brissard. Like his son's, his greeting was warm and friendly. He inquired if she had enjoyed her journey and was very interested to know she had driven up from the coast in Sarah.

Dinner proved an enjoyable meal, beginning with a delicious soup. Vicki marveled at the flavor, thinking wryly that Susie would have her work cut out to reach Madame Brissard's culinary standard when she married. The wine was extremely palatable, the conversation mainly about the present wine-making which was now under way and was to be continued in the great stone barn after dinner.

Like the cellars of the château, the barn was lit inside by dust-covered light bulbs illuminating huge vats, each more than six feet deep and twice as far in diameter. The air was wine-laden, coming from the first vat filled with grapes and giving a cloudy red juice. Vicki and Susie inhaled over the side while Robert and his father, wearing overalls, industriously cleaned out a second vat with wood alcohol.

Madame Brissard, no less industrious, was running a pipeline between the two vats; soon the juice was running from the filled vat directly into the empty one the two men had cleaned.

When the juice had been drained, the pulp that was left was carried to an emormous press. The great wheel started to revolve. This was the signal for Madame to roll up her slacks and take off her shoes and stockings. She then clambered into the vat, motioning for the two girls to do the same.

They obeyed and entered into the spirit of it by shedding their shoes and slacks, leaving their sweaters to fall to mini-skirt length before joining her in the press.

As she slipped inside, Vicki's first impression was one of delicious warmth around her feet and ankles. But after the first few tentative treads, the slippery juice clung to the soles of her feet making it difficult for her to keep her balance. Still the pails were emptied in and, heels were pressed down determinedly, sending up vapor-like fumes to curl eerily above their heads.

It was strenuous, this treading of the grapes, Vicki thought, but fun despite the ache beginning to develop at the back of her knees through the unaccustomed plunging of her feet. Wondering how Susie was faring, she cast a glance across the press. Madame Brissard was at the far end treading rhythmically like a machine with Susie midway between them. One look at Susie's face sent her heart in her throat. She was treading away as mechanically as Madame, but she looked tired and drawn.

"All right, Susie?" said Vicki, amid the creaking of the press.

Susie nodded and conjured up a smile, but Vicki was not convinced.

"Take it easy." Vicki's voice was low and out of Madame's hearing.

Susie, however, insisted upon keeping up with Madame, who had developed the knack through experience. Vicki's warning was ignored.

The rest of the evening was a nightmare to Vicki. More than once, she was tempted to slip over the side and ask Robert to persuade Susie to rest. It was only the thought of it distressing Susie, thereby doing as much harm as the over-exertion, that kept Vicki silent.

Feverishly, she found herself wondering how much longer the men would go on tipping in the pails, for the supply seemed unending. Beneath them the juice frothed between the slats. As time went on she wondered if it was worry over Susie or giddy reaction to the fumes that was making her feel lightheaded.

It was well after midnight when the men, having shovelled up the last of the pulp from the vat, watched the great wheel stop with a last defiant creak. The three women swung puce-colored legs to the ground and began to wipe them.

Susie had her face turned away, but Vicki thought she appeared to be fumbling when she put on her slacks. Vicki had changed and was about to put on her shoes when she looked again and saw her sway. Instantly, she ran toward her to catch as she fell. Then Robert was there lifting Susie up.

It was Madame Brissard who took control of the situation, bidding her son to carry Susie out into the air. Vicki hurriedly slipped into her shoes and followed them.

The courtyard was well lit and Susie had been placed on a chaise longue outside the barn. To Vicki the scene was a macabre one, with Robert, his white overall heavily stained with red juice, bending over Susie, who lay still. Her eyes were dark hollows in the chalk whiteness of her face; her hair was strewn over the pillow hastily pushed behind her head by Robert.

Madame Brissard, who had gone inside, returned brandishing smelling salts. "This will bring her around," she said, uncorking the small bottle in a business-like manner. "It wasn't at all necessary to ask your papa to phone the doctor at this hour, Robert. Mademoiselle has been overcome by the fumes. It is merely a passing out. Perhaps you will lift her up. It is usual for the person to sit up so that the head can be lowered."

"*Non*. Leave her until the doctor arrives," Robert said decisively as he chafed Susie's hands.

"Poof!" exclaimed Madame. "I don't know what all the fuss is about. She will be around when she has breathed in the smelling salts. The doctor is not going to like being called out for nothing."

She bent down to wave the smelling salts determinedly beneath Susie's pale nostrils while Robert, still chafing her hands, tossed Vicki a faint smile to reassure her. Now was her cue to tell him of her sister's suspected heart condition. He was nice, and the temptation to talk to him about it was great until she remembered Madame Brissard.

It came to her with poignant clearness why Susie had not told Robert. She was afraid of his mother. There was obviously no room for any kind of invalid at the Château Brissard. Looking at Madame's compressed lips and hard expression, Vicki felt a qualm when she thought of Susie sharing her home. Her eyes filled with tears when she looked down at her unconscious form. Could it be a heart attack? She could be overcome by the fumes and the effort she had made to keep up with Madame. Vicki had felt lightheaded herself.

Susie had never passed out before, to her knowledge. But she looked so still, and there was a faint blueness around her mouth.

Before she could conjecture further, a car swept into the courtyard to pull up behind Sarah. Instantly the scene changed for Vicki. Once again she was on the mountain road watching an angry Frenchman leave his car. The car door slammed in the same arrogant manner as before. He strode purposefully toward them carrying a small black bag.

Vicki stiffened. Amidst the chaos of her thoughts she took in the wide shoulders in evening dress, the lithe easy grace, and the firm disturbing features which masked an iron will. With his temperament, his eyes should have been dark and flashing instead of a penetrating blue. She had hoped to have seen the last of him, but deep down she had known they would meet again. Numbly, she watched Robert greet him cordially.

"Guy! I never expected to see you. Aren't you due to go on a lecture tour?"

"That is so. However, Doctor Molineux is ill, so I am

helping Janera for a few weeks." Already the keen eyes were focused on Susie's still figure. The small bag was placed on the ground; hands confident and controlled hitched up the knife-edged crease in his slacks as he stooped to lift Susie's eyelid to peer inside.

In spite of her antagonism toward him, Vicki could not deny that his swift comprehension and cool approach was giving her confidence in his ability to help Susie.

His examination was brief but thorough, his acknowledgement of Madame's presence with an amused glance at the smelling bottle, charmed even her practical heart.

Almost coyly, she said, "I must apologize for my son. He had no right to send for you at this hour. Mademoiselle has only fainted."

"Susie was taking part in the wine-making when she passed out," Robert cut in swiftly. "She could have been overcome by fumes, so I thought it wise to send for medical aid."

The doctor nodded comprehendingly. "You did right, *mon ami*. It could have been serious. I shall need a tumbler of water for when she comes around." He looked pointedly at Madame Brissard who, taking the hint, went indoors to fetch it. Then he was looking down at Susie again.

Vicki surveyed the scene on a wave of despair willing life into the silent, still figure. The pressure of tears persisted in her throat, threatening to choke her. After what seemed an age, Susie gave a small moan and opened her eyes.

Bewilderedly, she gazed at them each in turn; the doctor on one side, Robert and Vicki on the other. Vicki, in order to reassure her, winked with a lightness she was far from feeling. It worked. Susie's expression cleared, and the fingers of the hand Robert was holding curled around his.

Then the doctor was bending over her. "You passed out, *mademoiselle*. How do you feel?"

"Tired, I think," she said weakly.

He smiled. "Then we will try a pill."

"There, you see?" Madame Brissard, who had glided up with the tumbler of water, cried triumphantly. "I told you she did not need a doctor, Robert."

The doctor looked from mother to son enigmatically. He had taken a bottle of pills from the small bag, extracted one and gave it to Susie along with some water. Madame's remark, like Vicki's presence, was ignored. Madame Brissard drifted away with the glass now she was no longer needed. Robert bent over Susie, who looked up at him adoringly.

"I'm sorry to have caused you all this trouble," she said meekly.

Gently, Robert pushed the hair from her damp forehead.

"You scared the life out of me, *chérie*."

"But, darling, it was only a faint."

Neither noticed the doctor's swift glance, but Vicki did and wondered what it meant. She was not left long in doubt, for, after filling a tiny box with pills from the bottle, he wrote rapidly on the lid and addressed Susie in measured tones.

"*Mademoiselle*, I want you to take one of these pills twice a day, no more, no less. You are also to rest and no more winemaking. *Comprenez?*"

Robert answered for her. "Give the pills to Vicki. . . . *Pardon*, Guy, I forgot you had not been introduced. My fiancée, Mademoiselle Susie Kendon, her sister, Vicki. Doctor Guy Ransart, my very good friend who is also a surgeon."

"*Enchanté*." A bow, and the blue gaze slid from Susie to flicker over Vicki with the merest suggestion of a glint, but he did not reveal the fact that they had already met. Evidently the incident was not important to him. Yet, Vicki thought, slightly piqued, if he had forgotten her, he was sure to recognize Sarah, having parked behind her in the well-lit courtyard.

The box of pills was dropped into her hand and she accepted them politely, aware that Robert was speaking again.

"Susie is all right, isn't she, Guy? It was nothing serious?"

The firm mouth quirked into a smile. "You worry too much, but then you are in love and it is to be expected. I suggest you carry your fiancée indoors where she can rest long enough for the pill to work before you take her home."

"You're coming in for a drink, are you not?"

"*Merci*, Robert. I have left guests. Some other time."

Susie was swept up into Robert's arms. "Thanks, Guy. Don't forget you promised to be best man at our wedding," he said over Susie's head.

"I am not likely to forget such a delightful engagement," was the smooth reply. "*Bonne nuit,* Robert, Mademoiselle Kendon."

They answered, and Vicki was about to follow them inside when firm fingers gripped her arm.

"One moment, *mademoiselle*," the doctor drawled with a commanding air, and she was pushed down gently on to the chaise longue still warm from Susie. For breathless minutes she felt her heartbeats echo in her throat alarmingly. He hooked an empty bottle crate forward with the tip of a well-polished shoe, set a foot on it and leaned toward her with one arm along his bent knee.

"You knew your sister had a heart condition, *mademoiselle*?" he queried on a thoughtful look.

Her eyes were on the hand resting on his knee, noticing the sprinkling of fine hairs on the back below the immaculate cuff. His calm self-assurance annoyed her intensely. He was altogether too confident. Also, he had her at a disadvantage, for the heated performance in the wine press had destroyed her make-up, and she felt anything but presentable. "Then it was not a faint," she said at last evasively.

"You did not honestly think it was?"

"I was hoping it was," she corrected him.

Vicki was surprised she could answer him so coolly, for since his arrival at the Château her thoughts had been chaotic. That direct gaze of his was churning her inside in a way she found incomprehensible.

In his capacity as a surgeon he was used to sudden drama and knew infinitely more of what lay beneath the surface than she. She braced herself for his next remark without lifting her eyes.

"Is Mademoiselle's heart condition congenital?"

Vicki paused, reluctant to answer. The man was a menace! He already knew too much about Susie, as a doctor. Yet what could she do? He was the kind one could not put off by clever evasions. But she was fighting on Susie's side. There was a short silence. Unconsciously responding to his intent study of her lowered head, she raised her eyes to look straight into his. Their gaze held no longer than the sense of shock shooting through her veins with mercurial swiftness. She stiffened and decided on frankness.

"No, she was not born with it. When she was younger, she had a bad attack of rheumatic fever leaving her with a heart murmur."

"*Pauvre petite!*" He appeared to digest this, then exhaled a long breath. "You knew this, yet you allowed her to do what she did tonight?"

Vicki bristled. How dared he criticize her? He was going too far even in his capacity as a doctor. "My sister is of an age to do as she pleases, but even she will not be so foolish as to overtax her strength again after what happened tonight," she said coldly.

For tantalizing moments he continued to study her flushed, angry face; her hair a halo of spun silk, her eyes dark and flashing with resentment.

She could have explained the reason for Susie's reluctance to disclose her heart weakness, but this man, being a friend of the family, would only scoff at her fears. He might even form the opinion that she herself, in her eagerness to see her sister married, had suggested her silence in the first place.

"How old is she?"

"21."

"And she has had no attacks before?" His tone was purely professional.

"Not to my knowledge."

His eyes narrowed. "I cannot understand Robert allowing her to do anything so strenuous."

"He doesn't know. Susie thought, as I did, that she had outgrown the weakness. My sister and I are very close. If she had experienced any similar attacks she would have told me. Fortunately she wasn't particularly fond of sports and so did not over-exert herself while at school. She will tell Robert when she gets around to it."

"He might decide to talk to her parents about it when they attend the wedding," he said thoughtfully.

Vicki's lips tightened on a remembered pain. "We have no parents. My father is dead, my mother married again and is somewhere abroad."

"So, you play *la mère*. You can't be very old yourself."

"I'm 23."

An eyebrow raised on a slight smile. "*En effet!* I would have said 18. But no matter. I want you to see that Mademoiselle takes the pills as I have prescribed them. I also think it is a good idea for her to have a check-up in the near future."

Vicki swallowed. "Has the condition deteriorated?"

"Not necessarily."

"And they can marry?"

"Of course."

Vicki shuddered with relief and the cool night air. She had worked herself up to a glowing heat while treading the grapes and, in her mental stress, had not noticed the cold breeze until now.

"You feel the cold, *mademoiselle*. A thousand pardons for keeping you in the cold night air," he said with instant polite attention. "Come, into the Château."

Escorting her firmly across the courtyard with a light grip on her arm, he left her at the door.

CHAPTER THREE

The cackling of geese awakened Vicki; she lay listening to the familiar sounds of a farm, her mind recalling the events of the previous evening. Deliberately making light of it, she had told Susie that the doctor had advised a check-up. To her relief Susie did not appear to be upset. They had returned to the Jasseron farm in the small hours and had been enjoying a warm drink left by Madame Jasseron.

Susie, fully recovered from her collapse, sat on the kitchen table swinging her shapely legs as she drank. "I wonder why he has suggested a check-up. It was only a faint, wasn't it? Anyone could have passed out pounding away in a fume-filled press."

Vicki looked thoughtfully into her steaming cup. She saw no point in upsetting her sister until she had actually been examined. So she said carefully, "I know what you mean. I wasn't feeling too well myself toward the finish. I think we'll be walking like someone with two wooden legs after all that goose-stepping!"

Susie agreed, curving her hands around her cup. "Should be interesting," she had mused, "being examined by a dishy surgeon. Quite a lady-killer, isn't he? If you like them tall and handsome. Personally I prefer Robert's type, although he might be inclined to grow fat and bald later." Yawning delicately, she had rambled on. "Strange that Robert never mentioned Guy Ransart before, seeing they're such good friends. Do you think he was jealous of me meeting that handsome piece of humanity?"

Vicki stifled a yawn. "I don't know and I'm afraid I don't care. I'm tired and it's almost three o'clock." She had shivered, feeling little benefit from the warm drink.

"Thanks for telling me about taking a warm coat. The air can get really chilly here at night. I can't seem to get warm. I must be needing my bed."

It seemed she had only just closed her eyes when the cackle of the geese had woken her. Her watch said eight o'clock but she did not feel at all like getting up. It was the aroma of baking bread that aroused her, reminding her of Madame Jasseron already at work in the kitchen below. It was not Vicki's intention to add to the French-woman's chores. They were causing her enough extra work as it was.

The ache in the back of her legs made her wince when she stood up and moved about stiffly as she washed and dressed. Her head felt woolly after only a few hours' sleep which normally would not have affected her. A peep into Susie's room found her fast asleep, so she made her way downstairs to a breakfast table laid for two.

Madame Jasseron was putting large brown eggs away, fresh from the nest.

"*Bonjour, mademoiselle,*" she said, with a pleasant smile. "I trust you slept well."

Vicki, feeling better for the warm greeting, replied politely, following Madame's French quite easily. "I hope we did not disturb you coming in so late last night—or rather this morning."

Madame hastened to reassure her. "I never heard you, and I'm sure my husband did not. Being early risers we go out like a light when we go to sleep at night. You could have stayed in bed if you wished."

Vicki shook her head. "That's sweet of you, but we're making you enough work already. Susie will be staying in bed. We joined in the wine-making at the Château Brissard and Susie fainted. It was the fumes, I think. Robert sent for the doctor; she has to rest. I'll take up her breakfast, *madame*. I should also like to help with your chores if I may."

Madame Jasseron gave a French shrug. "Do not worry about me, I can cope. I like being active and am enjoying your company." She began to grind the coffee, motioning Vicki to a chair at the table. "Sometimes we take paying guests in the summer. Not many, a couple now and then or students. It all helps. So Mademoiselle Susie fainted. I hope she is feeling better this morning. Which *médicin* attended?"

"Doctor Ransart. I believe he is a friend of Robert's."

"That is correct. They shared the same tutor with another neighbor, Mademoiselle Molineux. She is also a doctor and shares a practice with her papa. Doctor Ransart is a very talented surgeon."

"He is not married?" The instant Vicki asked the question she wanted to withdraw it. What did it matter to her whether the man was married or single? Yet she found herself waiting breathlessly for the answer.

"Not yet," was the reply as Madame Jasseron made the coffee. "It is rumored that he will eventually marry Doctor Janera Molineux when he returns from his lecture tour."

Vicki stirred her coffee, wondering about the sudden change in her outlook. Yesterday, she had been full of enthusiasm for the holiday and change of scene. This morning she was listless, thoroughly disheartened and ill. The worst of it was that she could not account for it. Susie's collapse and the consequences had upset her, but she was over that now.

Her appetite was nil, her throat so parched that she could have gone on drinking. The coffee was delicious and she drank it, watching Madame Jasseron set out an attractive tray for Susie; fresh, crisp croissants, clear honey, coffee and fruit.

She covered it with a cloth. "I will take Mademoiselle Susie's tray upstairs, then I must go shopping." Madame Jasseron picked up the tray. "A friend is picking me up at the gate, so I will say *au revoir*." She paused to look at Vicki's pale face. "You do not look too well either, *mademoiselle*."

"Late nights don't agree with me," Vicki said flippantly, helping herself to a second cup of coffee. "I'll be all right, *merci, madame*. The coffee is lovely."

She sipped it, finding it soothing to her aching throat. Madame Jasseron, she decided, was a charming woman and would have made a wonderful mother with her gentle air and kindliness. Her coffee finished, Vicki cleared the table before returning to Susie.

She was finishing her breakfast when Vicki entered the room carrying magazines and her pills. "How are you feeling?" she asked brightly.

Susie put down her cup on the tray before her. "All right, but you look peaky."

"I feel it," Vicki answered. She dropped the magazines onto the bed and taking out a pill from the small box, gave it to her sister.

Susie swallowed it and drained her cup. "I don't need the magazines because I'm not staying in bed. I have to pay a visit to the village dressmaker today to try on my wedding dress."

"You're not going," Vicki said firmly. "If I know Madame Jasseron she will inform your dressmaker that you're not well and have to rest. Besides, the doctor might call."

Susie's eyes expressed surprise. "Why should he? There's no reason for him to call, surely." The surprised look faded, giving way to one of dismay. "Oh, Vicki," she wailed. "You didn't tell him about my attack of rheumatic fever?"

"Darling, the man's a doctor. You can't keep anything from him—not this one, anyway. There's nothing to worry about. Doctors are supposed to keep quiet over everything concerning their patients. Besides, he said there was no reason why you shouldn't marry."

"Very nice of him, I'm sure." To Vicki's sensitive ears

there was a hint of sarcasm in the young voice. "Now Madame Brissard will know all about me and think the worst."

"Not necessarily. The doctor might have told Robert had you not been fit enough to marry, but you are. That's all that matters at the moment. We can tackle anything else afterward. And don't forget you'll have Robert behind you. I do think you should tell him, though. Madame Brissard might expect you to do chores when you're married that she could give to someone else."

Susie dabbed her mouth petulantly with her table napkin. "All the same, I'd rather she didn't know."

"Don't be silly, dear. She would find out if you had a baby and might be affronted because you hadn't told her."

Susie suddenly capitulated. "Very well, I'll tell Robert and leave it to him to tell his mother if he wishes. But not until after the wedding." She watched her sister picking up clothes hastily flung down, and her expression softened. "I was too tired last night, to be neat and tidy. You're awfully good to me, Vicki. I'll never forget what you've done for me."

Susie would have been even more grateful had she known what the effort was costing her sister. Each time she bent down, the shooting pains in her head were shattering. She made a valiant effort to appear normal and even managed a smile.

"It doesn't sound like you, apologizing for being untidy! Come on, snap out of it. You're supposed to be a prospective happy bride." She surveyed the tousled head and pretty, pink cheeks. "What about combing your hair and looking presentable in case your Robert comes dashing in?"

Taking the tray, she smiled at Susie's hurried efforts to follow her advice. She had reached the door when a masculine voice called from below:

"Anybody home?"

Ignoring her sister's frantic gesture to keep him out until she could tidy herself, Vicki called down impishly, "Come on up, Robert. It's the first door on the right at the top of the stairs."

In the kitchen, she washed the dishes and did several chores she could see needed doing, aware of the muted sound of voices and laughter upstairs. The pain in her head and throat had not lessened. It was vying with the pains in her legs. When Robert had gone, she would go upstairs to her room for aspirins.

The sun spilled through the open door and beckoned her outside. In the far corner of the farmyard a giant oak tree had a seat around its girth. She walked across to it, hoping the fresh air would remove the feeling of faintness. Instinctively she chose the side hidden by the massive trunk from the farmhouse. The sound of a car aroused her and, turning in her seat, she peeped from behind the tree. Her heart lurched to see the big green car slide to a halt and Guy Ransart uncurl his length from behind the wheel.

Robert, on the point of leaving, met him at the door of the farmhouse. The two men greeted each other. Robert cast a look around, presumably for herself, before they went indoors.

She leaned back against the tree and closed her eyes, letting the quiet peace wash over her. The next thing she knew was that something heavy was being thrust on her knee accompanied by a doggy whimper. Vicki opened her eyes dully. Gaston, his chin on her knee, was looking up at her with concern in his gentle eyes. His presence meant that Monsieur Jasseron was working nearer the house. She patted his head.

"Go back to your master, *vite*," she said in rapid French for the dog to understand. "*Vite!*" she repeated, when he was reluctant to go.

The dog had not been gone long when she heard Robert and the doctor leaving. The first car shot away, and she waited for the sound of the second one. It seemed to take an age; she had neither the will nor the inclination to see whose car it was. Since Gaston had awakened her from a short troubled sleep, she had felt drugged with pain.

Her temples throbbed and she wished the car would leave. Restlessly, she pushed her hair from a burning forehead and opened her eyes to look up into the blue, intent gaze of the doctor.

The shock of seeing him made her sit bolt upright with an audible gasp of surprise. Her heart beat in thick strokes, and she was bereft of speech.

"*Pardon, mademoiselle,* for startling you, but I thought you had heard me approaching."

"I—I had no idea you knew I was here," she stammered on her first steady breath.

His cool gaze traveled slowly over her before he half turned to look behind him. And there was Gaston, tongue lolling happily, eyes dancing at his own cleverness, sitting behind him.

"I didn't until Gaston insisted upon bringing me. I think he sensed your reluctance to be seen, for he ran toward the tree repeatedly until I got the gist of what he meant." His eyes narrowed. "I wonder why he was so anxious for me to come?"

But Vicki had not heart him. She had the feeling of floating in space and made a last desperate attempt to lean back against the blessed support of the tree. It was farther back than she thought. She swayed and was held firmly between strong hands.

Then she was scooped up and carried indoors as easily as if she was a child. Upstairs her room door, slightly ajar, was kicked open. She was lowered gently on the bed. With the feeling of something solid beneath her, she gave up the fight for consciousness and knew no more.

When she opened her eyes again, the doctor was sitting on the bed watching her, his face set. She was fully dressed but for her shoes. Her throat felt as though a brick had been rammed down it to lodge in her chest.

"*Comment allez-vous*?" he queried without a smile.

"It's my throat. . . ." she began, thickly and painfully.

Her chin was taken between a thumb and finger. "Open your mouth. Wider please," he said, and placed a small flat instrument on her tongue to peer in her throat. Placing the back of his hand against her flushed forehead, he said quietly, "You have a throat infection. I am going to give you a shot of penicillin."

His touch was surprisingly gentle. At last, he replaced everything in his bag. Dazedly, she wondered how long she had been out. Long enough for him to fetch his bag from his car, evidently.

"I'm sorry to be such a nuisance," she managed on an apologetic note, watching the stern profile. "Like Susie, I've never fainted before."

"Don't apologize for something you can't help," he said, crisply. "I could be partly to blame for keeping you talking last evening in the cold night air after you had been steaming in that wretched barn." He snapped the bag shut, and Vicki had the idea he would have liked someone's neck to be between the clasp. "Ever had tonsillitis?"

"No, only measles."

He shot her a keen glance and gradually his mouth curved upward into a charming smile transforming his stern features in a way that jolted her heart. "You have been very lucky, *mademoiselle*. It won't be long before you are up and about again."

"But I can't stay in bed," she protested weakly. "Poor Madame Jasseron will be worn out with two invalids on her hands."

He said firmly, "Your consideration for others does

you credit, *mademoiselle*, but I am afraid there is no alternative. I will tell you when you can get up. You're young and resilient and will soon be on your feet again."

For the next two days Vicki could have cared less. Her throat had been so painfully swollen that she was surprised at liquids slithering down. On the third day she felt much better. On the fourth she felt well enough to get up after breakfast. Guy had called to see her each day. His visits had sent her spirits soaring, and on the fourth morning, she knew a tranquillity of mind she had not known for years.

Thank goodness lying in bed did not disturb her hair. Before she left the thick, unruly waves had been expertly styled and thinned to a natural look with curls clustering around her small ears and along her forehead in becoming bangs. Through the hand-mirror, her skin was clear and pinky with no sallowness to mar it; her neat unaccented eyebrows gave her a soft, appealing look.

"You're looking better this morning, and very pretty," Susie remarked, as she entered the room with an armful of gladioli and fern which she arranged artistically in a colorful vase. "Another bouquet from Madame Brissard. Everyone has been so concerned." She gurgled, "We are a pair, aren't we? First me fainting away, then you. I don't know what Madame Jasseron thinks about us, but she's been wonderful."

Vicki agreed. The Frenchwoman could not have treated them better had they been her own daughters. In a way, the fact that she had fainted had bolstered up Susie's morale in regard to herself. Her rest in bed had done her a world of good.

Bright as a button, her endless chatter about her forthcoming marriage had taken Vicki out of herself. She watched her arranging the flowers, a task she did remarkably well, and said thoughtfully:

"You haven't been so bad yourself, keeping me amused with your company."

Susie shortened the stem of a particularly fine bloom before putting it in the vase. "You haven't kept me from seeing Robert. He says he will be busy right up to the wedding arranging everything so that we can enjoy our honeymoon." Her mouth, beguilingly curved in dreams, straightened into adult seriousness when she stepped back to look at the flower arrangement. "There, isn't that pretty? At least I can arrange flowers. I wonder if Madame Brissard can." She sighed. "She's bound to be good at it. She's so efficient in everything."

Vicki looked at her drooping shoulders and dejected air impatiently.

"I've never seen anyone so aware of their own short-comings as you. I'd like to see Madame Brissard handling a classful of youngsters and keeping them happy and well-behaved as you did. If that's not being efficient, I don't know what is." She spoke cheerfully, quelling a faint twinge of uneasiness at her sister's downcast air. "You're not worried about living at the Château after you are married, are you, Sue?"

"Not really."

Vicki let it pass, but she was not deceived. Susie was evidently thinking that discretion was politic at the moment.

"Have you discussed the idea of a place of your own with Robert?" she asked carefully.

"Not directly." Susie picked up discarded pieces of stems from around the vase. "I don't want to worry him. Plenty of time when we return from our honeymoon."

"Yes, you lucky girl. A honeymoon in Paris," Vicki teased.

The dreamy look was back again. "Don't remind me of it," she said blissfully as the sound of a car was heard below.

Susie smiled. "That sounds like the man you're expecting," she said impishly. "I'll send him up."

"No, stay, Susie. . . ." Vicki cried, slightly agitated. But Susie had gone. Nervously, Vicki straightened the bedspread with slim white hands. She must be weaker than she thought to allow the doctor's visit to turn her into a bundle of nerves. Suddenly, she was facing the fact that his natural, urbane courtesy, his cool masculine approach, were becoming more precious with every visit. It was wrong to allow her emotions to become involved because she had discovered the man had a human streak in him after all.

She heard the slam of a car door. Susie's voice followed with light footsteps taking the stairs singly, instead of masculine ones taking every other one.

The sudden appearance in the doorway of an elegantly beautiful woman took some moments to register. Her brain said, about 25, leaf-green cashmere sweater over suède skirt and matching loose jacket, exquisite handmade shoes, chestnut hair and amber eyes. She was impeccably groomed with the enameled look of having spent hours in a beauty parlour. Her greeting, like her manner, was cool.

"*Bonjour, mademoiselle.* I am Doctor Janera Molineux. Doctor Ransart is away for a few days. I hope you are feeling better." She sat down on the bedside chair, crossing long slim legs gracefully before picking up Vicki's wrist in beautifully manicured fingers. The amber eyes held a mocking look. "Your pulse is working overtime. Were you expecting our very attractive surgeon, or did I surprise you by my unexpected appearance?"

Vicki's dark eyes widened at the woman's unexpected outspokenness. Was the remark spontaneous with no malice aforethought? She doubted it. The amber eyes were too guarded. So she had claws beneath those marvelously long fingernails.

"You're wrong on both counts, doctor," she answered perversely. "I was overexcited by the thought of being allowed up today. I feel so much better."

The doctor released her wrist in an offhand manner and shrugged elegant shoulders. "Tedious, this lying in bed, is it not? You may get up this afternoon. Tomorrow, if you feel equal to it, you can get up in the morning. You are taking pills *mademoiselle*?" She reached for a half-bottle of pills from the bedside table and looked at them thoughtfully. "I'll make out a prescription for more, then you will have no cause to bother Doctor Ransart when he returns." Extracting a pad and pencil from her bag, she wrote out the prescription and gave it to Vicki with a cool smile. "I try to save him needless demands on his time when I can. It is so good of him to help out while Papa is indisposed." She snapped her bag shut.

So that was that, Vicki thought grimly, but the woman showed no intention of leaving.

"You are here for your sister's wedding, *mademoiselle*?"

Vicki did not know why she resented the woman; unless her question proved her previous assumption that she was jealous of Guy Ransart's dealings with other women, be it only patients.

"Yes," she answered amiably. "It was sheer bad luck that I contracted this infection."

The lady doctor agreed. "It is not many visitors who are fortunate enough to acquire the services of a surgeon."

Vicki, knowing that the remark was deliberately intended to relegate her to the tourist class, kept cool with an effort and returned her serve. "I hope the bill won't be consistent with his position, or I shall wish I had an ordinary doctor."

"Doctor Ransart will charge no fee. He is a close friend of Robert Brissard," was the lofty reply. She stood up with a remote air. "*Au revoir, mademoiselle*. Take care."

Take care, Vicki echoed beneath her breath when Doctor Molineux had departed on a wave of delicious perfume. What did she mean exactly? Take care of her health in case her precious surgeon had to call again? She would certainly do that. She wanted no further visits from Doctor Molineux or her surgeon.

CHAPTER FOUR

By the end of the week Vicki was more herself again. Doctor Molineux had called once when Vicki was going to the village with Susie for a last fitting of her wedding dress. The dressmaker was reputed to be excellent, having worked for years for a famous Paris fashion house until she married.

Vicki left Susie for her fitting and walked in the main street where delicious small stores and gay cafés beckoned. There were old-fashioned signs hanging over store doorways with immaculate shuttered windows above, gay with window boxes.

Entranced, she gazed into windows filled with mouth-watering pastries and boxes of liqueur chocolates. She bought a box tied with blue ribbon for Madame Jasseron, and mingled with the crowd.

It was Saturday, the village was full of weekend shoppers from outlying farms. Stalls were set along the sidewalks, and pedestrians only were allowed in the narrow streets. In the bubbling market one could buy poultry, eggs, an endless variety of cheeses and thick fresh cream which was poured from huge jugs into the customer's containers.

The gaiety was infectious, she discovered, when later, she went with Susie to eat at one of the delightful cafés amid laughter and the tinkling of glasses. The fresh trout was delicious, so were the tender steaks and scallops served in rich cream sauce with truffles. After lunch they strolled up a gentle slope away from the bustle of the village to a small plateau to enjoy a panoramic view in the exhilarating air.

The village below looked enchanting with its half-timbered houses surrounded by vineyards so green against the fir-clad hills. The sun was warm and it was pleasant to linger in the quiet green peace. It proved to be an enjoyable day. In the evening they dined at the Château Brissard. Madame Brissard was charming and Susie appeared to be more relaxed.

Vicki was surprised how easily she slipped into the French way of life, although some things were completely strange. There was the continental quilt which was far too short to cover both the toes and the shoulders at the same time. Then there was the way the French invariably slept with their windows tightly closed and shuttered. She marveled, too, at the bed linen monogramed with the family initial and the unfamiliar square instead of oblong pillows.

On Monday, at Susie's suggestion, they made a trip into Nice with Sarah. There were one or two last-minute purchases Susie wanted to make before her wedding the following weekend. Nice was a wonderful shopping center and a veritable delight for women shoppers, she said.

They arrived in Nice about noon in glorious sunshine. The gentle rustle of palm trees and the soft wash of the Mediterranean on the pebbly beach was accompanied by the sudden change into much warmer air.

Lunch was leisurely with a panoramic view of the blue sea from their table by the window. The meal over, they went out into the brilliant sunshine, eager to explore the exciting stores and wide streets.

They made their purchases, but discovered that the lovelier items were too expensive. Susie, however, found what she sought, a cream leather-look roomy purse that opened out to carry bulky items to zip back into a neat square shape again. Vicki was thrilled with a small white turban in jersey, useful in the high breezes. After their shopping, they went to the flower market to spend a happy hour among exotic blooms and fascinating plants.

The flower market, separated from the beach by broad terraces, was held beneath an enormous roof. Every variety of flower was displayed and arranged in a miracle of color. The roses and lilies were superb, and the dried everlasting flowers, so skilfully arranged, had their quota of admiration.

Both girls were passionately fond of flowers, so it was not surprising for them to stroll away each with an armful of blooms.

The big green car drew up silently beside them.

"*Bonjour, mesdemoiselles,*" said Guy Ransart. "You have the look of two nymphs from the woods with your bouquets."

With athletic ease, he left the car and was standing looking down at them, the sun shining on his thick, crisp hair. He was looking very cool, very professional, in a well-cut light gray suit, green pin-striped shirt and sober tie.

It was Susie who spoke. "Doctor Ransart! We hardly expected to see you here in Nice."

His gaze flicked over her torrent of fair hair with a Frenchman's appraisal of her youthful freshness. Then he was looking intently at Vicki, aware of a spiritual quality about her even in her walk.

"Why not? I attend the hospital here on occasions," he said. "You have recovered, Mademoiselle Vicki, from the attack of the wicked tonsils?"

Vicki found his gaze disconcerting, but she managed to say coolly,

"Yes, Doctor Ransart. Your pills were wonderful."

His smile was utterly charming. "Modern science works wonders in medicine today. You are here for the day?"

"No. We return tomorrow."

An eyebrow rose attractively. "You are with a party?"

"No." It was Susie who answered on a dreamy smile. "We're doing some last-minute shopping before the wedding."

The blue eyes took on a glint. "Ah, the wedding! So

you come to Nice to have a last fling at the carnival, *non*?"

"Carnival?" They cried in unison.

"But of course. A water carnival."

"It sounds fun. What luck we came today!" Susie was all a-bubble.

"You are not to go alone. I will take you," he said firmly.

Vicki suddenly felt as gay as her smile. "It's very kind of you, Doctor Ransart, but we couldn't impose upon you."

"You will not impose. My work at the hospital is finished. I return home tomorrow." He drew back a cuff to consult his watch. "There is ample time for a drive along the coast road. You will find it more enjoyable than walking in the sun. *D'accord?*"

"Agreed," they echoed, and slipped into the back seat of the roomy car.

They purred along the coast road with a breathtaking view; the blue Mediterranean was topped with immaculate navy vessels, yachts, and every conceivable craft in readiness for the carnival. In his deep, pleasant voice, Guy told them about the Nice he remembered as a boy with no ugly apartment blocks, deplorable camping sites, or disfiguring billboards. But like everywhere else, Nice was changing.

The leisurely drive was enchanting with the steep walls on one side gay with bougainvillea; wild roses and geraniums and the sea on the other. The car was air-conditioned and pleasantly cool, but it was a welcome break from sitting when Guy drew up at a hotel on the headland.

Guy seated them on the terrace decorated with colorful tables and chairs and ordered drinks. There was a sprinkling of people at the tables, and the waiters were eager to greet fresh arrivals. Vicki watched the occupant of a nearby table receive his drink. The waiter moved away and much to her surprise, the man hailed Guy delightedly.

Middle-aged and slightly built, he had square-cut features and reddish brown hair. He was dressed in beige slacks and a cream silk shirt with tan silk scarf tucked in the open neck.

Guy was standing with a brilliant smile. "Gerard! It's good to see you again," he said, whipping a chair from nearby. "Come and join us."

The man came forward to cast a jaded eye over Vicki and Susie. "Delighted too. Are you collecting pretty girls?"

Again the brilliant smile. "*Mon dieu, non!* May I introduce Mademoiselle Susie and Mademoiselle Vicki Kendon, two of your countrywomen. Mademoiselle Susie is soon to be Madame Brissard." He turned to them suavely. "May I present Gerard Standon, my former tutor and very good friend."

A sandy eyebrow raised and a quick smile made the newcomer appear good-looking in a rakish kind of way. His look at Susie was full of appraisal. "So you managed to hook Robert. I was delighted when he wrote to me of his approaching marriage to an English miss," he said, sitting down with his drink. "Shows his good taste. I hope you don't mind me giving you away?"

Susie beamed. "Of course not. Lovely to have one of my own countrymen."

"That's probably what Robert thought when he wrote and asked me. May I congratulate you, Miss Kendon? You have an excellent man in Robert Brissard." He turned to look at Vicki sitting quietly beside him and gave a small appreciative whistle. "What did you do in London that you're still single? Go about in dark glasses?" He lifted a slender hand. "No, don't tell me, you're engaged, but he can't afford to buy you a ring."

Vicki laughed and colored as she met his teasing eyes. Whatever she was about to say was never uttered, for Guy cut in almost brusquely,

"How long have you been back?"

"This week. I was going to look you up. It seems years since I saw you."

"Six months, *mon ami*, with no word," Guy remarked dryly.

Gerard moved uncomfortably. "I was going to write, but somehow I never got around to it. I had even reconciled myself to staying home for good, but Robert's letter made the pull too strong for me and I returned."

"So you have decided?"

"Yes. I've sold my apartment. I'm not going back."

"I'm delighted. You can dine with us tonight. No other engagement have you?"

Gerard shook his head and tossed off part of his drink. "How is Janera?"

"Fine. Her papa is indisposed, so I'm helping out. How are you?"

The older man appeared to shake himself out of some unhappy thought.

"So-so. I'll pop in one day at your consulting-rooms for a check-up."

Guy's keen eyes were instantly alert as they took in the sallow skin and dull eyes of the other man. "You can call at the hospital here in Nice tomorrow before I leave for home. I'm going on a lecture tour soon and might not have an opportunity of seeing you for a while. Shall we say ten-thirty tomorrow morning?"

Gerard leaned back in his chair, fingering his glass and looking at it thoughtfully. "I'll be there. You're good to me, Guy. I feel better already. Those years I spent tutoring you were the happiest of my life."

"They were happy years for me also," was the reply.

Vicki, looking at the two men, sensed a bond between

them that was rare. Nice to leave happy memories behind. She would not be there long enough to leave any. Anyway, what was she bothering about? She wanted no connection with the place except for Susie.

Susie, as usual, was the chatty one when they dressed for dinner that evening in their hotel room. She was wearing a sleeveless aquamarine dress, Vicki was in tailored white jersey.

"I'm looking forward to this evening out with our surgeon," Susie remarked as she clipped large aquamarine studs in her ears. "The man has definite sexual magnetism despite that air of 'keep off the grass'. Don't you think so, Vicki?"

Vicki was sweeping possible hairs from the shoulders of her dress with a miniature clothes brush. "I don't intend to think about him at all. As far as I can see, your Adonis is a dedicated doctor who, one day, will give the woman he chooses a checkup before he marries her. As it appears to be the worthy Doctor Janera, they'll probably compare notes when it's completed."

Susie gurgled with laughter. "I don't know about you, but I don't like the woman. She's as hard as nails—one can see that by looking at her."

"But beautiful."

"So is an oil painting. You can't sleep with it, though." Susie held up her chin to see the effect of the studs in her ears.

"Susie!" Vicki cried in mock disgust. "You're getting earthy."

"And so is our surgeon. He's not as ascetic as he appears to be. That aloofness is cultivated. He's 100 per cent male, fighting fit, and he's also a Frenchman."

Vicki was brushing the blue-clad shoulders lightly with the small brush. "Don't forget your Robert is a Frenchman."

"That's what I mean. I'm going by what I know of Robert." Susie rolled her eyes; Vicki, chuckling, reminded her that time was running short and they must not keep the great man waiting.

Both men were already waiting in the hotel lobby when they went downstairs. Vicki's heart reacted strangely when she saw Guy in a smart dark suit. He would not be in evening dress because he knew they could only be wearing something informal. Very clever, she thought, then pulling herself up for being waspish, she gave both men a warm smile.

They were seated in the back of Guy's car with the two men in front. Leisurely, they slid along the Promenade des Anglais and within a short time were pulling up at a large white building. They were whisked up in an elevator to dine on the roof garden in the soft evening air.

The food and wine was delicious, and Vicki felt drugged with the splendor of it all. They sat long over the meal watching the scintillating necklace of lights around the bay reflecting on the water.

They talked, or rather Susie did, so naturally the subject was the absent Robert. Gerard recalled several amusing incidents from his youth, and Susie was insatiable. Consequently, Vicki was not surprised to find herself in the front seat beside Guy when they again entered the car.

Listening to Susie's chatter, she fell to wondering what the man at her side was like when young. Impossible to think of him as a small, grubby boy, but she could imagine that thick hair being tousled above a daredevil gleam in his eyes. She recalled Susie's remark that he wasn't as ascetic as he looked and tried to suppress an inward trembling at the thought of him as a lover. She had taken several glances at his profile, terribly aware of his magnetism and charm.

Her visit was turning out so much different from wha

she expected. She had looked forward to seeing Susie again, having long intimate talks with her, seeing her married before going off quietly herself to Paris. She had thought of finding a temporary job there and widening the horizon of her freedom by roving around for a while before picking up the threads again in London. It would not be the same without Susie, and she was beginning to wonder what her life would be like without Guy.

As if thinking about Susie had triggered off his own thought in that direction, he said, in a low confidential tone, "I want you to bring Mademoiselle Susie to the hospital here tomorrow morning at nine-thirty for a check-up."

For a moment the unexpected request churned her inside. She stiffened and said very quietly, "Could it not wait until after the wedding?"

"It could, but this way no one will know about it. That is what Mademoiselle Susie wants, is it not?"

"In a way," she answered guardedly, then added perversely, "I don't see any reason for a checkup at all. She has never collapsed before; it might be an isolated occasion."

There was a short pause, and she knew he was weighing up the challenge in her words. "Mademoiselle Susie is about to be married and anything can result from it. If she has a pronounced weakness, and it is known, one can act upon it should the need arise and perhaps save her life."

Vicki's first reaction was to tell the man to mind his own business, especially when it was most unlikely that he would be her doctor. But she could not deny that there was some truth in what he said.

Before she could answer Gerard's voice came banteringly from the back seat. "What are you two whispering about?"

Guy's only answer was to stop the car with a clear view

of the beach below. They looked down to see dancing going on amid much laughter and gaiety. Lanterns were strewn through the trees; the craft on the water were illuminated by colored lights. A large navel vessel out in the bay sent up fireworks. The display was spectacular and impressive, spraying the calm water with coins of brilliance while on the beach the dancing grew wilder.

Vicki's eyes were drawn to a group of young men who had encircled a laughing girl. She had to kiss them all before they would release her. Their car was then surrounded by young men forming a circle and shouting for *les demoiselles*.

Quite unperturbed, Guy cast a look around and honked the horn. The young men, startled by the unexpected piercing blast, broke the circle and Guy, reversing expertly, shot away.

"Why spoil the fun for our two pretty companions? All the young men wanted was a kiss," Gerard said lazily from the back seat.

Quietly and firmly the answer came. "It would not have been very wise. *Les demoiselles* are not familiar with this locality and the fun can be quite rough."

"Perhaps you're right." Gerard peered toward the sea at the lighted craft bobbing on the water. "I think we would have been all right on the water."

"That's precisely where we are going in a very short time, *mon ami*. But not in that *mêlée*," Guy replied.

He continued along the esplanade and parked opposite a deserted strip of beach. Vicki and Susie made their way down toward the water where a naval launch waited.

"Doctor Ransart?" The sailor standing by touched his cap; they clambered aboard and shot across the water to a large naval vessel.

Vicki and Susie were helped up a ladder to land on a deck where other guests were seated to enjoy a full view of the regatta.

Then Guy was introducing them to the captain, a well-built jovial type. "Captain Richard Holt, Mesdemoiselles Vicki and Susie Kendon. Gerard you already know."

Other guests arrived behind them, and they were taken to empty seats with Guy pausing for a few words with the captain. Vicki and Susie were seated between the two men. A waiter appeared with drinks to inform them that a buffet supper would be served later.

The fun on the water was now fast and furious, with the usual amount of horseplay. Motorboats streaked between other craft miraculously missing by inches, streamers were thrown and music floated across on the warm night air. All the vessels carried lights and presently fireworks went up from the shore.

And through it all sat Vicki, ever conscious of Guy smoking a small cigar by her side. This evening, there had been no curtness or coolness in his manner. He was perfectly friendly and charming, procuring two light deck rugs to drape across their shoulders to stop the chill from the water.

Some of the guests were wearing evening dress. It occurred to her that Guy had known this, yet he had worn an ordinary suit out of consideration for herself and Susie. As always, he was impeccably groomed, wearing his clothes with an air, never looking as though they meant anything to him.

Her attention was drawn to a boat not far away. Two young couples in it were acting the fool when suddenly the boat overturned to throw them into the water. They were in no way alarmed as they laughingly struck out for the shore. Vicki shared a smile with Guy to find him studying her intently. She felt her color rise and was thankful for the dim lighting, turning to accept the second Martini from the hovering waiter.

Later, they were all strolling into the buffet when a

firm hand closed on her arm. She halted watching the others move ahead and heard Guy's deep voice above her ear.

"You will see that Mademoiselle Susie keeps the appointment at nine-thirty tomorrow, won't you?" he said softly.

Vicki bit her lip. "I'll tell Susie, but let her decide," she answered without looking up at him.

"Even though you know your influence could count a great deal?"

She said firmly, "I will not have Susie worried on her honeymoon with the threat of ill health hanging over her."

"Is that the only reason?"

She shot him a swift glance, saw the set jaw and unsmiling gaze.

"What do you mean?" she asked.

For the fraction of a second a swift, unguarded look of anger rippled over his face. It was gone before she could convince herself it had been there. "I think you regard me as the demon king who will rush in at the last moment and forbid the marriage. Do you not?" Because what he said held an element of truth, Vicki was too confused to answer. He continued coldly, "Such a course was never farther from my mind. Furthermore, it may comfort you to know that Robert loves his fiancée far too deeply to allow ill health to come between them."

She moistened dry lips, feeling put down by his clever deduction. It was several minutes before she was able to say quietly, "I hope, should the tests not prove negative, that you keep the result from her until after the honeymoon."

His face was entirely without expression as he looked down at her for a long moment. Then, with a curt little bow, he motioned her forward to join the others in the buffet.

The rest of the evening was an ordeal for Vicki, trying to be spontaneous and natural when, with every fiber of her being, she was aware of Guy's forbidding presence.

He was natural enough, even bantering at times, with Susie and Gerard. He was attentive and courteous to herself; but she sensed a new barrier between them, a barrier far more formidable than his habitual one of cool politeness.

By the time she sank into bed that night at the hotel she had cultivated an intense dislike of him. It was pure bad luck that they had to meet him at all. The sooner he went on his lecture tour, the better. She snuggled down into bed and tried to relax, irritated beyond measure to find that all she remembered was the way he had looked at her. Nothing else.

CHAPTER FIVE

The possibility of complications had not once crossed her mind when Vicki had set out on the journey from London to the Jasseron farm. There had been no reason to doubt that Susie could have outgrown her heart weakness until her collapse at the Château Brissard. The idea that there could be something seriously wrong struck Vicki like a mortal blow. Even the knowledge that Robert loved Susie too well to allow ill health to come between them did not help. Strong though his love for her might be, it was powerless to right anything that might be wrong with Susie's heart.

Vicki had hidden her anxiety from Susie, making light of it when she had taken her to the hospital that morning in Sarah. It was only when her sister had been swallowed up by the wide hospital entrance that she began to tremble with apprehension. The morning was fine, the sun warm and rich, but Vicki was cold inside.

They had grown closer together through the years with a rare harmony unhampered by partings or petty jealousies. Vicki's love for Susie was such that she had given her up to Robert wholeheartedly, knowing she was going to be happy—but for how long? Every minute seemed an hour as she fixed her eyes on the hospital entrance like a condemned man watching the clock.

The constant trickle of outpatients was broken occasionally by bunches of pretty nurses coming off duty while others stepped daintily in. Eventually, her gaze wandered to the parking lot, not realizing until she saw it that she had been inadvertently seeking Guy's car. It was parked by several other opulent ones. As she stared at it, she offered up a silent prayer for Susie.

Susie unexpectedly appeared in the hospital entrance

running toward her, feet and hair flying. "It wasn't too bad. In fact our surgeon was quite pleased to say I have nothing to worry about," she announced joyfully as she slipped into her seat beside Vicki. "After I had the test I told him how I had tried to compete with Madame Brissard that night in the barn. He said I'd been very foolish and made me promise never to do it again." She sighed. "Pity the man's already spoken for. He would have been ideal for you, Vicki. Think how nice it would be for you to marry and settle down here, too." She turned suddenly to see Vicki's stricken look. "Why the tears?"

Vicki shook her head hastily and dabbed her eyes. "Don't take any notice of me. I'm . . . crying because you're going to be so happy." Putting her handkerchief away, she swallowed on a lump in her throat and jested weakly, "Pity your Robert isn't a twin, then I could have obliged and made it a double wedding!"

They were leaving the parking lot when Vicki braked to allow another car to enter and waved to Gerard Standon.

"Poor man," Susie said sympathetically. "He looks ill."

"He looks dissipated to me," Vicki said, not unkindly, looking both ways before swinging out onto the main road. "I've a notion that the man has received a blow large enough to make him slide. Probably been jilted."

"I wonder if the lady doctor Janera Molineux had anything to do with it. He was her tutor along with Robert and Guy," Susie said thoughtfully.

"I haven't a clue. In any case, I could be wrong," Vicki replied, her thoughts already elsewhere. "I think it will be a good idea to make our way back to the farm after lunch. It will give you plenty of time to call in on your beloved—and for goodness' sake, tell him about your test."

Vicki slept well that night. She spent the following morning with Susie on the gentle mountain slopes enjoying the sleepy, almost deserted countryside in the warm sun. It was another of those sunny, tranquil days which Vicki had experienced since driving from the coast; when time paused to hover with a breathless hush, as though the hurry and bustle of the world outside was, as yet, unknown, giving one a feeling of peace and security.

Mountains, she decided, were the ideal place to recover from the mental stress of everyday life. She was acquiring a taste for simple country pleasures and found it well worth exchanging the amenities of city life to indulge in a quiet one where one glowed with health and contentment. It was good to see Susie so happy, too. The only cloud on her horizon was her sharing a home with her future mother-in-law.

They had been invited to spend the afternoon and evening at the Château Brissard. They arrived soon after lunch to find Robert waiting for them. Maman, he said, had left for a garden *fête* where they had a stall. She had gone ahead leaving him to take them along. It was held in a well-preserved château not far away from the Château Brissard. Robert was telling Susie, who sat beside him in the car, all about it. Vicki, in the back seat, heard him refer to it as the Château de Venaud, but paid slight attention. She was interested in several groups of picnickers along the roadside who were taking advantage of the weather to indulge in a veritable banquet. Unlike the English, the French picnicked in style with cloth-covered trestle table, the lot.

The Château de Venaud was of 18th-century design, and Vicki's first glimpse of it through the trees of the parkland was very impressive. Built of stone with a carved façade and twin towers, it was as well-preserved as the magnificent gardens surrounding it.

The spacious courtyard with its clock tower topped by a weather vane was filled with stalls and side shows. They parked the car and made their way through happy jostling crowds to Madame Brissard's stall. She was doing good business with willing helpers and was much too busy to say more than a few words to them, so they mingled with the crowd and joined in the fun.

Vicki loved the organized chaos, the bouquets of happy faces and the delightful background music provided by a concertina playing lilting French tunes. She was parted from Susie and Robert by the crowd. When she saw them again they were so absorbed in each other that she had not the heart to butt in.

She enjoyed herself nevertheless, taking her turn at a side show where one had to trap a dummy fox as it shot out of a drainpipe. By sheer luck she made it and was presented with a prize, a delicious small replica in brown suède of Topo, the captivating mouse puppet with its two prominent front teeth.

"Bravo, *mademoiselle!*"

Her heart did a somersault. Guy Ransart, high, wide and handsome, in a gray suit, was looking down at her.

She gurgled happily. "I wasn't aware you attended garden *fêtes,* Doctor Ransart."

"I don't," he said dryly. "This one came to me. It has been held at the Château de Venaud for generations."

Her dark eyes with their slight outward tilt widened up at him.

"It is your château?" she asked breathlessly.

"Did not Robert tell you? Where is he, by the way?"

"They are around somewhere," she said vaguely.

"Ah, you are being discreet about leaving the lovers together. Would you care to look over the château, *mademoiselle?*"

"I'd love to," she answered, on a cloud. The unexpectedness of their meeting had scattered her wits, but she managed to walk sedately beside him allowing him to steer her through the crowd. "I remember Robert mentioning something about the Château de Venaud on the way here, but I didn't connect it with you. Actually, I wasn't paying much attention to what he was saying. I was too engrossed in the scenery."

A picture loomed between them of a mountain road and two cars within inches of crashing. She wondered, gazing at his firm profile quickly, if he was remembering that she had the same excuse for missing the one-way sign at the foot of the hill. He made no comment but preceded her politely into a lofty hall and up a beautifully carved staircase to the upper regions of the château.

Leisurely, he opened doors leading into spacious rooms; exquisitely furnished, combining elegance with comfort and beauty in an unpompous way. To her surprise, the bathrooms were a dream of modern delight with every convenience. She liked the light fruitwood paneling with the prevalence of curves in the mouldings of wall and door panels and the rich floral effect of the upholstery.

The long, elegant *salons* on the ground floor with their huge fireplaces conjured visions of a log fire on frosty evenings bringing to life the beautiful tones of the furniture and furnishings. There was no time to linger, but she would have liked more than a peep at the very masculine room her host obviously used as an office-cum-study with its charming desk and discreet furnishings.

They had walked at last into the main *salon* which, he said, was in daily use. It was highlighted by wall-length curtains providing a wonderfully warming background for the Directoire furniture, splendid Bessarabian rugs and Audubon prints on the walls.

"A touch of genius in mixing the old with the new," she said, looking around in admiration.

"You like it?"

"It's fabulous," she breathed. Lightheaded with so much elegance and beauty, she went on, almost to herself, "There's something about *le style français* that is irresistable and utterly charming."

"Like our scenery," he said, a devilish twinkle in his eye. So he had remembered that first meeting on the mountain road!

"What do you think of our country?" he asked, seating her in a chair in the sun by the transparent curtained window.

"The whole atmosphere is relaxing," she replied, thinking it was hardly the term to describe his presence and its effect on her emotions. Her heart was thumping like a teenager's on her first date.

Gone was the protective, cool front she had worn through the years at the airport where the attractive male staff, devastating in their uniforms and mostly married, had badgered her for dates. Gone, too, was her former dislike of the cool, courteous Frenchman now pouring her a glass of wine from a cut glass decanter. She accepted it politely and managed not to spill it.

He leaned nonchalantly against the window frame to look down at her slim figure as she sat with both dainty feet together. "How does it feel to know there is no cause to be concerned now with Mademoiselle Susie's health? There is, of course, the small weakness rheumatic fever usually leaves behind, but I think she appreciates the importance of not overdoing things. You are happy, *non*?"

"Very happy. I only hope she is as happy in her marriage." Vicki paused, knowing she ought to enlarge on her reply, knowing he could have no idea she was against Susie living with her future mother-in-law. He could misunderstand.

He did. "I think you can leave that to Robert. He is a splendid fellow, and they are very much attached to each other." A pause, then, "Is it because Mademoiselle Susie is marrying a Frenchman that you have doubts? You do not imagine Frenchmen making good husbands?" Vicki stared aghast at the way he had misconstrued, watching his mood change to one of icy politeness as he went on,

"You have no doubt heard that the average Frenchman also acquires a mistress. Do not some Englishmen do likewise? And why? Because they have married indiscriminately instead of marrying with the heart. There is also the lustful type which abounds in any country." His deep voice had quickened in an alien way. Now it slowed down, his blue eyes glinting darkly. "And the cold type of woman who can drive a normal man away." He straightened. "When two people are truly mated there are no such problems. I'd say Robert and his fiancée are two of these more fortunate people."

Vicki was shaken because, unwittingly, she had pierced his calm exterior. She knew doctors had to be careful in their choice of a wife and had imagined him choosing one by a process of elimination and deciding on the worthy doctor Janera. So he must love her. A spasm of something akin to jealousy shot through her. Susie had hinted at hidden fires beneath the immaculate exterior. He was probably banking them up until he married his lady doctor.

There was a choked feeling in her throat; she had the urge to escape. She put down her unfinished glass of wine having lost the taste for it and said stiffly, "I have no objections at all to Robert. I like him very much and have no doubt that he will make Susie very happy."

"You will be lonely when your sister marries?"

"Naturally. I shall miss her, but I shall get over it."

"What is your occupation, *mademoiselle*?"

"I am a secretary at an air terminal."

"Ah, you have a dashing pilot waiting for your return, *non*?" This with his eyes on her ringless hands.

"No." She stood up, clutching her purse. "I must be going. My sister will be looking for me."

His smile held a glint. "Your sister, along with Robert and Madame Brissard, will be in the small *salon* for refreshment. I will take you to them, then I have to leave."

"Refreshment?" she echoed. "Surely you don't provide everyone with refreshment?"

"A large *salon* is cleared of furniture and a trestle table is set down the middle for the organizers and helpers. The smaller *salon* is for my personal friends."

A manservant met them as they left the *salon* with a bouquet of roses, gladioli and carnations, beautifully arranged. "For Mademoiselle," he said with a bow.

"*Merci*, Paul," Guy said, as Vicki accepted them.

"They are beautiful," she said, eyes shining, when the manservant withdrew. "Thank you—and thank you for showing me around. It's very kind of you."

"It has been a pleasure, *mademoiselle*," he answered, and walked with her to the small *salon*.

There was dancing in the courtyard later, and all the young people joined in. The music was provided by the concertina; the atmosphere was lighthearted and full of gaiety. Yet Vicki was not in the mood. She had joined in the dancing, flitting from one partner to another without coherent thought. In bed that night, she wished achingly for the wedding to proceed quickly without a hitch. Further than that she did not care one way or the other.

Thursday morning brought rain. Vicki opened the shutters of her room to the scent of rain-washed air and damp earth. Robert called to take Susie to the church to discuss wedding arrangements, so Vicki spent the morning writing letters and helping Madame Jasseron with the chores. She thought the gentle Frenchwoman did not look well and made her sit down while she prepared the midday meal. Robert would keep Susie out for the day, and Monsieur Jasseron did not come in from the fields until the evening, so there were only the two of them for dinner.

They lingered over their coffee. Madame Jasseron had eaten sparingly, and Vicki had not done much better. She appeared to have lost her appetite.

"I think it is the change of life affecting me," Madame said, confidentially. "I never had children and wanted them so much."

"Have you told your doctor?" Vicki asked in concern.

Madame shook her head. "We have no faith in doctors, my husband and I. Years ago when we consulted our doctor about my failure to conceive, he merely shrugged his shoulders and advised us to adopt a baby. It was not like having one of our own, you understand?"

Vicki nodded visualizing Madame Jasseron's anguish through the years as she saw her friends starting their families and knowing that she herself was barren.

After dinner, she persuaded Madam Jasseron to rest in her room while she did the dishes and left everything ready for the evening meal. When, after a wash and change, she peeped into her room to find Madame fast asleep, Vicki slipped on a white raincoat and scarf to brave the weather.

She had decided to take a run to an old town perched high in the hills behind the farm, that had fascinated her since her arrival. It was dominated by an old castle that simply begged to be explored.

The rain had stopped when she set out in Sarah, and the sun peeped out between darkly tinged, ominous clouds. Everywhere was the stillness of a place after rain. There were no toilers in the vineyards, now a yellow green after giving up their grapes. But the rain had brought out the mimosa in all its golden glory. Vicki loved mimosa and had bought it eagerly when it appeared in the stores to brighten the winter gloom. Whenever she bought it in the future, it would bring back poignant memories of a dream country so easy to love suspended in time.

The road ahead was an upward incline which Sarah did not appear to take with her usual exuberance. It was probably one of her off-days, too. Sometimes when Sarah had these moods it was a sure sign of trouble ahead. She had a nose for it. Vicki sincerely hoped not and left her, ignoring the disgruntled protest when she braked before the entrance to the town.

She walked between narrow streets of mellowed houses to find the town center vibrating with life. It was market day; stalls were everywhere, making it difficult to get around. It was too congested to enjoy the novelty of a strange town, so Vicki wandered on to join a small group of people at the entrance to the castle.

This also proved to be disappointing, for the interior was dark, sinister and depressing. Vicki finally emerged to pouring rain. The stores and cafés were full to overflowing with people taking shelter. By the time she reached Sarah, Vicki was drenched. Slipping inside, she switched on the windshield wiper and watched it make little difference to the sheet of rain continually dousing it.

Sarah was stubborn and started off eventually on what sounded like a muffled sneeze. She slithered on the downhill road, for the deluge had made the asphalt as slippery as an ice rink. The bends in it, which on ascending had appeared gently curving, were now nightmare twists on blind corners. Vicki's eyes began to ache as she tried to pierce the curtain of rain. When an unexpected fall of earth and stones bounded down on the road a few feet ahead, she stamped on the brake and forgot to steer.

Sarah skidded across the road and finally skidded to a halt at an ominous angle with her offside wheels deep in the rain-soaked earth. Vicki clambered out, shaken but unhurt. Looking back, she saw the small landslide causing the trouble was only a small heap of rubble. She could easily have driven around had she not lost her nerve.

She called herself all kinds of a fool. Her scarf felt as

heavy as wet seaweed and the rain dripped from the end of her nose. She thought expectantly of a phone booth. Disconsolately, she looked around, wondering in which direction to turn, when she saw the approaching car—a dark shape in the downpour. It pulled up promptly, the door flew open and a deep voice exclaimed, "Mademoiselle Kendon! *Montez donc!*"

Dazedly she obeyed and slid in beside Guy Ransart and whipped off her sodden scarf. "It's Sarah," she gasped. "She's stuck at the side of the road!"

"Sarah?" he repeated on a frown. "You mean Mademoiselle Susie?"

"No, the car. We call her Sarah."

He kept a straight face, though not without effort, leaning across her to see that the door was tightly closed. "I'll send someone along later to tow her in. Whatever are you doing out on a day like this?"

Vicki, mopping her streaming face, felt a large masculine handkerchief thrust into her hand as her own became waterlogged.

"I've been to visit Castle Clair. It was very disappointing, so dank and musty." She shivered at the memory. The next moment a small flask of brandy was pushed beneath her nose.

"Drink," he commanded. "It will save you a chill."

The smell of it made her recoil until she saw his grim look. Then she noticed the dark patches on his shoulders and his damp hair drooping in curling tendrils on his forehead. He was obviously on his rounds and was impatient at the delay. Not wanting to hinder him further, she swallowed a mouthful of the fiery liquid. It made her cough, but he insisted on her taking several more gulps before he returned it to the first aid box.

Heat flowed through her veins. She returned his handkerchief and was running her fingers through her flattened locks when he gripped her shoulder.

"You're soaked," he said. "Take off that raincoat."

He helped her to struggle out of it before reaching over to the back seat to pick up a car rug. She was very much aware of his nearness as he draped it around her shoulders. For breathless seconds he regarded her intently, taking in the dark pools of her eyes, her face glowing from the rain, and her hair curling becomingly around her small head in damp waves.

"I have a call to make, then I'll drive you to the farm," he said, turning to start the car with the manner of one not welcoming the delay.

Chilled by his brusqueness, she said stiffly, "I'm sorry to have to take you out of your way, but it's entirely unnecessary. We're sure to pass a garage, soon, and all you need to do is to drop me off. They will do the rest."

His only reply was to concentrate on his driving, content to let the windshield wiper tick away the silence. Vicki bit her lips. He would be the one to pick her up, she thought grimly. Firmly, she decided on no more complications during her stay in France if she could possibly avoid them. Not that there could be any concerning the man sitting beside her.

His future, like his career, was already mapped out in his agile brain. A lecture tour to make the lady doctor aware of his absence, then a return to her welcoming arms and marriage. In a way they were two of a kind, both immaculate and diamond-bright, products of a medical machine. Their children, if they had any, would grow up with every material advantage minus the cuddling and love that parents with a less exacting career would provide. Vicki trembled at the thought of his children. A choked feeling came into her throat, and she cast around blindly for something to say to stop her painful flow of thought.

"How is Mr. Standon?" she asked, in a small voice. "We saw him the other day at the hospital."

He swung the car around onto a rough track. "He will be all right eventually. He neglected his health and now has to pay for it."

"Poor man! He's not married?"

"No," he said laconically.

She waited for him to enlarge upon the clipped syllable, but he said no more. Minutes later he pulled up at a farm gate and turned up the collar of his raincoat. "Sorry I have no magazines for you to peruse while you wait, but I will not be long. There is a car magazine in the glove compartment."

He stepped out into the deluge to stride along a rutted road to the farmhouse.

She picked up the magazine he had mentioned, casually turning over the pages. Admiring the sleek automobiles, she wondered if he was buying a new one for his honeymoon. Restlessly, she tossed it back into the glove compartment. A glance at her watch told her the fading light was not due to rain clouds but night closing in. Her thoughts strayed to Madame Jasseron; she hoped she felt a little better when she awoke. She had grown fond of her, and it worried her to think her illness could be something serious. Her thoughts were still on the Frenchwoman when Guy returned.

He opened the car door, bringing in a rush of damp air. Then he was wiping his streaming face and hair on the handkerchief she had used and she felt idiotically pleased about it.

He had started the car when she said, "I'm rather worried about Madame Jasseron. She hasn't looked well these past two days. This morning she appeared to be in pain; her stomach was slightly distended. When I mentioned a doctor, she wasn't keen." She looked at his dark, clear profile revealing nothing of his thoughts and tacked on hastily, "I don't want to detain you, for I know you must be very busy with calls, but I would feel happier if you could just drop in casually to see if she is all right."

"What about Monsieur Jasseron? Does not the fact that his wife is in pain suggest him calling in a doctor?"

"He doesn't know. Madame is doing her best to keep it from him." She paused, about to tell him more, but decided that what Madame Jasseron had told her was in confidence. As he said nothing, she wondered if she had been wise in telling him at all. "It may be nothing and we could arrive to find her well—but she looks so dreadfully tired and spent," she tacked on lamely.

Against her small husky tones, his deep voice sounded strong and vibrant. "It is not unusual for a woman approaching middle age to look that way. Most women tend to become a little anemic as they grow older. I don't recall seeing her name in Doctor Molineux's files, but since you're so concerned I will come in with you.

Monsieur Jasseron, visibly upset, met them at the door of the farmhouse. "*Le médicin*," he exclaimed. "Ah, I am so pleased that Mademoiselle has brought you to look at my wife. She is so sick. Come, I will take you to her."

Guy flickered a glance at the surprised Vicki before taking the stairs two at a time followed by Monsieur Jasseron, who thanked her first for bringing him.

Vicki went into the kitchen to prepare a meal for Monsieur Jasseron. His raincoat and leg coverings had been flung on a chair to drip into a pool of water on the tiled floor. He must have dropped them there to look for Madame, whom he usually found putting the last touches to their evening meal, when he came in. He went upstairs to find her in bed. When Guy arrived he had naturally thought she, Vicki, had brought him. Poor Monsieur Jasseron!

She picked up the soaked things to hang them in a recess to dry and mopped up the water. The big kettle was boiling, and there was an appetizing smell of a pie baking in the oven when Guy entered to find her laying the table.

His smile was tinged with mockery. "Madame Jasseron is in an advanced state of pregnancy," he said, slipping a long, narrow hand inside his raincoat to draw out a pad and pen. Rapidly, he wrote, tore off the sheet and placed it on the table. "Perhaps you will see that this is filled as soon as possible. When I called at that farm earlier on I phoned to arrange for your car to be picked up. Your . . . Sarah should be delivered first thing tomorrow morning."

"Oh, thank you," Vicki said dazedly. She was still trying to take in the news of Madame Jasseron having the baby she had longed for so much. "It's like a miracle," she said, dark eyes shining.

He lifted a brow. "A miracle, *mademoiselle?*" he queried, replacing pad and pen inside his raincoat.

"Yes. You see, Monsieur and Madame Jasseron have been so disappointed that they have been denied children. Now they are really having their baby. I'm so happy for them."

"One of the main reasons for a woman being unable to conceive a child is when the fallopian tube is blocked. Did she not seek medical advice?"

"Oh yes. She was advised to adopt a baby if she wanted one."

He shrugged broad shoulders. "Then whatever it was has cleared up. Madame is to get her wish. You like children, *mademoiselle?*"

"I adore them and, of course, they are awfully essential to a happy marriage. I'm going to love Susie's." She looked at him, her dark eyes more appealing than she knew. "She will be able to have children, won't she?"

Before he could answer Monsieur Jasseron came in, his florid face beaming.

"One moment, doctor. You must join us in a toast before you leave. This is a very happy and proud moment for my wife and me," he cried excitedly.

Guy looked swiftly at his watch and seemed about to

refuse, but Monsieur Jasseron had already procured a bottle of champagne and glasses.

Guy's glance at Vicki as he passed her glass was both tolerant and amused at his host's excitement. He lifted his glass.

"To Madame," he said.

"To Madame," they echoed.

The toast drunk, Monsieur Jasseron picked up the bottle. "A drink for my wife. It will not harm?"

Guy put down his glass. "I doubt if anything can harm Madame Jasseron in her present ecstatic state, except too much work. You do understand, Monsieur Jasseron, that your wife must take things easy from now on?"

"I will hire a regiment of servants," he declared rashly.

Guy laughed with a flash of white teeth. "That won't be necessary. Too little activity can be as harmful as too much. Madame Jasseron must be active to a certain extent but she must not overdo it. *Comprenez*?"

Monsieur Jasseron made a shrugging gesture, lifting open hands palms upward. Then, thanking Guy again as though he had taken a hand in Madame's condition, he bade him *au revoir* and ambled off happily to take his wife her drink.

Vicki, busying herself at the table, said without lifting her head, "You didn't answer my question about Susie having a baby."

The reply came in almost a drawl. "You worry too much about others. Put that champagne bottle away in case Monsieur Jasseron decides to get drunk on his victory. He's in a mood to celebrate. Incidentally, Madame is well enough to get up. I have given her a pill and left enough for her to take until you have the prescription dispensed. Your sister will be all right. *Au revoir*, Mademoiselle Kendon."

Susie shared Vicki's pleasure when she heard about Madame Jasseron.

"I've been thinking, Vicki," she said when they made

their way to bed that night. "I wish you would stay until Madame has her baby, then you would be here when we come back from our honeymoon. I'd like that," she said wistfully.

"If Madame Jasseron asks me to stay I will, if it means so much to you," Vicki answered thoughtfully. Guy Ransart would be away soon on his lecture tour and somehow the suggestion had its appeal.

Madame Jasseron did ask her to stay the next morning. After breakfast, Vicki was about to follow Susie upstairs to get ready for a trip into town when Madame stopped her. She appeared to be much better. The drawn look had left her face leaving a happy, serene expression.

"I wish you could stay with me until I have the baby," she said. "My husband has engaged a woman from the village to work in the dairy each day so you would not have to help with a lot of chores." She sighed. "To tell you the truth, *mademoiselle*, I'm scared. I'm no longer young and things could so easily go wrong."

Vicki hugged her warmly. "You're as jittery as Susie is. She is scared to death that something will prevent her from marrying her Robert. Nothing is going wrong for you, and to prove it I'll stay until it's all over. And I must not forget your prescription when we are in town this morning. I'm going to call in at the wool store for baby patterns and wool. Believe me, *madame*, you'll have no time for morbid thought." She looked toward the kitchen doorway at the sound of a car. "That sounds like Sarah."

She moved into the courtyard to see Sarah entering it almost coyly. And well she might, for she had been cleaned and polished to an immaculate degree. A young man in workman's overalls with a beret perched provocatively on his dark hair poked his head through the car window.

"Mademoiselle Kendon?" he inquired politely. Then, as Vicki smiled and nodded, "Your car, *mademoiselle*."

"*Merci*," she said. "If you will wait a moment while I fetch my purse I will pay you."

"*Non, non.*" The young man was adamant.

"Then you must accept a tip, and I will pay your garage," she insisted.

He grinned. "I understand—*mon garage*." He bowed from the waist. "I am Doctor Ransart's *homme-à-tout-faire*. At your service."

Vicki caught on quickly. *Homme-à-tout-faire* translated into English meant man-of-all-work. So Guy Ransart had not phoned a garage—he had asked his man to pick Sarah up instead. She watched the man leave with mixed feelings. She would have preferred to pay a garage instead of being in debt to Guy Ransart.

CHAPTER SIX

The trip into town in Sarah was made joyous by Susie, who was starry-eyed and full of her wedding the following day. Vicki felt her happiness along with Madame Jasseron's as though it were her own. She went to the *pharmacie* with Madame's prescription, leaving Susie to collect her wedding dress from the dressmakers. She did her shopping, stopped for wool and patterns for baby clothes and was depositing her purchases in the car when someone hailed her in English.

It was Gerard Standon. He strode forward looking slimmer but minus his jaded look. "Hello, Miss Kendon. How are you and your pretty sister?"

"We're fine, thanks. As a matter of fact I'm waiting for Susie. She's collecting her wedding dress for the great day tomorrow."

He gave a mock sigh. "Ah me, to be young and in love!"

"You're not so old," she said, borrowing his easy smile and feeling a bond between them because he was one of her countrymen.

"I feel old when I meet someone young and glowing like you. What about having a coffee with me?"

"I'd love to. Not too far away, though, because Susie will miss us."

They strolled across the square to a small café with tables beneath gay awnings. "She is sure to see us here," he said seating her. He sat down himself, gave the waiter the order and placed folded hands on the table to look across at her. "I hope you're not leaving directly after the wedding."

"No, I'm staying for a while."

"I'm pleased to hear it. Maybe we can meet occasionally."

Her pause was barely perceptible, but she knew he noted it.

"I don't see why not. If you live in Nice, it won't be very often," she said frankly.

"I don't," he answered on a wry smile. "I happened to be in Nice when we first met. Not engaged or anything, are you?"

"No. Why do you ask?"

"Because you appeared to be cagey about seeing me. Don't you enjoy going out with men?"

"I don't mind. Why should I?"

"I don't know. But I do know I would like to meet you sometimes, if I may. You don't bore a chap with idle chatter, and I've reached the stage when I like a pretty woman to be intelligent, too."

"Thanks very much," she said flippantly. "I'm glad you didn't say you preferred an intelligent woman to a pretty one. It would have been a severe blow to my ego."

His experienced eyes roved over her smiling face with calculated appraisal. "An unusual combination," he mused, as though to himself. "Dark eyes and tawny hair. You're more than pretty, you're one of the daintiest morsels I've had the pleasure of feasting my eyes on."

The waiter's arrival with the coffee coincided with Susie's.

"I wondered where you were," she said brightly. "I saw you over Sarah's top when I was putting my dress and wedding presents away." Excitedly, she sat down beside Vicki. "I've had two more presents. Hello, Mr. Standon. Better, I hope?"

"Yes, thanks." He addressed the waiter, who still hovered. "Another coffee, please, for Mademoiselle." The waiter departed, and Gerard looked at Susie with amusement. "You have the look of a mischievous puppy. All ready for the great day tomorrow?"

She gurgled, "Who wouldn't be?"

"Look out!" Vicki said, on a light laugh. "The man is tossing compliments around like confetti."

Gerard sat back with an air of content. "Guy is giving a bachelor party at his lodge in the hills tonight for Robert. I'm looking forward to it. It will be like old times."

He accepted the coffee politely from the waiter, passing it to Susie and casting them a shy grin of experienced charm. Vicki felt its appeal and wondered if he was a bachelor from choice or because the woman he wanted had been denied him.

"So Doctor Janera Molineux will not be going," she said.

Fleetingly the smile left his face to return to a mouth gone awry.

"No. Strictly for males. When her papa is well again I wouldn't be at all surprised if she and Guy didn't announce their engagement."

The ache in Vicki's heart made her smile brittle. "That leaves you the only bachelor. I'm surprised some pretty Frenchwoman hasn't hooked you before now."

He shrugged. "Maybe I don't happen to be the marrying sort, or I could have been too busy having a good time. A car takes you to the bright spots so easily, and it's a gay country."

So he was not giving anything away. But the shadow on his face brought there by the mention of Janera told more than he admitted. It was quite possible that he was in love with her. He was not all that much older. He could have been in his early 20's when he took the job as tutor to Guy, Robert and Janera. That would make him not much over 40, and Janera in her late 20's.

Then suddenly Janera was there, a slim shadow across their table.

"Mind if I join you?" she said. "I'm simply gasping for a coffee."

Instantly Gerard procured an extra chair and she sat

down, chic and expensive-looking. She had an aura of elegance about her created by that intangible asset, a really exclusive perfume. "I hope I'm not intruding," she said sweetly, surveying all three with delicate uplifted brows. Casually, she drew forth a leather cigarette case and handed it around. Everyone refused politely, but Gerard was there with his lighter to oblige.

"We weren't exactly in a huddle," he said drily. "How's Papa?"

"Improving," she answered, leaning across to his lighter. Inhaling, she leaned back in her chair and looked at him obliquely. "How are you?"

"Very well," he said briefly.

"Guy said you were back to stay." She bestowed a brilliant smile on the waiter when he brought her coffee, but the smile she gave Gerard was less bright. "You're thinner," she said.

"Perhaps I want to look my best for the wedding tomorrow."

"Of course." She looked at Susie. "Thanks for the invitation. I'll do my best to be there, but I'm feeling terribly tired at the moment."

As he watched her drink her coffee, Gerard looked and sounded hostile.

"Guy is helping you out, is he not? Surely he gets through more work than your papa does. You shouldn't be so tired."

She loosened her coat from elegant shoulders. "I didn't go to bed until the small hours. I went to a party with Guy last night. The man's indefatigable, as fresh as the dew this morning. I'm as limp as a puppet."

"Never mind," Gerard said sardonically. "Guy will probably have bags under his eyes in the morning after tonight's party."

Vicki dismissed the pang brought on by the linking of Guy's name with Janera's and concentrated on the odd pair in front of her. For they were behaving oddly. As old friends they could naturally take liberties in bantering with each other, but these two were more like battering rams drawing in their horns between thrusts.

It seemed to Vicki that Janera had deliberately mentioned attending a party with Guy in order to provoke Gerard. But Gerard had not risen to the bait. He chatted with Susie and herself while Janera drank her coffee and listened until she was drawn into the conversation. As Vicki expected, Janera was the first to make a move and they all followed.

Saturday morning dawned with a mist hovering. Vicki, entering with the wedding dress on her arm, found Susie peering anxiously through her bedroom window. She had taken it to press out the creases and now hung it on the closet door.

"Good morning, poppet. It's going to be a glorious day when the mist clears," she said reassuringly. She touched the folds of the dress almost reverently. "It's a lovely dress; you're going to look ravishing."

Her own dress, utterly feminine in blue, had a fluid sensual appeal in a subtle combination of suède and pure silk. Topped by a hood lined in white silk, it clung to the slender lines of her figure becomingly. Gerard arrived on time to give the bride away and Vicki, with a lump in her throat, thought she had never seen Susie look so lovely. Her dress, in a medieval style in white lace with a full length veil, suited her to perfection. The sun shone as Vicki had predicted.

Everything went smoothly, with the bridal party calling first at the town hall for the civil ceremony before proceeding to the church. During the ceremony, Vicki held Susie's bouquet, ever-conscious of the tall figure of Guy standing by Robert.

At last it was all over, photographs were taken, and the bride and groom were whisked away to the reception. Vicki was helped into a car by Guy who slid in beside her.

He gave her a charming smile as he took in the youthful curves of her figure, the sweet tranquillity of her face and the liquid brightness of her eyes, for Vicki was trying hard to suppress the tears.

"May I say how lovely you look, *mademoiselle*? You almost outshone the bride," he said softly.

She wondered if he had said the same to Janera who, in church, had looked delightful in pale lemon. The thought steadied her as nothing else would, and she was able to answer him perfectly naturally.

"*Merci*," she said. "We are fortunate to have such a heavenly day."

He agreed. "The weather certainly makes a difference, although I doubt if the bride or groom would have noticed it particularly. They were far too engrossed in each other."

"Frenchmen don't usually marry late, do they?" she asked curiously.

"The majority don't. Some take longer to catch than others."

"Like you?" she said, then wondered why on earth she had said it.

"*Eh bien,* my time will come," he said. "It has probably come already."

Vicki felt her heart jolt with pain. She was annoyed with herself for mentioning it when she was well aware of his being practically engaged to Janera. She sank back into the upholstery of the car with a sense of shock, for not until that moment did she realize that all the see-sawing of her emotions, her utter restlessness was due to one thing and one thing only. She was in love with the man at her side, the man who held a definite attraction for her from the day they met. She loved his long supple strength of limb, his eyes dark blue in anger, the way his defined lips curved into a smile, and his constant courtesy and gentleness.

The smile she gave him was bright, her voice as light as

it was possible to make it. "I hope you will be very happy," she said.

"No doubt about that," he answered.

Then the car was at the Château Brissard. They walked inside together and by the time they reached the *salon* where Susie and Robert stood to welcome them, she had her feelings under control. The long table with name cards in each place was ablaze with silver, cut-glass and marvelous flower arrangements. Champagne flowed amid the tinkling of glasses and the muted sounds of small talk. Guy proposed the toast, and everything went off smoothly.

Later, Vicki went upstairs with Susie to help her into going away clothes. Soon she was looking chic in a three-piece suit of jersey wool in turquoise with white accessories.

Susie's departure left an empty void Vicki did her best to fill. She dispatched wedding cake to friends and thought bitterly of a mother who could heartlessly relinquish all claim on her two daughters.

She found a great friend in Madame Jasseron, who introduced her into the French way of cooking, using butter with almost everything and enriching the simplest fish dish with a clot of cream. She accompanied her to the market, where the custom seemed to be to ignore goods on show and demand others from some mysterious place beneath the counter.

Arguments between customers and vendors were often heated but of short duration, for the average housewife would not be put off by questionable goods. She simply marched off in high dudgeon to the next vendor. Once Vicki witnessed an argument *en plein air*. Hot angry words were accompanied by wild gesticulations. Then, as everyone gathered around to enjoy it, the parties concerned were shaking hands. All was well!

Gradually, Vicki slipped into a world of drowsy contentment where time drifted along as casually as the horse-drawn tilted carts still used by the older generation, and where farmers milked their cows in orchards surrounded by strutting fowl.

When Monsieur Jasseron's van was awaiting spare parts, Vicki loaned him Sarah in which to make deliveries of his farm produce to the market. Since then Sarah had behaved very oddly. Normally at her best when a man was in command, she became sulky, grumbling when she was taken out in the early hours after requiring endless persuasion to start.

Beneath Vicki's gentle handling, she had been serene and obedient. Now she was like a harnessed mule kicking out, impatient and not at all herself. She could resent being used as a van and regarded it as a bit of a comedown. Then one day Monsieur Jasseron said she had been making rude noises, so Vicki decided to take her to a garage for an overhaul. The one recommended by Monsieur Jasseron was two kilometers away. So, one afternoon, when Madame Jasseron was resting, Vicki set out for the garage. Sarah, however, kept stalling and spluttering; eventually, when they came within sight of the garage, she came to an undignified halt.

Vicki gave her a reassuring pat and walked to the garage asking for a tow in. The man at the garage instantly obliged and examined Sarah's innards methodically. It would take him two to three hours to fix her—depending, with a shrug, on how many customers he had to contend with in between.

Vicki, knowing that time was not important to these friendly people, guessed it would be the following day before Sarah was delivered. So, thanking the man, she strolled in the direction in which she had come until a bus arrived.

The first vehicle to pass was a truck followed by a car traveling quickly. To her surprise it pulled up.

"*Bonjour, mademoiselle.* You have walked a long way and had better accept a lift to wherever you are going," Guy Ransart said smilingly.

"I'm not going anywhere. Sarah has given up; I've taken her to the garage for repairs. As it will take a while, I was strolling along until the bus passed," she explained, her disappointment over Sarah forgotten.

"If you are not in a hurry to return, you can accompany me on my rounds. I promise you will enjoy it."

She still hesitated at the open door. "Won't I be in the way?"

"Not at all."

She slid into the spacious seat beside him; his nearness and well-groomed fragrance set her heart beating in thick painful strokes, and senses long deprived of masculine companionship clamored outrageously inside her.

The car slipped away smoothly and, to Vicki, the day took on a magic quality. Soon the main highway was left behind, and they purred between vineyards and olive groves along roads sometimes so narrow that there was barely room for the big car to pass.

Guy slowed down while several goats crossed the road, stepping daintily as they searched for scraps. He waited for them to file into a field on the opposite side of the road before he drove on.

"You have seen how wine is made. Today you will see how brandy is distilled," he said. "Most of the people around here barely scratch a living from the soil, so the red wine they produce is as valuable to them as honey is to bees. It is not only a means of entertaining; it is also a food. They drink it to restore lost energy, to warm them after cold hours of toil in the fields, and as an aperitif to lift their spirits when misfortune has cast them down."

He pulled off the narrow road and braked. They walked between vineyards where the last of the grapes were being gathered amid much talk and laughter. They walked slowly along cobbled lanes between little carts drawn by small donkeys, and women walking with the easy grace of models. Children swarmed by on chubby legs pulling tiny handcarts of grapes while older ones successfully balanced baskets on their heads.

"*Bonjour, monsieur le médicin*," they said, greeting Guy from all sides. The children repeated it, their mouths blue with grape juice. Guy ruffled the small heads as they passed.

The small procession continued to a stone cave-like structure. Like the farmhouse nearby it was probably centuries old. Inside Vicki watched grapes being fed into slowly rotating rollers to break them in the process of making wine which was later barreled. The grapes were then crushed in a press with slatted sides to force the juice into a tub below.

Vicki was given a glass of last year's vintage which she found remarkably good. A smiling *vigneron* was pleased when she told him so and he explained that when all the juice was extracted from the grapes, the dry pressings went on to the distillery to make brandy.

Then Guy, who had left her there while he visited the farmhouse, returned and they walked down to the car. "Enjoying it?" he said, looking down at her with a smile that turned her heart over.

"Enormously," she answered, the wine glowing in her eyes as they shone up at him. "Do they make all the grapes into wine?"

His hand shot out to grip her elbow as she slithered on the cobbled road—puce colored and slippery from grapes trodden underfoot.

"No. Certain grapes are gathered earlier on to be stowed away in dark caverns or cellars where they are left to mature during the winter months. From Christmas onward until spring they are sold in perfect condition."

"It must be a hard life wresting a living from the soil,"

she said, slightly dizzy from the wine—or was it his nearness?

"But one which they all enjoy. They are mostly their own masters, growing what they choose and harvesting it happily in their own time. Consequently, their nerves do not become frayed at the edges like those who live in large cities."

They continued to another farm. This time, while Guy went into the farmhouse to see the farmer, his wife took Vicki to the cellars and, among donkey harness, farm implements and cobwebs, offered her a glass of rich red wine.

There Guy joined her after attending to his patient. Bending his head to enter, he gazed at her mockingly as she sat drinking the wine on an upturned barrel. "I hope you have not emptied the barrel," he teased. "You must leave room for the brandy later!"

They were on the fringe of the village when Guy stopped at a barn adjoining a farm. Inside were several tar boilers bubbling merrily in a sooty atmosphere. Guy explained that they contained the pressings left over from the wine making. The boilers, black and sticky, had thick stove pipes and a maze of copper piping. Youths, black as chimney sweeps, were carrying in armfuls of special pine logs to feed the fires. Each time they opened a stove door to throw in more wood, they were greeted by belching smoke and flames. Guy kept Vicki firmly in the doorway.

She was fascinated by the small Dante's Inferno. Presided over by obese men stripped to their perspiring waists, they appeared to be enjoying every minute of it. Commanding her to stay put, Guy strode over to the biggest of them, a man with a large girth and smile to match. Guy took hold of one of his soot-blackened arms, said something unprintable and proceeded to treat the burn on the muscular flesh. Then he bandaged it up, stressing the importance of keeping the wound clean and well wrapped.

They were offered a glass of the clear liquid trickling from the tar boilers. To her surprise, it was pure proof spirit, satin smooth with ten times the potency of the wine.

They drank and watched the last of the fires being replenished with logs. Then it happened. Vicki had returned her glass when she gave a cry of pain and clasped her face with trembling hands. She shook her head dumbly when Guy's fingers closed on her wrists in an attempt to drag them down. When he did so her eyes were streaming with tears.

It was the work of seconds for him to whip out his handkerchief and, lifting an eyelid, use it to dislodge the small fragment beneath it.

"*Pauvre enfant,*" he said. "I'm terribly sorry this had to happen."

He placed an arm about her, walking to the car and helping her inside before going around to the driver's seat. "It will sting for a while," he said, turning to rest an arm on the wheel and look down at her with concern. "Being a spark, it stuck to the lid. Can't feel any more of them, can you?"

She shook her head, continually wiping her eye which insisted upon watering. Suddenly he was bending over her and lifting the now swollen lid before taking the handkerchief from her to wipe the corner of her eye with her handkerchief. For moments he was so close that she could see his strong springy eyelashes, blue eyes and thick hair in a straight line across his forehead.

"Thank you, *monsieur*, for taking it out," she managed, quelling an almost uncontrollable urge to touch the firm brown cheek with the tips of her fingers.

"You will certainly not forget our wine making or brandy distilling," he said.

Those were not the only things she would never forget, she thought grimly, leaning her head back against the upholstery.

Once on the highway, he speeded up. "There's no point in collecting your car from the garage when you are in no state to drive. They can deliver it."

At the garage he slipped from the car and was back in a few minutes to tell her the car would be delivered the next day.

She thanked him and the rest of the journey was made in silence.

Madame Jasseron was concerned to see Vicki's blood-shot eye and insisted upon her resting while she prepared supper. After supper Vicki decided to go straight to bed. The injury to her eye had brought on a headache, and she was thankful to slip between the cool sheets.

A movement by the bed awakened her. Guy was there, his tall figure narrowing the dimensions of the room as he hovered above her.

He smiled and sat down on the bed facing her. "I'm sorry to wake you, but I think these eyedrops will ensure a better night."

He held a small phial in his hand and directed drops into her eye. "They will sting at first until the burning ache is soothed." He replaced the dropper and placed the phial on the table nearby.

Gradually, she felt the pain beneath the swollen lid ease.

"Thank you, *monsieur*," she said huskily. "As you said, the burning is already receding."

He rose to his feet pushing his hands into his pockets and said thoughtfully. "I'll leave the drops so that you can use them again tomorrow if the eyelid is still painful." He scanned her pale, strained face, noting the shadows beneath the dark eyes. "You have a headache? I will leave you a sleeping pill."

"No, thank you," she said hastily. "I do have one but I shall sleep now that my eyelid feels more comfortable." She swallowed, wishing there was a pill to make her immune to his presence. "You have been very kind."

He moved abruptly, picked up the small puppet Topo from the dressing table, and said, "I find the whole incident most regrettable. Had I not taken you with me it would not have happened." He replaced the puppet on the table. When he turned his expression told her nothing. "I would like to make it up to you by taking you out for dinner one evening."

To her disgust, her face flamed with color. "That is very kind of you, *monsieur*. The accident was not your fault; I was fortunate in having you to attend to it so promptly. You don't have to ask me out just because you feel responsible."

"You don't want to come?" he asked swiftly.

But Vicki was too sore to accept what was obviously an invitation to appease his conscience. "It's not a matter of not wanting to come. I will not accept an invitation given from a sense of duty."

For a brief unguarded moment a strange glint appeared in his eyes. Then it faded and he was regarding her with an odd expression. He made a small bow. "Mademoiselle Kendon, will you do me the honor of dining with me on Saturday evening at seven?"

There was a short silence while they measured glances. She saw a slow smile curve his lips; a boyish quirk of amusement, so far removed from his usual somewhat cynical air of detachment that it rocked her heart. And because she could not resist him, she found herself smiling, though rather tentatively.

"Very well, *monsieur*. I cannot refuse after all your kindness," she said at last demurely.

Again a bow, this time a mocking one. "A well returned shot. We are now what you call quits. A sound note to leave you on, is it not? *Bonne nuit,* Mademoiselle Kendon. Sleep well."

She heard him going swiftly downstairs, heard his deep voice followed by the voices of Monsieur and Madame Jasseron, then the sound of his car. A few moments later Madame Jasseron appeared.

"What a charming man he is," she said warmly. "He was quite concerned about your eye. While you were out Monsieur Standon called. He is phoning again in the morning."

Before she went to sleep, Vicki wondered about the two men. Gerard Standon was no problem. She still thought that he was bitter over some past hurt and had called up solely for company. She could go out with him offering a warm sympathy and knowing his company would not create complications. Guy was far more disturbing. His charm was smooth as silk and deadly as dynamite. She had never met anyone remotely like him before, never been so stirred by a look or gesture. She had only to hear his deep voice to become a bundle of conflicting emotions.

Vicki tried hard to convince herself that the delicious dissolving of her bones at his nearness was not love. It was the kind of feeling a teenager might have for a favorite film star or someone else equally unattainable. She had imagined love to be a gentle magic sensation amidst an aura of dreams. Instead she was plunged into turbulent waters, to be bruised and battered by a cold look from a man who had no idea of her struggles.

She snuggled down in bed, knowing she had been wrong to stay on and wishing with all her heart that Guy Ransart was already far away on his lecture tour.

CHAPTER SEVEN

When Vicki awoke the next morning her headache had disappeared, and her injured eyelid looked and felt normal. She washed and dressed and was not surprised to find Madame Jasseron already about to make coffee.

"It's no use," she said, when Vicki remonstrated with her for not sleeping in. "I'm much better now I'm taking the pills Doctor Ransart prescribed. Besides, I can't stay in bed."

There was a card from Susie. She had written to say everything was wonderful. Vicki passed the card to Madame Jasseron, who was pouring coffee beans into the grinder. "Ah, what it is to be young and in love!" she sighed as she returned the card. "You have that delight yet to come, *mademoiselle*."

Vicki laughed. "I might end up being a spinster."

Madame shook her head. "You are far too chic and pretty. You might marry a Frenchman!"

Vicki buttered a croissant and applied honey. "What, with all the competition from your wonderful French girls?" she exclaimed, a picture of the elegant lady doctor flickering in her mind.

"And why not?" Madame Jasseron ground coffee industriously. "You have the advantage of being different because you are English. Your accent is very attractive, and you have much kindness of heart. It shines in those dark eyes of yours and, one day, you are going to steal some man's heart just like that." She clicked her fingers.

"You're awfully comforting. I'm not really keen about marriage, but thanks for cheering me up," Vicki said lightly.

"It is you who cheer me up, *mademoiselle*. With you here I do not worry so much about the coming baby."

She poured boiling water on the freshly ground coffee. "I can't believe it is true after all these years. *Mon mari*, he thinks I shall have the baby with no trouble at all!"

"He could be right. It will help you enormously if you can think that way, too," Vicki said gently.

"I try," said Madame Jasseron.

It started to pour with rain about nine o'clock and at ten Sarah arrived back. To cheer up Madame Jasseron, Vicki took her for a run to the market. Madame enjoyed going to market, for after shopping, there was always a little chat with friends in a café nearby. Bits of scandal and the latest news were chewed over with hot rolls and coffee laced with brandy or rum. Madame Jasseron came in for her share of teasing with sly innuendoes and much back-patting and laughter.

They returned to the farm with Madame Jasseron brighter and too full of other people's problems to give a thought to her own. Around half past two she went to her room to rest, and Vicki prepared the evening meal. Today it was *pot-au-feu*: two pounds of brisket, two carrots, a large potato, a tiny bay leaf and a small clove of garlic. The whole was put into a stewpot, and with the lid tightly fastened, cooked slowly for at least four hours. The liquid made a delicious soup; the meat was sliced and served on its own. She had put it in the oven when the phone rang. She heard Guy's deep voice. "*Bonjour, mademoiselle*. How is the eye? I trust it is better."

"*Bonjour, monsieur*," she answered, breathless with surprise. "It's much better, thanks. The inflammation has gone."

He sounded amused. "Did I surprise you? Surely you did not think I would not inquire?"

"I didn't expect you to call. You did leave the eye-drops, for which I was very grateful. It's very kind of you to call when you're so awfully busy," she said on her second wind.

"It's all part of the job," he replied. "Don't forget our date on Saturday. *Au revoir*, Mademoiselle Kendon."

"*Au revoir*, Monsieur Ransart," she answered, replacing the phone to feel herself quivering.

Gerard rang up soon after. "Hello, Miss Kendon. What about dining with me tonight? That is, if you're not doing anything. There's quite a good hotel at the end of a pleasant drive, and they have excellent food. It's used mostly by residents who have a permanent reservation."

"I'd like to come," she answered.

The rain had stopped when Gerard called for her that evening. Stars blinked in a purple sky, and the rain-washed air was like champagne as they walked to his car. She liked his friendly smile and look of appraisal roving over her sleeveless dress in cream jersey with its matching coat. He was wearing a good-looking brown suit, beige shirt and brown tie. His eyes, crinkling at the corners, were clear and healthy, his face not so strained.

"You're looking much better," she said, settling down in her seat beside him.

"I feel better," he replied. "Guy has changed my pills and they're working wonders. Done much sightseeing?"

She told him about visiting the brandy distillery the previous day without mentioning her accident. She had no wish to talk about Guy. She was out to enjoy herself for the evening and shut out all thought of him, although she knew his name was sure to be spoken.

"Did you see the glassblowers? Their factory isn't far from the distillery."

It occurred to her that Guy would probably have taken her there if not for the accident. "No, I didn't," she answered. "It sounds interesting."

"It's only a small factory. The glass made there is similar to Venetian, but more durable. What do you think of this part of France?"

"I love it. The people are very likeable and the atmosphere is so friendly. Then there's the climate, that's friendly, too."

"Thought of getting a job here?"

"I don't think so. I've nothing to keep me here. Did you come in the first place with the intention of staying?" she asked curiously.

He turned the car from the main highway and they started to climb.

"I was a math teacher at the local elementary school, spending my summer vacation touring France. I liked it so much here, I went no farther. I was 24, saw an ad in the local paper for a tutor and answered it."

"I know you were tutor to Guy, but how did you happen to tutor Robert and Janera Molineux?"

"Guy's grandparents thought it would be good for the boy to have young company during his lessons. He was 12 when his parents and former tutor were lost in a plane crash. His father was a keen flier and owned his own plane. I don't know all the details, but all three were killed when the plane crashed in the Alps. Robert and Janera were neighbors."

Vicki, although interested, refrained from asking further questions. Gerard went on to talk of English families who were settling down in the hilly regions around them. They eventually stopped at an unpretentious but pretty hotel in a narrow street.

Inside, Vicki was surprised at the spaciousness of the dining room. They were escorted to a table by an affable waiter. Vicki sat down in full view of the room and entrance. The tables were filling rapidly and the clientèle were smartly dressed. The waiter brought them aperitifs and while Gerard studied the menu, Vicki stared at a couple who entered the room.

The woman, Janera Molineux, was gliding toward them in a black velvet evening cape, toggle-fastened. Her hair was piled high in a *diamanté* band. She walked sedately, her physical movements in tune with the languid flowing cape. Pausing at their table, she appeared to allow Gerard a moment for appraisal before she bestowed a brilliant smile on them both. By the time she had greeted them, her companion had joined them. "It's Papa's first time out since his illness," she said brightly.

Vicki looked with surprised interest at a short, plump man whose small black eyes and smart black moustache were the most impressive things about him. His round face wore a perpetual calculating expression. He was evidently a man who found food a diverting pastime he richly enjoyed. He spoke excellent English.

Two more chairs were brought, and Janera and her papa sat down. As Gerard had said, the food was excellent, the wine had just the right degree of smoothness and the coffee was perfect. Doctor Molineux was both amusing and entertaining, making light of his acute ulcer attack which was now gradually retreating under treatment.

Vicki listened most of the time, noticing that Gerard never looked directly at Janera, unless politeness demanded it, when he answered her questions. She had shed her cloak on the back of her chair to show a black dress in billowing, transparent silk organza with full floating sleeves gathered into sparkling crystal cuffs. One could see the delicate straps of her low-cut underskirt beneath the high neckline, and Vicki guessed it must have cost a pretty penny.

Her father was no less well groomed; his broad shoulders fitting squarely into a well-tailored, dark gray suit. His glance strayed often to Vicki's small face with its potentialities for beauty with a pleasure which ran deeper than admiration.

Gerard must have noticed it, for he remarked on it when they were returning in the car.

"Doctor Molineux has taken to you. He could hardly take his eyes away," he said.

"What happened to Madame Molineux?" Vicki asked curiously.

"She died years ago."

"He's quite a man, isn't he?" she mused. "He's also very well read and most amusing company."

"He's been around a bit."

"Don't you like him?"

"Let's say he doesn't like me."

She gave him a swift glance. "And why not?"

"He has his eye on bigger game for Janera. His one ambition is to have Guy for a son-in-law."

Her heart gave a painful jerk. "What's so special about Guy?"

"His breeding and his wealth. He has another château in the Loire valley, a villa in Cannes and an apartment in Montparnasse. Years ago, Janera was quite a tomboy. When she knew Guy was going to be a doctor she made a bet with him that she would become one before he did. She didn't, of course, but she carried it through and did very well for herself."

"I'd say she's still doing very well," Vicki said pleasantly.

"Janera is what her father made her."

"And that's why he does not approve of you; he thought you had designs on his daughter. Do you really like Janera, Gerard, or shouldn't I ask?"

"I like her. I always will, but that's as far as it goes."

"How do you know if you've never told her?"

"I could have done years ago if I hadn't always felt I wasn't good enough."

"Why? Because you weren't wealthy?"

"Partly. It's too late now. The irony of it is, I stand to make quite a bundle with my writing."

"Then why not tell her?"

She saw the sideways pull of his mouth, and his answer struck her like a blow.

"It wouldn't be any good. I really think she and Guy are in love with each other."

Poor Gerard, she thought. Her heart echoed, poor Vicki.

Madame Jasseron was looking very fit and well from taking life easy, although she was a woman who could not sit still and do nothing. She was knitting for her baby, helped by Vicki, and they were turning out some delightful small garments between them. One afternoon Vicki was pressing a coat she had made, when Madame Brissard called.

"Ah," she said pleasantly. "You are busy preparing for the baby. I am delighted for Madame Jasseron. She has been so disappointed through the years because there was no baby. Now she has her wish. That is very chic." She picked up the small garment knitted in white wool. "You have threaded it in pink ribbon for a girl, *non*?"

Vicki smiled, "We can always change the ribbon if it happens to be a boy."

"So you can. I suppose one day I shall be making them for Robert's children. Which brings me to my reason for calling. I am going to Robert's house."

Vicki blinked. "Did you say Robert's house?"

"*Pardon*, I should have said Robert's and Susie's house. Susie does not know about it yet. That was why Robert was so busy before the wedding arranging things. I wonder if you would like to see it. It's part of our estate and not far from our own château."

"I'd love to. I'll leave a note for Madame Jasseron. She is resting in her room and may be down before I'm back." Vicki felt torn between a desire to rush upstairs to change, and to kiss Madame Brissard. Swiftly she took in Madame's smart black slacks and white top with a scarlet chiffon scarf and decided to go as she was in her green slacks and cream sweater.

Madame Brissard's car drew up at a pink stone villa where white louvered shutters gleamed among a profusion of geraniums and wild rose climbers. Vicki left the car to stand gazing at it in admiration.

"You like it, *mademoiselle*?" Madame Brissard asked as she stood beside her.

"It's lovely!" Vicki breathed. "Susie will be delighted." A warm feeling toward Madame Brissard washed over her; the last worry over her beloved sister was swept away by the sight of the pretty villa.

Putting her arm through Madame's, a gesture she would not have imagined in her wildest dreams a week ago, she marched her into the villa.

The entrance hall had one mirrored wall, giving the room larger dimensions by reflecting the French wallpaper and delightful mosaic floor. Like all old farmhouses, the living quarters formed the heart of the villa. Over 60 feet in length, it was subdivided into living room, dining room, study and kitchen by sliding partitions. Both living room and dining room had a southern exposure with picture windows framing magnificent views and glass mobile walls opening out onto a terrace.

The elegant furniture, soft wall lighting and subtle contrasts in color and arrangement created an aura of sophisticated warmth. The villa had been built years ago with the intention of presenting it to the eldest son on his marriage, Madame Brissard said. Later, when the young couple had a family, they would take over the Château and the *grandpère* and *grand'mère* would retire to the villa.

"I doubt whether Susie will ever want to leave it," Vicki said.

Madame Brissard agreed. "Robert has become attached to it. He has worked so hard modernizing it. Fortunately the structure was sound, so there was no problem in removing walls and enlarging windows. Robert employed a few highly skilled men, doing the rest of the work himself, helped by his papa."

They flung open the windows, aired the bed and flicked a duster over the house. It was furnished down to the last detail, even to gay Irish linen tea towels.

"Robert is not the only one who has worked hard," Vicki said. "There are lots of things here a man would not know about. I would like to thank you, Madame Brissard, for what you've done. I think everything is beautiful. I'm sure Susie will think the same when she sees it."

Madame Brissard smiled. "She is a sweet child, but she does not appear to be very strong."

Vicki said carefully, "I think she has been driving herself too hard. She admires your efficiency and feels awfully inadequate herself in comparison."

"But that is absurd," Madame said. "Someday she will be efficient too. *Eh bien*. It will come." She spoke kindly, more than a little pleased that her new daughter-in-law should admire her qualities.

"She is very clever at handling children and adores them," Vicki said loyally.

Madame Brissard agreed. "So does Robert. His papa and I are very happy for him. I'm not saying that we would not have preferred him to marry a French girl, but we are content, if he is happy. And you, *mademoiselle?* Are you not disappointed because your sister married a Frenchman?"

"Goodness, no," Vicki said frankly. "All I care about is Susie's happiness. Thanks for showing me the villa. I think she's a very lucky girl."

Later, dropping Vicki off at the Jasseron farm, Madame Brissard gave her a key to the villa. "Now you will be able to visit any time you wish," she said.

Vicki accepted it happily. "I'd love to keep it aired."

"So you can, but no hard work. Papa is looking after the garden. We would like you to come to the Château tonight for dinner."

"I'm awfully sorry, I have a date."

"Another time then," Madame said. "Don't leave it too long."

Vicki promised. She had never liked Madame Brissard as much as she did at that moment. She spent Saturday morning doing her chores and the afternoon washing her hair for her dinner date with Guy that evening. The week since Susie's wedding had gone faster than fall leaves in a September breeze. The letters she received from friends back home were only a reminder of a way of life another world away.

Through the years she had skimmed along on the surface of life, accepting dates occasionally without making any deep attachments. Vicki was not hard in any way, but her parents' divorce had made her wary. It was unbelievable that she, who had remained unaffected by attractive men, devastating in their uniforms, should find herself bowled over by an arrogant Frenchman who had laid aside his aloofness long enough to take her out to dinner. She remembered the look of concern on his face when he had taken the grit from her eye; not concern for herself but because he blamed himself for her accident.

She had been wrong to accept his invitation, but the charming smile, the humorous glint in the blue eyes had been suddenly endearing. In a nebulous way she had given him the answer he wanted.

Monsieur Jasseron arrived around five. He had been making deliveries in the town and carried a pretty crib for the expected baby. Since the news of the coming event he had been as enthusiastic as his wife over preparations. Madame Jasseron had risen from her afternoon siesta feeling out of sorts. Vicki had persuaded her to take one of the pills Guy had prescribed for such occasions.

It was the periods of being unwell that gave Madame her doubts about having the baby. Naturally, she was none too pleased with her husband. He should wait until she had actually had the baby before buying a crib. But Monsieur Jasseron had hugged her and laughed happily as he carried it upstairs. Poor Madame had sent her eyes heavenward, looked at Vicki with a French shrug and followed him upstairs.

Perhaps she had borrowed Monsieur Jasseron's light-heartedness, for Vicki found herself humming that evening when she looked through her small wardrobe for a suitable dress for dinner. She decided on a slim-fitting tailored dress in red with an inch band of multi-colored braid around the high neck and short sleeves. Her face was flushed when she looked in the mirror. The red dress gave her sparkle and the fillip she needed. She was slipping into her cream coat when she heard the car. Grabbing her bag and gloves, she tripped lightly downstairs and flung an *au revoir* on her way out to Monsieur and Madame Jasseron.

Their meeting was one of delicious intimacy none the less heartbreaking because he was entirely unaware of it. Oblivious of the flutter he had caused, he leaned over to test her door, saying in that deep, charming voice that she felt iron beneath, "How is your eye? Not having any trouble with it, are you?"

She had drawn back automatically into the upholstery when he had reached across her. Appreciating its support, she said,

"It's fine now, thanks."

"And Madame Jasseron, is she taking her pills?"

"Yes. She had one this afternoon because she was not feeling too well. I wish the time would pass more quickly for her. She is so convinced that something will go wrong, and she will not have the baby."

"Most of Madame's upset is emotional. In her case it is

advisable to let nature take its course. She is fortunate to have you staying with her. Know anything about babies?"

"No."

"Now is your chance to learn. Afraid?" he asked, raising a brow.

Meeting his eyes for a split second, Vicki realized he was laughing at her flushed face.

Her lips thinned. "Why should I be? It's a perfectly natural function, is it not?"

He gave his attention to his driving. "It is. Don't worry, we have an excellent midwife in circulation capable of dealing with any emergency."

Gradually, Vicki's heart settled down to normal after experiencing the sense of shock his appearance gave her. She wished despairingly that she could borrow some of his coolness, but she could only cling desperately to her pride. It was quite an effort to smile and make casual conversation. "Aren't I fortunate to have escaped your mistral? I believe it can be shattering on occasions."

"One learns to live with it. We are protected here by the hills. Robert and Susie should enjoy their first one, for they can fasten the shutters and cling together beneath their feather quilt."

His glance came back to her face. There was a bantering challenge in his blue eyes, a gleam of laughter that set her pulses hammering. A fugitive thought passed through her mind of sharing a feathered quilt with the man at her side. She flushed scarlet, sure that he could divine her thoughts. The amusement deepened in his eyes. "Does the thought of the mistral bother you?"

"Not particularly. I loved walking over the hills back home and battling with the breezes. It was wonderfully refreshing after spending the day in a heated office," she answered, thankful that he was concentrating on his driving. "I don't care for winds that bowl me over."

"Are winds the only things that have bowled you over to date?" he asked wryly.

"No, your country has, but then I have not yet experienced your mistral."

She knew it was not the answer he expected, but he made no comment. He had been traveling quickly, slowing down when they approached the town ahead. It was one she had not seen before because it was away from the main highway. Leaving the car, they walked along pedestrians-only streets past mullioned windows to the sound of bubbling springs in the small market square. The *patronne* met them at the door of the inn where she had been saying goodbye to a party of people.

"*Bonjour, mademoiselle, monsieur*," she greeted them, leading the way indoors where the air was impregnated with the savory cooking aromas. A waiter escorted them suavely to a table in a dining room filled with a varied but generally prosperous clientèle.

Two elderly ladies at the next table, very *soignée*, were sipping aperitifs daintily between pink mouths, allowing them to slide leisurely down their long, elegant throats.

Vicki found each course a gastronomic adventure which left her toward the end of the meal with a radiant glow. She had grown used to Guy's presence partly because he was an excellent host and partly because, as a surgeon, he was accustomed to putting people at their ease.

Over coffee she felt him regarding her with a shrewd, interesting eye. Slowly, his gaze slid over the cap of tawny waves of hair around her small, neat head before coming to rest on her soft, pink lips smiling a little tentatively beneath his scrutiny.

Slowly his mouth curved into a smile. "Red suits you, *mademoiselle*. You should wear it more often."

"*Merci, monsieur*," she answered, gaiety bubbling inside her like extra calories. "Tell me about this exciting country of yours."

He raised a brow. "You are interested, or," mockingly, "is it because it is new and therefore a novelty? The nights, soft and mysteriously romantic, the château harbouring a prince who will swoop down one dark night to carry you away on his white charger. Is that how you see it?"

She had stiffened at his tone. "No, it is not. Not being a gregarious type of person, I love the countryside. Nor am I a silly romantic or a cynic. When one's parents are divorced the rose-colored glasses are discarded. My interest in your country and in your delightful people is genuine."

"In that case I will tell you about it with pleasure," he said in no way abashed. "You have missed the summer with the flower-drenched countryside enchanting the eye. Yet, to me, the long mild fall presents a countryside even more beautiful. You have seen some of the delightful old towns and villages among miles of pine and beech forest; the many castles perched high on rocks so tempting to climbers. You are, no doubt, aware that you can sail, canoe, water-ski, play tennis, ride or swim and sunbathe. We have long hot summers with the sun often shining 12 hours a day. What do you like most about it?"

She pondered carefully. "Your wild flowers, I think. There are so many of them, even in fall."

"You would enjoy the gorgeous blue carpet of violets in February and March. April brings the jasmine and orange blossom with the inevitable crop of weddings in its wake." Here his voice had again held a mocking inflection. "The rose harvest is particularly beautiful with the valleys a riot of pink blooms, though only one of the species is selected for its scent. The *rose de mai*, in itself a nondescript flower, has an exquisite perfume."

"In other words a plain Jane with an alluring perfume—which goes to show what it can do for women. I wonder if that is why your countrywomen lay such store by perfume?" she said lightly.

He considered this for a moment, his eyes tracing the delightful curve of her face from brow to chin. Her lips were parted in a smile revealing white teeth, and the dimples in her cheeks held his gaze for several moments bringing a glitter between his narrowed lids.

"A Frenchwoman wears her own particular brand of perfume, regarding it as an essential part of her freshness and feminity. She does not rely upon perfume to make her attractive, for she has the instinctive gift of highlighting her good points by camouflaging her bad ones. She cultivates every feminine wile and even in *pantalons* still remains a *femme fatale*."

Vicki thought fleetingly of Janera and said, "In short, she displays all her charms with the male ever in mind."

"Not blatantly so, but in a delightful way. The permissive society of today, you will agree, is a man's world where he can satisfy his needs with no strings attached. Yet with all men, this is not so. Most men prefer a woman to remain something of a mystery. A woman who covers her charms is much more exciting to a man than one who flaunts herself in her birthday suit. There is nothing left to discover. A man climbs a mountain because the view from the top is a challenge. The climb would not be the same if there was nothing at the end of it. *Comprenez?*"

"Perfectly, *monsieur*," she said demurely.

He produced a slim case from his inside pocket. "Cigarette?" he asked.

She accepted one, obeying the urge to prolong their talk. He applied a lighter, then chose a small cigar for himself. Then sitting back in his chair, he said, "The perfume you are using is provocatively elusive. What is it?"

"It's nothing more exciting than English eau de cologne," she replied, almost apologetically, remembering Janera's exclusive scent.

"I like it," he said, studying her speculatively. "What exactly are your duties at the Jasseron farm? They are not heavy, I hope?"

"No, Monsieur Jasseron has engaged someone to work

in the dairy. I help Madame in the house. They are lovely people, and so happy now the baby is coming. Monsieur brought home a crib today, but Madame wasn't pleased."

His smile was tolerant. "Madame Jasseron is superstitious like most country folk. She has no wish to tempt fate. There is a superstition that if the mistral continues to blow after six in the evening, it will continue for three days."

"And does it?"

He blew a fragrant line of smoke above his head. "Would it upset you if it did?"

"Not really. One can become resigned to it like other unpleasant things one has to tolerate from time to time."

He stretched out a long arm to tap the ash from his cigar. "Tell me, *mademoiselle*," he said in a dangerously soft voice, "do you regard me as someone unpleasant who has to be tolerated?"

Vicki felt the blood rush beneath her creamy skin. The question was so unexpected that she floundered hopelessly beneath his gaze.

"You have given me some bad moments where my sister was concerned," she managed at last.

He frowned. "But you knew she had a heart murmur."

"We both hoped she had outgrown it. When you insisted upon a test, I knew that if her heart was affected seriously you would not have hesitated to tell Robert."

"It would have been the correct thing to do."

She shook her head. "I don't agree. Not in Susie's case. She loves her Robert so much that she simply couldn't face life without him. I preferred her to marry him and take her chance."

His frown deepened. "But you must see that, as a doctor, I only wished to ascertain that she was not in need of instant medical attention."

"I appreciate that. You can't help seeing everything from a doctor's point of view."

He did not look very pleased. "I am a doctor only when working, *mademoiselle*. Tonight, like every time I am off duty, I am a man, very much so."

Her heart moved queerly beneath her red dress. Tonight she was feeling very much a woman, an emotion entirely owing to his presence.

"I meant no offense, *monsieur*. I am only too grateful for what you have done for Susie. As it happens, you have cleared her mind of the uncertainty of her heart condition. She was on top of the world on the day she left the hospital."

His expression cleared. "Are you not a little envious of her happiness?"

"No. Only very happy for her. I shall miss her awfully at first because we have always been together." She gave a mock pained smile. "I decorated our apartment when she came here to teach, with the thought of giving her a pleasant surprise when she returned. It wasn't wasted, though. The young couple I leased it to were delighted with it."

"It was your own apartment?"

"Ours," she corrected him. "It was our father's house, a three-storey terraced one. When he died we had it converted into three self-contained apartments keeping the ground floor one for ourselves."

"You will be lonely when you return, *non*?"

"We have plenty of friends."

"But no special one?"

She smiled, and he looked at her oddly. "If you mean male, no."

He crushed out his cigar. "Is this your first visit to this town?"

"Yes," she answered.

"Then you have not visited the monastery on the hill?"

"Is there one?" The remains of her cigarette joined his cigar butt in the ashtray.

"The ruins of one. It is said to be haunted. I've never seen a ghost, but local people swear to its existence. Most of the way is uphill but quite pleasant. It will help to digest our meal, if you are interested."

"Well, yes, if you like."

He raised a tantalizing brow. "Are you scared of ghosts?"

Suddenly her eyes danced. "Not if you aren't."

He evidently did not think the question merited an answer, for he said lazily, "Shall we go?"

In the moonlight, the town gave the impression of having strayed from the Middle Ages with its narrow, medieval and twisting streets, leading to an earthen path with an upward gradient.

Leaves crackled beneath their feet and nocturnal scents rose with all the mysterious reserve of flowers at night. To Vicki, the air held a breathless magic, minutes borrowed from time which, even if repeated, would never be the same again. Tall trees lined the path linked together with lights. Vicki watched them meandering through the branches; a striking jewelled necklace strung through the air to converge into the shadows of the monastery at the top of the hill.

"The view from the top is a panoramic one in the daylight," Guy was saying conversationally. "The vineyards and fields remain much the same as when the monks were here. The grape harvest is said to be particularly heavy. There is a story attached to it. It is said to have occurred centuries ago at a famous abbey not many miles from here. It was spring and the vines which the monks tended with such care were full of young shoots. A young monk thoughtlessly left the gates open and donkeys roamed in. They nibbled away all the fresh vine shoots. The monks were left to visualize a bleak year ahead without their wine harvest. But to their surprise and delight several weeks later, the vines were again covered with fresh green, young shoots much stronger than the first. The donkeys had inadvertently pruned the vines—something the monks had never thought of doing. The result was a bumper crop of better quality grapes."

"So after that everyone pruned their vines. Where does the ghost come in?" Vicki asked curiously.

"That is another story. The monks loved their life at the monastery so much and were so deeply content that their spirit returns. There are rumors of strange sounds emanating from here in the night. The monks have been heard chanting their prayers and singing joyously as they used to while working in the fields."

"Then they are happy ghosts," she said gaily, moving closer to his side. As they approached shadows deepened against the irregular outline of the ruined monastery. The air, so utterly still, pulsed palpably with life because of Guy's presence. Only the walls, and the bell tower which had called the monks to prayer were standing.

They walked forward through the thick stone entrance into the derelict ruin, stark and eerie in the moonlight. Guy pointed out the bakery kitchens and chapel; their feet echoed on what remained of the tiled floors.

Vicki suppressed a shudder. There was an uncomfortable aura about the place. It was nothing evil, but similar to the old castle she had explored the day she had been caught in the rain. It was the kind of sensation that brought the moisture to her temples, making her nerves as taut as violin strings. The sudden dull thud somewhere near sent her heart rocketing, and she gave an audible frightened gasp. He had kept a light hold on her arm, only allowing her a peep into each recess, but now he drew her to his side.

"Did it scare you? It was probably a stone dislodged by the last mistral. That is why you are only allowed a peep into each room. It is wise to keep clear of the walls," he said, "although they look safe." She looked up to see the sky above. "It's all right, there is no roof to fall in on us, and stop trembling." His arm slid around her slim shoulders.

Vicki had been quivering inwardly for a while with no idea that it showed. The walls apppeared to tower above her suffocatingly and menacingly. When footsteps echoed from the direction of the ruined chapel, she tore herself away from his arm to run. Instantly his arm shot out to hold her fast. "*Doucement!*" he said softly above her ear. "It is more sightseers eager to see the ghosts."

And so it was—an elderly couple with an old man as guide relating to them the history of the ruined monastery emerged just ahead in the moonlight.

Vicki was conscious of the warmth of Guy's hand on her arm in its firm impersonal hold and the uncontrollable leap of her pulses at his nearness. She had to leave, and quickly. When she turned to retrace her steps he walked beside her. Their descent was quicker and never had lights seemed more friendly than those beckoning from the little town below. Soon they were again in the warmth of the car. They had spoken little on the way down, and she had slipped into her seat, very aware of him beside her.

She felt strangely unnerved and not a bit like herself. "There's something to be said about modern buildings," she said, to break the silence. "At least there is nothing morbid or frightening about them. This monastery gave me the creeps, like Castle Clair I visited the other day."

His uncompromising, "*Vraiment?*" as he started the car made her realize the reason for his cold reaction to her words.

"I didn't mean anything disparaging about your château. I think it's charming and you've modernized it. . . ." She bit her lip to stop herself from rambling on, knowing she was making things no better. The icy silence which followed made this perfectly clear. What an idiot she was! It was her own fault she had gone to the monastery in the first place. The air of relaxed friendship between them had gone as though it had never existed. If indeed it had. The wine he had in congenial surroundings may have only temporarily thawed him out. In any case, he had taken her out to dine because he had felt responsible for the injury to her eye. She sank further into her corner, beginning for the first time to envy Susie. At least she was happy and content knowing her love was returned.

Years of taking care of Susie had given Vicki little time to think about herself and her own future. Now she was beginning to discover she had problems of her own; the biggest one being the tantalizing figure sitting beside her. She had not the slightest idea how to cope with him.

CHAPTER EIGHT

Vicki knew his image was stencilled on her heart for all time when the next day went by without the intrusion of Guy. His piercing blue eyes, his wiry masculinity, his charm—all had the power to set her heart pounding frighteningly.

Through him, her whole life had burgeoned and flowered into something so sweet, so ecstatically wonderful that it scared her. He filled her thoughts completely, leaving no room for anyone else. Tonight had shown her how much he really meant to her. It was wrong, she would have to fight with all her strength to destroy his power over her emotions.

As she was brushing her teeth before going to bed, she was surprised by a knock on her bedroom door. It was Monsieur Jasseron, agitated and extremely worried.

"It is my wife," he said, in a hoarse whisper. "She has been sick and has a pain in her chest. I am phoning for the doctor."

As he went downstairs, Vicki went in to Madame Jasseron, who was lying in bed weakly wiping the perspiration from her forehead.

"I have an awful pain in my chest," she gasped. "I can't understand it. Before I was pregnant, I never had a thing wrong with me, but now something is happening all the time."

Vicki laid a cool hand on her forehead. "It could be a touch of indigestion," she said gently. "I'll fetch you one of your pills."

Hurriedly, she went downstairs to the kitchen, found the pills and filled a small glass with water. Madame swallowed the pill and lay back on her pillows looking spent and drawn.

"I hope the doctor won't mind coming so late," she said.

"It's not even 11, so stop worrying," Vicki reassured her, annoyed with herself to find her heart quickening at the thought that it might be Guy. It was not. It was Janera. She came into the room wearing beautifully soft, white leather boots and a short white fur jacket over a turquoise sweater and tights—informal wear for a doctor but nonetheless elegant.

Surrounding them with her own particular fragrance, she asked what the trouble was and turned down the bedclothes to examine her patient. A beautiful manicured finger pinpointed the trouble spot. Madame Jasseron winced.

"Tender, is it not?" Janera put back the bedclothes. "You are too tense, Madame Jasseron. You must learn to relax. I will give you a prescription for a stomach mixture and a few tranquillizers." She scribbled a prescription which she gave to Vicki. "I understand you are staying with Madame until she has her baby."

"Yes," Vicki replied wondering if she was deliberately making her feel inferior or simply stating a fact. She led the way downstairs still wondering, while Janera had a few words with Monsieur Jasseron, then she walked with her to the door.

"Do you find it boring here, *mademoiselle*, after London?" Janera had paused in the doorway.

"As a matter of fact I am enjoying it," Vicki said, sensing a tenseness in the Frenchwoman's attitude.

"But you will be pleased to return home, *non*?"

With anyone else Vicki would have replied spontaneously, but there was something about the doctor that put her teeth on edge. She had a feeling the woman was not being friendly. There was a reason for her prolonged leavetaking. She did not have to wait long before she discovered why.

"I am in no hurry," she answered.

Janera gave her a searching look. "I had occasion to call at a farm today; the farmer asked if your eye was better. I believe you trapped a spark when you were there with Monsieur Ransart."

"That is so." Vicki matched her coolness.

"I suppose, like any other single girl, you find Guy attractive?"

Vicki decided to be diplomatic. "The doctor was very kind. My car had broken down and he drove along and offered me a lift."

"He is very courteous. He could do no other. Robert Brissard is one of his closest friends."

Vicki knew what she was implying. There was nothing personal in Guy's paying her any attention. It was a favor on his part through his association with Robert. She stiffened, thinking wryly that a little determined dignity would not achieve much with the Frenchwoman but it could bring about a kind of mutual respect for each other.

"I am well aware of that. I am also unlikely to misconstrue his friendliness."

Janera's smile was a little tight. "So many women take the attentions of a bachelor as having only one meaning. *Bonne nuit, mademoiselle.*"

Vicki sent her on her way with an equally cool response. She locked the door and climbed the stairs to find Monsieur Jasseron at the top.

"My wife is feeling a little better. It could be the pill you gave her," he said, somewhat relieved.

"I'm glad," she said. "Say *bonne nuit* for me and tell her I hope she has a good night and you, too. Call me if you need me. *Bonne nuit, monsieur.*"

She stood by the open window in her room for a long time, breathing in the exhilarating air and thinking about Janera Molineux. So she had claws where Guy was concerned. Well, she had no occasion to sharpen them on herself; he would probably forget her existence.

Tuesday morning brought the promise of another fine

day. Vicki was up early to prepare Monsieur Jasseron's breakfast and make his sandwiches for lunch. He said Madame had a fairly good night and was feeling a little better. Later Vicki took her breakfast upstairs, much to that lady's embarrassment. Smiling at her vehemence, she placed the daintily laid tray on the bed.

When she went again for the tray, Madame Jasseron had eaten and was looking brighter. "And now I am getting up," she said determinedly and, although Vicki protested, she did so.

Vicki opened the windows, cleaned the bedrooms and went out to feed the fowl and geese. The latter were becoming quite friendly, much to her relief. There was a lump of sugar for Shandy the horse, a beautiful creature from good bloodstock. Monsieur Jasseron had bred quite a few first-class horses in his time. Shandy was the only one left. Since he had known about the baby, Monsieur Jasseron had talked of breeding them again. Who knows, he had said, it could be a son. Vicki hoped it was, and refused to share Madame's pessimistic attitude that anything could go wrong. Mid-morning, she took a tray to the woman in the dairy. She was Italian and had recently joined her husband, one of the many sun-tanned laborers darting along the country roads in trucks to the many building sites.

Maria was in her twenties, dark and heavily built. She was hard-working, quick and clean, but she gave one the impression that she had grown up without love, for she had no tenderness. She accepted her coffee and talked in a voice devoid of expression. Yes, she liked it here and soon she would send for her three *bambini*. There was no light of love in her eyes when she spoke of her children. She could speak quite good English, having worked for an English family before she was married. But Vicki did not find her likeable. She would be good for Madame Jasseron because she was not *sympathique*.

After lunch, Vicki went to the village to have

Madame's prescription filled, as Madame did not feel up to the jaunt.

"Perhaps you would go to the town when you have done your shopping," she said. "I need more wool for the baby's shawl and only Montmères in the town stock it."

So, after lunch, Vicki set out in Sarah, giving Maria a lift home on the way. She dropped Maria off and sailed on, with Sarah in a much happier mood since her visit to the garage. The countryside was a blanket of mimosa; the sun shone minus the overpowering summer heat. Of course, in the summer, there would be no one out shopping. The stores would be closed and houses shuttered against the intense heat. In the fields the ploughs would be silent, the bullocks and donkeys resting in their stalls.

Here life was pleasant. To the gregarious type of woman, Vicki supposed, it was sadly lacking in gaiety. They would say Monsieur Jasseron was a good man, but dull. Yet Monsieur Jasseron, when one really knew him, was full of humor and charm. Since the news of the baby, he had shed years from his age. He was exercising his baritone voice, which, through the past years, had been lulled into silence because he felt his wife's disappointment at being barren. He had eaten well of the farmhouse fare, drinking the rosy wine, the product of his own vines. In his lighter moments, he waltzed Madame around the kitchen until they collapsed into a chair happily with Vicki looking on. Madame apologized for his behavior, and Vicki had felt both humble and lost in their happiness.

She was shaken rudely out of her thoughts by a truckload of laborers honking behind her on the narrow road.

"*Bonjour, mademoiselle!*" they shouted as they passed.

"*Bonjour, messieurs,*" she replied. Sarah had moved out of their way haughtily, squeezing herself against the side of the road with a small shudder of revulsion. She was no doubt remembering her own fall from grace when Monsieur Jasseron used her to take his produce to market.

Vicki watched the truck disappear around a bend in a road that hitherto had known only donkeys and mules as daily traffic. Now even the narrowest country roads reverberated to the sound of trucks and jeeps used in building operations as more and more people sought the sun.

In the village stores, everyone asked kindly after Madame Jasseron. Had she had the baby? *Non?* Not very well? A bit under the weather maybe. Ah well, with kindly French shrugs, it was to be expected at her age. Everyone was *sympathique*.

Madame from the *boulangerie* sent a large fruit pie. Madame at the *pharmacie* where Vicki presented Madame Jasseron's prescription sent raspberry leaves for raspberry leaf tea. You simply poured boiling water on the leaves in the manner of making ordinary tea. *Comprenez?* They were excellent for relaxing the muscles during childbirth.

Monsieur from the flower shop, who dealt only in the most expensive blooms, sent a bouquet of red carnations and fern. And because Vicki, looking so young and sweet, had flushed prettily on receiving them, she had been presented with a half-opened rose.

How deliciously sweet and considerate they were, she thought, walking to Sarah with her purchases and gifts. There had been no malicious or acid remarks about Madame Jasseron's small miracle, only a sincere desire to help and sympathize with her in her *maladie*.

The town was but a short run from the village, the approach to it rising gently as the outline of mellowed stone houses appeared on the hill. Leaves were falling from the plane trees in the square onto deserted cobblestones. The sharp click of metal balls colliding told her that the local inhabitants were in the Mairie indulging in their favorite pastime of *pétanque*—the French game of bowls.

At the shout of "*Bravo,* Gerard!" she peered inside to see Gerard Standon. He looked as French as his companions in a T-shirt, slacks and rope-soled espadrilles. She watched him bowl expertly to another round of applause. When the game was finished he came over to her looking very pleased to see her.

"Come for a drink in the bar," he said, and, holding her arm lightly, piloted her to it.

Vicki settled for a glass of the local red wine and found it extremely palatable.

Gerard raised his glass. "As the locals say, *à l'amitié!*"

Vicki laughed. "I must say you appear to have made plenty of friends. Is this what you do all day, play *boules?*"

"Good lord, no. Besides the script-writing I told you about, I also write educational books for children. I find this a wonderful way to relax from my writing." He looked at her thoughtfully.

"What's the matter? Have I a smut on my nose?" she asked, moving uneasily beneath his scrutiny.

He grinned. "I was wondering how you feel about a temporary job here. I'm in need of a typist at the moment. I have a mountain of work. What about it?"

She shook her head. "I couldn't possibly leave Madame Jasseron, much as I would like to help." She paused, then murmured, "Shouldn't you be working instead of playing *boules?*"

"I should, but this is an important match and I like the company."

She noted two very English moustaches among the clientèle at the bar. "I see quite a few Englishmen share your love of *boules.*"

"The one with the very handsome handlebar moustache is a retired Army colonel. His pal is ex-air force. You won't find either Guy or Robert here. Guy is no snob, but it would simply not occur to him to hobnob with the peasants in a game of *boules*. Robert, before he was married, was too tied up in the family estates to come to town except for a haircut."

To prevent any further mention of Guy, she said impulsively, "Did you know Robert and Susie have a villa near to the Château Brissard? Robert has done wonders with it."

Gerard smiled. "I know the one you mean. Robert told me there was a villa waiting for the son of the family when he married."

"I have a key if you would care to see it," she said.

"That's very sweet of you. What about tomorrow afternoon?" he answered.

"Shall I call for you?"

"No. I'll see you there around three."

Vicki laughed. "Five minutes ago you were saying about being piled under with work. Can you spare the time?"

He grinned. "I can always spare the time to look over the love nests of one of my favorite pupils, especially when the guide is his very charming sister-in-law. By the way, the name is Gerard."

"And mine is Vicki."

Arriving back at the farm, Vicki gave Madame Jasseron her presents from the villagers; the carnations were placed in the center of the table at supper. Monsieur Jasseron admired them and said with a twinkle:

"We are about to have another addition to the family. I've put Nanette in the barn. I noticed tonight that she was producing milk, so it won't be long before she presents us with a small billy or nanny goat."

Vicki's small white teeth bit on a piece of crusty bread thoughtfully. "What do I do, *monsieur*, if Nanette has her young one while you are in the fields and Madame is resting?"

"Nothing except give her corn. The offspring will be

better left alone for the first couple of hours. See that Nanette has plenty of drinking water handy, won't you, *mademoiselle*? And don't worry. Nanette should come through all right. She is not yet three. It is nice and comfortable for her in the straw."

Thursday morning passed with Vicki peeping into the barn at intervals to check on Nanette. Around 11 she saw Shandy the horse and Gaston the dog at the barn door looking in curiously. To her delight, she found Nanette standing in her corner with a proud but protective air, her newly arrived offspring at her feet. With a laugh of pure joy, she ran to hug Nanette, telling her what a clever girl she was to produce such a delightful offspring. Then she was moving cautiously to murmur endearments and stroke the still damp, tiny black-and-white head of the new arrival.

It took only a few minutes to provide Nanette with corn and plenty of water before going to tell Madame Jasseron. When they returned to the barn about ten minutes later, the newcomer was standing up on thrust-out, sturdy little legs, although she could not have been more than half an hour old.

Vicki gurgled as she hugged her. "I hope your offspring comes as easy, *madame*," she said, watching the Frenchwoman bend over her own bulge awkwardly to pat Nanette.

Monsieur Jasseron, who had been to the barn on his way to the house, was beaming when he entered the kitchen. Placing a muscular arm around Madame's thickened waist, he said roguishly, "It's a nanny. What shall we call her?"

"We'll think about it," she said. "Now be off with you to wash and change or dinner will spoil."

He sniffed appreciatively. "It smells *très bon*," he said, eyeing the pan.

"It's always *très bon*," his wife replied.

He kissed the side of her neck, and she raised the wooden spoon she was using threateningly, lifting her eyes heavenward at a smiling Vicki who was laying the table and chuckling at Monsieur's sudden exit.

When Vicki left Sarah in the drive to Susie's villa, she stood for several moments with dreams in her eyes looking up at the house. A tantalizing vision came before her: of sharing it with someone who adored her, being alone with him there in the silence of the hills, with only the music of the wind amid flower-scented, sun-washed days. Heavenly to sit at his feet at the close of day and listen to his deep tender tones as they made plans; best of all, to have his children, a son so like him that he would jolt her heart each time she hugged him.

The cool key of the villa in her hand was a touch of sanity, a reminder that her dreams had been triggered by Susie's marriage. She uttered a silent prayer that Robert would always cosset and adore her, treating her always as a bride.

She opened the door, remembering that Gerard was arriving at three. Her watch said half past two—just half an hour to make herself useful. She hummed as she dusted and opened windows, happy because Madame Jasseron was so much better.

She leaned out of a bedroom window to shake out her duster. She drank in the clean air and admired the view of clear blue skies, above a smiling countryside nestling contentedly against gentle hills. Beneath her window, the garden, well planned and neat, had been weeded. Not far away was the compost heap, mostly of weeds. She must remember to burn it before she left. The mistral, if it arrived, would scatter it far and wide to take root among the vineyards and olive groves.

She watered the pretty potted plants, not forgetting those outside the villa. How lovely it would be in the

summer with the rambling roses and jasmine in full
bloom hugging the façade of the villa. Her gaze traveled
to the climbing roses reaching to the open bedroom windows before she wandered down to the compost heap.

If she had paused for thought, she would have been prepared for the flare-up when she set a light to it. The sun
had dried out the moisture. Flames suddenly shot into the
air with a fierce whoosh and crackle. Sparks flew far and
wide alarmingly.

As she stepped back from the heat, her heart almost
stopped beating when, horror-struck, she saw fugitive
sparks igniting the climbing roses clinging to the villa
walls. The bedroom windows were wide open; it would
not take long for the flames to travel up to the billowing
curtains. She was galvanized into action. Leaping forward, she clawed frantically at the strong thorny tendrils
in an effort to dislodge them from the wall. The smoke
from the fire was all around her, smarting in her eyes and
making her cough. She tugged as if demented, ignoring
the cruel thorns digging into her hands. At last, her eyes
red-rimmed from the smoke, her hands torn and
bleeding, she succeeded in tearing away the last of the
lighted tendrils.

As she stamped them out underfoot, she was aware of
her slacks being singed at the bottom in the process. Oblivious to her scorched bleeding hands, she lurched into
the villa for water to douse the fire before more harm was
done. She was carrying out a second pail of water to
make sure the fire was out when Gerard arrived in a con-
vertible.

He was out of it in a flash to stare incredulously at her
red-rimmed eyes and dishevelled appearance, pieces of
rambler sticking to her sweater. "Good lord!" he cried.
"What happened?"

"I nearly burned down the villa," Vicki croaked, pushing back tendrils of hair from her hot forehead with the back of an injured hand.

She could not avoid wincing when he took hold of her hands, gentle though he was. His dismayed whistle did not help.

"These hands need treatment right away," he said firmly.

The smoke had parched her throat, and she felt horribly sick and ill, but she would not give in. "They'll be all right when I've cleaned them up. I'm afraid I shall have to sit down for a minute, Gerard. I'm sorry."

"Sorry be hanged," he said grimly, noticing her pallor. "This is no time to be polite. Come on indoors."

Half carrying her into the *salon*, he lowered her into a chair. With strong determination, she swallowed convulsively in an attempt to ward off the sickness. A cold sweat broke out on her forehead; the pain in her hands was almost unbearable. Never had water tasted so good as Gerard held some to her lips. Her thanks were barely audible as she lay back with closed eyes.

Nothing was clear after that. There was a floating sensation in her head, and she kept her eyes tightly closed in an effort to dispel it.

"*Mon dieu!*" The exclamation came on a sharp intake of breath.

Vicki opened her eyes, feeling her hands lifted gently by Guy, who was kneeling at her feet. He had placed them on a towel and was wiping away the blood from the cuts and scratches.

"A glass of water for a sedative, *s'il vous plait*, Gerard," he said, his face set grimly. "These hands must be intensely painful."

Her pulse was beating overtime. She was powerless to hide it from him since his thumb was already on it. She wanted desperately to tear her gaze away from his, but she was equally powerless to do that, too. Their gazes clung, with every fiber of her being responding to his nearness, the pain in her hands momentarily forgotten. The contact ended when Guy rose abruptly to his feet as Gerard returned with the glass of water.

She was given the sedative, and Gerard was dispatched for a bowl of water. "I hope that helps," Guy said. He hitched immaculate trousers to kneel again at her feet, this time with tweezers at the ready. "I'm afraid I am going to add to the pain. Your hands are full of thorns. I will try to remove them as painlessly as I can if you can manage to hold your hands perfectly still."

He dealt with several small ones while he was speaking, moving on swiftly to others more deeply embedded beneath her skin. Vicki clenched her teeth and made not a murmur when he had to remove a broken piece of nail rather low on her finger. She removed her gaze from the crisp hair so near her own and concentrated on the window. The pain in her hands accelerated by the burns was almost unbearable, but to Vicki it was a small price to pay for saving the villa.

Then it was over. Guy was on his feet again to wash her hands in the bowl of water Gerard had brought. She caught Gerard's half wink when Guy passed him the used bowl with a polite, "*Merci.*"

Soon Guy was addressing her in a cool, trenchant voice.

"And now, *mademoiselle,* perhaps you will tell me how your hands managed to get into this state?"

He listened, dabbing cotton wool soaked with something that stung on her cuts and scratches before applying jellied cream to her burns.

Her voice trailed off lamely when she finished to watch him put the last bandage in place. The pain in her hands had eased slightly and a delicious lassitude washed over her. Whether it was the sedative or his nearness, she was too hazy to define. He placed everything back in his bag, dropping the used cotton wool in an ashtray to be disposed of later. His every movement betrayed his rising anger.

At last he said sharply, on a censorious note, "Was it necessary for you to assume the role of *femme-à-tout-faire*? Aren't you doing enough by helping Madame Jasseron without coming here to do chores too?"

"I wasn't asked to do any chores here. Madame Brissard gave me a key to come when I felt inclined. I did no gardening. It was my own fault that I burned the compost heap. I'm glad I saved the villa, though."

"The villa! *Ma foi!* The villa could have been rebuilt," he said explosively. "But you. . . ." His eyes took in her thick tawny hair. "Can you imagine what would have happened had your hair caught fire? Don't you realize you could have been so badly burned. . . ." He struck a clenched right fist into the flat of his left hand in righteous anger. "I have seen third-degree burns that I shall never forget. . . ." He broke off with an audible breath of exasperation and snapped his bag shut. She had shrunk back in her chair before his tirade, looking small and defenceless.

The blue eyes centered on her pale face and lost their fire. "Is the pain still acute?" he asked quietly.

She gave a pale smile. "They feel much better, and thank you for dressing them for me. I realize how foolish I was and how right you are to be angry, *monsieur*."

Gerard, coming in at that moment, sensed the atmosphere. "Are you still calling each other by Monsieur and Mademoiselle? Isn't it time you called each other by your first names?" He waved a negligent hand. "Vicki, this is Guy. Guy, this is Vicki."

Guy did not smile. His features merely relaxed. "Were you here when it happened, *mon ami*?" he asked curiously.

Gerard leaned back against a nearby table to face them. "No. When I arrived our heroine was flinging a final pail of water on the ashes before she collapsed."

Guy's eyes narrowed. "You carried her in here?"

"No, I slipped up there."

Guy frowned. "Slipped up?" he echoed.

Gerard laughed and folded his arms. "I meant it literally, of course. I made a mistake and so missed the opportunity of picking up a cute little number. To be quite candid, the state of her hands frightened me. I hardly dared touch her. That's why I phoned for you."

"You agreed to meet here?"

"Yes," candidly. "Vicki was going to show me the villa. I met her in town yesterday. She told me she had a key to the villa, and we made arrangements for me to come at three to look around."

Guy's glance from one to the other was wary. "You are in the habit of meeting?"

"I'd like to think we were," Gerard replied. "But no. Yesterday we met accidentally in the town."

Guy picked up his bag. "You had better take this while I carry Vicki to my car. Her hands are not fit for her to drive. Robert will, no doubt, be pleased to show you around when he returns."

He almost thrust the bag at Gerard before turning to scoop Vicki up in his arms and stride to his car. Gerard opened the car door, dropped the bag on the back seat and stood aside for Guy to lower his burden into the front seat.

Gerard looked down at her sympathetically. "Sorry our afternoon has ended so painfully for you. I'll be calling to see you tomorrow, Vicki. Meanwhile, I hope the hands don't hurt too much."

She nodded, too confused to speak. Guy lifted a hand and the car shot away. In the following silence, she stole a glance at his set profile. He was like a stranger; she sensed the anger in him. Was he angry because she was becoming something of a liability and a nuisance?

She voiced her thoughts. "I'm sorry for being so tiresome," she said quietly. "You have enough to do without running around attending to me."

He did not appear to be listening, then, "You came here for your sister's wedding, helped out with the wine-making at the Château Brissard and caught a chill. You go presumably to look after Robert's villa and are nearly burned to death. You would have been wise to have returned home after the wedding instead of becoming involved in other people's problems." He shot her an exasperated look. "When Madame Jasseron has her baby, what then? Do you plan to wait until your sister starts a family, to be used again?"

Vicki sat very still. His cold clipped words were like metallic pebbles aimed at her heart. So he did find her a nuisance and was actually telling her to leave. The pain in her hands was nothing compared to the pain lurking around her heart.

She said slowly, "I happen to be very fond of Madame Jasseron, and I know my company means a lot to her in her present condition. As for waiting until my sister starts a family, surely that is my business?" She swallowed on a choked feeling. "I did not send for you, *monsieur*, on the first occasion when I was ill. Gaston fetched you. This time, it was Gerard much against my wishes. Next time, I will take great care you are not inconvenienced."

He said dryly, "Your hands will keep you out of mischief for a week. Madame Jasseron has someone to help her, I believe, so you will have nothing to do but allow your hands to heal. Madame will be all the better for keeping active."

Vicki bit her lip. "You don't have to concern yourself with me. I can manage. I know you resent me for some reason, perhaps because we started off, rather unfortunately, as enemies. Apparently I was in the wrong then, and I still am."

She was too upset to see how near they were to the farm, for she was seeing only a blur of tears. When he pulled up at the farm gate, she said hurriedly, "It isn't necessary for you to open the gate. I can manage."

He left the car and strode around to her door before she could attempt to open it with her bandaged hand. Her eyes were dry when she unfolded herself from her seat clinging desperately to her pride. To her dismay, he stood squarely in her path to hold out a hand.

"The key to the villa, please. You will be indisposed for longer than the honeymooners will be away. I can return it when I call at the Château Brissard on my way back."

She stiffened. "As I said before, it is none of your business," she replied tartly.

Softly, menacingly, he said, "I am making it my business. The key please."

Vicki holding her purse awkwardly between bandaged hands, relinquished it when his fingers closed around the top. She watched him open it and remove a key. He held it up with raised eyebrows. She nodded briefly, and he slipped it into his pocket before returning her purse.

Making no attempt to move, he looked down at her for a long moment.

"One minute," he said, and leaned inside the car to open his bag. Swiftly he transferred a few tiny pills from a glass bottle into a tiny box, then straightened from the car. "Sleeping pills," he said laconically. "Take one tonight in case your hands keep you awake."

She wouldn't allow him to drop them into her purse.

"Thank you, but I don't take sleeping pills," she said.

He merely slid the purse from her hands, opened it, dropped in the pills and closed it again.

She accepted it with the urge to hurt him as she had been hurt.

"You must send me a bill, *monsieur*. It must be steadily mounting up by now."

He looked furious, wheeled around, opened the gate and gave her a stiff little bow. "*Au revoir, mademoiselle*," he said.

It had been "Vicki" at the villa. The *"mademoiselle"* was the last straw. "*Au revoir, monsieur*," she answered, returning his serve, and walked blindly to the house.

CHAPTER NINE

Monsieur and Madame Jasseron were volubly upset when they saw Vicki's bandaged hands. Madame sent her to her room to rest and fussed over her sympathetically. Sympathy, however, was the last thing Vicki wanted. While she rested that afternoon, she became convinced of one thing. When Madame Jasseron had her baby and was up and about again, she would return home.

Susie would be all right in a home of her own; they would correspond. She refused to think ahead when she would have to visit Susie. By then Guy and Janera would be married and might have moved to Nice where he could commute daily to the hospital. When his honeymoon was over, he would have a waiting list of patients to attend to. She could then make short flying visits without the risk of running into him.

Vicki left her room just before supper feeling unrefreshed, her spirits lower than they had been for a long time. Monsieur Jasseron poured her a glass of wine while Madame put the finishing touches to the meal.

And how Monsieur teased her! "I'm all on the *qui vive* to do anything for you, *mademoiselle*," he exclaimed, his eye twinkling. "You will not be able to wash your face without help."

"Of course she won't," Madame said. "Stop embarrassing *la pauvre petite*. I shall look after her."

Vicki remembering how she had struggled with a damp face cloth before coming downstairs, smiled. She was drawn into their brand of humor willingly as some of the ice melted around her heart. She could move her fingers stiffly in the bandages and managed to eat her dinner without help.

Sarah arrived around seven, delivered by Guy's man.

Not long afterward Monsieur and Madame Brissard came.

"Guy called to deliver the key to the villa and tell us about your accident," Madame Brissard said. "We were so sorry. Monsieur Brissard had no business leaving the compost heap to be blown about in the wind."

"It isn't all that serious," Vicki replied, trying to make light of it and not wishing to bring trouble to Monsieur Brissard. "It's very sweet of you to come. I ought to have minded my own business."

"You only did what I should have done, *chérie*. Guy positively glared at us. I think it would have given him the greatest pleasure to throw Monsieur Brissard on the compost heap and set fire to him," Madame exclaimed, with a thread of annoyance.

"Oh dear! It was all my fault. Poor Monsieur Brissard!" Vicki looked apologetically at Monsieur Brissard.

Monsieur Jasseron had seated the visitors, and Madame had passed around the wine.

"*Eh bien*, it will pass." Monsieur Brissard raised his glass. "To your swift recovery, Mademoiselle Vicki, and my sincere regrets for having caused you so much pain."

Vicki drank part of her wine, then raised her glass once again.

"Shall we drink to Madame Jasseron to wish her a speedy recovery too?" she said, anxious to change the subject.

Gerard called at half past eleven the following morning to take her out for a drive. Vicki was glad of his company; Guy might call to dress her hands and find her out. She had no wish to see him again. It was altogether too painful. As they zoomed along a sunlit road, Gerard said conversationally, "You must come at Christmas. In the town a special market is held for the sale of poultry, rabbits, piglets, pigeons and all Christmas fare. At night, a

Christmas tree is lit up in the square and carols are sung."

"Sounds lovely," Vicki said wistfully, but she knew she would not be there. Guy would be at the Château by then with his wife. Unhappily, she looked ahead to see the town on the hill. The cluster of restful old houses, stores and quaint turrets reminded her that they were not far away from the Molineux' villa where they had their office.

The thought occurred that Janera might not yet have left the office with Guy already on his rounds. If that was so, she could ask her to dress her hands. Guy would be almost certain to visit the farm that day to dress them for her. Fervently, she hoped he would call while she was out. Nothing could persuade her to see him again is she could avoid it.

"Do you mind if we stop at Doctor Molineux's office to have my hands dressed? I shall miss Guy if he pays a visit to the farm this morning while I'm out," she said casually.

Gerard shot her an amused glance. "Did he scare you yesterday? He's a wonderful fellow and an excellent surgeon. He's a heart specialist and his lectures are always well attended. His next tour is one he has been asked to do by special request."

Vicki had a sudden vision of Guy, tall, immaculate and vital, holding his audience with that deep musical voice of his explaining an interesting point. She had not wanted to talk about him, but she had to carry on with the conversation or Gerard would think it strange.

"Not really," she said. "He had a right to be angry with me."

Gerard said thoughtfully, "I don't think his anger was directed against you. He was angry because he thought you were being used."

"But I wasn't. I was there to show you around the villa," she reminded him.

"That was another thing he didn't approve of. In France such meetings arouse suspicion."

She flung him a wide-eyed glance. "But that's ridiculous!"

"I agree, but these people wouldn't regard our relationship as casual."

Vicki looked through her window to see the first villa leading to the town. The trees overhead still gave a rich shade, whereas in England they would be practically leafless by now. The Molineux residence lay just ahead. Gerard braked to slow down and stop at the side of the road.

Vicki left the car to walk the few yards to where the two-storey villa slumbered in the morning sun. The courtyard was at the side of the house leading to the waiting room. To her infinite relief, no familiar big car was parked on the cobbles. She opened the waiting room door and stepped inside. Pale green walls were lined with white chairs; two low glass-topped tables supported magazines.

There was utter silence with no sign of anyone around. Facing her were two doors and she walked across to open one. Instead of the surgery she expected, she saw a corridor containing still more doors. Opening the first door to her left, she found herself in a small conservatory overlooking the garden. In it were four basket chairs and a table. One of the chairs had a dent made in the cushion. There was a newspaper dropped on the floor beside it and a small tray which had obviously contained coffee and biscuits on the table.

Vicki was about to beat a hasty retreat when someone came suddenly around the corner. To her dismay, it was Doctor Molineux, his smile stretching his moustache into a thin line.

The small black eyes looked at her boldly. "*Tiens!*

Who have we here? Mademoiselle Kendon! *Montez donc*," he exclaimed.

Reluctantly, Vicki stepped farther into the room, feeling an idiot beneath his appraisal.

"I came to ask Doctor Janera to dress my hands; it appears she is not around. I can call again," she said, uneasily.

"She is out, but I shall be *enchanté* to be of service, *mademoiselle*. This way, *s'il vous plaît*."

She was ushered out of the conservatory along the corridor and through a doorway into the surgery she had tried in vain to find. He washed his hands at a small basin in a corner of the room, dried them, and procured fresh dressings and cream. He asked her how the accident had happened as he attended to her hands.

He seemed very slow after Guy's experienced and economical movements, but she was thankful it was not Guy. A few moments later she was beginning to have doubts when the doctor kissed each hand, now free of bandages, to murmur, "Such small hands to be hurt so much."

At last the dressings were in place and he straightened. "*Ça va?*" he said.

"Much better, thank you," she answered.

She was poised to take her leave when he asked her to stay for lunch.

Politely she informed him that Gerard was waiting for her and fled. Guy had called when she was out, Madame Jasseron informed her on her return to the farm. Gerard stayed for dinner. Vicki took the news, aware of Gerard's thoughtful gaze on her flushed face. She made light of it, telling Madame Jasseron of calling in at the surgery in town.

Janera called the following day to dress her hands. By the weekend they were well on the way to recovery. The newlyweds arrived at their villa late on Saturday night.

Susie phoned the following morning to talk excitedly about her new home.

"What a wonderful surprise!" she gurgled. "It's absolute heaven. We're giving a small party tonight for a house-warming. Do come early, Vicki, so we can talk."

"Very well, Madame Brissard," Vicki promised, banteringly.

But Madame Jasseron was not well on Sunday morning. Vicki prepared dinner and in the afternoon called Susie to tell her she would not be there until late because she did not like leaving Madame Jasseron. Monsieur Jasseron was no use when Madame was ill. He was too upset to be of help. However, when Madame came downstairs after an afternoon's rest she was much better.

Vicki prepared supper, leaving it for Monsieur Jasseron to serve and went to her room to dress for the evening out at the villa. Her wardrobe was really inadequate for such occasions. There was nothing else but her white sleeveless jersey dress. It looked immaculate but young and unimpressive. White, however, was one of her best colors. It brought out the delicate texture of her creamy skin and was a foil for the liquid darkness of her eyes. She was careful to put liquid make-up on her hands to cover the scratched and dried skin and was ready to go downstairs when she heard a car.

To her surprise it was Gerard. "I called to see if you would like a lift to the villa," he said.

"I don't mind," she answered lightly. "If you don't mind bringing me back."

Gerard was wearing his brown suit and was in a gay mood. "How are the hands?" he asked, when they were on their way.

"Much better, thanks," she replied, then, as something suddenly occurred to her, she added, "Have you any idea who is going to the housewarming?"

"Personal friends of Robert's, I suppose. Guy is away in Cannes, and I don't know if Janera is going."

Vicki knew an inward relief to hear Guy would not be there, yet beneath it there lurked an emptiness.

At the villa a happy Susie and Robert greeted them. Vicki was surprised at the change in her sister in two short weeks. Gone was the look of uncertainty, to be replaced by one of confidence. The coltish angles of her neck and face had filled out in a softer, mature loveliness. She looked positively radiant in a little sleeveless dress of multi-colored silk.

Robert, too, looked younger and carefree as he poured out drinks. Monsieur and Madame Brissard were there with two other couples whom Vicki had not met before. They were Robert's uncles and aunts from Menton. Vicki was being introduced to them when Janera arrived. She kissed Robert's cheek, accepted a drink and stood talking to him. She was wearing a brown dress threaded with gold. The heavy beaten gold necklace and broad bracelet on her slim arm completed a picture of casual elegance. Gerard joined them, so Vicki had time for a word alone with Susie. They sat down together on the sofa and, after Susie had asked how Madame Jasseron was, she said urgently, "Stay behind when the rest of the guests have gone tonight for a little chat. Robert will run you home. I want to hear all about the fire. Robert's mother told us how you saved the villa from being burned down. Bless you!" She gave Vicki a swift kiss on the tip of her nose and rose to her feet. "I must see how dinner is getting on." She wrinkled her nose happily. "Robert has engaged a woman daily from the village."

To Vicki's surprise, Janera came to sit in Susie's vacant place, carrying her own drink and one for Vicki. She gazed down at Vicki's hands as they curled around her glass. "Your hands are much better," she said chattily. "I use make-up on mine, too. It hides the veins on the back and improves them tremendously."

"I agree," Vicki replied. She was at a loss to know how to deal with the new friendly approach. It was affecting, but not affecting enough to clear all doubt regarding her friendliness.

Janera shot her an oblique look from beautifully made-up eyes. After a moment she smiled, "I'm odd man out tonight. Guy was unable to come. He is at the hospital in Nice for an important consultation."

She finished her drink and placed the glass on a small table nearby. Vicki had not touched hers, but she put it down beside the empty glass, having lost the taste for it. "Bad luck," she said.

Janera looked around the charming room. "This is a delightful villa," she said. "Robert has excellent taste."

Again Vicki agreed. She refused a cigarette from the smart leather case Janera offered and watched her light one for herself. She saw no prospect of being rescued from the Frenchwoman whom she felt was only condescendingly making polite conversation. She had mentioned Guy as if she was already engaged to him, she thought, maintaining, in spite of her pain, an austere detachment.

Anything personal to do with the lady doctor left her cold. Let her marry her surgeon and glide about the magnificent château with its regiment of servants and lovely grounds. She would never reach the heights of happiness that Robert and Susie had.

Thinking about Susie brought her in person, but she was not alone. Vicki felt her heart miss a beat before it thundered on. Guy was strolling beside her, hands thrust into his pockets in an easy relaxed way. He greeted everyone courteously, giving her a cursory glance before strolling to Robert.

Vicki had the sensation of being in high wind with all the breath knocked out of her body. Everyone else in the room faded away to form a backdrop against which his clear-cut features, blue eyes and strong determined jaw mocked at her defenses. Then pride came to her aid in the form of Janera who, with commendable swiftness, drifted to his side to catch his arm.

"*Chéri*, now you can take me in to dinner," she said, smiling up at him.

He gazed at her with his charming smile, and everyone made a general move to the dining room. Vicki found Gerard at her side and seated next to her at the table, with Susie and Robert on her right. It was an oval table with Robert and Susie in the center. Robert's parents sat next to their son, then Guy and Janera with the aunts and uncles completing the oval.

The meal was cooked excellently and served promptly by an elderly woman, obviously the capable kind, in a spotless overall. Vicki ate mechanically with apparent enjoyment for the benefit of Susie without tasting a thing.

When the meal was over, they all returned to the *salon* to look at colored snapshots taken on the honeymoon in Paris. Vicki was sitting on the fringe of the assembled company in order to avoid contact with Guy and was the last to receive the snapshots when they were passed around.

They were all very good. Several beautiful scenes of the river Seine included a delightful one of Susie taken in a pretty gingham dress on the deck of a *bâteau mouche*. Later, most of the guests drifted away with Robert and Susie to look around the villa, leaving Monsieur and Madame Brissard to pass the last of the snaps to Vicki.

She was too interested in them to notice someone lowering himself into the vacant chair beside her. But the arm reaching out a hand beneath an immaculate cuff for the snaps shook her into an awareness of his presence. Lazily, he dropped them onto a small table well within his reach.

With a voice sounding so much quieter than the uneven thump of her heart, she said, "Are you not interested in looking around the villa?" A faint hostility had crept into her tones, and she knew he noticed it.

Being Guy, he ignored it, reaching for her hands before he answered. "I have seen it in all stages of conversion. Your hands have healed very quickly," he said, bending a thumb back slightly in order to examine a scratch around the base.

She was reminded of the last time he had held her hands; they had been torn and bleeding, his thumb on her pulse to discover it beating erratically. It was beating much the same now. She drew her hands away before his fingers could move down to it.

His only reaction was a slightly raised eyebrow which gave her the feeling of having behaved churlishly.

"How is Madame Jasseron?" he asked.

She wondered if Susie had told him of Madame not feeling well, then decided it did not matter. He was merely making polite conversation. The presence of Monsieur and Madame Brissard lent substance to a scene she felt was strangely unreal. It was with dismay that she saw them leave their seats and head for the garden. Guy had settled himself in his chair, stretching out his long legs comfortably. Knowing he was waiting for a reply, she resisted the urge to make some absurd excuse to follow them.

"She wasn't well this morning, but she was much better this evening when I left," she said at last stiffly.

"She will remain unwell, I'm afraid. She is much too tense. The stomach nerves react to that tenseness resulting in spasms of indigestion which can be very upsetting. How is her appetite?"

"Very good really." She almost jested that her cooking could be upsetting Madame Jasseron. Since coming to France, Vicki had collected many recipes and delighted in trying them out at the farm when Madame was indisposed. But Guy had taken on his familiar impersonal manner that did not encourage flippancy.

"See that she has plenty of easily digestible food. As I shall probably be on my lecture tour when she has the baby, I have alerted my colleagues at the hospital in Nice to be ready to receive her if the need arises."

Vicki's dark eyes widened with concern. "You think something will go wrong?"

He gave a French shrug. "Madame Jasseron is no longer young. A first baby is always a bit of a gamble. As I told you, the local midwife is excellent in her sphere."

"But Madame Jasseron will not go to hospital under any circumstances. She is fully determined to have her baby at home. The mention of her going to hospital would convince her that something was wrong," Vicki said huskily.

Vicki felt his distaste of her pursuing a subject she knew little about. The pause ended when he said, "The midwife is a reliable diagnostician and also a good administrator of anesthetic. In short, she is as capable as a doctor." His look was tinged with mockery. "Your sister is looking very well."

Vicki took the abrupt change of conversation to mean that as far as he was concerned the subject was closed. It upset her a little, for there was so much she wanted to ask him. For one thing, she was so anxious for nothing to go wrong that she was ready to cooperate in every way to ensure that Madame had her baby.

She hoped that Madame not wanting a hospital had made an impression on him. It was a pity he would be away, for Madame Jasseron had faith in him which would help a great deal when the time came for her to have her baby.

"Susie is thrilled about the villa," she said. "She never expected a place of her own."

"Yet the Château Brissard is roomy enough for them to take up residence there. Was it not modern enough?"

"Being modern doesn't enter into it. All young couples are happier in a place of their own."

"Then, unlike you, she does not object to living in a château?"

"I never said I did. I believe I said that some old buildings gave me the creeps. I imagine surroundings are of secondary consideration when one is with a beloved partner."

"Even a haunted monastery?" he teased unexpectedly.

His sudden change of mood as he turned on the charm took her unawares. She much preferred his impersonal approach. It was much easier to contend with. She had only to reach out a hand, and she would be touching his thick cap of hair which sprang into natural waves about his well-shaped head.

She was saved from replying by the imperative ringing of the phone.

"I'll answer it," he said, on his feet in one fluid movement. "It could be for Janera."

He strode into the hall. She heard his voice, crisp and to the point. When he reappeared, he came no farther than the threshold.

"*Pardon*, I have a call. It sounds serious and I might not return. Please convey my apologies to Robert and Susie. *Au revoir*, Vicki."

She replied, loving the sound of her name on his lips. The rest of the evening passed uneventfully. Vicki did not feel in the mood for staying behind when the guests had left, much as she would enjoy a chat with Susie and Robert. Yet, by talking to them, the tantalizing image of Guy could be dismissed more readily.

When the guests were leaving, Robert lingered at the door to have a word with his parents. Susie seated Vicki on the sofa, then went upstairs to return with a present in her hand.

"For you, dear," she said.

Vicki opened it to find a white gossamer nightdress and

a bottle of Paris perfume. "How sweet of you both," she said, a little choked. "I never expected you to think of me on your honeymoon. Thanks, it's lovely."

While Vicki replaced it in the pretty box, Susie exclaimed in horror at her hands. "Your poor hands! They must have really hurt you."

"They're much better, and I did nothing heroic. It was my fault the creepers caught fire. I never should have burned the compost heap in the first place," Vicki answered dryly.

"If that had been me, I would have lost my head completely and let the villa burn down. I'm glad it didn't, of course, but it was an awful price to pay. They won't be scarred, will they?" She looked anxiously at Vicki, who laughed.

"There's nothing to leave scars. The scratches will fade away; the burns were only superficial, so those will go, too."

Susie shuddered. "You might have been burned to death!"

"Nonsense. That's what your precious surgeon said."

"Guy?" Susie hugged her knees and rocked herself too and fro contentedly. "I've been telling Robert, we shall have to find you a husband. It's wonderful being married. I wish you could find the same happiness. I know you haven't much faith in matrimonial bliss since the parents were divorced, but falling in love makes all the difference if it's the right man."

Vicki looked at her fondly. "Seeing you happy is enough for me at the moment."

Susie wrinkled her nose. "I was telling Robert what you said about Guy giving his intended a check-up before he married her and then comparing notes with Janera on the result."

"You didn't!" Vicki wailed in dismay, then froze in horror to see Robert entering the room with Guy. How much had he heard? The door had been left ajar and

Susie's voice was youthfully clear. Her gaze met Guy's across the room, but it was impossible to tell whether he had heard. To her dismay she felt the blood rushing beneath her clear skin. Her heart pounded away frighteningly.

Susie, however, saw nothing amiss. Taking it in her stride, she went forward lightly to greet him. "Guy, I'm so glad you came back. Come and sit down while Robert fixes you a drink. We kept Vicki here for a chat, now you can join us."

Catching his hands, she pulled him forward to a chair. Vicki remained a statue on the sofa and accepted a drink she did not want. Thank heaven for Susie, who sat beside her beaming happily.

Robert stood, a drink in one hand, the other thrust in his pocket. "Was the call serious, Guy?"

Guy swallowed part of his drink as though he was in need of it.

"A heart attack—old Villiers. Unfortunately, it was his last."

"I'm very sorry," Robert said sadly. "He was a grand old chap. In his 80's, wasn't he?"

"84. It was fortunate I was at hand. It would have been an ordeal for Janera had she answered the call."

His softened tones were a knife thrust to Vicki's heart. He evidently loved her, by the way he spoke. Vicki's fingers closed convulsively around her glass. If it was possible for him to care for someone, then Janera was the ideal choice. They had such a lot in common regarding their careers. She would fit into his circle too, with her sophisticated elegance. A curious calm settled over her. She could stop torturing herself. She had final proof that Guy was not for her, never had been. He was Janera's. All the same, she wished the lady doctor had more spontaneous warmth, for Vicki loved him so much that all she wanted was his happiness.

She drank enough to ease the restriction in her throat,

then put it down. She had to remember to keep her dignity at any price. Robert was talking about Paris with Susie looking up at him adoringly.

Vicki closed her eyes, imagining the small open-air cafés, the fascinating market places, boulevards and squares, the magnificent splendor of the Sacré Coeur and the glory of Notre Dame. A delicious dreaminess swept over her.

"Come on, sleepyhead. It's the farm and bed for you." Robert was bending over her smiling as he added, "Unless you would like to stay here for the night?"

"Oh no, thanks, Robert. I must go in case Madame Jasseron worries about me." Vicki was now very much awake and gathered her gift box and evening purse hurriedly.

"I'll take you home." Guy was also on his feet, tall and unsmiling. For some reason, Vicki was terrified.

She looked appealingly at Robert. "I'm sure Monsieur . . . Guy is tired after driving from Nice and answering that call. I'd better go with you, Robert. We can't take him out of his way."

Robert looked from one to the other and Guy put in smoothly, "A kilometer or so out of my way is nothing. It will save you from moving your car, *mon ami*. So if you are ready. . . ." He gave a mocking little bow and motioned her forward with a wave of his hand. There was no humor in the eyes that met hers for several seconds; they looked menacing and dangerous.

Clutching her evening purse and gift box like a lifeline, she managed to stroll unconcernedly with Susie to the door. The two men came behind.

"You will come to see us, won't you, Guy, before your tour starts?" Robert was saying.

"I can't promise," was the cool reply. "Perhaps you will come and dine with me. I have had little time for entertaining this last year, but when I return from the lecture tour we will have a shot at bringing back the old days when the Château was never without guests."

Susie promised to call on Madame Jasseron as Vicki kissed her and Robert before sliding into the car. Guy took his seat, started the car, and they both waved before they shot away.

The car hummed along; neither of them talking, Vicki because she did not know what to say and Guy . . . well, he looked as congenial as a glacier. She longed to reach out a hand to smooth away his tension.

He had hardly enjoyed a very relaxing evening, not having arrived until eight and then attending a call that had ended so tragically. At length, she said, sympathetically, "I'm sorry you weren't able to do anything for Monsieur Villiers. Had you known him long?"

"All my life," was the brief reply.

"Perhaps you would rather not talk about it. It must be one of the heartbreaking incidents your job entails from time to time."

"It was. I have known him intimately. He was a close friend of my grandfather."

"Then you must be feeling his passing keenly."

To her surprise he suddenly turned the car off the highway, switched off the engine and turned toward her, his arm on the wheel.

"You don't really think so, do you?" The steel thread in his deep voice sprang from anger leashed within him.

She quivered with apprehension. "What do you mean?" she whispered weakly.

"Oh, come now," he said, regarding her speculatively. "Surely a man who would be callous enough to give his chosen bride a check-up before marriage is not capable of deep emotion."

Her heart leapt in her throat. So he had heard! She felt terrible. He had been upset at the old man dying and had called to see Robert before going home to an empty house. But instead of having a quiet talk with his friend he had heard her very uncomplimentary remarks which had been more or less in jest.

What could she say? Vicki cast about desperately for something, but found nothing. In the dimly lit interior of the car, his eyes blazed at her, demanding an answer. Her fear at his anger was offset by a desire to confound him by speaking the truth.

"Aren't you attaching too much importance to a statement made in jest?" she asked, amazed at her calmness.

He blazed, "*Ma foi!* You expect me to make light of the fact that you not only regard me as inhuman, you actually make it known to others. Your opinion of me is of no consequence, but your sister has repeated it to one of my closest friends." Savagely sore and angry, he leaned over her, his face inches from her own. "You have made a personal remark about two people you know practically nothing about."

Vicki recoiled in her seat, rebelling inwardly. Antagonism had been between them from their first meeting, flaring up at the slightest provocation. There had to be a climax and this was it. Meeting his dark, contemptuous gaze, she said hurriedly,

"I regret that Susie has told Robert, but since you know he will not repeat it, no harm has been done. I am sure Susie will not repeat it either."

A slight unpleasant smile curved his well-cut mouth. "Does that mean you believe what you said was true?" His fingers gripped her shoulders cruelly and he turned her around to face him roughly. "Does it?" he repeated.

Vicki knew he was waiting for her apology, but one glance at his thinned lips and tight expression stopped the words from reaching her lips.

She felt his hands pinning her down, rendering her virtually helpless. "You have a short memory, Vicki," he said softly. "On the evening you dined with me you accused me of seeing every situation through the eyes of a surgeon. I corrected you by saying that when I was off duty, I was a man, very much so."

He bent his head to take her lips in a long, pitiless kiss. In vain she tried to move her head as she gathered every scrap of resistance against him, but to no avail. When his mouth slid down to her neck, she was gasping for breath. She was spinning around in a vacuum at the mercy of lips that, to her utter humiliation, punished unmercifully. He moved to her mouth again, crushing it beneath his own while his hand caressed her breasts beneath her coat. Gradually her defense ebbed away, leaving a shattering sense of shame.

When, at last, he lifted his head, she was too hurt to define the expression in his eyes, an expression she saw through a mist of tears. She was released to fall back, shuddering, against the upholstery of the car. It was reversed, and the rest of the journey to the farm made in a painful silence.

CHAPTER TEN

Monday brought two visitors to the Jasseron farm. The first was the midwife. She was a tall, sturdily built Scot with light hair and gray twinkling eyes. Madame Jasseron's doctor had asked her to call, she said. Vicki knew Guy had sent her with the idea of keeping an eye on Madame and, at the same time, to give her confidence. She had evidently been well briefed, for she said, kindly, "I believe it is your first baby, Madame Jasseron, but you have nothing to worry about. I will take care of you. I am sure you will be all right."

Madame Jasseron was certainly much brighter when the midwife left. When Susie visited in the afternoon, she proudly brought out all the tiny things they had made. Susie brought a layette for the baby and begged to be allowed to take home the crib Monsieur Jasseron had bought to decorate it.

In the days that followed, Vicki tried to erase Guy's image from her mind. She knew it was an impossibility, for she loved him as one only loves once in a lifetime. Over and over again, she asked herself if it was infatuation. One could not hate a man one minute and be sick with longing for him in the next. A week had passed since that fateful night. She had stumbled into the farmhouse still trembling from his kisses, to gaze into the mirror at her pale face and tumbled hair.

Yet, for all her humiliation at his hands, she still remembered how his touch had thrilled and shaken her to the depths. Sometimes, in an unguarded moment, she wondered how their friendship would have developed had she not fought with him over Susie. For it had been Susie, whom she loved so devotedly and protected with such loyalty, who had been partly responsible for the hostility between them. Yet, if it had not been for Susie, they might never have met. So her thoughts ran on until she wondered how long she could bear it.

Fortunately, her days were filled with work. One of the smaller bedrooms had been cleared for a nursery. She had spent one day clearing out the attic to find a baby chair and a rocking horse. Happily she had painted them white to match the woodwork in the nursery. The walls she had painted in eggshell blue with the heat of the summer in mind. Susie returned the crib trimmed beautifully in white nylon and lace, finished off with a huge bow of blue ribbon. The bow could always be changed to pink if it happened to be a girl, she said. Monsieur and Madame Jasseron were delighted with it.

Susie settled down contentedly into married life. Robert left the villa early in the morning to work on the Brissard farm estate and returned home in the evening for dinner. Susie was helping Madame Brissard with the bottling of the wine. They appeared to be getting along splendidly, for which Vicki was very thankful. The woman Robert had engaged at the villa did the housework and cooking, leaving Susie to fill in her time as she wished.

Vicki spent her time between the villa and the Château Brissard looking after Madame Jasseron, who was now nearing her time.

Vicki hadn't seen or heard anything of Guy. At the villa, one evening, she was told he had begun his lecture tour. There had been a queer ache inside her when she realized she would never see him again. She longed for Madame Jasseron to have her baby, so that she could leave and begin to pick up the threads of her old life.

Gerard called to date her. He had managed to enlist the services of a girl in the village who could type. She came in on weekends for several hours, so he was managing to get his work done.

Madame Jasseron did not go shopping in the village now that she was in an advanced stage of pregnancy. So

Vicki went alone, calling in at the coffee shop to inform Madame's friends who gathered there of her progress. One market day, she had spent an enjoyable time with them and was thinking of leaving when Janera walked in.

Vicki was sitting at a small table in a corner overlooking the room. It had been Madame's favorite place, but most of her friends had left when Janera came to take an empty chair.

"Mind if I join you?" she asked amiably.

"Not at all," Vicki replied. Having come to terms with herself over Guy's relationship with the lady doctor, she could even find Janera bearable. Life was easier when one learned not to get too involved, a maxim she had used before coming to France. In the future it would always be that way. She had learned her lesson.

The few occupants of the other tables in the café all knew Janera and there were greetings from all sides. Janera acknowledged them as she sat down and asked Vicki if she would like another coffee before she ordered.

"*Merci*," she said. "I can't stay. I have to call at the villa with things I have bought for Susie."

Janera ordered a coffee and restlessly lit a cigarette. She appeared to have mislaid her usual *sangfroid*. Yes, Vicki decided, Janera seemed to be nervous. For one thing she was smoking too much. It was evident by the stain on her fingers. She exhaled a column of smoke and accepted her coffee with a brilliant smile.

"She is very happy, your sister. One can see that," she said, thoughtfully. "Yet they knew each other so little before they married. Me, I've loved the same man since I was eight years old. Fantastic, you say, *non*?"

"Not really," Vicki answered, wishing she had left when she saw Janera first coming through the doorway. She might persuade herself that the mention of Guy did not hurt any more, but she had no desire to test herself by hearing Janera confess her love for him.

Janera studied the tip of her cigarette. "Grand'mère used to say there would be no wedding if the women did not do a little pushing. I am inclined to agree."

"Grand'mère could have been right. I take it that you have done no pushing. Perhaps, like me, you think the man should do most of the running," Vicki said wryly.

Janera's eyes became friendly and warm. "I certainly do. When I began to practise as a doctor, I vowed I would not marry until I was 30. After that, I would willingly give up my career for the more satisfying role of wife and mother. I have two more years to go and find I don't want to wait any longer."

Vicki gathered her things together. "Then the answer is obvious, isn't it? You will have to do that little bit of pushing. Now if you will excuse me, I must fly."

Driving away from the village, Vicki told herself she must be the only woman on record who told another how to attract the man she herself loved.

Vicki and Madame Jasseron grew very close when they sat together making baby clothes. The Frenchwoman told of her marriage with Jean Jasseron. She had been 18, he 24, when they had first met. She had liked his warm brown eyes, blunt square features and gentle hands. He had a seriousness of manner sadly absent in the village boys with whom she had come in contact in her work as assistant to the local vet.

They had married within six months of meeting and Madame, wildly happy, had looked forward to starting a family. Jean had no parents. An uncle had set him up in the farm when he was 18 and left him to make his own way. When their second year of marriage failed to produce children, Madame was shattered. The rest Vicki already knew.

Vicki imagined her walking to the village proudly swinging her basket in the early days of her marriage—then, as neighbors' babies came, losing her happy swing when she remained barren. It had been doubly hard for Madame because her husband had never known a family, and she had longed to give him one. Poor Madame Jasseron! Everything had to come right for her. It had to.

One night Vicki was awakened by a muted roar. The house appeared to heave like a storm-tossed vessel. She raised herself up on an elbow to look at the time. It was half past four. The shutters creaked and rattled outside her window. Now she knew why it had to be closely barred and shuttered at night. It was to keep out the *mistral*.

She lay listening to the gale force wind recalling Guy's teasing remark about Susie and Robert clinging together beneath their feather quilt when the *mistral* came. Thank goodness they would be doing just that. Susie would not be alone. Robert did not leave for work on the farm until five-thirty. It was Nanette's baby's first *mistral* too. But she would be in the barn snug and warm with her mother and the other goats.

She must have drifted off to sleep, for she was roused by a knocking on her bedroom door. Hurriedly slipping on her wrap, she opened the door to see Monsieur Jasseron. He was fully dressed and had obviously been outdoors fastening everything down.

"It's my wife," he said. "I think the baby is coming. I am going to call the midwife."

He went downstairs while Vicki went quickly into their room. Madame Jasseron lay sweating in her bed and giving occasional short painful gasps.

"Are you all right, *madame*?" Vicki asked, bending over her anxiously. "Monsieur Jasseron has gone to phone for the midwife."

"I'm glad," she gasped. "The pains have been coming more or less all night. Now they are coming at shorter intervals and are more pronounced."

Vicki patted her hands reassuringly. "Hang on. I'll get dressed and put the kettle on."

Before she reached the bedroom door, however, Monsieur Jasseron was there.

"I can't get through," he said. "The wind must have blown the line down."

"Then one of us will have to fetch her. Shall I go or you, *monsieur*?" Vicki said firmly.

"I'll go," Monsieur Jasseron said without hesitation. "The *mistral* will blow you away."

"Get away with you," Vicki laughed. "If it is behind me I can get there all the quicker."

While Monsieur Jasseron was away, Vicki boiled water and put towels handy. The hours ticked away and still he did not come. When someone did eventually arrive it was the midwife. She was at a train accident several kilometers away; Monsieur Jasseron had stayed to help. It was dreadful, she said, with people lying injured all along the track.

Madame Jasseron was still in labor at lunchtime. It was a real tragedy that the telephone wires were down, Vicki thought in dismay. It could not have happened at a more crucial time. She prepared lunch and took a tray upstairs to Madame's room. Then, finding she could not face any food herself, she drank coffee thirstily.

When she collected the tray, the midwife drew her aside.

"I think Madame Jasseron should go to hospital," she said. "It isn't a straightforward case. It's a difficult birth, and I don't want to lose the baby."

Vicki's heart dropped. "But you can't do that! Madame will be upset. Besides, Nice is miles away and anything could happen on the way."

"Then we must have a doctor. I can't take the responsibility myself."

Vicki flinched when she heard Madame Jasseron moan. "I'll go and fetch him," she said.

Slipping on her white raincoat and a scarf, Vicki, buffeted by the strong winds staggered across the courtyard to the garage. On the way to the Molineux' villa the wind tore at the car, battering the windows; Sarah keeping valiantly on as if she knew what was expected of her.

To her dismay Vicki found the Molineux were at the train crash. The maid promised to tell Doctor Molineux when he returned. Vicki sped away. It was half an hour before she reached the scene of the train disaster, where the wreckage spread for about half a mile along the track. Ambulances were darting to and fro taking stretcher cases to the hospital, and firemen were using acetylene burners to free victims from the wreckage.

Fighting against the wind, she staggered to a young policeman directing an ambulance toward stretcher cases.

"Doctor Molineux?" she shouted above the wind.

He gave a shrug and shook his head. She stumbled on. When she saw Doctor Molineux, he was supporting a man trapped by wreckage. Firemen were trying to burn free the lower half of his body.

Vicki tapped the doctor on the shoulder. "Please, doctor," she said, above the wind. "Madame Jasseron is in labor and needs a doctor. Can you come?"

He shook his head. "Not yet," he said. "She had better go to hospital. I believe there is a bed for her there."

Vicki was near to tears. "But she can't. In any case, the telephone wires are down."

"Then ask one of the ambulances here to collect her. Tell them I sent you," was the reply.

"You don't understand . . ." Vicki began, but the doctor was already giving his attention to his patient. She stood there literally wringing her hands. Either way it could be too late. It was a long journey to Nice; if the doctor did eventually see Madame Jasseron the time factor would be about the same. She looked around for Janera, but saw neither the lady doctor or Monsieur Jasseron.

Realizing that time was precious, she made her way back. She struggled against the wind to where she had seen the ambulances, only to find them gone.

What to do now? She stood like a slender stalk swaying in the fierce onslaught, in so much anguish that when her scarf was torn away, she made no attempt to chase after it. Slowly, she turned her back to the wind, trying to keep her balance. She had never felt so helpless in her life as she looked on the scene of disaster. Many of the helpers appeared to be searching through the wreckage for belongings, giving the impression that most of the passengers had been accounted for. Then her eyes were drawn to a big familiar car with a tall, broad-shouldered figure standing beside it wiping his hands.

He was looking less immaculate than usual, and his hair was dishevelled by the wind. Vicki tried to call his name as she let the wind sweep her toward him. Then she was in his arms clinging to him and gasping for breath.

"Guy!" she gasped. "Thank heaven!" For blissful moments she leaned breathless against his broad chest. And when, at last, she lifted anguished eyes to his, he gripped her arms.

"What is it?" he asked sternly. "Why are you here?"

But her relief at seeing him was too great. Tears welled in her eyes and brimmed over. "It's Madame Jasseron. . . ." she began, then could not continue.

"Come into the car," he said, leading her to the door.

When he slid in beside her, Vicki had managed to compose herself. Swiftly, she told him about Madame Jasseron. He listened, his face grave.

"I had no idea you were back," she tacked on at the end of her story.

"I arrived early this morning, heard about the train crash and rushed over. Most of the passengers have been released from the wreckage; there are sufficient doctors and nurses to cope. What exactly did the midwife say?"

"That it was a difficult birth, and she did not want to take the responsibility."

"Doesn't sound too good. How long has Madame Jasseron been in labor?"

"All last night and today."

They shot away with Vicki putting her hand on his sleeve. "Sarah is here. I can't leave her behind. Monsieur Jasseron is helping somewhere, but he came in his van."

"Your car can be collected later. There is not a moment to lose if it is not already too late." With that he speeded up. Vicki had to cling to her seat as he shot around bends as if the devil was after him. "Let's hope the road is clear," he said as the car ate up the miles.

It was. They arrived at the farm with Vicki feeling bruised, battered and completely exhausted. The midwife opened the door, her face clearing when she saw them.

"Oh, *monsieur*," she said. "Am I glad to see you!"

"What's wrong?" he demanded.

"Everything. The baby is stuck. It's a shoulder birth and the arms are protruding."

"*Mon dieu!*" he exclaimed. "Then it is too late. The baby will be dead."

"The heart is still beating," the midwife assured him. "That is why I thought the best plan was for Madame to go to hospital for a Caesarian operation."

He frowned. "A Caesarian is out of the question. The child's protruding hands are sure to be infected now and hours would be wasted on the journey." He gazed speculatively at the midwife's tense expression and went on urgently, "You can administer anesthetic?" She nodded eagerly. "Then *vite!* Let us hope it is not too late."

Hot water was carried upstairs in the minimum of time; and Vicki, taking the weight off her shaking legs, sat down in the kitchen to wait. She closed her eyes, sitting as though suspended in time, her heart already beginning to ache for Madame Jasseron if the baby failed to survive. Outside, the *mistral* roared eerily, filling the kitchen with ghosts. She could see Madame Jasseron putting the last touches to the evening meal, her husband creeping up behind her to kiss the back of her neck. Monsieur filling the house with song, waltzing his wife around the room and carrying in a crib with the joy of heaven in his eyes.

Tears gathered in her eyes when she remembered wishing Madame Jasseron an easy confinement on the day they went into the barn to see Nanette's baby kid. But it was proving anything but easy. Everything had gone wrong from the start, with even the *mistral* against her. And poor Monsieur Jasseron, who, thinking everything would be all right for his wife with the midwife and herself in charge, had stayed to help the victims of the rail crash. At least he had been spared the agony of suspense.

The wind still whistled and moaned. She looked at her watch. Four o'clock. Two hours to go before it blew itself out or continued for three days, if the saying was true. What did it matter how long it continued? The harm was done and she hated it; would always hate it for what it had done to Madame Jasseron.

Someone at the door brought her to her feet. Monsieur Jasseron entered, closed the door and leaned against it, looking tired and weary.

He replenished his lungs before saying on a slow smile, "I intended to give a helping hand until more help was forthcoming, but you know how it is at times like this. I've been running people home who lived locally and were not too badly hurt. How is she?"

Vicki swallowed and knew with a hopeless despair that it would be cruel to raise his hopes. She tried to speak, but could voice no words that made sense. All she could do was to shake her head numbly, fighting back the tears.

Then it came: a thin wail as though borne on the wind. Gradually it grew into a lusty yell, and they both looked up to the ceiling. Monsieur Jasseron's face lit up the room. Then he was up the stairs with Vicki a close second.

He flung open the bedroom door. Guy stood there as he held the baby by its feet in the air. It looked like a skinned rabbit, but it was perfectly formed and yelling at the top of its lungs.

Guy grinned. "*Félicitations, monsieur*. You have a fine boy."

He laid the baby down gently on the bed. Monsieur Jasseron took Guy's hands, wet as they were, and kissed them humbly. Guy's smile was white, his forehead damp with sweat. Vicki wanted to stroke back the damp dishevelled hair and wipe his face, for his boyish look tore at her heart. For a moment his eyes met hers before giving his attention once more to Monsieur Jasseron.

"Out of the room, *vite!*" Both of you!" he commanded.

At the door, Monsieur Jasseron turned. "My wife?" he asked. "How is she?"

"Madame is asleep," came the reply, and they both left the room.

In the kitchen, Vicki began preparing a meal. She was laying the table when Guy appeared followed by Monsieur Jasseron, who had washed and changed.

"A drink before you go," he cried happily.

Guy shook his head. "*Merci.* I must be off."

"I'd like to thank you, too," Vicki said sincerely. "You have been wonderful."

He regarded her without expression. "I would not be here if it had not been for you." Monsieur Jasseron looked from one to the other with a puzzled frown until Guy captured his gaze. "Yes, *monsieur*, you have the little English miss to thank for the safe delivery of your son."

Monsieur Jasseron's reaction to this was one of stupefied surprise changing gradually to one of elation. Grabbing Vicki's arms, he kissed her soundly on both cheeks.

"Monsieur!" Guy barked so suddenly that she was released instantly. "You can collect Vicki's car. I will take you to where she left it."

Vicki stood for a while after they had gone, trying to catch up with all that had happened. She was so bemused that she could have sworn that Guy had looked angry because Monsieur Jasseron had kissed her. She was mistaken, of course. He was eager to be away, having spent most of the day at the scene of the rail disaster. Only then did it occur to her, with a jolt of her heart, that he might not have had anything to eat all day, either.

Doctor Molineux called to see if Madame Jasseron had been taken to hospital. He apologized for being unable to leave the crash scene to attend to Madame Jasseron, but he knew she could be taken care of at the hospital. It was also unfortunate that Janera was away, staying with friends in Nice.

Vicki told him everything that had occurred, and he went upstairs to see Madame and the baby. When he came down again, he was all smiles.

"A beautiful baby," he said. "Madame Jasseron was lucky to have the services of Monsieur Ransart. The midwife had informed me that his skilful handling saved the child's life." Vicki felt her face suffuse with color at the mention of Guy and was aware of the doctor's intent regard. "Monsieur Ransart," he went on smoothly, giving him the correct title for a surgeon, "broke his lecture tour to perform an operation at the hospital in Nice. He was still in the building when the hospital was alerted about the rail disaster, so he went to help."

He went on to talk of the difficulties of childbirth, but Vicki scarcely heard him. She was thinking of Guy being in Nice and Janera going to spend a few days there with friends. She had gone to meet Guy, of course. Maybe he had already proposed. Vicki put the thought from her mind and concentrated on what the doctor was saying.

Monsieur Jasseron returned with Sarah as the doctor was leaving and was congratulated on a beautiful baby.

For the week following, the farm was never free from visitors.

Susie and Robert called along with his parents, Susie thrilled because she had decorated the crib with a large blue bow for a boy. At times, the farmhouse was so packed that Vicki found herself running around like a demented hornet to supply everyone with refreshment. And how she loved it; happy to have her days filled, leaving no time to think about Guy. She was usually so tired at night that she was asleep almost as soon as her head touched the pillow. Like Monsieur Jasseron, she trilled happily as she did her chores, loving to watch the lines of freshly laundered white diapers drying in the sun.

The day Madame Jasseron came downstairs for the first time was a happy one. Vicki made a special dinner for the three of them. She hastened her chores in the morning and spent the afternoon baking and cooking the dinner. Madame came downstairs helped by her husband in his best suit, his broad face freshly shaved and beaming.

A bottle of champagne was opened. Monsieur Jasseron proposed a toast to their new son and heir. They had decided to call him Victor Guy Jasseron. Victor after their beloved Vicki, and Guy, after the surgeon who had saved him for them. To Vicki, it was the happiest night she had known as she seconded the toast with tears pricking her eyelids.

"We will never forget what you have done, Vicki," Madame Jasseron said, sincerely. "The most wonderful part about it is that the midwife says there is no reason why I should not have more children."

"Why not?" Vicki said happily. "I think a girl would be nice. It would be good for Victor because I am sure he is in danger of being spoiled."

"Sounds interesting," Monsieur Jasseron remarked with a twinkle in his eye.

"Get away with you!" Madame Jasseron said with a blush. She was looking ten years younger since having the baby. She was wearing a plain navy tailored dress with a round neck and three-quarter sleeves. Vicki had styled her hair into soft waves about her head, clipped white studs on her ears and clasped a white beaded choker around her neck. The whole effect was quite charming, the light from the candles bringing out the coppery glints in her hair. Vicki congratulated herself on thinking about the candles, set in triple candlesticks on each side of the long table.

Afterward, when she had stacked the clean dishes on the kitchen dresser, she slipped on her coat, whistled to Gaston and went for her evening walk. Since Madame's confinement she had not been outside except to do the shopping. Tired though she had been most evenings, she had taken a short walk before going to bed to digest her meal. It had become a habit.

She had heard nothing from Gerard. He had phoned to say he would be away at the television studios supervising a play he had written. Janera also appeared to have vanished into thin air. Which brought her thoughts inevitably to Guy. Nocturnal scents from the wild roses in the hedges and the mimosa in yellow cushions on the hills filled her nostrils as she recalled him talking about the beauty of fall. But the tranquillity of her surroundings failed to revive her drooping spirits as she walked, listlessly trying to whip up a spark of enthusiasm for planning her future.

She ached to see him again. The dreams she might have spun around him were ended before they began; and she knew she was a fool to think about him at all. He was a

Frenchman who had chosen a Frenchwoman for his future wife, a woman who was suited to him in every way. He evidently, she thought miserably, preferred the cool, elegant, sophisticated kind. With a pang, she recalled the strong features suddenly becoming young and boyish. As he held Madame Jasseron's baby aloft, his attractive brows drew into a mock pained smile as it yelled its way into the world. That was how she would always remember him, with the tendrils of hair clinging to his damp forehead, his blue eyes gleaming with victory over the battle he had won against tremendous odds.

Madame Jasseron continued to make good progress and spent more hours downstairs each day. It was quite an event when Vicki drove her and the baby to market for the first time. The village storekeepers were enchanted with *le petit garçon*, gazing down at his tiny plump face and pushing a finger into his small clenched fist. The café where they went later to meet Madame's friends was filled with ecstatic murmurings.

The day had begun dull and cloudy, but Victor Guy Jasseron had been like a small sun lighting up the features of all who saw him in the village. And when the sun shone on the way back to the farm, Vicki declared that the little one had brought it out.

That evening Robert phoned from the villa to say that Susie had a heavy cold. Also Luce, the woman he had engaged to do the cooking and the chores, had left that day to answer a summons from her aged *grand'mère* who was very ill. As she had no idea when she would be back, Robert wondered if Vicki would mind calling the next day while he was on the farm to see if Susie was all right.

Vicki left for the villa the next morning after doing a few chores, happy now that Madame Jasseron was fit to carry on with the help of the daily woman in the dairy. She washed the breakfast dishes, fed the fowl and collected the eggs. Nanette and her baby came to her for a cuddle and the tidbit she always carried for them. The nanny was both intelligent and affectionate. Vicki had grown fond of her as she had the rest of the farm animals. She would find leaving them very hard when the time came.

She found Susie in bed with smudged eyes and red nose. For the best part of a week she was really ill. Doctor Molineux called every day. He was inclined to linger longer each time he called, with Vicki divided by embarrassment and the fear of being alone with him.

She spent the day at the villa looking after Susie, cooking the evening meal. She left her with Robert in the evening to return to the Jasseron farm. Robert's parents had accompanied the aunts and uncles back to Menton and were staying there for a few days. Consequently, they were not able to help out.

The end of the week found Susie out of bed and walking around like a pale ghost. Doctor Molineux had finished his call with Vicki very politely refusing his invitation out to dinner. Those small black eyes of his saw far too much and it would not be long before he noticed that she was in love with his prospective son-in-law.

The week Susie had been in bed was one of intermittent rain. The second week, however, brought clear blue skies and a countryside green and sparkling. Luce came back to do the chores, so Robert agreed with Vicki that Susie should go out for a few days to cheer her up again.

So each day they went out in Sarah, sometimes for a picnic, sometimes for lunch at a garden restaurant where they dined off freshly caught trout within sound of the murmur of cool mountain streams.

Leisurely they explored the hills: so mysterious in shade, so enchanting in the sun, to linger above tumbling water crashing down on moss-covered rocks below. It was a week of happy relaxation for them both. It also proved beneficial to Vicki, for she had been feeling the strain after the hectic time of Madame Jasseron's confinement.

One of their favorite places for refreshment was a delightful small café at the entrance to a bridge over a waterfall. It was there on the Thursday afternoon as they lingered over coffee beneath the sun-dappled leaves of trees that Vicki told Susie she would soon be heading for new pastures.

"I'm going to miss you awfully, Vic," she said, rather downcast. "But you will come and see us often, won't you?"

Vicki agreed, wondering how she was going to bear even the fleeting visits she had in mind with Guy so near.

Monsieur and Madame Brissard senior arrived home on the Friday and, as they were to dine with Susie and Robert on the Saturday night, Vicki was also invited. She accepted with the idea of making it kind of a farewell dinner for herself. First, she had planned to tell Madame Jasseron of her decision to leave within the next few days. She would then slip away quietly.

Madame Jasseron was also upset when Vicki told her of her intentions. "It's been wonderful knowing you both and I shall hate saying goodbye, but I have to move on," Vicki said gently.

"But why?" Madame queried. "Why not stay on? We have writers living locally who would welcome an experienced typist."

Vicki shook her head. "It's very sweet of you, but I've made up my mind to leave. With Susie always in mind I have never really felt free to do as I want to. Now she is married, there is no reason why I should not go wherever I feel inclined. I shall come to see you when I visit Susie."

Susie called her on Saturday morning to say that Gerard would be picking her up that evening on his way to dinner at the villa.

Vicki replaced the receiver thoughtfully. Of course, Gerard had been invited to make the number even. There would be Monsieur and Madame Brissard senior and junior and herself making five. Susie, being the dear she was, had invited Gerard so that she, Vicki, would not feel odd man out.

There is always a sad hollow ache when one does something for the last time. Without any definite feeling she slipped on the sleeveless white jersey dress, her dark eyes deep unfathomable pools. Her tawny hair had become so easy to manage since staying at the farm. It lay around her small head in thick curled waves showing gold lights she had never noticed before. The week outdoors had given her cheeks a pink glow; her skin had the velvety bloom of a peach. But the glow was only on the outside. Inside there was a numbness which she felt nothing could penetrate.

Gerard was calling for her at half past seven, and she was ready on time. When at a quarter to eight he still had not arrived, Vicki decided to go in Sarah to avoid disappointing Susie. They were entering the courtyard at the villa when she recognized only too well a certain big vehicle parked outside the villa. Guy's car. "Oh, no!" her heart cried in dismay.

She braked and her breath fastened in her lungs. All the peace of mind she had cultivated during the past week, the calm brought about by her decision to leave as soon as possible might never have been. Never for one moment had she thought it possible for Guy to be there. Minutes passed in which she felt incapable of movement. Then an urgent desire to escape took possession. She had only to turn Sarah around and drive away, far away, but the thought of Susie stopped her.

They were all in the *salon* when she entered. Monsieur and Madame Brissard senior were seated on the sofa with Janera close by. Robert and Guy were standing looking down on them and everyone held a drink.

"No Gerard?" Robert queried, after greeting Vicki warmly.

"He's probably been delayed," Susie chipped in, standing with Vicki's coat on her arm. "Sit down, Vic, while I remove your coat. Robert will give you a drink."

Vicki sank into the nearest chair, thankful that she was far enough away from the tall, overwhelmingly masculine figure leaning so nonchalantly against the fireplace. Mechanically, she accepted a drink from Robert and answered Madame Brissard's inquiry about the Jasseron baby, aware of Guy listening with interest to her answer. With cold fingers curved around her glass, she leaned back in her chair aching for Gerard's support. He was charming, gregarious and fun to be with, so different from Guy with his clipped comments, enigmatic looks and indefinable proud bearing.

Janera, dressed in dusky pink silk jersey drifting to the floor from a high bodice of pin-tucks, was laughing up at him with a remark that sent his thick attractive eyebrows into a humorous peak on his forehead.

They awaited Gerard's arrival until eight-thirty before trooping in to dinner. Vicki was seated by Susie with Janera on her other side between her and Guy. She thought this an excellent arrangement since it kept her out of his line of vision, and, more important, him out of hers.

The conversation was mostly about the absent Gerard, who was apparently becoming one of the top television writers. They had reached the coffee stage when the phone rang and Robert went to answer it in the hall. He was back in minutes, his expression grave.

"It's Gerard," he said. "He is in the hospital in Nice. He collapsed on the set during the filming of his play."

Guy was on his feet instantly. "I must see if there is anything I can do."

He was walking to the door when Janera drifted across the room to cling to his arm. "Take me with you, Guy, please," she entreated in husky tones.

Vicki watched them go, Janera still clinging to Guy's

arm. If anything could convince her of their relationship that ought to, she thought despairingly. Poor Gerard! She wished with all her heart that he could meet someone who would make him happy. She hated to think of him being alone and unhappy and wondered about the collapse.

Vicki was up early the next morning to pack and say goodbye. She was having breakfast with Monsieur and Madame Jasseron when the phone rang. It was Janera phoning from the hospital in Nice.

"*Bonjour,* Vicki," she said. "You will be pleased to hear that Gerard came around early this morning from his collapse. The poor idiot had been working all day in a hot studio without having eaten a thing. Guy has phoned Robert to let him know. He was told that you were leaving the country today. Is that so?"

"It is," Vicki said firmly. "It's awfully good news about Gerard. Thanks for telling me."

"I thought you would be pleased." Janera sounded very cheerful and, in the next breath, gave her reason. "Too bad you are going so soon, for you will miss my engagement party next Saturday."

Vicki's fingers closed tightly on the receiver. "Congratulations," she said. "I wish you much happiness."

"*Merci,*" was the bright reply. "I wish you *bon voyage.*"

Vicki put down the phone, her own unhappiness swamped by her pity for Gerard. When she told Monsieur and Madame Jasseron the news they begged her to stay until the engagement party. But Vicki shook her head, numbly aching to get away, glad she had been spared the ordeal of seeing Guy and Janera together. There was so much she had to put behind her that all emotion dried up inside at the thought of it.

She cuddled the baby for the last time and went to say farewell to all her farmhouse friends. Then she was driving away in Sarah with Monsieur and Madame Jasseron waving her off and wishing her *bon voyage*.

There were a few clouds scurrying across the sky and the weather appeared to be changing, but she was not alarmed. She doubted whether even an earthquake could shake her out of her present lethargic state.

When she drew nearer to the Château Brissard church bells were ringing in the valley below. Their sound smote her heart with the thought that soon they would be ringing for Janera and Guy. Her pale lips spoke the words her heart echoed. "Be happy with your Janera," she whispered.

Monsieur and Madame Brissard sent her on her way with a bottle of vintage wine, telling her not to leave it too long before coming again. At the villa, Susie loaded her up with all kinds of fruit and a packaged lunch for the trip. In vain, Vicki protested that she had more than enough from Madame Jasseron.

"Perhaps you can share it with some Romeo on the way," she said, trying to be cheerful. "I wish you'd met someone here, Vic. Did you know Gerard has come around and that it was only a collapse through not eating? Guy called us this morning from the hospital."

Vicki wondered if she knew of Janera's engagement, but she doubted whether she could tell her in the light tone she had adopted to leave Susie, so she said nothing about it.

"I'm glad it was nothing serious," she said. "I'm quite fond of Gerard."

They had strolled to the door with Susie peeping out into the garden. "Robert is around somewhere—and that reminds me." She caught Vicki's arm. "Come into the kitchen. I have a present for you from Robert. I told him that your old transistor radio wasn't very good; he's bought you one."

In the kitchen, Susie picked up an attractive cream

leather case and switched it on. Swinging music filled the room, an old familiar tune to which Susie swayed her hips. Wrinkling her nose, she said,

"Reminds you of the old days when we went dancing, doesn't it?"

Vicki nodded brightly, and they listened until the tune ended. Susie turned the dial and there came the sound of masculine voices. With a lurch of her heart, Vicki saw that they were not coming from the set but from the garden visible through the French window.

Two men were walking slowly to the villa along the garden path. The second one, taller than the first, had his hands thrust into his pockets as he strode along with an easy grace. Robert and Guy. Guy must have arrived under cover of the music from the radio.

Vicki panicked. "I must go, Susie." She gave her a swift kiss. "Say goodbye to Robert for me."

Susie stared, looked from her to the men who had paused in the garden. "But here's Robert now," she said in bewilderment.

Vicki, however, was at the door.

"Your radio!" Susie cried, running after her.

Safely in the car, Vicki began to breathe more freely.

"Thank Robert for me," she called to a puzzled Susie, who waved her off and blew kisses.

Not until she was clear of the villa did Vicki give a deep breath of relief. She could not have faced Guy again without giving herself away. Poor Susie had been at a loss to account for her sudden departure; she could not explain. Tears blocked her throat as she tried to visualize a future without Guy: living through the agony of knowing she would never see him again, going on from there.

The next instant, however, she was dumbfounded. A big car following behind quickly had entered her mirror. Guy's car. She froze and pressed hard on the accelerator. It was obvious from the start what the outcome would be, but Vicki was not giving in without a struggle. He was angry because she had not said goodbye. There was no other reason why he should come after her. This was awful! She could not face him. She was sure to make a fool of herself, and the humiliation would be unbearable. The road was wide enough for two vehicles to pass but the bends made it dangerous for a car to pass at the speed limit. However, Guy drew level. "Stop the car!" he shouted.

A feeling, part anger, part fright, made her press her foot down harder, taking advantage of his slowing down to race ahead. He was close behind when Sarah did the unforgivable. She gave a sudden gurgling sound and stopped.

"Judas!" Vicki hissed. She heard the sound of Guy's car as he swung out and around to brake in front of Sarah. Then she closed her eyes to brace herself to meet him, appear uncaring. His car door slammed, and he was opening hers to peer inside.

"Follow me to the Château," he commanded. "I have something important to tell you."

Vicki took her time about answering, trying to read the keen blue eyes regarding her so aloofly. Like Sarah, she was rigid, but she knew the trembling could start at any moment.

"You can tell me here," she declared stubbornly.

"If I told you here you might not be in a fit state to drive on," he said, unsmilingly. "So, *vite*! To the Château!"

His arrogant command stiffened her defenses as nothing else would. "It's not that easy," she said sweetly. "I didn't stop the car. Sarah decided to go no farther. As I imagine she is partial to a male sitting on her lap, perhaps you could persuade her to move on."

She slid along her seat to allow him to take the wheel. Sure enough, after the second attempt, he had Sarah purring.

To Vicki's surprise, he backed swiftly to swing Sarah around in front of his own car. Her mouth thinned in a bitter line. So he was not going to take the risk of her running out on him! He was keeping a tag on her by tailing her from the rear.

On the way to the Château, Sarah behaved impeccably with Vicki attempting to work out what he had to tell her that was so upsetting. She could only surmise that it had something to do with Gerard. Could be the news of Janera's engagement had brought on a second collapse and that her presence could help his recovery.

She entered the drive to the Château and braked in the courtyard. Guy followed promptly and was out of the car as soon as she was. At the Château she was led into the *salon* she had admired on her first visit, to stand slim and forlorn in a sea of exquisite Bessarabian carpet.

He strode forward after closing the door and motioned her to a chair imperiously. She gritted her teeth and was going to refuse when she saw his blue eyes. He had the look of one whose feelings were tightly controlled, yet ready to snap at the drop of a hat.

She sat down and looked up at him appealingly. "Is it Gerard? He's worse, isn't he?"

His face darkened and set. Pushing his hands into his pockets, he gazed down at her. "What would it mean to you if he was?"

"Very much," she replied without hesitation, adding, "As a friend."

He looked at her for a long moment and then drew an audible breath.

"And you ran away from the villa, not because of me, but because you wanted to get to the hospital in Nice in visiting hours in order to see him?"

She clung to his words like one clings to a lifeline. "You could say that," she said, and began to tremble at the disbelief on his face.

Savagely he barked, "So you were going to push his fiancée aside to weep on his shoulder?"

Vicki blinked, unwilling to believe her own ears. "You . . . m . . . mean he and Janera are engaged?"

He frowned. "Surely you already knew that. Janera phoned you from the hospital this morning to tell you."

Something so wonderful was happening that Vicki had to take it in slowly. "She didn't say it was Gerard."

Enlightenment dawned slowly in his eyes. "You thought I was the fiancé, *non*?" His handsome mouth curved into a smile, and his eyes held a roguish glint. "That was why you ran away when you saw me at the villa, wasn't it?" he asked softly.

Vicki tried to shake her head and only succeeded in moving uneasily in her chair. The look in his eyes was sending shivers down her spine. She had difficulty breathing. Then, like an eagle, he swooped her up into his arms.

At first, his kisses were as cruel as the ones he had showered on her as a punishment weeks before. Then, although his mouth grew more gentle, it still demanded the response she was too shattered to give. His hold slackened, and he lifted his head. She saw the puzzled frown and her eyes glowed shyly up at him. Slowly, her arms reached up to clasp his neck, her body curved to his, and she gave him her lips. If it was a dream, she thought wildly, may she never awaken.

But the firm mouth on her own, the strong heart beating into her breast was no dream. It was heavenly reality. His lips moved into the youthful curve of her neck. It was a long time before either of them spoke.

It was Guy who broke the ecstatic silence to speak above her ear in deeply moved tones. "I cannot believe it," he said. "To me, marriage has always been a union I could never enter into lightly. I had to find the woman possessing all the qualities I was looking for. Until I did, I refused to think about it. Then, when she failed to materialize, I resigned myself into becoming dedicated to my work. And what happened? You came along with your dark eyes flashing dislike and a fierce determination to protect a beloved sister from a wicked surgeon." He rubbed his chin against her temple. "I was irritated beyond measure to find a slip of a girl disliking me so thoroughly. I found myself inclined to shrug it off as being of no importance. Then a dog, whose love you had won by your gentleness, led me to you. I found myself drowning in dark eloquent eyes and that was it. I have never been the same since."

She smiled, "That was when I was beginning to capitulate—until Janera came in your place. I was shattered to discover how much I had looked forward to your visits."

His mouth moved on hers in a quick kiss before he looked down into her flushed face. "And there was something about your first meeting with Janera that convinced you of our relationship?"

Somehow she could not tell him of Janera's taunts. "I think you contributed to it yourself with your praise of your countrywomen."

His smile was white and boyish. "I was fighting against your charms. The desire for you was tearing me apart."

"You were doing the same to me," she admitted happily.

"Then you love me?"

He was humble and so unlike himself that she could not answer for several moments. Then she said, slowly and clearly, "I love you so much that the thought of losing you makes me shudder."

His arms tightened about her. "And you will marry me as soon as I procure a license?"

"Oh, yes," she whispered, her eyes filling with tears.

"What is it, *chérie*?" he asked, with the anxious look of a lover.

She swallowed. "My parents, Guy. They loved like we do, yet it ended in divorce."

He looked at her tenderly. "Love, *mignonne,* is a gentle flame which a married couple can keep burning only if they forget their claims on each other. They should always be lovers, never married people, especially when they are in bed."

"Guy!" she exclaimed, blushing furiously.

He laughed. "If the thought of sharing my bed makes you blush what will you do when it happens?" he teased.

"Love you and go on loving you," she said.

"Forever?"

She nodded, loving the feel of him against her as he kissed her with a lingering tenderness. There was no shrinking. She returned his kisses with a passion equal to his own, knowing that the gentle flame would always burn brightly for them.

TO MY DEAR NIECE

To My
Dear Niece

Hilda Nickson

Strong-willed and imaginative, Vanessa had no problem deciding what to do with Puck's Hill, the rambling country house she'd inherited from her eccentric great-aunt.

She was so busy reclaiming the gardens and setting up a gardening center that she forgot to worry about the conditions attached to the inheritance – conditions known only to the trustees.

And she refused to admit to herself that she was in love with her next-door neighbor, Ian Hamilton, who was obviously helping her because he wanted to buy Puck's Hill! The house became just like a millstone, keeping Vanessa from her love.

CHAPTER ONE

The letter from Aunt Maud arrived on one of those rare, still misty mornings in early summer that give promise of a fine, warm day. The dew was wet on the grass, the distant trees mysterious and aloof, the world silent, ethereal, and unspeakably beautiful.

Coming in from an hour's weeding for breakfast, Vanessa picked up the letter from the hall mat. The name—Vanessa's own—and address were written in a thin rambling scrawl and were barely decipherable. Vanessa's father had been born in this house, and the mailman brought into the world by her grandfather. Everyone for miles around knew the unconventional Dr. Woodrow and his pretty wife who was a leading soprano in the local operatic society.

Vanessa went through into the large kitchen. Hester, an elderly, distant relative who acted as general help and housekeeper was setting the breakfast trays. No one ever ate breakfast in the same place. It was an eccentric household. Her father came of a family of eccentrics—or so they appeared to the more conventional. Great-Aunt Maud, who had never married, lived virtually alone in a large old country house called Puck's Hill: its grounds overgrown with weeds because Aunt Maud would not allow chemical weed-killers in case these poisoned the birds; Uncle Ted who owned a private zoo; a cousin living in a converted windmill in Norfolk on the edge of the marshes; her mother, hopeless at ordinary household skills, but an accomplished pianist and with the voice of an angel. One could continue. Even herself, filling the role of chauffeur/gardener at home. Not that she considered herself odd. It was a job she had drifted into, having had no other immediate plans for a career. She had been educated at a boarding school. It was typical of her father that when people asked what she was going to do "when she left school", he would answer:

"Do? Do? Why, she's just going to be herself. She's not being educated merely to earn money; she's being educated so that she can live a full and happy life."

Vanessa could see now the sad smiles, the wise shakes of the heads. Fresh from the home of a friend whose parents had a beautiful garden to the wilderness which passed for the same thing at home, she had set about up-rooting weeds, making flower beds, tending the stretch of grass which had once been a lawn in the days of old Joshua, her grandfather's gardener. Turning a wilder-ness into a thing of beauty had given her an immense amount of satisfaction. Then she began to drive her father on his rounds or out on emergency calls, and to run her mother to and from rehearsals and opera performances.

Life was good—or had been until her father had taken on a junior partner. Vanessa had fallen in love with the young doctor, but not he with her. Yesterday, he had married the equally young and very pretty district nurse. When they returned from their honeymoon they would be living much too near the Woodrows' house to make it easy for Vanessa to forget him. Not that anyone had ever known how she felt. She had kept it completely to her-self—simple enough, surrounded as she was by people who were always preoccupied.

She had her own breakfast in the big conservatory. Her mother would doubtless have hers in the bath; her father, with a book, in front of the French window of his study which overlooked the herb garden; and Hester, in the kitchen.

Halfway through her breakfast Vanessa took out Aunt Maud's letter. Accustomed though she was to her great-aunt's scrawl, she still had difficulty in deciphering its contents, but two sentences stood out like banner headlines. *I have not been so well of late.* And: *I would dearly love to see you, child, if you could possibly come down for a few days.* Vanessa folded the letter thoughtfully, her features relaxing into soft lines. Dear, funny little Aunt Maud! She was sweet, but as tough and as independent as they come. Vanessa had been fond of her since childhood when she used to spend school holidays in the rambling old house full of passages and tiny rooms. Aunt Maud had devised treasure hunts in the untidy garden, and built fairy and elfin houses. She had taught Vanessa to appreciate nature; to learn about insects, birds, butterflies and all tiny creatures by seeking them in their natural habitat, by sitting with quiet patience, watching and waiting. Waiting for them to appear, and then watching what they did and how they lived.

Vanessa made a swift decision. She would go to Aunt Maud. Tomorrow. She would send a wire saying she was coming on the ten-thirty train. Another of her aunt's eccentricities was not having a telephone. It would be folly to trust the mail. She finished her breakfast, then went outside again. She would tell her mother and father when she saw them. A family consultation about her decision was not necessary; neither would it be expected.

"Poor Aunt Maud," was her father's comment when she told him as she drove him on his morning round. "She must be 90 if she's a day. Go and see her by all means, my dear. Have you any money?"

"Not much."

"Oh. Well, I'll write you a check when we return. You can cash it in the morning."

"Thanks, Father. I hope you'll be able to manage."

He smiled. "I can't promise to weed the garden or spray the roses, but otherwise, we'll manage. Kenneth and Julie are due back at the end of the week anyhow."

"Yes. Yes, I know."

When she told her mother the news at lunchtime, her

mother simply murmured absently: "Yes, all right, dear. Give Aunt Maud my love."

And so with 50 pounds in her pocket, Vanessa caught the ten-thirty train to Cringlewood, a small country town deep in the heart of Suffolk. Barn Hill, the tiny village where her aunt lived, was some 20 miles from there. If the little branch line had been closed down, which was more than likely, she would have to hire a taxi to take her the rest of her journey.

Puck's Hill, she mused. It was the name Aunt Maud had given to the house. She was rather puckish herself, Vanessa thought, with her wizened, weather-beaten features and crinkly smile.

It took the train a little over two hours to reach Cringlewood. As she expected, the branch line to Barnhill was now closed. Vanessa knew that buses ran only about twice a day, and these were unlikely to have been increased. She was searching for a taxi when a girl about her own age with long dark hair approached her.

"Are you Vanessa Woodrow?"

"Yes," Vanessa answered in a surprised voice. The girl was a complete stranger to her.

With a swift smile the girl held out her hand. "My name's Freda Hamilton. Ian knew you were coming, so he asked me to meet you."

"Ian?" Vanessa queried with a brief handshake.

"My brother. He was around at Puck's Hill yesterday when your telegram arrived."

"You and your brother are friends of Aunt Maud?"

Freda Hamilton nodded. "Ian especially. My car's just outside. Shall we go?"

Vanessa fell into step with the other girl. "How is my aunt?" she asked, trying to remember whether she had ever met any friends of Aunt Maud.

"She's—not too good, I'm afraid," was the answer.

"So we're glad someone has come. Actually, you're the only relative your aunt seems to talk about."

Vanessa felt a twinge of conscience. Her mind had been so preoccupied in battling against her hopeless love affair that she had not written to Aunt Maud quite as often as usual.

"She does have other relatives, of course," she told Freda, "but not all of them understand Aunt Maud's funny little ways." It was the kindest way she could put it. "Anyway, she and I have always kept in touch, though I must admit I haven't written to her lately. I didn't know she was ill; naturally, otherwise—"

She broke off as they emerged from the station yard and her companion pointed to a green station wagon.

"That's my car. It used to be Ian's, but he let me have it and bought another one."

"How long have you and your brother lived in Barn Hill?" asked Vanessa as they drove out of the pictur- esque town with its narrow cobbled streets, half-timbered stores and houses, and the colorful, straggling market.

"Not very long, I suppose, in terms of country life. About five years."

"And you've known my aunt all that time? She never mentioned either you or your brother."

"For the simple reason that we haven't really known her for very long. Your aunt has always been something of a recluse, hasn't she? Or so they say in the village. We rarely saw her, either."

It was true. Aunt Maud's home and garden had been her world; though at one time, the children of the village were always welcome in her wild garden. But as she had become older, she had kept more and more to herself.

"How did you come to meet her, then?" she inquired.

"Ian went to see her one day. She asked him to stay to tea, and after that he was a frequent visitor."

"And you?"

"Oh, I didn't visit her quite as often as Ian did. They—found things to talk about."

Vanessa had detected a slight hesitation before the other girl answered and was about to ask her what sort of things her brother had discussed with Aunt Maud, but Freda Hamilton went on:

"Ian and I wondered whether you'd care to come and have lunch at home with us. You'll find things a little disorganized at Puck's Hill."

But Vanessa was anxious to see her aunt as soon as possible.

"That's very kind of you," she answered, "but if you don't mind I'd rather go straight to my aunt's. If things are as disorganized as you say, then it's high time someone did something about it." Anxiety lent a sharp edge to her voice.

There was a pause, then the other girl said quietly: "Yes, of course. I understand. I just thought it would give my brother a chance to—to meet you. But if you're staying for a few days—"

"I shall stay for as long as my aunt wants me."

Though the other girl was very likeable, and it was good to know that Aunt Maud had found someone to keep an eye on her, Vanessa could not help feeling slightly irritated. She frowned, trying to find out why. Was it really a guilty conscience about her own family; that their eccentricities caused them to be lacking in caring enough for each other, even for someone old like Aunt Maud? But then this applied also to her aunt. Each of them seemed to have one thing only, besides themselves, that they cared about. Her father had his medical practice and was a good doctor, but the rest of his time he lived in his own world. Her mother had her singing. Aunt Maud had her house and garden, but the world outside—apart from Vanessa herself—might not exist.

This Ian Hamilton. How had he managed to gain Aunt

Maud's confidence sufficiently to become a regular visitor? Few people had, if any, so far as she knew. It was strange. Who was he? What had he and her aunt to talk about? His sister appeared greatly preoccupied with him—Ian this, Ian the other. He was obviously a person of some importance to her. It had been he who had asked her to meet Vanessa herself. Why? Why should he concern himself with her arrival? Perhaps Aunt Maud had asked him to meet her, and he had delegated the task to his sister.

Vanessa concluded that it was he, this man she had not even met, who was the cause of her irritation. She could almost hear him accusing her of neglecting her aunt. Well, she was here now, and there was no need for this Ian Hamilton to concern himself any longer.

She became aware that they had almost arrived. The car was driving through the cool avenue of trees which formed part of the estate bordering on Aunt Maud's property. Vanessa realized that she had followed her aunt's lead in not taking much interest in the rest of the people who lived in the village. All she knew of the ownership was that the estate belonged to a wealthy land-owner who used the woods with its house—aptly named The Lodge—as a country retreat, breeding pheasants for the sheer joy of killing them. He was known simply as the Colonel, though whether he had ever actually commanded a military unit was doubtful. But even this limited knowledge had been gained from snatches of conversation Vanessa had heard in the village stores. His name was never mentioned in Aunt Maud's house. A wicked man like that who bred God's creatures for the pleasure of killing them was beneath her contempt. Vanessa caught a glimpse of a deer. Had the man added deer-shooting to his nefarious pastimes?

But the trees were thinning out. A few minutes later Freda Hamilton turned her car through a wide gateway which led up a twisting drive to Aunt Maud's house. Vanessa was appalled at the neglect. The rank weeds, now eight or ten feet high, had thick stalks and umbrella-like leaves shooting up from the earth like nuclear monsters.

"Good heavens!" she breathed. "I had no idea it was as bad as this. What's happened to Joe Simpkins who used to do the gardening?"

"He's still here. It's simply more than he can cope with. He keeps an area near the house clear, then tackles as much of the rest as he can. Your aunt won't allow—"

"I know. I'm not entirely ignorant of my aunt's ways," Vanessa felt stung to interpose.

"I'm sorry." Freda Hamilton brought the car to a halt outside the front door of the old gray stone house with its porticoed entrance.

Vanessa sensed that she had given offense. She turned to the other girl.

"Do forgive me if I seem put out. I'm so worried about my aunt. I write to her regularly as a rule, but I'm afraid I've had problems lately and—"

Freda gave a swift smile. "Never mind, you're here now."

Vanessa nodded. "It was extremely good of you to meet me. Perhaps we shall see each other again."

"I hope so," the other girl responded.

They said goodbye, and as the car disappeared down the drive Vanessa looked after it for a moment. A charming girl, even if she did seem rather under her brother's thumb. Where did they live, she wondered. And what did both she and her brother do?

The outer door of the house was flung back. Vanessa turned the knob of the vestibule door and stepped inside the wide hall that narrowed into a long passage with doors on either side. Immediately, a dusty, musty smell pervaded her nostrils. She wrinkled her nose and frowned. Dust lay thickly on the Jacobean oak furniture; the once colorful carpet was badly in need of cleaning. What had happened to Miss Gould, the companion-help Aunt Maud used to have?

Vanessa was about to climb the stairs when a door opened at the farther end of the long passage. Miss Gould herself appeared.

"Your aunt's expecting you, Miss Vanessa."

Vanessa went toward the woman, almost as small and frail-looking as Aunt Maud and was struck at once by the tired look about her eyes.

"You look as though you could do with a rest, Miss Gould. How is my aunt?"

Miss Gould shook her head sadly. "Not too well, miss. I wanted to get a nurse in, but she wouldn't hear of it. She just keeps drifting off, sometimes for a few minutes, sometimes for longer periods. At times she rambles, at others she's surprisingly lucid. She keeps asking for you, miss. I'm glad you've come."

"Is she in any pain? And has the doctor seen her?"

"Oh yes, he comes every day, sometimes twice. She doesn't seem to be in any pain. The doctor says it's her heart—and just old age. She's 93, miss. But if only she would eat, I'm sure she'd gather a little more strength."

"Is she asleep now?"

Nancy Gould nodded. "I've only just this minute left her. Do you know what I think, Miss Vanessa?" Vanessa shook her head. "I think your Aunt Maud's decided she's had enough of this world and has simply made up her mind to leave it."

Vannessa felt her heart contract sharply. "Oh, don't talk like that, please!"

"It's true, my dear. You know what she's like. Once she's made up her mind to a thing—"

"I know. But I hope you're wrong. I'll go up and see her. Would you like me to stay with her for a while? You must have lots to do."

Nancy Gould nodded. "If you would, Miss Vanessa. I've hardly dared leave her side for weeks now."

Vanessa's conscience smote her again. "For weeks? But how long has she been ill? I received a letter from her only yesterday. I could tell by her writing that something was wrong, but—" She broke off in distress. "Oh, I do wish you had written to me, Miss Gould."

"My dear, I wanted to. She kept saying you'd be writing in a day or two. Then when weeks passed and no letter came, she made me bring paper and pen and insisted on writing herself. If she hadn't, I had quite made up my mind to drop you a line myself. If her condition had become really serious—urgent—I would have telephoned or sent you a wire. As it is, Dr. Upson says she might continue like this for a year or more. He wanted her to have her bed brought downstairs, but she wouldn't hear of it."

Vanessa sighed worriedly and went upstairs. She tapped softly on the green-painted door, but there was no response. She opened it quietly and closed it behind her. She walked on the balls of her feet toward the great double bed. At the foot she paused, and her heart as well as her conscience smote her. Dear, sweet, fragile Aunt Maud! She looked tinier and more puckish than ever, but weak and ill. Tears gathered in Vanessa's eyes, but suddenly her aunt's were wide open and looking straight at her.

"Hello, child. There's no need to tiptoe. I heard you arrive, and I heard you come into the room. I have to pretend to be asleep sometimes, otherwise I'd never get any peace. Old Nancy hangs around me as if she were afraid I'd run away."

Vanessa blinked, and for a brief moment, hovered between laughter and tears. She moved swiftly to the bed and dropped on her knees, putting her arms around the tiny figure.

"Oh, darling Aunt Maud! Why didn't you write to me before? I'll never forgive myself for—"

"Child, child—" The thin fingers clasped around Vanessa's hand. "It's all right. I knew you'd come."

Vanessa brushed her cheek against the velvet soft one of her aunt. "I'd have come much sooner if I'd known you were ill."

"Ill? Who says I'm ill? I never heard such nonsense. Stop fussing, child, and tell me what you thought of Ian Hamilton. One of these days I shall close my eyes and quietly slip away. But ill? Never."

Vanessa brought up a chair and sat down. "I—didn't meet him. His sister met me at the station and drove me here."

"But didn't you have lunch with them?"

Vanessa shook her head. "She did ask me, but I wanted to come straight home to you."

"Tut, tut, child. But no matter. You will meet him soon."

Her lids closed heavily. Vanessa eyed her aunt anxiously. Was she, in fact, slowly losing her hold on life, and not, as she had said, merely pretending to be asleep? Then the bright blue eyes were wide open again.

"Well? Don't look at me like that. You're getting to be as bad as Nancy. Go down and get yourself some lunch."

"Very well, Aunt Maud, if you're sure you'll be all right. But what about your lunch? You must eat something."

A thin hand waved her away, and before Vanessa left the room, the tired eyes closed again.

Vanessa went downstairs thoughtfully. How ill was her aunt really; how close to the time when she would close her eyes for the last time? Tonight, if the doctor came, she would have a word with him. Meanwhile, she would help Nancy put the house in some kind of order and look in on Aunt Maud from time to time.

After a hasty lunch, Vanessa cleaned and polished the hall, then went to the village stores while Nancy tidied the kitchen. She was making preparations for dinner when there was the sound of a car outside.

"That will probably be Dr. Upson, Miss Vanessa," Nancy said.

Vanessa whipped off her apron. "I'll let him in. I want to have a word with him."

She had never met the doctor, and he looked younger than she expected, but he had that air of confidence and authority that most doctors have. His dark, straight hair was parted at the side, his features were fine and clear-cut, and his face tanned more like that of a man who lived an outdoor life—an interesting, rather than a strictly handsome face. His lean figure moved easily as he walked toward her carrying a basket of fruit.

He thrust the basket into her hands. "For both you and your aunt. How is she?"

A little taken aback by his unceremonious greeting, she glanced at the delicious-looking peaches and grapes sitting on huge oranges and grapefruits.

"Well, I—was hoping you could tell me that."

"Oh? I thought you could draw your own conclusions—aside from having a chat with the doctor."

Vanessa was beginning to feel somewhat exasperated. "I certainly do want to have a talk with you, doctor. Drawing one's own conclusions is not good enough with someone like my Aunt Maud. I want to know—"

She would have gone on, but the doctor's eyes widened, and the rather grave features relaxed into something like faint amusement.

"Did you call me doctor?"

She stared at him. "Aren't you—"

"I'm afraid not. My name is Ian Hamilton."

Vanessa drew an angry breath. "It might have saved us both some embarrassment if you had introduced yourself, Mr. Hamilton."

His eyebrows shot up still farther. "I'm not embarrassed. You shouldn't jump to conclusions so readily. I've come to inquire about your aunt—and see her, if she's—"

"My aunt is asleep. I don't think she should be disturbed," she told him swiftly.

Ian Hamilton gave her a steady look. For a split second Vanessa felt something within her crumbling, then her lips came together firmly. He might have his sister under his thumb and have somehow managed to gain Aunt Maud's regard, but he was not going to win her over so easily!

"I'll take your word for it," he said, in a tone which clearly cast doubts on her truthfulness. "But if your aunt asks for me at any time, I hope you will let me know."

"Naturally. And now if you'll excuse me—"

She was appalled at her own rudeness. Why had she taken such a dislike to this man? It was quite unlike her.

A noticeably steely look came into his gray eyes. Then he turned and went back to his car without another word.

As his car crunched its way down the drive, Vanessa sighed heavily and went indoors again. She couldn't think what had come over her. She had not even thanked him properly for the fruit.

She took the basket upstairs and quietly opened the door of Aunt Maud's room, hoping that she was indeed sleeping. But the blue eyes were wide open.

"I heard a car," she said at once. "Who was it?"

Vanessa noted mentally that her aunt missed absolutely nothing.

"It was Ian Hamilton," she was forced to answer. "He brought you this basket of fruit. Isn't it lovely?"

"Ian?" demanded Aunt Maud. "Why in heaven's name didn't he come up?"

"I—thought you were asleep."

Aunt Maud eyed her fiercely. "So you prevented him from coming up to see me? Why?"

Vanessa shook her head quickly, thinking she had better humor her aunt.

"No particular reason. I've told you, darling, I thought—"

"You didn't try to find out whether I was asleep or not, did you?"

Vanessa did not know what to say. This cross-questioning was quite unlike her aunt. But she was saved from replying by Aunt Maud speaking again.

"What did you think of him?" she quizzed.

This, too, was difficult. "Well, I—only spoke to him for a few minutes."

"Mm! You didn't like him, did you? That's easy to see. But no matter. He and I exchanged a few sharp words the first time we met, I remember. Take the fruit downstairs, child, and eat it yourself. I hope you thanked him nicely."

Once more Vanessa was saved from answering an awkward question. This time by Aunt Maud closing her eyes.

Dr. Upson arrived a short time later. Vanessa spoke to him while Nancy was persuading Aunt Maud to eat a little dinner. He confirmed Vanessa's fears that her aunt was having periods of unconsciousness, rather than merely pretending to be asleep as she said.

"Your aunt has had a good game," he told her. "She has led a very active life, as you may know, even if she has stayed to herself. She's kept this huge place clean with very little help, as well as doing a great deal of the gardening."

"Yes, I know. So you—don't think she'll ever get up again?"

He shook his head. "No, I do not, Miss Woodrow, though how long that obstinate heart of hers will continue to tick over, I can't tell you. Will you be staying with her long?"

"As long as she needs me," she assured him.

Vanessa wrote to her parents saying that she would be

staying with Aunt Maud for an indefinite period. She helped Nancy spring clean the entire house and took turns sleeping in the dressing room attached to her aunt's bedroom, in case she wanted anything during the night. It soon became evident that day and night were one to Aunt Maud. Dreams and reality, past and present, were merged into one in her confused mind.

Repeatedly, she spoke to Vanessa by name. Once, she murmured—and Vanessa did not know whether she was awake or asleep.

"Vanessa, don't ever sell Puck's Hill. Promise me."

"Darling, of course I won't."

Vaguely, she wondered whether her aunt had made out a will, or if not, who was her nearest relative. Vanessa's father? But she put aside any serious thought of her aunt's passing. It was too unhappy to contemplate.

She was in one of the village stores one morning. The proprietor asked how Aunt Maud was and made one or two comments on her life. The other customer in the store was a young man whom Vanessa had never seen before, but as new houses were being built in the village all the time, this wasn't surprising.

When she went out, however, the young man followed her. "Can I give you a lift back to Puck's Hill, Miss Woodrow?" he asked.

She looked at him in surprise. "How do you know my name?"

He grinned disarmingly. "Didn't I hear Mrs. Green call you by it just now? Anyway, the whole village has heard about the charming niece of Miss Woodrow of Puck's Hill who has come to stay."

Her lips curved in amusement. "Flattery goes right over my head, Mr—"

"Kendal's the name. Miles Kendal—but please don't call me Mister."

He was very likeable, she decided. "In that case, my name is Vanessa," she told him. "But we're not likely to meet very often. I'm helping Miss Gould look after my aunt. When she's—better, I shall be going home."

"That would be a pity when we've just met—your going home, I mean," he added hastily.

Vanessa smiled and said she must return to Puck's Hill, but Miles Kendal said persuasively:

"Look, why not come into the Swan and have a sherry with me or something? I can't say have a coffee because, as you know, we don't have a restaurant in the village. I met your aunt once and thought she was a wonderful woman."

At this, Vanessa found her resistance weakening. "You've met my aunt? How?" she queried.

He took her arm. "Come and have a drink and I'll tell you. I know you must want to get back, but if you let me drive you, you'll be there quicker than if you hadn't met me and had to walk."

Vanessa laughed. "All right, you win."

The Swan was a homely sort of place with its oak beams, low ceilings and interesting examples of copper ware. They sat in the little parlor, whose floors and furniture gleamed with years of polish.

"How *is* your aunt, really?" Miles Kendal asked gravely when they were seated and served. "Do you honestly think she will get better? They say she's getting on for 100."

Vanessa shook her head sadly. "Everyone's life has to come to an end some time, I suppose. But I'd rather not talk about it."

He smiled. "I understand. I think it's wonderful that you've come all this way to look after her. She must mean a lot to you—and you to her, I imagine."

"We are fairly close, I suppose." She told him how she used to spend her holidays with Aunt Maud, and the sort of games they used to invent. Miles Kendal listened with close interest.

"You're not her only niece, are you?" he asked.

"Oh no, but my father is her only nephew."

"Her next of kin, in other words."

Vanessa frowned, hating the expression now that her aunt was nearing the end of her life span.

"Why do you say that?" she asked, an edge to her voice.

"I'm sorry," he said swiftly. "It's just that—I felt I wanted to warn you, as it were."

"Warn me?" she echoed.

He smiled faintly. "I didn't mean to sound dramatic. I realize you don't want to dwell on things, but your aunt has a sizeable bit of property there. Some people, with no sense of rightness or delicacy of feeling are already hovering around her like—well, vultures, wanting to buy the place."

Something inside Vanessa contracted sharply. "Who do you mean exactly?"

He shrugged, as if unwilling to mention anyone's name. Then he said, "Well, I expect you'll meet him sooner or later, if you haven't already. I mean Ian Hamilton. He's already made your aunt an offer."

Vanessa drew a swift breath. "So that's it!"

Miles Kendal nodded. "That's it. I take it you and he have met?"

"We certainly have. But Aunt Maud will never sell. I'm sure of it."

"Maybe he's hoping she'll change her mind."

"Then he doesn't know my aunt. She'll never change her mind, and—" She broke off, unwilling to repeat her aunt's injunction never to sell. "But as a matter of interest, why does he want to buy such a big place? Has he a family?"

"If you mean has he any family of his own, he isn't

even married. He and his sister live together in that place called The Lodge. But I expect you know that."

Vanessa shook her head. "No, I didn't."

"No? Well, of course, his place is more or less a playground. Or should I say a sportsground. You must have heard of the Colonel."

"I have—to some extent."

The news that Ian Hamilton was now the owner of those acres of private woodland in which defenseless birds were hunted, made her dislike him more than ever.

"His little hunter's paradise adjoins you aunt's place, as you may know," Miles Kendal went on. "The man is just land-hungry. And what he'd do with Puck's Hill if he acquired it, heaven knows. Pull it down, I expect."

"Not if I can help it," muttered Vanessa determinedly. She rose to her feet. "If you don't mind, I really must be going."

"Don't look now," Miles said as they left the Swan and went to his car, "but there's Hamilton and his sister now in that expensive-looking car across the road."

"I don't want to look," she said angrily. "And I wish to goodness he'd keep away from Puck's Hill." How the man had managed to win her aunt's confidence, she didn't know, but she vowed he would never win hers.

She would have pretended not to see them, but to her surprise Miles Kendal gave them a wave, a smile and called out, "Hi, Ian!"

Vanessa was almost forced to look their way. After all, Freda had been kind enough to meet her at the station. And so she gave a slight wave, being careful to look at Freda only. She could not help noticing, however, that there was no answering wave for Miles from Ian. He looked decidedly put out. Miles chuckled as if something were amusing him and put his hand under Vanessa's elbow to help her into his car.

"Do you know Ian Hamilton very well?" she asked.

Miles shrugged. "Well, you know how it is. One has to keep on something like friendly terms with people, even if one doesn't agree with what they do or how they live."

Vanessa did not agree with him. "I shall never make any pretense of liking him."

Miles started the car and cast an amused smile at her. "As bad as that?"

"Why should one pretend? I think I disliked him before I even met him. I know that sounds terrible, but it was the way his sister kept talking about him; as if his word was law. Then he came to see my aunt and let me think that he was the doctor, and—oh, I don't know—"

"*I* do. You find him generally irritating. He affects me that way too, so you're not alone. I think it's that superior manner of his. But I'm surprised you don't like him—in a way—because most of the women hereabouts, including his sister, are absolutely mad about him."

"Really? Perhaps that's what's wrong with him. He expects every woman to come running. If they don't, it doesn't please him. It's made him conceited."

"I'm glad you're not taken in by him, anyway," answered Miles, turning into the driveway of Puck's Hill.

Characteristically, Vanessa began to feel guilty about her attitude toward Ian Hamilton. She shouldn't have spoken like that about him to someone else, even though she did dislike him. After all, there must be *something* likeable for Aunt Maud to have such a high regard for him.

Miles Kendal was eyeing the fantastic weed growth flanking the drive.

"Heavens! I wouldn't like to be the person who takes on this little lot. Couldn't you persuade your aunt to do something about it?"

"She won't have chemical weed-killers used," Vanessa answered. "And in any case, I wouldn't dream of bothering her about it while she's ill."

"No, of course not," he murmured, in a conciliatory tone. He halted the car outside the front door and opened the door of the passenger side for her. When she thanked him, he said, "It would be nice to see you again. May I?"

She hesitated. "I'd like to, of course, but I'm afraid I can't make any arrangements while Aunt Maud is so ill. I might see you in the village some time when I'm shopping, but in any case I'm not here permanently, so—"

He put his hand into an inside pocket. "Tell you what. Let's say same time and place next week. If you can't make it, don't worry—maybe you will the week after. If there's ever anything I can do any time, here's my address." He gave her a card.

She glanced at it briefly, then thanked him and said goodbye.

But exactly one week later, Aunt Maud passed peacefully away in her sleep. Vanessa telephoned the doctor from the booth a short distance from the house. With him, within five minutes, came Ian Hamilton. Vanessa was too shaken with grief to resent him. In the days preceding the funeral, she was grateful to him for the way he took charge of everything, and to his sister for all her help. After the interment, she turned to thank them both, Ian in particular, feeling rather ashamed of her original opinion.

"I don't suppose we shall ever meet again," she told him. "I shall be returning as soon as I've helped Nancy put the house to rights. But I would like you to know how grateful I am for all you've done. I hardly know how to thank both you and Freda."

Freda murmured, "Only too glad to have been of help."

But Ian said stiffly, "I shouldn't bother to try. Anything I did was for your aunt's sake."

Vanessa felt decidedly snubbed. Even Freda gave her

brother a protesting glance. To hide her feelings, Vanessa moved on to speak to one of her aunts.

Actually, few of Aunt Maud's relatives had attended the funeral, though Vanessa had notified all those whose whereabouts were known to her. Vanessa's mother had stayed away, saying she detested funerals. Though her father had driven down, he had already left again. Vanessa wished they would all go—Ian and Freda included, though during the past week she had grown to like Freda very much indeed.

But soon all had left, leaving Nancy and Vanessa alone again.

The day after the funeral Vanessa caught the train into Cringlewood. Aunt Maud's lawyer had asked to see her. Vanessa could not think why, as it was most unlikely that her aunt had any money to leave. The house would surely be left either to Nancy or Vanessa's father. She hoped, to the former, as Nancy was more in need than her father. But Aunt Maud was just as likely to leave it to the National Trust, or a wild life preservation society. Perhaps she herself was a trustee or something like that.

The lawyer, a bright and surprisingly young man, began by offering his sympathy to Vanessa on the death of her aunt.

"She was a very interesting and unusual woman."

"Eccentric," Vanessa supplied with a slight smile.

"Yes, I suppose you would say that, and like all eccentrics she left a rather unusual will. You will not be surprised, I'm sure, to know that she left a considerable sum of money to a local bird sanctuary, also to her friend and companion, Miss Nancy Gould. To her relatives she left absolutely nothing—with one exception—yourself. Even so, there are conditions attached."

"Conditions? What sort of conditions?"

But the lawyer shook his head. "That I am not allowed to tell you. It's to be held in trust for six months, after which time, my fellow trustee and I will decide whether or not you are entitled to it."

Vanessa couldn't help smiling. "Aunt Maud always did like playing games. But I didn't know she had any money."

"Oh yes. It's a very considerable amount. Your aunt accumulated it simply because she never spent any—or very little."

"And if I don't fulful the conditions?" Vanessa queried.

"Then the money all goes to the bird sanctuary. But there's something else."

"Yes?"

"Your aunt has left the house and the entire estate to you—unconditionally."

CHAPTER TWO

"To me?" Vanessa echoed. She could scarcely believe it. "But—but why me?"

The man behind the desk smiled. "You're too modest. I would have thought it was obvious. She left the thing she valued most to the person for whom she had the highest regard."

But Vanessa shook her head in denial. "You're very kind, Mr. Oliver, but I'm sure it would have been more appropriate if Aunt Maud had left the house and land to Miss Gould. What on earth am I going to do with a house that size?"

"I'm quite sure your aunt knew what she was doing, Miss Woodrow. You'll do the right thing with it, I've no doubt of that. There's no need to worry about Miss Gould. Your aunt has left her well-provided for."

Vanessa felt too bewildered for the time being to think straight. Mr. Oliver rose and held out his hand.

"You'll soon get used to the idea. And if you have any problems, I'll be glad to advise you in any way I can."

She shook hands with him and thanked him. Then as she reached the door, he added,

"By the way, Ian Hamilton was a very great friend of your aunt. I'm sure he too will be happy to give you any help or advice you need."

Vanessa smiled politely and descended the spiral of stone steps, vaguely trying to assess how she felt about Ian Hamilton—and why, and at the same time hazarding a guess as to his opinion of herself. But her thoughts either way did not progress very far. As she stepped out onto the sidewalk she almost collided with Ian.

"Good morning," he said, not looking in the least surprised to see her. He glanced upward to the lawyer's office window. "I see you've paid your visit to Mr. Oliver."

"Why, yes. Do you know him?"

"Of course. Your aunt mentioned to me that he was her lawyer. Have you—heard some good news?" he queried.

"I—I think so."

"What do you mean—you think so?" he demanded.

She fought a swift reaction to his interrogation. "I mean I'm not sure yet. I haven't had time to think about it. A large house like that—all those grounds. It's a terrific responsibility."

"That's so." He glanced at a nearby clock. "Look, it's almost lunch time. Would you have lunch with me and maybe talk about it?"

She hesitated, then almost, it seemed, against her will, she thanked him. He put his hand under her arm and marched her off down the street. She was beginning to get a glimmering of what made Ian Hamilton tick for some people—the strong, forceful personality of the man. That and more. Much more.

He led her through a doorway sandwiched between a hardware store and a gardening store, then up a flight of stairs.

"This is the place to come if you should ever be in town and need a meal," he said. "It's quiet, unpretentious, the food's good—and it's licensed. I don't think much of any place if you can't have a glass of wine with a meal if you want it. It's called the White Horse."

Now he was telling her where she should eat, she thought. His taste might not be the same as hers in the least, though he seemed to take it for granted that it would be.

But when they reached the top of the stairs, and he led her into the restaurant she was agreeably surprised. The place was beautifully and very tastefully decorated with clever lighting, flowers on every table and a deep pile carpet on the floor in a rich wine color. It was evident that he was a regular from the way he was greeted by name by the head waiter and by the girl who served their meal.

"You like it?" he asked, as her gaze flitted from one point of the decor to another.

She nodded. "It's very nice. But whether I shall come here very frequently, if at all, depends on their prices. I have very little money, I'm afraid. Unless I get a job of some kind—" She broke off. "I'm sorry. I was thinking aloud. I hadn't meant to trouble you—or anyone—with my problems."

"That's all right," he said quietly. "Perhaps you wouldn't mind telling me the news from your aunt's lawyer. I take it from the little you said earlier that she has bequeathed you her house and land."

"That's so." She told him the rest. "I don't know what the conditions are with regard to the money in trust, but I don't really want my aunt's money, and—"

His eyes opened wide. "You can't really mean that."

She gave him an angry look. "Of course I mean it. The only thing is, I don't know how on earth I'm going to keep up the place. Even if I do get a job, what I earn will only keep me. It won't pay for anything to be done on the house or—"

"Or what?" he prompted.

"Or even heat the place adequately in winter."

"You certainly have a problem. Do I take it that you intend living at Puck's Hill?"

"Of course. What else? I'm sure that's what Aunt Maud would have wished."

"I expect so. I thought you might consider selling the place. As you say, it's a large house; certainly too big for either one or two, supposing Miss Gould stayed on with you."

Vanessa frowned. Into her mind with startling clarity came the things Miles Kendal had told her—that Ian Hamilton wanted to buy Puck's Hill, that he had already made her aunt an offer, and that he was land-hungry.

"I shall *never* sell Puck's Hill," she flung out emphatically. "Not to anyone."

Ian inclined his head and gave her a calculating look.

"That's how you feel at the moment, I'm sure, but it might be a different story in a few months' time. However—" he went on swiftly, as an angry denial sprang to Vanessa's lips—"I take it you're going to take up residence and do the best you can for the house and property. What sort of a job do you have?"

Vanessa drew a deep breath. "I work for my parents—or did. My father is a doctor, as you probably know, and I act as his secretary, do the gardening and drive the family car."

A hint of a smile curved at Ian Hamilton's mouth. "It sounds as though you'll be very well equipped to look after Puck's Hill. But won't your father miss you?"

"He will understand. And he won't miss me so much as he might have done some months ago. He—has a new partner now who—who has just married, so—"

"I see. You talked of getting a job around here, but somehow I don't think you'll find it necessary."

She gave him a puzzled look. "What do you mean?"

"Oh, you'll think of something," he said evasively, and as if to assist him the waitress came with their second course.

So much for the "help and advice" Mr. Oliver said Ian Hamilton would be happy to give, Vanessa could not help thinking wryly to herself. All he was interested in, seemingly, was the future of Puck's Hill. Well, she had promised her aunt she would never sell, and she would keep that promise. But how was she going to live without getting a job, and if she was out at work all day how was she going to be able to look after the place?

"Don't look so worried," Ian told her. "You'll make out, I'm sure of it."

If Vanessa had not been so puzzled by this and his other rather ineffectual remark, she would have been irritated. But somehow she couldn't help feeling that such banalities from him were out of character.

"I shall have to do some hard thinking, anyway," she answered.

He gave her a steady look. "Well, when you arrive at some conclusions, I'll be interested to hear them," he said, much more characteristically, Vanessa thought fleetingly. Then he went on, "Meanwhile, as you're in town why not take the rest of the day off. I'll show you around?"

Vanessa hesitated. She felt sure he would be the most uncomfortable person to be with. On the other hand, there was no bus back to Barn Hill until four-thirty.

"We could include a look around some of the stores," he added disarmingly.

Vanessa could not resist a smile. "You make it difficult for me to say no. But I would like to get home about five-thirty. Nancy will be expecting me by that time. I wouldn't like her to worry about me. As you probably know, we don't have a phone."

He nodded. "I'll get you back all right, but you should think seriously of getting a phone. I tried to persuade your aunt, but she said she'd managed all these years without one and would continue to do so."

Vanessa's eyes gleamed. "No one could ever persuade Aunt Maud to do anything she didn't want to do."

Ian eyed her keenly. "And what about you? Are you just as obstinate?"

"I can be—yes," she told him, "if obstinate is the term you would use for someone who knows their own mind and won't allow themselves to be maneuvered first this way, then that."

He made no comment, but Vanessa could guess what

he was thinking and was glad. She did not know whether she was considered to be obstinate or not. But she had certainly been brought up to make her own decisions: once having felt a course of action was right, to stick to it and not allow herself to be talked out of it. She hoped he realized that no power on earth would persuade her to sell Puck's Hill.

She knew Cringlewood a little, but that was all. Ian showed her the more interesting buildings in the old part of the town: the merchant's house dating back to the 15th century, now a museum and art gallery; the Elizabethan Theater, recently restored; an old coachhouse inn; a narrow, cobbled street with its pink and whitewashed houses and stores that sold and displayed all the old crafts and artists' materials; and finally the ancient market square, still in use with its wonderful floral and plant displays.

Now they were on foot. Presumably on a sudden impulse, Ian bought a bouquet of sweet-smelling freesias and thrust them into her hands.

"In memory of Aunt Maud," he said as if he was afraid she might misconstrue the gift.

"Thank you," she said. "I'll put them on her—"

"No, don't," he cut in sharply. "She wouldn't like that at all. Put them in your room, or at any rate somewhere in the house."

He was an odd sort of person, she concluded. Difficult to know, difficult to understand, difficult also, she surmised, to please.

"Well, now for the stores," he announced. "We have only three large ones, but they sell pretty nearly everything among them. All have a top floor tea room."

Each of the places had some very beautiful things—china, glasswear, furniture, fabrics and, naturally, clothes. Afraid of boring him, she was careful not to wander too long among the many dresses, coats, suits and hats, but Ian obviously sensed this.

"Go on," he urged. "Don't mind me. Take all the time you want."

But some of the clothes were so fabulous, so smart and so desirable, and Vanessa had so little money, it was really depressing to linger. She sighed at the recollection of her meager wardrobe and turned away.

"A cup of tea would suit me better at the moment—and it is getting late."

"This way, then," he said briskly.

During tea she suggested that she should catch the bus home, but he wouldn't hear of it.

"I'm your neighbor," he said. "Remember?"

She was not likely to forget. But she had been in danger of forgetting how poor defenseless creatures were hunted down on his land and shot. How *could* Aunt Maud have liked him? she wondered again.

"What's on your mind?" asked the object of her thoughts.

She gave a slight start. What a disconcerting man he could be. There was not a flicker of the eyebrows, or a look or gesture which he missed. But she was not to be led into disclosing her musings.

"It's on my mind that I ought to be getting home—if you don't mind," she answered.

"All right."

He rose immediately, much to her inner annoyance. She had not expected him to take her up quite so quickly and had intended finishing her cup of tea. But now she had no option but to follow his lead.

He spoke very little as he drove through the Suffolk countryside. From time to time, Vanessa stole a glance at his stern profile, and the uncompromising mouth and jaw. A man to be reckoned with, she thought. He was a good, competent driver, courteous to other road users, calm and unruffled in the face of some blatant bad driving. Vanessa found herself watching his strong hands on the wheel in strange fascination. She was so entranced, she hardly even noticed when they drove through his woodlands. Afterward she was annoyed with herself. She had meant to ask him one or two questions about himself and his property—whether he had been related to the Colonel, whether he had bought the land or had it bequeathed to him, and just exactly what he did—besides hunting. But he deposited her at the front door of Puck's Hill and made off, giving her barely enough time in which to thank him.

Vanessa had two visitors that evening; Miles Kendal and Freda Hamilton. Miles was the first to lift the great, old-fashioned front door knocker.

"I would have called sooner," he said, "to offer my sympathies on your aunt's death, but I didn't want to intrude on a private and family affair."

"That's all right. But it's nice to see you." She invited him in.

"I've been thinking about you," he said as he stepped inside. "In spite of your aunt being so ill, her death must have been a great blow to you. I know how fond you were of her."

Vanessa led him into the small sitting room, a favorite of Aunt Maud's which she used instead of the large living room, because it overlooked a quiet part of the garden. Here, she could open the French window to put out food for the birds and the squirrels and sit and watch them. This was one area of the garden that was relatively free from the rank weeds which choked the rest of the grounds. Aunt Maud dug them up herself, but still retained all the wild flowers which other people called weeds.

"Yes," Vanessa said in answer to Miles. "It was a wrench, but Aunt Maud's personality was so strong it almost seems as though she's still here."

Miles frowned slightly. "It will be like that for a while until you get over it."

Vanessa gave him a glance of faint surprise, but she made no effort to contradict him. Aunt Maud had set her seal so firmly on this house and garden; her influence would always be felt.

"What—will you do now?" Miles asked after a short silence. "Will you be staying on here or—has your aunt left the place to someone else?"

Vanessa smiled. "No, she's left it to me—and I'm glad. At first I think I was a little overwhelmed at the thought of owning all this—the responsibility and so on. But now I'm glad. I don't think I would have liked anyone else to have it. They might have been tempted to sell it or something."

Miles eyed her uncertainly. "You mean—you're glad because of the affection you had for your aunt?"

"Of course. What else?"   He was still puzzled. "Do I—er—take it your aunt left you a sufficiently large sum of money to pay for its upkeep?"

Vanessa laughed shortly. "No, as of this moment she hasn't."

"Good lord! Then what on earth are you going to do?"

"I don't know yet," she told him cheerfully. "I haven't had time to think." It was useless telling him of the sum of money left in trust for her, she thought. She might never get it, not knowing the conditions under which she would be entitled to it.

Miles looked at her curiously. "But it's terrible, really, leaving you this great house with the grounds in such an appalling condition; no money to do anything about it. Just think of the heating too, in the winter."

"Winter is at least six months away," Vanessa told him. "Now I've recovered from the first shock, I regard it as a challenge."

Miles shook his head. "That's all very well, Vanessa, but you have to be practical."

"I will be," she assured him. "But let me offer you a cup of coffee."

He thanked her and followed her into the big, old-fashioned kitchen.

"You're not alone in the house, are you?" he queried as he watched the preparations.

She told him about Nancy. "She's probably in her room. If she comes down, I'll introduce you."

"Is she staying on with you?"

She nodded. "Aunt Maud left her a legacy. We talked things over earlier this evening after I'd come back from seeing the lawyer. She wants to remain as before and make this her home. In return for a couple of rooms, she'll support herself and help with the work of the house. An ideal arrangement."

Miles shook his head. "You mean your aunt has actually left a sum of money to her—and not to you, her own "flesh and blood" as they say? It sounds monstrous to me."

"It isn't at all," Vanessa answered. "In fact it would have been appropriate if my aunt had left Puck's Hill to her instead of to me."

Miles gave her a long look. "You know, Vanessa, you're an extremely generous person. In fact, you're quite a girl. The only thing I'm afraid of is some people taking advantage of your good nature."

"Such as—whom?" she queried.

"Well, Ian Hamilton. I bet he's already made some kind of approach about your selling Puck's Hill."

She laughed briefly. "He has, as a matter of fact. I ran into him outside the lawyer's office."

"What?" Miles Kendal gave a sound of derision. "I knew it. And don't tell me that your running into him was accidental. It's my guess he knew you'd be seeing the lawyer this morning and was hanging around waiting for you to appear. He probably asked you out to lunch, I shouldn't wonder."

Vanessa's eyes widened. "I must say you're making

some very accurate guesses. He didn't look very surprised to see me and did take me out to lunch, as a matter
of fact. But don't worry about Puck's Hill. I shall never
sell it—and I told Ian so." She picked up the coffee tray,
and Miles followed her to the other room.

"I'm glad you made it plain to him, anyway. But tell
me; was it laid down in the will that you mustn't?" he
asked.

She was interrupted by a knock at the front door, so
excused herself to answer it. It was Freda.

"I came to say how pleased I am that you're staying on
at Puck's Hill," she said.

"That's kind of you. Come on in. You're just in time
for a cup of coffee."

Vanessa led her into the small sitting room. "You two
do know each other, don't you?" she asked.

Freda looked very surprised to see Miles there. They
both nodded. Miles looked oddly amused.

"Miles came to offer his condolences," Vanessa explained to Freda. "I suppose your brother told you my
news?"

"Yes, he did. But if I'd known you had someone with
you, I'd have come another time."

"Don't mind me," Miles said. "I shall be pushing off
pretty soon, anyway."

There was a rather strained silence. Vanessa sensed
that the other two had no great liking for each other.

After a while, Freda turned to Vanessa. "I suppose it's
too soon for you to have any ideas as to what you're going
to do with the place?"

Miles sipped his coffee. "Maybe she's just going to live
in it. I forgot to ask, Vanessa—and I'm sure you won't
mind. Have you by any chance a private income of your
own?"

She shook her head. "Enough to live on for about
another week, that's all."

"Good grief!" he said expressively.

"If I'm any judge," Freda said, "Vanessa won't be content just to 'live in it'."

"But what else, for heaven's sake? You're not suggesting she should take in lodgers?"

Vanessa laughed. "Maybe I'll start a fruit farm or something."

"First get rid of the weed," Miles told her, "—And that'll cost a fortune in chemical weed-killer."

Vanessa frowned and made no reply. Even if she could afford a chemical weed-killer, she couldn't possibly use one when her aunt was so much against them. She didn't know what the answer was at the present moment, but she did not want to start a discussion—possibly an argument—with Miles. Freda, she noticed, was saying nothing on the subject. But Miles was looking at Vanessa questioningly, so she had to answer him.

"Maybe I'll team up with Joe Simpkins in digging them out by hand," she said with a laugh. "After all, 'if seven maids with seven mops'—" she quoted.

"Yes, and that's just about the size of it," Miles said emphatically. "Like seven maids with seven mops trying to sweep the seashore free of sand. I tell you, Vanessa, without money you've got a pretty near impossible task here."

"Have some more coffee, Miles," was Vanessa's answer.

But Miles shook his head. "I must be going, but I hope you'll let me visit again."

"Of course."

Vanessa excused herself to Freda and showed Miles out. "Thanks for dropping in. It was nice of you," she said sincerely.

He grinned. "Pity we were interrupted." Then he paused for a moment before he went on, "I—er—should watch out for Freda, if I were you. She's a nice enough girl, but—well, she does tend to echo her brother. She'll probably act as his—sort of emissary."

"With what object?" she asked quietly.

"Well, you know. He wants this place. Oh, neither of them will ask you right out, but they'll try to con you in various ways, you'll see."

But Vanessa couldn't accept that entirely. She felt sure Freda was genuinely trying to be friendly. She gave a light-hearted laugh.

"Well, thanks for the warning, anyway."

"When can I see you again?" he asked, his hand on the door handle of his car.

"I don't know. I think I'm going to be pretty busy. Just drop in when you're passing."

"Thanks, I will—and maybe we can go for a drive some time, or have an evening out in town."

"That would be nice—but I'd better go now because of Freda."

Freda had stepped outside into the garden. "Sorry to have kept you waiting," Vanessa said.

"That's all right. I only hope I didn't intrude too much."

"Of course not."

But Freda obviously had something on her mind. "Do you like Miles Kendal?" she asked.

Vanessa shrugged. "Well enough. Why do you ask?"

Freda frowned. "I should be wary of him if I were you."

Vanessa almost laughed aloud—two people using almost the same words to warn her off the other!

"What makes you say that?" she asked.

"Didn't you know? He's a property developer. He's hoping to buy Puck's Hill at a giveaway price."

Vanessa could no longer hide her feeling of amusement.

"What's the joke?" asked Freda.

"Well, *he* says that Ian wants to buy it; that he's already made my aunt an offer."

Freda drew an angry breath. "Yes, he has, but only because—" Then she broke off. "I'm sorry. It's really none of my business. Ian would be furious if he knew I'd so much as mentioned it. Let's talk about something else, shall we?"

"As you like."

So Miles Kendal and Ian Hamilton were business rivals, concluded Vanessa. Both wanted to buy Puck's Hill. For a moment she did not know whether she was amused, angry, or hurt. Neither had been really honest with her. Miles least of all.

"What on earth will you do with all this weed?" Freda was saying, a note of despair in her voice as she glanced around the grounds.

Vanessa shook her head and looked at it; growing from the earth like monster rhubarb with its thick, fleshy stalks, huge umbrella-like leaves, more and more fronds uncurling both at the base and up the stalk. Wild rhubarb she used to call it as a child.

"Dig it up, I suppose, little by little," she answered.

Freda shook her head. "Really, Vanessa, you're as bad as your Aunt Maud!"

"Maybe," Vanessa answered laconically.

Freda glanced at her swiftly. "Vanessa, I'm sorry. I didn't mean—"

"That's all right, I know you were only joking," Vanessa told her. "All the same, I do have a loyalty to Aunt Maud. I wouldn't like to do anything she'd disapprove of. I shall just have to feel my way. After all, there *are* parts of the garden free of this stuff. I don't know whether chemical weed-killers harm the birds or not, but in any case I couldn't affort to use them."

"No, I suppose not," murmured Freda.

Conversation flagged after that. Vanessa wanted to be

alone to think things out, and make plans. Freda seemed ill at ease, so Vanessa was not sorry when she departed.

Nancy was in the kitchen washing up the coffee cups. "You shouldn't have done those," Vanessa told her. "I don't want you waiting on me."

Nancy smiled. "I'm not waiting on you, am I? Only washing up."

Vanessa picked up a cloth to dry them. "We must have a talk, Nancy, you and I—make plans."

"I thought we'd had our talk, Miss Vanessa. Any other plans you make will suit me."

"Well, to begin with, you must stop calling me 'Miss'. You're not my servant. Just call me Vanessa."

"All right, if that's what you want. But if I were you, I wouldn't try to make too many plans tonight. Leave it until morning."

"But I can't stop various things from running around in my mind. What I was thinking was, if you're going to pay your way here as you want to, then you must have Aunt Maud's little sitting room for yourself. The thing is, would you find the housework too much on your own?"

"Good heavens, no, Miss—I mean, Vanessa. I know the place was in a pretty bad state when you arrived, but then I had your Aunt Maud to look after. She wasn't very demanding, but I used to spend quite a bit of time in her room. Why do you ask? You're not going away, I hope?"

Vanessa shook her head. "It's just that I shall probably be spending a good deal of my time outside. I must do something to start earning some money."

"Such as?" queried Nancy with a sidelong glance. "I hope you're not reneging on what we said earlier this evening. If I'm going to carry on as before and do the housekeeping, I can surely buy food for the two of us. Your aunt left me enough money to keep both you and me put together for the rest of our lives."

Vanessa gave her a grateful hug and said no more. But

she could not live on Nancy's legacy indefinitely.

While it was still light Vanessa had a good walk around the garden area and the rest of the grounds. There was the large barn which had possibilities. Its only purpose at the moment, apart from housing a few garden tools, was to provide a nesting place for the many swallows that came regularly every year. In the past Aunt Maud had sometimes given parties in it for the village children. Vanessa stood and regarded the place. It was big enough to hire for village dances—bingo, too, whether or not one approved of such a futile pastime. It was worth considering.

Quite close to the barn was a large greenhouse. She was reminded of the one at home; bright with pot plants. Perhaps she could make money by raising plants from seeds and selling them. But she had no money to buy glass for the many broken windows; and in the winter she would have to buy fuel for the heating. It was all very difficult.

What *had* Aunt Maud expected her to do with Puck's Hill except just live in it? It was only with the greatest difficulty that Vanessa ploughed a way through the weeds which choked the grounds beyond the small area of garden. On one side, separating the grounds from the road which ran through the village was a high wall. Along the surface grew Virginia creeper, ivy and other evergreens. At intervals there were trees: great oaks, chestnuts, sycamores, and a large number of common beech. On the opposite side was a wide ditch and hawthorn hedge, and at the lower end which bordered on Ian Hamilton's land was a straggling line of Scots pines—self-seeded from the Colonel's woods.

Vanessa went as near the boundary as she could, half expecting to see Ian himself strolling beneath the trees with a gun in his hand; the typical squire who idled his time "huntin', fishin' and all that." Dusk was falling now, however, and she could not see very well, but it looked as though considerable clearing was being done. She wondered why.

When she went indoors again, Vanessa wrote to Hester asking her to pack her clothes and other personal belongings and send them to her; and also to her parents telling them about Aunt Maud's bequest and her decision to make Puck's Hill her home.

She concluded that the only thing she could do which was not going to cost money, was to work outside. So the following morning after tidying her room, she went in search of Aunt Maud's gardener, Joe Simpkins. She found him about to start mowing the small lawn at the back of the house. He was a man of about 40 and looked tough enough for anything. She said good morning to him and told him that she was now the owner of Puck's Hill and would be living there.

"I take it you're willing to stay on?" she asked him. Nancy had offered to pay his wages for the time being.

"Certainly I am," he told her. "I've worked for your aunt ever since I was 16, an' it suits me fine. I've got my own bit of garden where I grow my vegetables and so forth. My wife does three days a week at the Lodge, so we manage fine."

She explained to him briefly the necessity of earning money in some way.

"I haven't made any definite plans yet," she told him, "except perhaps to rent the barn for various purposes, but the first problem is to get rid of some of this weed. Maybe you'll help me to clean out the barn one day when it's too wet to work in the garden."

But at the mention of the weed, Joe had started slowly shaking his head.

"You'll never get rid of all that stuff without weed-killer, miss. I've been trying for years, but it's futile. Your aunt—"

"Yes, yes, I know—the birds. But in any case the cost of weed-killers would run into hundreds of pounds—and I just haven't got hundreds of pounds. So together, you and I will just get digging—if you don't mind."

"I don't mind. I'm used to it, and while I'm doing one job I can't go doing another. But what about you, miss? It's much too heavy work for you. The roots of these things go deep."

"I'm used to hard work, too. You are speaking to a fellow gardener, Mr. Simpkins. I've been doing little else for the past two years. So I'm afraid the lawn and the flower beds will have to be neglected for a little while until we can afford more help."

He shrugged. "Just as you say, Miss Woodrow, but don't call me Mister. My name's Joe."

"Right, Joe."

He produced a spare spade, but she found uprooting the obstinate weed to be hard and tiring work. Warm work too, as the sun was now blazing down. After about an hour and a half Vanessa felt as though her back was breaking. She was thinking longingly of a cup of coffee and a short rest when she heard Nancy call out. When she turned, she saw Ian Hamilton standing there watching her.

"You look busy," he said unnecessarily.

She felt in the pocket of her jeans for a handkerchief with which to wipe the perspiration from her face, but couldn't find one. Up to now she had simply used the back of her hand. With what seemed like a cynical smile, Ian took a handkerchief from his pocket and gave it to her.

"Clean this morning. Unused."

She hesitated momentarily, then as she felt a trickle of moisture run down her nose, she thanked him and mopped her face.

Nancy was setting out a small wicker table and two garden chairs under the shade of a sycamore.

"Coffee's ready, Miss Vanessa!" she called out.

"Thank you, Nancy." She noticed that the older woman had called her Miss once more. By force of habit, or because of Ian Hamilton's presence? But for whatever reason Vanessa said nothing for the moment. "Would you care for a cup of coffee?" she asked Ian politely.

"Thanks. That would be very nice."

She had half expected him to decline and wondered why he had called. But she led the way to the chairs and sat down thankfully.

Ian regarded her in speculative silence for a moment or two, then remarked, "You're doing a very noble job of work there."

She sighed. "I don't see anything 'noble' about it. It's a first essential."

Vaguely, she knew she was deliberately misunderstanding him. She had the feeling he had been trying to be complimentary, but somehow she simply could not stop herself from feeling faintly antagonistic toward him. She was wondering why, when Nancy brought the coffee—all set out on a tray for Ian's benefit, Vanessa did not doubt. She and Nancy did not usually bother with such formalities.

"You've only brought two cups, Nancy," she said, glancing at the tray. "Mr. Hamilton is joining us."

"The other cup *is* for Mr. Hamilton, Miss Vanessa. I'm having mine indoors, and Joe will have his in his usual place."

"Nancy—" Vanessa began in an admonishing tone. But Nancy affected not to hear and called to Joe to come to the kitchen for his coffee.

Vanessa suppressed a sigh. "Black or white, Mr. Hamilton?"

"White—but strong," he answered, "and two good spoonfuls of sugar."

Evidently he expected her to sugar it for him. "Is that to your liking?" she asked. A hint of sarcasm was in her voice, as she offered him a cup of dark brown coffee, particles of demerara sugar dissolving on the surface.

"Looks fine," he answered.

She offered him a biscuit, but he declined. "I'll have a smoke, if you've no objection."

He pulled out a pipe. I might have known it, she thought. He didn't look the type to smoke cigarettes. She poured her own coffee and sweetened it while he filled his pipe. He paused in the act of striking a match.

"I'm sorry I haven't a cigarette to offer you."

"I don't smoke, thanks."

He struck his match and drew on the smooth brown pipe. "Have you made any plans yet, or thought any more about getting a job?" he asked.

He sounded almost schoolmasterish, she thought, or as if he were her guardian or something. She tried to remember that as a friend of Aunt Maud he had a certain interest in her.

"I don't think I shall look for a job, anyway," she told him. "There seems to be more than enough to do here—"

"If it's only digging out weeds, eh?"

"Well, it's a job which in my opinion has to be done," she answered sharply.

He gave her a swift, sidelong glance. "But not necessarily by the sweat of your brow, surely?"

"How else? Chemical weed-killers are out of the question."

"On what grounds?"

"If you were a friend of my aunt you must know how she felt about weed-killers."

He removed his pipe and looked at it thoughtfully for a moment.

"Yes, I do know. But I'd like to know how *you* feel. I

know how costly a job it would be to clear this little lot by
sodium chlorate or something like that, but suppose you
had the money, what then?"

Vanessa frowned and thought for a moment. "I still
wouldn't," she decided suddenly.

"Why not? Because of your aunt's influence?"

"Not entirely, though she taught me more than any
other person to appreciate wildlife of all kinds. If there *is*
any possibility that chemical weed-killers would poison
the birds and other small creatures, then—"

"Well, some say they do, some say they don't, but it's
going to be the only way you'll get rid of all this quickly
without a lot of back-breaking work."

"I'm not afraid of work," she told him with determination. "Naturally, if I had the money I'd employ
extra labor. In the meantime, while the weather is good, I
shall carry on digging up the weed."

"And when the weather is bad?" he prompted.

But she felt she had answered enough of his queries.
"You're asking a lot of questions, aren't you, Mr.
Hamilton?"

"I'm interested," he answered smoothly. "And by the
way, the name is Ian."

It was on the tip of her tongue to retort that she did not
feel like calling him Ian, but checked herself. Why was
she so tempted to be rude to this man? She counted ten
and answered his query, ignoring for the time being the
reference to his first name.

"When the weather is wet, I might get Joe to help me
tidy up the barn."

"With what object? To rent it for barn dances or something?"

She gave him a surprised look. "Something like that.
How on earth did you guess?"

"It wasn't difficult. You mean that's what you are
thinking of doing?"

She nodded. "It wouldn't bring in very much money, I

know, but then, it wouldn't cost anything to clean up either. And it would be a start. I'd rent it to anyone who wants to hire it; for dancing, bingo, political meetings or anything."

"Not a bad idea, but of course there is the village hall, you know."

"Thanks for the encouragement!"

It was out before she could stop it, but Ian did not seem the least bit put out.

"Just reminding you, that's all. Any other ideas?"

"I thought I might make use of the greenhouse. I'm—fairly good with plants. I could grow some flowering pot plants to sell for Christmas and next spring."

"Ah now, that is a good notion. Long term—or at least, fairly—of course, but the idea does have possibilities."

"The only trouble is, numerous panes of glass are missing."

"That's no problem," he said promptly. "I'll get one of my men to fix those for you."

"It isn't the fixing I'm worried about," she answered. "It's the cost of the glass."

"That's no problem, either. I've got plenty of glass lying around at my place," he said in a voice which brooked no argument.

But Vanessa did not want to be indebted to him. "I'd rather pay my way—thanks all the same."

He did not give away his feelings by so much as the flicker of an eyelid, but he rose and knocked out his pipe.

"All right. I'll send you a bill. You can pay me when your plants begin to pay. Thanks for the coffee. I'll leave you to get on with your digging."

His tone implied that he thought her efforts rather futile. He strode off down the weed-flanked drive. Vanessa gazed after him for a moment or two angrily. Then all at once she found herself admiring the way he walked, his firm yet loose-limbed strides, the way he swung his arms and held his head. But this was ridiculous! She quickly picked up the tray and took it into the kitchen.

In spite of a rest at lunchtime Vanessa ached in every limb by evening. How on earth was she going to stand this day after day? she thought despairingly.

Fortunately for Vanessa's aching back—though in the light of a new day, she told herself she would get used to it—it was pouring rain the following morning. Joe said he could manage clearing out the barn himself. Vanessa took a good look into all the rooms of the house, beginning with the attic packed with the usual kind of bits and pieces. At this juncture Vanessa made no attempt to start sorting it out. That was a task which would take weeks. There was a various assortment of chiars with torn upholstery and protruding springs; an old sofa of the chaise longue kind; an ancient cabinet gramophone with no innards; trunks and pictures and piles of stuff which at the moment were unidentifiable.

As she went from room to room, some of them unfurnished, others filled with what could only be described as junk, Vanessa toyed with all kinds of ideas. Some rooms were large, others quite small. One could have the house converted into a number of apartments. But that would cost money. Not only did the idea not appeal to her but she felt sure Aunt Maud would not have approved. A guest house? But what attractions were there at Barn Hill apart from those of a pleasant country village? She could not think of anything which would not be too expensive.

She wandered into her aunt's room where there were drawers and cupboards that ought to be looked into and cleared out. Clothes and other personal effects could not just be left to rot. In the drawers of the dressing table was an assortment of underclothes of the old-fashioned kind. What Nancy did not want could go to a village rummage sale. In the top drawer were various trinkets and ribbons.

Nothing of any great monetary value, but Vanessa would keep them for memory's sake. The cupboard which passed for a closet was almost empty. Two coats; one light-weight, one heavy; two winter dresses and a summery one which Vanessa remembered quite well. Poor dear Aunt Maud! She had spent very little either on herself or on the house. On the floor of the closet were two pairs of shoes and a couple of empty boxes. Vanessa was about to shut the door again when she caught sight of an old-fashioned hat box tied up with a piece of string. She picked it up thinking it might contain old letters or other souvenirs.

She untied the string and flung back the lid, then almost dropped the box. In it were rolls of pound notes. On top of them was a letter addressed to herself.

CHAPTER THREE

Vanessa stared at the contents of the box for a moment, unable to believe her eyes. She carried it over to the bed and took out the letter to read it.

Vanessa child, here is a little money to tide you over for a few months until you find your feet. I know you've no money of your own. Bless you and keep you. Your Aunt Maud.

Vanessa felt tears prick her eyes. Dear, sweet little Aunt Maud! What sacrifices of personal comfort she must have made to have saved this. The money was in bundles of 50, and there were half a dozen altogether. If all the bundles contained the same number of notes, there would be 300 pounds. Not a fortune but enough for her to live on until she began to earn money: enough to pay for the repair of the greenhouse, employ extra labor for weed clearance, to buy plant pots and potting soil, to heat the greenhouse when the weather grew colder, to pay a year's taxes or anything else urgent which cropped up.

At the bottom of the box were old letters, some from Vanessa herself, others tied with black velvet ribbon were apparently love letters from someone called John. Why had Aunt Maud never married? Perhaps the letters would reveal the answer, but Vanessa felt it would be trespassing on her aunt's privacy to read them. For the time being she put them back in the box and went to find Nancy to tell her what she had found.

Nancy was not in the least surprised. "I had a feeling she would do something like that. She was certainly what some people would call odd in many ways, but somewhere hidden away she had a shrewd, practical streak. I've often seen her with that old hat box, but I would never pry into things that didn't concern me. Your aunt knew that."

"But where did the money come from?"

"I can only guess, Miss Vanessa. You know, at one time your aunt owned a lot of property in the village. Cottages, plots of land and so on. She'd collect the rents and never bother to put the money in the bank. And in later years she got into a habit of selling things. Jewelry, pictures, things of that nature. It started when we had one or two burglaries in the district. She said she wasn't going to have her bits and pieces stolen. As I said to her, they could steal money just as easily and that was a lot more difficult to trace than articles. But she wouldn't listen. She said she'd put the money where no thief would dream of looking for it. She was always afraid the house might one day catch fire, too. She said she could easily pick up her money, whereas she might not have time to go running around the house for various things."

Vanessa smiled. "It sounds just like Aunt Maud. But what happened to her cottages and other property? The lawyer didn't say anything about them."

"She sold those too, Miss Vanessa. A rare old profit she made in some cases. Plots of land, for instance, for building purposes. You know how values have risen. As the older folk who rented her cottages died, she sold those at a handsome profit too. Cottages she hadn't paid more than 100 for fetched a couple of thousand or so."

Vanessa smiled ruefully. "And I thought she was poor—apart from this old house."

"That was another of her notions. It was what she wanted people to think."

If the house had a telephone, Vanessa would have called Ian and told him not to bother about sending his man to glaze the greenhouse windows. She could now afford to have it done by a glazier.

Excited at the prospect of starting on her pot plant

project, she put on a raincoat after lunch and went into the village to see what flower seeds were available. But the stores that did sell seeds—the general store and the drug store—had a limited variety. There was a preponderance of vegetable seeds, wallflower seeds and annuals, but no cinerarias or other of the greenhouse plants she had had in mind, such as the popular winter cherry, browalia or exacum. With the vague idea of perhaps being able to raise and sell wallflower plants if she could clear a space outside, she bought several packets of these seeds.

An idea occurred to her as she walked back to the house. An idea which became a strong conviction. That was the use to which she ought to put Aunt Maud's land. For growing things. For growing plants which would bring color and beauty to the world, not those ugly weeds which choked everything else. She would grow tall spires of lupins, and delphiniums, scarlet and yellow geums, bright golden coreopsis and sunflowers, as well as all the wonderful half-hardy annuals which many people had not the time, space or heating to grow. Asters and petunias in their glorious array of colors, sweet pea plants, exotic zinnias, sweet scabious, gloriosa daisies and many more. A thousand and one things. Vanessa's imagination ran riot as she almost skipped back to Puck's Hill.

"All that, Miss Vanessa, on four packets of seeds?" Nancy quizzed jokingly when Vanessa told her excitedly about her plans.

Vanessa laughed. "Yes, I know. It sounds crazy, doesn't it? But I'm going to make Aunt Maud's garden into a real show place, you'll see."

"And how long do you reckon that will take you?" came a masculine voice behind them.

They swung around. Ian Hamilton stood in the open doorway of the kitchen, wearing a raincoat and a country cap, his pipe in his mouth, but unlit.

Vanessa recovered swiftly. "I don't know how long it will take, but whether it takes six months or six years, I shall do it."

He pursed his lips and inclined his head. "Well, as a step in the right direction I've come to find out how many panes of glass you need for your greenhouse."

Her chin went up. "That's very kind of you, Mr. Hamilton, but I have the money to pay for that to be done now."

"Oh, really?"

"Yes, I've discovered a little—nest-egg, as it were, left for me by my aunt."

"Ah, I thought it wasn't like her to leave you entirely without resources. But I take it it's not an overly large sum?"

She told him the amount, while behind her she heard Nancy putting on the kettle for tea.

Ian heard the sound too. "I always arrive at the right time, don't I? A 'cuppa' would be just fine."

Vanessa had to stop herself from retorting that he should wait to be invited. Nobody seemed to realize that this was her house. But of course, Nancy had been living here for so long.

"Yes, well—" Ian said, examining his pipe in his usual fashion, "I wouldn't be too ready to turn down offers of help, if I were you. Your money will melt quite soon enough, you'll find. My man will be here in the morning. If it makes you feel any happier, you can pay him for his time."

"I want to pay for the glass too," she insisted.

He regarded her in silence for a moment, then said reasonably, "It's been hanging about my place since goodness knows when. I'm only too glad to get rid of it. It was in danger of getting broken."

She did not know what to say to that. The natural, normal thing, of course, would be simply to thank him, but with Ian Hamilton she was anything but normal and seemed to have a natural antagonism. Evidently taking her silence for consent, he turned to leave. But at the same moment came the sound of the teapot lid dropping onto the teapot.

Vanessa roused herself to be polite. "Will you stay for a cup of tea, Mr. Hamilton?"

She fully expected him to refuse, as her attitude was anything but friendly. She was still calling him mister instead of his first name. Even asking him formally to have tea could be taken as a hint that he ought to wait to be invited. But Ian Hamilton appeared impervious to all these considerations.

"Thanks," he said.

She led the way into the library—one of the rooms she had not yet had time to attend to. But it had two comfortable chairs, a floor to ceiling window with a pleasant view and seemed a more suitable place to have tea than the larger living room.

Ian looked around the room with interest, his glance ranging up and along the rows of dusty-looking books, most of their titles all but obscured with age and use, and to the large Adams-style fireplace.

"It's rather a fine old house, this," he remarked. "I haven't been in this room before."

Nancy brought in the tea, then left again. "I haven't used it very much myself up to now," Vanessa answered. "And I can't remember Aunt Maud using it much either. I'm not sure yet what to do with it."

"How do you mean?" he asked.

Vanessa frowned a little. He had a habit of asking questions to which she had not even thought out answers for herself.

"Well, I don't believe in having rooms that are not used, nor books which are never read, for that matter. I must get around to having a look at these—find out what they are, whether they're worth keeping."

He took the cup of tea she offered. "You're very practical. Tell me, how far will your aunt's wishes count with you? You don't seem to me the kind of person who will allow sentiment to influence your decisions."

Vanessa thought for a moment. "I don't know that there's a very clear-cut answer to that one. I'm sure my aunt would expect me to have a mind of my own."

"I'm glad to hear you say that. I think you're right."

"Do you?" she came back swiftly. "Why?"

He took a sip of his tea before answering smoothly, "Well, I'm quite sure your aunt—from what I knew of her—would never want to bind you to anything or impose any restrictions on you. At least, not as far as the house and what you do with it is concerned. She has left it to you without any conditions, hasn't she—I presume?"

"That's right," Vanessa answered stonily. "If I wanted to, I daresay I could sell the house tomorrow."

Her words seemed to electrify him. He shot a sharp, piercing glance at her.

"I thought you said you'd never sell," he said accusingly.

"So I did, but circumstances might lead me to change my mind, mightn't they?"

She was not serious. She had no intention of ever breaking her promise to Aunt Maud. She was not quite sure what was making her say these things, except some inexplicable desire to provoke him.

His mouth hardened. He put down his cup and rose to his feet.

"Well, if you do happen to change your mind, perhaps you'd be good enough to let me know, or at any rate to put it on the open market; not let any Tom, Dick or Harry of a property developer have first chance."

"I would choose carefully, I promise you," she told him.

"Thanks for the tea," he said stiffly. "If you'll excuse me, I must be going."

He strode away without waiting for her to see him out. Vanessa sighed and stood with her arms crossed, each hand gripping the other tightly. What on earth was the matter with her? What had made her goad him in that way? Why pretend she might sell when she had no intention of doing so? She had not even entertained the idea that one day she might be forced to, if she could not earn enough money to maintain the place.

Then she told herself it was the way he had talked: telling her how practical she was, that she wasn't the kind of person to allow sentiment to influence her decisions, that her aunt would never want to bind her to anything. What had he meant by "anything"? Had he guessed that Aunt Maud had extracted a promise from her? She had found out one thing anyway. He still wanted to buy the house.

But although she justified herself, she went about for the rest of the day feeling very ragged and at odds with life.

After tea she began looking at the books in the library. It had occurred to her that she could use this room as her office or study. But it would need redecorating before she could feel really happy in it. She was not sure that she liked these floor-to-ceiling bookshelves. The stern, heavily-bound volumes towered above her intimidatingly. She would prefer low bookshelves containing bright, friendly-looking books backed by pale walls and perhaps wall lighting.

The books on the lower shelves were mainly classics—Dickens, Shakespeare, Thackeray, Walter Scott. These would rub shoulders quite happily with the books of more modern authors. There were a great many books on birds. These too she would keep. Those on the top shelves for which she had to climb on a stepladder, were frowning, dusty volumes of the history of the Crimea, the Boer War, the Great War. All very interesting, no doubt, if one had the time to plow through them. Vanessa felt sure there were collectors of such books who could put them to far better use than she ever would. There was little point in letting them remain forever where they were gathering dust.

She was glancing once more along the shelf containing the books on natural history and birds when she came across a book on plants. She reached for it eagerly and flicked over the pages, walking over to the window. Then all at once her attention was riveted by a drawing. It was of a plant called the *Heracleum mantegazzianum* or Giant Hogweed.

It was the weed Aunt Maud had in her garden.

Vanessa turned over the page to find the script. *The largest umbelliferous plant in the world. Habitat, Caucasus.* She read on. It was a biennial, so took two years to reach maturity. It grew from ten to 15 feet high—that was Aunt Maud's weed all right. Its sap could cause a rash on some people, sometimes taking the form of blisters. Involuntarily Vanessa looked at her hands. But fortunately, she was in the habit of wearing gloves for heavy gardening work. Naturally, the book gave no hints on how to get rid of the weed.

Vanessa sat back in the chair and tried to think. Like most weeds, it flowered, seeded and propagated itself by the seeds falling when they were ripe. If one dealt with the weeds before they flowered, this served to control them. But if one simply cut off the heads they would go on producing more flowers and seeds in an effort to propagate themselves. But cutting off the seed or flower heads could act as a sort of first aid measure. Yes, that was the first thing. None of these weeds must be allowed to flower and seed. Those which were not seeding would be first year plants which would flower next year. They were the ones which should be uprooted this year. Approached this way, the solution to the problem sounded simple. Joe, of course, had not identified the weed. Few people would, as it was not very common, and Aunt Maud had not bothered her head about it. Killing even an obnoxious weed was not in her nature. Vanessa remembered she would never even have flowers in the house because it was "unkind" to cut them or break them off. But in Vanessa's view these weeds were choking the very existence out of other plants and flowers. Like the bullies and dictators of life, they would take over completely if nobody had the courage to fight them.

By sundown the rain had cleared. The following morning, the air was dry and warm. Vanessa was explaining to Joe her discovery about the giant hogweed when to her surprise Freda drove up in her station wagon accompanied by Ian and two other men. The men immediately began unloading squares of glass from the back. Freda lowered her window.

"Lovely morning, isn't it?"

Vanessa went toward them. "Hello, there! Nice to see you." Feeling guilty because of her rudeness to Ian the previous evening, her gaze slid past Freda to include him in a smile. "I've been discovering things about this weed," she told him.

Ian inclined his head. "Such as?"

"Won't you come in and have a coffee, both of you. I'll show you where I found it," she said, still feeling penitent.

Freda and Ian exchanged a glance. "We haven't come to take up your valuable time," Freda said. "And we've just had breakfast, as I suppose you have. Actually, we thought you could use some extra help, but we don't want to intrude, if you'd rather not have us around."

Vanessa's conscience smote her harder than ever. "Oh, Freda, how can you say such a thing? I'm always pleased to see you. But as for using extra help, I can't keep trespassing on your good natures."

Freda grinned. "Say no more! Just tell us what you want us to do. Come on, Ian."

They got out of the car. "What have you been finding out about this weed, then?" he asked.

She told him, but as she was quite unable to remember the Latin name for it, still less pronounce it, she brought the book from the library and showed them the illustration and text.

"That's it all right," Ian pronounced. "And from what it says about the sap you'd better wear gloves when you handle it."

"I've brought some anyway," Freda said. "You and the men haven't, though, have you?"

"Well, neither they nor I need actually handle it," said Ian. "If we do the digging, you girls can pick it up and stack it ready for burning; that would be the best thing." Vanessa simply could not help the thought that he was like a foreman giving orders, but she did not want to say anything to offend him when he and Freda were being so helpful.

Ian was watching her face. "What's the matter? Have you got some other ideas?"

"I have, as a matter of fact," she answered. "I'd thought it a good idea to go around with some shears and cut the flowering or seeding heads off before they ripen and fall. That will at least save new plants from springing up next year."

"All right," Ian said as if giving his permission. "But watch out for that sap. And start at the far end of the grounds away from where the men and myself are working. For one thing there's no point in cutting off the heads of those we'll be digging up. For another, the sappy ends will probably dry out if left for another day."

He dropped the book onto the low table and strode out purposefully.

"By the way," Freda said as she and Vanessa followed

him, "congratulations on finding the little nest-egg your Aunt Maud left for you. I imagine it will make all the difference."

Vanessa admitted that it would. "At least I shall be sure of being able to pay the taxes and electricity bills for a year or so."

"And maybe get a phone?" suggested Freda.

"Perhaps," agreed Vanessa.

In less than no time at all Ian and one of the men, along with Joe were digging away at the weeds while Ian's other man began putting panes of glass in the greenhouse. Armed with a pair of shears and a short-handled scythe, Freda and Vanessa began slicing off the flowering and seeding heads.

"Ian and I were wondering whether you'd like to join a club that we're members of," Freda said as they worked. "We meet once a month and have the occasional party."

"What sort of club?" queried Vanessa.

"It's a Foresters'. There's a fair amount of forestry in the area, as you know. Ian is a forester, so—"

"Is he?" asked Vanessa curiously.

"Why, yes, didn't you know?"

"How should I? I did notice the other evening that some clearance had been done on your side of the fence, but it was getting dark."

"You must have a meal with us and see around the place. Why not make it Sunday lunch? You have to take a little break some time," she added, seeing Vanessa's hesitation.

"Yes, I—suppose so. It's just that I'm anxious to get the greenhouse into production. But perhaps we can talk later."

She moved in the opposite direction to Freda. As she grasped the tops of the hogweed and slashed at them before dropping them on the ground, it occurred to her that it would save time and a second handling if she and Freda dropped them into boxes or cartons as they went along. Then they could fill the wheelbarrow and take them to a central place for burning afterward. So she went inside the house and brought some of the cartons Aunt Maud had hoarded in the attic.

When she went outside again, she glanced over to the men and involuntarily, she stood and stared.

Surprisingly, following yesterday's rain, the sun was hot. Ian stripped off both his shirt and pants and was clad only in a pair of shorts and thick-soled canvas shoes. His back and arms were bronzed to a smooth, even tan; his muscles firm and strong. Lost in sheer admiration of the man's physique, Vanessa's gaze traveled to his equally brown legs whose calf muscles looked as hard as iron. She had never seen such a fine specimen of masculinity. She let out a sigh and gave herself a mental shake.

Such a smooth even tan with no lines of demarcation at all could have only been acquired by continuous and pro-longed sunbathing—possibly on some beach. In all prob-ability he'd been a rich playboy before he bought, or in-herited the Lodge, she told herself contemptuously.

But as she worked, she could not prevent her gaze from straying in his direction from time to time.

"Cuts quite a fine figure, my brother, doesn't he?" Freda said at once with a mischievous smile.

"He's certainly very tanned," Vanessa answered as carelessly as she could. "Where did he get it? The Mediterranean?"

Freda laughed. "Good heavens, no! Working mostly. Ian always strips like that when it's warm, and he's doing any outdoor work."

Once again Vanessa was put in the wrong about Ian Hamilton. She did not like it one bit.

By lunch time quite a large area had been tackled, the unrooted hogweed lying limp and defeated in the sun. Freda had brought enough sandwiches and fruit with her to feed an army. Nancy laid a table under the shade of the sycamore, adding a great bowl of fresh crisp lettuce and early tomatoes, smelling and tasting wonderful. She explained that she had bought them from a neighbor who had his own greenhouse.

"I think I might grow some another year," Vanessa mused. "I grew them at home. They're not much trouble when you're around all day to look after them."

"You mean instead of plants?" queried Ian.

"No, I was thinking of a second greenhouse. And when the tomatoes were finished, I could use it for chrysanthemums."

Freda laughed. "You talk like a real gardener. I've never known a girl like you."

But Ian's face was serious. "Amateur gardening is one thing, building up a paying concern is another—if that's what you want to do."

"I'm well aware of that," Vanessa retorted. "What I want now are some seed boxes, propagating medium and a few packets of seeds. If I can sow them during the next few days, they'll flower in time for Christmas."

"Such as?" asked Ian in a sceptical tone.

"Such as browalia, exacum, calceolaria and cineraria—though I doubt if *they'll* be ready in time for Christmas, actually," she added, meaning the two latter flowering plants.

Ian eyed her through lids half closed against the sun as it filtered through the outer leaves of the tree.

"I suppose you know you can buy seedlings at this time of the year? Not as cheaply as packets of seeds, of course, but you'd still make a considerable profit. With the right sort of treatment you might well have them coming into flower for Christmas."

"And what do you call the right sort of treatment?" queried his sister.

His lips curved at the corners. "Ask Vanessa. She's the expert."

If he was hoping to catch her out, Vanessa thought, he was much mistaken.

"Well, cinerarias and calceolarias certainly need time to develop a good root system and an adequate period of time outdoors before they're taken into the greenhouse. But if they could be potted singly now in three-inch pots and put outside in a shady place, then about the middle of July potted in five or six inch pots and into a 'cold' greenhouse in the middle of August, they might stand a chance. But it's no good trying to bring cinerarias on by too much heat in the early stages. Is there a nursery nearby where I can buy seedling pot plants? I might even get some cyclamen."

Ian nodded. "There's a good one just this side of town on the Barnley road. You can buy your plants, seeds and everything from them. Why not let Freda drive you out there?"

"Would you, Freda?" asked Vanessa.

"Of course," Freda answered promptly. "When would you like to go—in the morning?"

"Suits me fine, thanks."

It was sometime during the middle of the afternoon when Miles Kendal drove up in his car. Vanessa left her task to speak to him.

He surveyed the scene with some surprise. "What's all this? A village working party?"

Vanessa explained, and he grimaced. "Well, I'd wade in and help, myself, but I'm on my way to town and wondered if you wanted to go in for anything."

Vanessa suddenly thought how she'd love to be able to prepare some of her seed trays this evening if only she had all the necessary materials.

"There are one or two things I need," she told him. "Would you be coming straight back? And have you room in the trunk of your car for about half 100-weight of seed compost?"

He grinned. "Yes, I think so—and we can come straight back if you must."

"That's awfully good of you."

Vanessa went back to Freda and was vaguely aware that Ian had ceased his digging for a moment and was leaning on his shovel watching her.

"Freda, do you mind? Miles Kendal is going into town now. He's offered to run me to the garden center. If I go right away I'll be able to do some of my sowing tonight."

Freda glanced across at Miles, his arms folded, leaning on the hood of his car smoking a cigarette.

"No, I don't mind," she said quietly. "But if I'd known you were so anxious to get started *I* could have drivin you there this afternoon."

"I thought as Miles was going anyway, it would save you the trouble," Vanessa said uncomfortably.

"It wouldn't have been any trouble. But go if you want to."

Vanessa thanked her for all she had done, aware uneasily that neither Freda nor her brother liked Miles. But she reasoned that she couldn't be expected to dislike him simply because they did.

"Nancy will be bringing out some tea before long, I expect," she added. "But don't work any more, Freda. I'm sure you've done more than enough. Ian too, but you've both been a great help. It would have taken Joe and me a week to do all that's been done today."

"Think nothing of it," answered Freda.

Vanessa hurried indoors to change and to pick up some money. Before she came out again, she put a couple of pounds in two envelopes and asked Nancy to give one each to Ian's men. She simply could not have them working for her for nothing. Outside, she braced herself to go and thank Ian, knowing she would meet with his disapproval.

He listened to her thanks and her explanation of why she had dropped everything to go with Miles. His face was an expressionless mask, and he made no comment whatever. But the coldness of his gray eyes was enough to tell her what his opinion was.

Vanessa walked away from him, her chin lifted defiantly. She had not asked him to come. She had thanked him and had left money behind for his men. She refused to allow him either to intimidate her, or to dictate to her. But she could not put a name to the feeling buried deep within her.

Miles grinned widely as he opened his car door for her. "Friend Ian didn't look very pleased," he said.

Vanessa frowned. "Do you think it was rude of me to have left them? Even Freda didn't seem very pleased—though she said she didn't mind."

Miles tuned the ignition before answering. "Did you ask them to come and give you a hand?"

"No, Ian offered to send a man to put some glass in the greenhouse, but this morning he turned up with two men as well as Freda."

Miles turned the car and set off down the drive. "I—don't—like—the—sound—of—it," he said slowly.

She glanced at him swiftly. "What do you mean?"

"They're trying to get around you, Vanessa, as I said they would. In one way or another, they intend to get their hands on your property."

But Vanessa felt this was too sweeping. "Oh, I think they're trying genuinely to be helpful, Miles," she protested. "In any case I've already told Ian I shall never sell."

"I don't blame you," he said, turning the car into the road. "It's a very desirable piece of land. It's been a shame to see it going to waste. But purely as a matter of interest, why are you so adamant? The house is much too big for you, isn't it? And why spend all your energies on trying to clear that impossible weed?"

"The weed is not impossible," she answered. She told him what she had found out about it and her system for getting rid of it.

"That's quite a discovery," he conceded. "But it's still a mammoth undertaking unless you want to be dependent on people like Hamilton. Mind you, I'd have been along to give you a hand myself if I'd known you were going to get down to it in earnest."

She flashed him a smile of amusement. "But you wouldn't have been 'trying to get around me'."

She saw his eyebrows shoot up. "You know perfectly well that isn't true—at least, not for any ulterior motive. I just happen to like you. What made you say that, anyway?"

"Well, I understand you're a property developer. You'd like to buy my aunt's house and land too, wouldn't you?"

He frowned. "What do you mean—'you understand'? You knew from the start what my profession was. I gave you my card."

Vanessa realized that she had never properly looked at his card. She didn't know what had come over her since she had left home.

"I'm sorry, Miles, I was only joking. But seriously, have you ever made my aunt an offer for Puck's Hill?"

"Of course. Why not? But once she said no, that was that. I didn't try to pressure her."

"You haven't tried with me."

He smiled. "You've already told me you don't intend selling. That's good enough for me. If you were ever to change your mind, of course, I hope you'd let me know. Which brings me to my other question you haven't answered yet. Why are you so adamant about not selling when the place has got so many disadvantages? If you were to sell it, you'd have money to buy two houses—or one, and enough money left over to sail halfway around the world."

She hesitated for a moment, then told him quietly, "The main reason, I suppose, is because I promised Aunt Maud that I wouldn't."

"Oh, for crying out loud!" he groaned. "Death-bed promises! The very worst form of tyranny. You can never be released from them. The trouble is they're usually extracted under abnormal circumstances. Sometimes, of course," he amended swiftly, "dying people don't really know what they're saying or doing. I feel sure that was the case with your aunt. That place is going to be a mill-stone around your neck, but I don't suppose she realized it."

He had made such an interesting point; there was so much truth in what he said that for a moment or two Vanessa sat in thoughtful silence. Miles glanced at her uneasily.

"Don't get me wrong, Vanessa. It's you I'm thinking of. I've seen this sort of thing happen before. A person makes a last request, and the one left behind ruins their entire life trying to keep the promise. Often as not it's something that isn't remotely worthwhile. Dying people aren't normal; they're not responsible for what they're saying. Your aunt was obviously very fond of you. If she'd been in full possession of her senses when she made you promise never to sell, she would surely have left you some money for the place's upkeep."

"Oh, but she did. I forgot to tell you."

"Really?" He sounded more abashed than pleased, but when she went on to tell him the amount, he shook his head. "But if you don't mind me saying so, that's chicken feed. In fact, it could turn out to be worse than having nothing. It will only encourage you to put a lot of time and effort into keeping your promise and wear yourself out in the process. That's barely enough to live on for more than about three months by the time you've paid your taxes, electricity bills and what-have-you."

She told him her plans for renting the barn and propagating house plants to sell.

"I suppose you'll say all that's chicken feed, too," she said a little despondently.

He shrugged. "Well, I don't want to discourage you. There are no windows in the barn, are there? That means another outlay for you. Only on very hot nights will it be fit to dance with the doors open. Even then you won't find the village people willing to pay more than about ten shillings a night for the hire. Maybe in the winter for bingo, yes, but then you'll have to heat the place, won't you? And of course, your pot plants won't be ready for sale for another six months at least."

Vanessa tried to joke. "You'll have me in tears any minute!" But she really was beginning to feel like crying.

Miles's hand shot out. "Pay no attention to me, Vanessa. I didn't mean to put you off. It's just that I'm so concerned about you. I could stand in the sidelines and cheer you on. I could give you every encouragement by wading in and helping you as Hamilton and his sister have done, but that wouldn't be doing you any kindness. Quite the reverse. It would be better, in my opinion, if you'd put your aunt's wishes down to the wanderings of a sick woman. Really, Vanessa, she was a little eccentric at best, even you must admit that. Ask yourself seriously whether you really are doing the right thing by hanging on to the place. Sell it to Ian Hamilton, sell it to whomever you like. But don't kill yourself by trying to make it earn money so that you can keep a promise which—who knows—even your aunt might be regretting having asked you to keep—if you believe in life after death."

Vanessa didn't know what to say to such undeniably common sense. It was true Aunt Maud had been an eccentric. It ran in the family. Was she in danger of following literally in her aunt's footsteps, living in that great house in poverty, or at best just earning enough by raising plants to keep the place going and herself in food and bare necessities of clothing? She would probably become just as much a fanatic about her plants as Aunt Maud had been about her birds.

She put the depressing picture behind her as Miles drew up outside the nursery.

"I could leave you here to browse and buy what you want, then call back for you in about half an hour, if you like," he suggested.

"Are you sure I'm not putting you to a lot of inconvenience?" she asked him.

He gave her a smile. "Quite sure. Half an hour will be ample for what I want to do. But just take your time. I'm in no hurry."

He drove off, and she looked interestedly around. Attractive flower beds were laid out at the entrance, and a paved drive led to a large open-plan store where one could buy absolutely everything one needed for a garden. Vanessa decided she would be a regular visitor here. Then she realized she had no means of transport without possibly having to take two buses, one into town and another out again; those only at restricted times. But a car of her own was out of the question.

Knowing how many plants could be had from just one packet of seed, Vanessa did not buy more than two each of the kind she had planned, but as her eyes ran along the packets of seeds in the rack, all kinds of possibilities occurred to her. Her excitement mounting, she reached for one after another of the brightly colored packets depicting superb, larger-than-life-sized blooms, unblemished either by wind, rain or sun. She must think beyond Christmas to next spring. She would use the barn as a sort of store where people could come and buy their plants for the garden as well as for the house. There was no end to what she could grow and sell. She would buy a few geraniums and take cuttings, rear some colorful coleus. She simply could not fail.

She bought seed boxes and sowing medium; one pink, one white, and one red geranium, then wandered outside to where the boxes of seedlings were hardening off. The man who served her looked at her with surprise mingled with amusement as she bought four dozen cinerarias, calceolarias and cyclamen.

"You starting up a store?" he asked, nearer the truth than he imagined.

She laughed and said she was buying them for Christmas presents, which was also near the truth. Pot plants as presents were becoming more and more popular.

Miles opened his eyes wide too, when he saw the stack of items she had bought.

"You really mean it, don't you?" he said soberly, shaking his head.

"Well, yes, of course."

She found his lack of enthusiasm for her scheme rather dampening, though he meant it from the best of motives, she felt sure.

They stacked the things in the car. Miles drove her home again, but this time in comparative silence. Vanessa sat in silence too—a troubled silence. Would her enterprise be successful? It was all very well being able to rear plants, but supposing not enough people bought them? Had Aunt Maud been right to ask her to promise not to sell Puck's Hill? Miles had made a very good point about "death-bed promises". One could never ask to be released from them. Where, she asked herself, did respect for the wishes of a person one has loved end and sheer sentiment take over? At what point did determination become obstinacy?

Freda, Ian, and his men had left when Vanessa arrived back home. Joe was putting away tools preparatory to going home himself.

"Mr. Hamilton said to tell you he'll be along to see you some time tomorrow, Miss."

"Thank you, Joe. Goodnight."

She asked Miles if he would like some tea. He was eyeing the large area of unrooted weeds and the stacks ready for burning.

They've done well, haven't they?" she ventured against the speculative expression on his face.

He nodded. "Hamilton has, at any rate. If he can ever persuade you to sell, having this weed cleared will suit him fine."

"I suppose so." She cast him a mischievous smile. "Tell me, Miles, to what purpose would you put the house and land if I sold it to you?"

He looked at her seriously for a moment, then laughed suddenly.

"You've got me there, haven't you? I haven't thought a great deal about it. I can tell you this—I'd put it to a darned sight more practical use than Ian Hamilton would—and to be honest the giant hogweed, or whatever its Latin name is, wouldn't be much use to me, either."

At least he was frank. "Will you come in and have a cup of tea with me?" she repeated.

"It will be a pleasure."

She took him into the room which was to become her study-cum-sitting room and left him looking at the book on natural history while she went to make the tea. When she returned, he was eyeing some of the other books.

"Dry as dust most of them, aren't they?" he said. "What on earth are you going to do with them?"

"Sell them. At least most of them. Maybe to private collectors or libraries."

He smiled. "So your aunt didn't extract any promise about these. I take it you've no sentimental attachment to them."

"Silly, of course not! I shall simply have to use my instinct and discretion about things."

He put his hand on her shoulder. "That's the stuff!"

After tea he suggested they might spend the rest of the evening together.

"A movie and supper afterward—something like that?" he said.

But she shook her head. "Some other time, Miles, if you don't mind. After leaving Ian and his men doing my work for me, I don't feel justified in going out again now. I must make a start on my propagating."

He shook his head disapprovingly. "Doing your work for you, my foot! You're a dear sweet girl and more likely to be put upon than anything else. But what about making a firm date with me? As far as I can see, it's the only way I'm going to be able to see you for more than half an hour at a time. If the weather's nice on Sunday we could go for a picnic lunch."

"Sorry, Miles, I can't."

"Why not?"

She sighed, knowing what his reaction would be. "Freda Hamilton has invited me over there for lunch. I—couldn't very well say no."

"Couldn't you? There might come a time when you will want to. Are you free on Saturday, then? We could make it theater and supper."

"Yes, all right. Thanks very much."

She saw him out, then went back indoors to change before tackling the job of filling the seed trays and sowing her seeds. Her mind went over some of the things Miles had said, and thought too about Ian Hamilton. Both men professed to have her welfare at heart, or at any rate, in mind. Yet both men wanted Puck's Hill. Which of the two was the more genuine? Miles, who was trying to prevent her from making mistakes and running into failure, or Ian who was encouraging her and helping her?

CHAPTER FOUR

Vanessa had taken the precaution of picking up some fumigating tablets at the garden center so that she could sterilize the greenhouse. She wanted to make sure that no disease would attack her plants or seedlings. She sealed up the windows, lit two of the tablets, then closed the door and sealed it from the outside. It was early June, so danger of morning frosts would be over. As a precaution she erected a trestle table in the large kitchen and put her boxes of seedlings into three-inch seed trays there for the night. Tomorrow she would have to transplant some of the seedlings into three-inch pots so that they would develop strong roots to make good flowering plants. She must also get Joe to help her to make frames so that they could stand outside. And she would need peat with which to surround them. This was something she had not thought to bring from the garden center. If only she had her own car!

She was digging around beneath some trees the next morning in the hope of finding some natural peat when she saw Ian walking around looking at various things—their work of yesterday, the greenhouse, the frames Joe was constructing, and the newly cleaned out barn. Vanessa stood and watched him for a minute or two. Walking around as if he already owns the place. The phrase came unbidden into her mind, and she felt ashamed. Why did she resent Ian Hamilton so much? True, he was inclined to be high-handed, and he lacked the kind of charm Miles had, but— She broke off her thoughts abruptly. There was someting about Ian which both attracted and repelled her.

Then he scanned the garden and saw her, so she dropped the shovel and walked toward him.

"I hope you don't mind," he said, disarming her. "

hopped over the fence instead of coming around by the road."

"That's all right."

His glance went to where she had been digging. "What are you doing now?" he asked.

She told him. "It's the one thing I forgot to buy yesterday, and not having my own car—"

His face became thoughtful. "You ought to have a car of some sort. It's practically essential in the country. You can't be dependent on buses or—or other people. You should have a phone, too. Have you thought any more about that?"

She didn't answer for a moment. A certain pride forbade her from saying she hadn't the money for these extras. She was about to say that she hadn't really felt a serious or ugent need for either a car or the telephone when he forestalled her.

"If you're going into any sort of business, you simply must have a phone," he said. "And a car needn't cost you the earth. I know where you can get quite a good reliable utility van for around a hundred. You could spread the cost over 12 months with very little drain on your capital. As for peat, you never need to buy that. I've got a whole estate full—yours for the taking. In fact I'll send one of the men around with a few sacks full."

She felt he was thrusting solutions to her problems down her throat. She was not used to other people making decisions for her.

"Thanks very much," she said coolly, "but I have all the peat I want here for the time being. Please don't put your men to any trouble on my account. As to the car and telephone—I'm not in any hurry."

He drew an exasperated breath and looked as if he might say something explosive, then changed his mind. But his expression was stormy. He pulled two envelopes out of his pockets and handed them to her.

"These are the envelopes you left with money inside for

my men yesterday. They don't want payment for what they did."

"Don't they?" she flashed back. "Or have they returned it because you told them to?"

His jaw tightened. He drew another deep breath and expelled it forcibly.

"You really are the most difficult person I've ever met in my whole life!"

"And you, Mr. Hamilton, are the most—irritating and high-handed that *I* have ever met! Everyone is expected to jump to your commands."

He stared at her as if she had taken leave of her senses, as if it was incredible that anyone could think such things about him, still less say them.

"I'm sorry," he jerked out at last, but in a far from apologetic tone, and turned to stride down the drive in long, angry strides.

Vanessa sighed and wished she had better control of her tongue. Ian Hamilton seemed to bring out the worst in her. All the same she smarted for a very long time, his words running around and around in her brain. *You really are the most difficult person I've ever met in my whole life.* How could she possibly go to his house for lunch on Sunday now?

As she half expected, Freda paid her a visit that evening. Vanessa was working late, tackling the weed which flanked the drive. Ian and his men had done quite a considerable amount, but Vanessa felt it was important to clear the entrance to the house and barn as soon as possible. She was thinking of having some posters printed announcing that the barn at Puck's Hill was available for rent. As well as to earn a little money from the hire, she felt it would get villagers accustomed to visiting the place in preparation for the time when her plants were ready.

"Still hard at it?" queried Freda.

Vanessa smiled. She really liked Freda. "I think I'll

call it a day now, at any rate. Come and have a cup of coffee with me."

She knew what Miles would have said about Freda's visit. Whether it was true or not, she did not care. It was good to have someone her own age to talk to.

"I came to make sure you were still having lunch with us on Sunday," Freda said when they were drinking their coffee.

"Yes—if you're sure you want me."

"Of course we do."

Vanessa smiled ruefully into her cup. "I'm afraid I was very rude to Ian this morning."

Freda laughed. "So was he to you, I gather. You'll have to forgive Ian. He does tend to give the impression of being 'in charge'. He doesn't mean to dictate. It's just that he's so accustomed to taking responsibility, and being so fond of your aunt—"

"I'd—rather he didn't feel responsible for me, all the same," Vanessa murmured.

"He's only trying to help," Freda pointed out mildly.

"I suppose so, and I appreciate his efforts, really I do, but I didn't want the men to work for me for nothing. Why should they?"

"Well, as for that, Vanessa, they were already being paid by Ian, you see. And the whole idea was to give you a hand and try to *save* you a little money. You'll run out of it all too quickly, you know, if you don't watch out."

"You make me feel ashamed."

Freda shook her head. "No need for that. If you feel so strongly about giving the men something, why not just give them a token payment: about a quarter the amount you did originally, which was almost the equivalent of a day's wages."

But Vanessa was not quite convinced. "Are you sure the men didn't want the extra money?"

"Quite sure. They brought it to Ian to give back to you."

"Oh."

Freda looked at her downcast face. "Cheer up, we all make mistakes. I would just forget about this morning's little scene, if I were you. Ian won't want to be reminded of it."

"You're a great peacemaker, aren't you? I'm not usually so pigheaded. I don't know what's the matter with me."

"It's this house and everything. You've taken on a good deal."

"Don't make excuses for me," Vanessa told her. "I've been as stubborn as can be about the business of getting a phone. I wasn't entirely penniless when I came down here—at least, I had enough money to pay for the installation of a telephone. Of course then, I didn't want to use up my capital on something that didn't seem necessary. But there's been no excuse since finding the money Aunt Maud left me, and I did snap Ian's head off about it. About a car, too."

"Well, I expect he tried to sell you the idea of having a car before your mind was really ready to accept it," Freda comforted. "Anyway, I'll tell Ian to keep on the look-out for one for you. You don't have to have one, if you don't want to. Ian will understand."

Will he? wondered Vanessa privately. He considered her to be difficult. The most difficult person he had ever met in his whole life. The reminder of it depressed her beyond belief, but she smiled and thanked Freda.

"A telephone is the first step anyway. That will save me going to the booth. Maybe I can get firms to deliver things like sacks of potting soil and pots and so on. Meanwhile, if I want to go into town I can use the public transportation."

Freda pulled a face. "With two buses a day? And so far

apart you have to hang around wasting time instead of being able to come back when you're ready? Look, any time you want to pop into town just let me know. I'll either come in with you, or you can borrow my car."

Vanessa had rarely met such generosity. But she knew the misunderstandings which could arise if one took advantage of such an offer too often, or at an inconvenient time. She simply must get a van or small car of some kind before long. She smiled and murmured her thanks, but Freda made a shrewd guess at her thoughts.

"Look, Vanessa. Neither Ian or I want to force our help on you. We just want you to know you can call on us at any time. We're your neighbors, and we want to be your friends, too. And what are friends for if not to lend a helping hand? So you will let us know, won't you, if there's anything we can do?"

Vanessa had a sudden inspiration. "You could do one thing for me right away, if you would. Telephone the phone company and ask them to come and see me about getting the phone installed."

"I'll do that with pleasure."

But when Freda had gone, Vanessa wondered how far, in actual fact, Freda had been speaking for Ian with regard to their being friends. Freda had done her best to speak peace, but Vanessa couldn't help feeling that Ian was more angry than Freda would have her believe; that he was still angry, and had meant every word he had said this morning.

The weather, at any rate, was on Vanessa's side. By Saturday she and Joe had managed to clear several feet of weed on either side of the drive. She wished she dared spend some money on pot-grown roses, but she would need so many. She comforted herself with the thought that even bare earth looked better than rank weed. She would have almost forgotten about her date with Miles had not Nancy reminded her. Joe had finished work at 12 as he ususally did on Saturdays, and Vanessa thought she would have a change from digging.

"Good heavens, I almost forgot," she said when Nancy reminded her.

Nancy eyed her shrewdly. "You can't be very keen if you nearly forgot," she said.

"Oh, I had been looking forward to going to the theater," Vanessa assured her.

"I meant you can't be very keen on Miles Kendal as a person," pursued Nancy.

"I like him well enough, but that's all. What else?" asked Vanessa.

"What else is there usually, between a man and a woman?" Nancy queried pointedly.

But Vanessa shook her head swiftly. "I'm not getting any of those kinds of notions about Miles Kendal or anyone," she said firmly. "And I'm quite sure Miles hasn't any ideas about me beyond ordinary friendship."

Later on, Vanessa was not quite so sure of that. Not only was he extremely charming and attentive, but over supper he began to talk in wistful terms about a real home of his own.

"I don't mean just a bachelor apartment like I have at the moment, but a house and a garden and—well, all that goes with it, like a—wife and children."

They were sitting side by side at a table. His hand reached out and grasped hers. Just how much significance there was in this, Vanessa dared not think, but she felt the only thing to do was treat him lightly.

She laughed. "In that order?"

He turned his head and eyed her seriously. "Let's just say, at the moment, that until—a few weeks ago, I was quite content with my bachelor apartment and bachelor life."

Vanessa thought she had better not ask him why a few weeks ago.

"What do you mean?" she asked.

His shoulders lifted. "Well, you know, taking different girls out, generally living it up. But there comes a time when a fellow starts thinking about growing roots, if you know what I mean."

Vanessa tried another tack. "What about your parents, Miles? Wouldn't you be happier living with them rather than on your own?"

He shook his head. "Heavens, no, not where they live."

"Which is?"

"Australia. They emigrated about two years ago, but I decided to stay here. They sold their house for capital and wanted me to go with them, naturally, but—well, I was engaged at the time, and—"

Vanessa knew a swift reawakening of her own only recently healed wounds.

"Oh, Miles, I'm sorry. What happened?"

"She married someone else, but not to worry. I'm well over the little episode now. But what about you, Vanessa? How is it that an absolutely marvelous girl like you is still free?"

"I suppose because I've still to meet the right person. Like you I've—had my disappointments."

"I just can't believe it—a wonderful girl like you. Attractive, intelligent—"

She laughed. "Easy on the compliments! You'll have me getting a swollen head."

"Not you."

When he drove her back to Puck's Hill, he seemed in no hurry to say goodnight. But when she asked him in for coffee, he declined.

"Let's just sit here and talk for a while. Somehow that house depresses me."

Vanessa admitted that it was not very homey. "But it will be by the time I've finished with it."

"I'm sure." His arm slid across her shoulders and his lips brushed her cheek. "I'm sure you're a wonderful homemaker, but a house like that was meant for a staff of servants."

His lips found hers, but Vanessa's mind was too occupied by what he had just said to respond very much. Sometimes she felt Miles was so right, her courage failed her. She pushed against him.

"Please, Miles, if you don't mind. I'd rather go in now."

Very slowly, he removed his arm. "I expect you're tired—and no wonder."

"I am rather—but it's been a lovely evening, Miles. Thank you so much."

He walked with her to the door of the house. As she was about to say goodnight to him, he suddenly put his arms around her and pressed his lips hard on hers. But Vanessa had never been one to indulge in this sort of thing lightly.

"Please, Miles—"

"What's the matter? Don't you like me?"

"Of course I like you, but—"

"But you're tired. I understand." He put his hands on her shoulders and gave her a long look, a fond smile on his face. "I can't tell you what this evening has meant to me. When can I see you again? Soon?"

She gave him a faint smile in return and nodded, but felt vaguely uneasy at the change in him. At the present moment, she did not want anything deeper than ordinary friendship from any man.

"The phone company is coming to install my telephone on Monday," she told him evasively. "I'll give you a call, then you'll know my number."

"You—do want to see me again?" he queried, a note of anxiety in his voice.

"Of course. But at the moment, with so much to do, I'd rather not make too many arrangements in advance. You're always welcome to drop in. But now I really must go in."

She made her way inside wondering whether Miles always behaved in such a way when he took a girl out for an evening, or whether he was becoming serious about her. She hoped not. She liked him well enough, but that was all.

She slept late the next morning and was awakened by Nancy with a breakfast tray. Vanessa sat up sleepily as the older woman poured out a cup of tea for her.

"This is terrible. It's I who should be doing this for you," she protested.

"Nonsense. You're working hard. You need someone to 'mother' you. In any case, I had my breakfast over an hour ago."

"Mother me?" Vanessa laughed. "I never had this kind of spoiling from my own mother."

"Maybe you didn't work so hard, either." Nancy looked down at Vanessa, her face serious. "Are you sure you're doing the right thing by trying to make this place earn money? Don't you think you're taking on too much, doing work which is much too heavy for a woman? You should be thinking of getting married."

"Married!" For a split second Vanessa experienced small stabs of something like pain. Then she laughed. "Don't you start, Nancy. You sound almost like Miles Kendal."

Nancy stared at her. "You don't mean he's asked you to marry him?"

"No, not yet—and I'm not saying he intends to, but he was making some very odd noises last night."

Nancy shook her head gravely. "I wouldn't trust that young man any farther than I could throw him. No, Ian's the one for you, Vanessa."

At this, everything within Vanessa seemed to freeze.

"Now you're talking nonsense. Ian Hamilton is the very last person I would marry. But there's no need to worry. He is the one person who will never ask me."

"I'll leave you to eat your breakfast." Nancy answered and left the room.

Vanessa gave a long sigh as she tackled her toast and honey. Ian Hamilton did not even like her, nor she him.

Dressing to go to the Lodge for lunch Vanessa could not help wishing she had bought more clothes. After changing her mind several times she chose a dress she had bought last year and which she had scarcely worn; a simple, easy-to-wear white dress with groups of narrow pleats from neck to hem. She was wondering whether to walk around by the road, or pop over the fence dividing the two properties when Freda drove up.

"I thought I'd better collect you," she said. "It's a long walk by road. Walking through some parts of the woods can be tricky, especially while there's so much clearance being done."

Vanessa was consumed with curiosity to see what the Hamiltons' home was like. Freda drove in what amounted to a semicircle—left, left through the village and left again through an open gateway which in the Colonel's time was always closed, along a winding drive flanked with beautiful specimen trees and evergreen shrubs, to the house itself made of red brick and rich cedar, blending together perfectly. Running the entire length of the house was a veranda gay with red geraniums and fuchsia, while the surrounding garden was an absolute picture—smooth green lawns, colorful flower beds, roses and pergolas against a background of trees. Vanessa let out an involuntary exclamation of admiration.

"Oh, Freda, when I think of my wilderness!"

"Yours will soon be every bit as nice as this the way you're progressing," Freda comforted.

"Do you sit out here much?" Vanessa asked as they mounted the wooden steps to the veranda.

"Not really," Freda told her. "We prefer the back of the house. Come and see."

Vanessa had subconsciously geared herself to meet Ian as soon as she arrived. There was still no sign of him as she followed his sister into a wide, carpeted hall and through a pair of very beautiful glass doors to a large sun-lounge, its sliding doors opening onto a paved patio.

"Oh, how lovely!" cried Vanessa.

A fountain played in a small pool, cascades of color overflowed from hanging baskets, and spilled out of urns and flower troughs. White-painted garden furniture added a touch of elegance as well as luxury. Inside the sun-lounge were comfortable basket chairs, palms, ferns and other graceful plants.

"Make yourself at home," invited Freda. "I'll just pop into the kitchen to see how lunch is getting along."

Vanessa sank into one of the lounge chairs, and for a moment or two allowed their comfort to take possession of her. Then she rose and went to sit on the edge of the raised pool to watch the goldfish darting like flashes of copper light hither and thither. She trailed her fingers in the clear water, warmed by the sun and became lost in a vague, misty world of dreams; one of happiness and heart's desire, love and peace. Then, without actually seeing him, she became aware of Ian standing a few yards away. She looked up to find him watching her, an odd expression on his face.

"Hello, Vanessa," he said quietly.

CHAPTER FIVE

Vanessa rose slowly, her gaze riveted to his face. "Hello, Ian."

He moved toward her, and the brief moment of something which had been beyond understanding passed.

"You look very charming this morning," he said in a faintly mocking tone. "And so relaxed there by the pool."

Sensing an underlying sarcasm, she chose not to accept the compliment. "It's so restful and attractive out here, I'm afraid it emphasizes the state of my place."

"You have the satisfaction of creation still to come," he answered. "This place wasn't the way I liked it when—Freda and I first came to live here."

She noticed the hesitation, as if he had been going to say something and then changed it. She realized how little she knew about Ian Hamilton and his sister.

"Did you buy the place or—inherit it?" she asked.

He stared at her for a moment. "What made you think we'd inherited it? The previous owner was no relative of ours."

An unexpected relief washed over her. "I—don't know why I thought that. This house and the woodlands have always been considered to be a sort of hunting ground and—"

"And you considered me to be a rich playboy," he finished, as she hesitated, seeking for her next phrase.

"I hadn't really thought much about what you were," she answered coolly.

"And you're not interested."

His tone was accusing. "I didn't say that," she flashed back at him.

For a moment there was a sharp silence between them, then as if remembering his duty as host, he relaxed.

"Sit down, won't you, and let me get you a sherry—or is there some other drink you'd prefer?"

She sat down on the padded seat of the white wrought-iron sofa. "A sherry would be very nice, thank you."

He went inside and reappeared almost immediately with a tray on which was a decanter and glasses. He poured out two glasses and handed one to her, then sat half turned to face her. They sipped in silence for a minute or two, then feeling it was up to her to show some interest in the home of her host and hostess, she asked, "Was this sun-lounge and patio here when you bought the house or have you had them added?"

"Half and half," he told her. "There was a veranda of sorts, but it was rather gloomy and depressing with a tiled roof and a wooden rail around in the real hunting lodge style. The patio was just a neglected yard, the paving cracked and uneven, the various outbuildings bare and ugly. But it had a sunny exposure, and I firmly believe a place in which one can relax is essential. So we had a glass roof and sides put in the veranda, sliding plate glass doors along the entire front, as you can see, and some new floor covering. Then we laid colored paving slabs out here and covered the outbuildings with either trellis work or decorative bricks. A few plants and climbers did the rest."

"Not to mention this elegant garden furniture," Vanessa said wistfully.

"They were Freda's idea. In fact, she bought them. I would most likely have made do with canvas chairs and a homemade table of some kind."

Vanessa was about to ask him why he and his sister had chosen to live at Barn Hill, and why they lived together rather than with their parents, when Freda joined them, and with her a young man with fair hair, wearing slacks and a white open-necked shirt. Freda made the introduction.

"Vanessa, meet a friend of mine, Harry Davidson. Harry, this is our new neighbor, Vanessa Woodrow."

A very special friend? Vanessa wondered as she shook hands with the young man. At any rate, she felt he would be a welcome addition to the small luncheon party.

The meal was served in the oak-panelled dining room, furnished in the Jacobean period which Vanessa found so mellow and satisfying to look at.

"You like the room?" Ian said, seeing how she glanced around.

She nodded. "Very much. I like old furniture—or rather, antique furniture."

"Do I take it you wouldn't settle for the reproduction kind?" he queried.

"I would if it was well made. Why not? It isn't the period in which things are made which counts, but the craftsmanship and design. Did you—buy the furniture with the house?" she queried, still curious as to why a brother and sister should be living together.

Ian shook his head. "The Colonel took his furniture with him to the Isle of Wight. All the furniture in the house was chosen at various times by either Freda or myself. Fortunately our tastes don't clash too violently, although Freda prefers the more modern look. If she shows you her own rooms after you'll see what I mean."

It was a pleasant and most enjoyable meal. Ian sat at the head of the table looking very much a family man as he carved the Sunday roast. Vanessa couldn't help wondering why he was still unmarried. Freda, she guessed, would not remain single for much longer, judging from the expressive glances she and Harry exchanged from time to time. But in the event of her marrying, what would happen to Ian? Would he live in this house alone?

Vanessa tried to control her thoughts better. For all she knew Ian might already have someone he was hoping to marry, someone who lived in another part of the country perhaps. But why another part of the country? she asked herself. It could be a girl in the village. She had not known Ian and his sister long enough to know much about them; neither did she know many people in the village. As well as the cottages and terrace houses, there were some quite big houses here and there.

"Freda has been telling me what a heroic job you're doing at Puck's Hill." Harry spoke to Vanessa across the table. She smiled.

"Well, it did seem rather formidable at first, but now I've found a way of tackling that giant hogweed. Thanks to the help I've had from Freda and Ian, it doesn't seem nearly as hopeless. There's still an awful lot of work, though. I've realized that even more after seeing Freda and Ian's lovely house and garden."

"There's quite a considerable amount of land there, isn't there?" pursued Harry. "You're not going to try to cultivate it all, are you?"

"I'm aiming to clear the whole area of that hogweed, anyway," she answered. "After that, I'm not sure. I might develop my plant growing into a sort of nursery business, or just add more greenhouses and grass the rest."

"A nursery business? Why not grow trees?" suggested Harry.

An alert glance passed between Ian and his sister.

"What sort of trees?" asked Vanessa.

Harry shrugged. "Oh, any kind. Christmas trees, for instance. Much less trouble than growing roses or whatever it is you have in mind. Ian could—"

The rest of his sentence was cut short by Freda.

"*Harry*, Vanessa doesn't know you're a forester. He simply can't help trying to sell the idea of trees to everyone," she explained to Vanessa. "Unlike Ian, he works for the Forestry Commission, but he's got trees on the brain."

"Haven't we all," murmured Ian. "But Vanessa is more interested in plants and flowers."

Vanessa wondered what Harry had been about to say when Freda had interrupted him.

"I wasn't thinking of growing roses, actually," she answered him. "Just things like perennials—herbaceous border plants and maybe shrubs. But the idea of growing Christmas trees is intriguing. I must think about that."

After lunch Ian and Harry gallantly said they would do the washing up while Freda showed Vanessa the rest of the house.

"Coffee on the patio in half an hour," Ian told them. "So don't start chatting and forget the time."

Freda made some tart rejoinder and led the way upstairs. "I'll show you the kitchen and other downstairs rooms last—when they've done the washing up."

"Is Ian always so domestic?" asked Vanessa.

"Oh yes. He calls it a fair division of labor. I do the cooking, he does the washing up—when there's no one else to do it. Our daily help works from nine to four, five days a week. Evenings and weekends we have to do our own chores."

Vanessa ventured to ask, "Why are you and Ian living together? Are your parents still living?"

"Oh yes," came the surprising answer. Vanessa had thought perhaps they were both dead. "They live in Hampshire—the New Forest. Father is a head forester there. It's just that Ian wanted to have his own woodlands and carry on his own forestry business. He bought this place and—I thought I'd like to come too. I wanted a change. In fact I wanted to recover from a disappointing love affair. You know the sort of thing—I was in love, he wasn't, so I thought I'd get away: keep house for Ian and help him with the secretarial work. And I'm glad I did. Because now I've met Harry and he's in love with me and vice-versa. A much more satisfactory state of things."

"Yes, indeed," Vanessa siad fervently. "And I'm very glad for you. Have you fixed a date for your wedding?"

Freda shook her head. "Not yet. Ian would hate to hear me say this—but I would like to make sure things are going to work out happily for him too. I'd hate to leave him on his own."

"Is there—anyone?" Vanessa felt encouraged to ask.

Freda gave a little smile, giving a slight shake of her head at the same time.

"I have an idea that there is, but he hasn't said anything, so I just keep on hoping."

Vanessa wondered who the mysterious woman was and what kind of lover Ian would be: whether he would "rush a woman off her feet" or gently woo, be jealous and possessive, or easy-going. She decided he would be anything but easy-going.

Vanessa loved the house. It had four large bedrooms and two smaller ones, with two bathrooms, and a large square landing housing linen cupboards which would be many a housewife's dream.

"Roomy, and at the same time compact," was her verdict.

"It's a shade on the big side for two, of course," Freda said, "unless you do a lot of entertaining—which we don't at present. But it went with the property, and it was a property Ian was looking for primarily. One with woodlands or room to develop. It will be an ideal family house, though," she added.

Vanessa noted the way Freda said *will be*, not *would be*, as if she was 100 percent certain of Ian's marriage. As if, indeed, it were a *fait accompli*.

The two guest rooms were simply but extremely tastefully furnished; one in a décor of blue and gold, the other in grey and pink. A guest would sleep peacefully in either room. Ian's room was in muted shades of green with fine Regency furniture; a comfortable armchair, plenty of books—several, Vanessa noticed, on his bedside table, with antique maps and one or two curious wood carvings to add a truly masculine touch. A fascinating room. Vanessa would like to have lingered—to look at some of the book titles, to see the view from the window and to sit for a while in Ian's armchair. Why she didn't know, unless it was to know him better through his possessions.

Freda's room was completely feminine in pink and white, with light, modern furniture, a white carpet, pink walls and pretty curtains.

"Quite a contrast to Ian's, isn't it?" laughed Freda, then she added, "I expect Harry's room is essentially masculine. The problem is, whose taste is reflected when one marries? A mixture would probably look awful, neither one thing nor the other."

Vanessa agreed that this could be the effect. Then she said without thinking how it could be taken, "For myself, I'd prefer Ian's room."

It was not until she met Freda's amused glance that she realized what she had said. She felt her cheeks coloring. "I didn't mean that. What I did mean was, of the two—yours or Ian's, Ian's would be more to my taste. I don't think I'd want a purely feminine room."

But Freda only laughed. "It's all right, I know what you meant. But it did sound rather funny. On the whole, I think my home and Harry's will be a mixture. Periods don't really clash if the designs are good."

They made their way downstairs, and Vanessa thought the sitting room the most beautiful she had ever seen. The whole tone was so restful. The color scheme was green and gold with panelled walls and alcoves. The wall lights had twin fittings. At one end there was a grand piano, a sheet of music on the stand as if someone had recently been playing, the easy chairs and sofa were commodious and comfortable-looking. There were one or two interesting pieces of fine furniture which could well be Sheraton.

"Who plays the piano?" she asked.

"Ian. He plays quite well. I thing he wanted to do it

professionally at one time, but for various reasons it didn't work out."

"Was he terribly disappointed?"

Freda thought for a moment. "A little frustrated perhaps at the time, but he soon recovered. And now I think he's rather glad. Once an art becomes a person's work, it's no longer a relaxation, is it?"

"I suppose not."

"At any rate he enjoys playing in what leisure time he can get."

"Do you think he could be persuaded to play this afternoon? I'd love to hear him."

"If you're really keen, he might. But he hates playing to an audience who only listens out of politeness."

The kitchen was used also as a breakfast room and was a joy of varnished timber and copper brightness. A room adjacent which had probably been intended for a breakfast room was set aside for Freda's own use. "I do my dressmaking and keep all my own bits and pieces in here," she explained. Ian had his study. This again reflected Ian's personality; his love of good furniture and a pleasing color scheme. The house also had a downstairs cloakroom where raincoats and jackets could be hung, and all kinds of articles deposited which would normally make a house look cluttered.

Ian called out that coffee was ready, so they went out to the patio.

"Well, what did you think of the house?" Ian asked as they settled down to coffee.

"I love it. It's a perfect dream," she answered. "If only I could transform Aunt Maud's house to something like it!"

"Oh, you'll get it the way you want it in time," Freda murmured.

"What sort of place is your aunt's?" queried Harry. "A rather big rambling house, I suspect."

"Yes, it is. All sorts of things could be done with it, but it will never be the compact, useful size that this house is," Vanessa said.

"What will you do with it, then? Convert it into apartments or something like that?"

Vanessa shook her head. "I—don't somehow think Aunt Maud would like that."

Harry gave her a thoughtful look. "You—er—set a great deal of importance on what your aunt would have liked or disliked?"

Vanessa did not quite know how to answer. Neither Freda nor Ian were taking any part in the conversation. Ian was eyeing her thoughtfully as if waiting to hear what she had to say. But suddenly Vanessa wanted his opinion on the subject on which Miles had been so adamant. "What do you think, Ian?" she asked him. "how far should the wishes of the dead influence the lives of the living? How seriously should one take a promise made to the dying?"

His expression became alert, then a slight frown appeared between his brows. "I very much doubt," he said thoughtfully, "whether it's right to make distinctions between the living and the dead. A promise is a promise and should be kept. I don't believe, myself, in making promises unless I intend to keep them."

"But, Ian," interposed Freda, "people often do intend keeping such promises at the time, but—"

"I know. But there are people who make them without the slightest intention of keeping them; who make them rashly, or, which is the more usual, make a promise to a dying person in order to placate them in the same way that they tell lies or half truths to children. But from whatever motive, a promise should be honored no matter to whom it was made, or under what circumstances."

Vanessa thought how uncompromising he was. Such strength of purpose was almost frightening.

"On the other hand," he went on, "if we're speaking in

general terms, I firmly believe that one should never allow tyranny from either side of the grave. If we're speaking specifically of Vanessa and her aunt, I would say that Vanessa should do what her conscience dictates."

"Oh dear," Freda said. "What a heavy burden of responsibility that could turn out to be! Are we to take it, Vanessa, that you—made your aunt certain promises?"

Vanessa nodded. "I promised her I would never sell Puck's Hill—and I have every intention of keeping my word."

This brought a swift exchange of glances among the other three. Ian drew a deep breath and knocked out his pipe on the heel of his shoe. There was silence for a moment or two, during which Vanessa experienced a faint feeling of regret that Aunt Maud had not left her house to someone else. She did not wholeheartedly want it.

Harry was the first to speak. "You know, it's a very debatable point really, whether or not a person should be bound for ever to a promise made to someone who's dying. I don't mean that one should make promises lightly, but they can be made on a wave of emotion such as pity or sorrow, or to give a dying person peace at the last. The dead can impose tremendous burdens on the living—sometimes unwittingly, of course. But is it right for a person to be carrying a burden too great for them? There is a time, surely, when a promise becomes no longer binding?"

"Certainly there is," agreed Ian. "And I would suggest that, if the time comes when Vanessa finds that that house is, or has become a burden, then she should consider letting it go. Her aunt was far too fond of her to want her to feel that the place is a millstone around her neck."

He had used the same phrase that Miles had. Was he really hankering after the property for himself?

After they had talked a little more and finished their

coffee, Freda suggested that Ian might show Vanessa around the grounds. Sensing that Freda and Harry might like some time alone together, she said she would love it. She did genuinely want to see the place, but somehow did not feel entirely at ease in Ian's company.

He rose and glanced down at her feet. "Will you be all right in those sandals, or would you like to borrow a pair of Freda's walking shoes?"

But Vanessa assured him that her sandals were not as flimsy as they looked and that she was used to them.

"Mm," he said disbelievingly. "Well, we'd better go through the house and out at the front anyway. It's a bit rough around by the sheds."

He succeeded in making her feel something of a nuisance. She wanted to retort that she didn't mind whether it was rough or not, but he stood waiting for her to precede him, so she meekly went through the house as he had indicated.

But once outside, her admiration for the beauty of the garden dispelled all raggedness. She gave a huge sigh.

"Oh, Ian, do you think I'll ever have a garden half as lovely as this?"

He didn't answer for a moment, then he said gruffly, "Of course you will. The main thing is not to try to do too much at once. You need more help, of course."

But she shook her head. "I simply can't afford to pay for any more help at present, so I shall just have to be patient. There's a lot I can do toward improving the garden area near the house, anyway."

"I suppose so," he answered.

She glanced at his unsmiling face and wondered what was wrong. She so often seemed to displease him. Or was it that he did not really like her very much? She told herself that she didn't much care whether he did nor not, that the feeling was mutual. But she knew in her heart that that wasn't true.

Soon they left the garden area and were walking along

wide grassy paths beneath mature beeches, oaks and chestnuts. Vanessa's gaze wandered upward to the leafy canopy. "I think I'd like to have more trees," she murmured. "But of course it takes years and years for them to reach this height."

"Some trees grow more quickly than others, of course,"

The lines of his face had softened. Evidently it pleased him that she liked trees.

"Your—won't have these lovely beeches and chestnuts felled, will you?" she asked.

He smiled faintly. "Not all of them, naturally. But you mustn't be too sentimental about trees. There's a time to plant and a time to harvest, just as in other growing things. We've done quite a bit of felling already."

"Yes, I noticed."

"The main thing is to keep on planting. The area we've felled will be prepared for a nursery bed to receive young plants."

"Why do you say that? That the main thing is to keep on planting? For commercial reasons?"

"Not entirely, though of course it is my living. If one just kept on felling timber and selling it without re-planting, one would soon be out of business. Besides, the country needs timber. But there's something else attached to it. The feeling, or instinct, that for every tree one fells, another should be planted in its place."

She smiled. "I like that. It's good. Do you buy plants or sow seeds of trees?"

"Both, at present, but in time I shall grow from seed only. I don't know how much you know about forestry, but not all trees are allowed to reach maturity before being used commercially. Young chestnuts, for instance, are used for fencing, for pit props, and, or course, the thinning of Norway spruce for the inevitable Christmas trees."

"It all sounds marvelous."

They arrived, eventually, at the boundary fence of her own land where they stood silent for a moment or two. For some inexplicable reason Vanessa suddenly hated the fence. It was like a barrier, one she did not want. She looked at Ian's grave face and wondered what he was thinking. Then, eyeing the hogweed still to be dealt with, she said, "I suppose that horrible stuff encroached on your land too?"

He nodded. "To some extent, but of course we were able to tackle it before it became too rampageous. And in your aunt's time, our men hopped over the fence and cleared a yard or two there to prevent further encroachment too soon."

Viewed from this side of the fence the task of dealing with the monster weed appeared insuperable. Vanessa felt swamped in her own inadequacy. How long was it going to take her with help from only Joe Simpkins? A long, long time. She was only just beginning to realize fully the enormity of the task she had set herself. Not only that, but the land ought to be productive as soon as possible. Perhaps Ian would like a strip for tree planting. He wanted more land. She could now see it taking her years to cultivate the whole of the estate and develop a full-scale nursery business, employing a lot of labor as she had envisaged, though vaguely.

She sighed heavily and voiced some of her thoughts aloud. "You know, I can't help feeling that this land ought to be put to a better use more quickly than I shall be able to." Then she had a sudden inspiration. "Come to think of it, I didn't promise Aunt Maud anything about the land—only the house. I suppose I could sell part of the grounds and just keep enough to develop a small nursery business."

His eyes widened swiftly and his glance sharpened. "That sounds to me awfully like compromise. I'm quite sure that if your aunt wanted you not to sell Puck's Hill, she was referring also to the land. Don't you realize what was behind her request to you not to sell? This land of yours is a very desirable piece of building land. It has road access, and it's well drained. It's not too far from a town, while at the same time being in pleasant country surroundings. In addition, building land is at a premium. Before you know where you are somebody like Miles Kendal will slap a block of apartments or something here."

He paused to fill his pipe. Vanessa was so surprised and so staggered by the way he had taken her up that she could not think what to say to him. But before she could say anything he spoke again.

"Oh, I know people need houses and all that, but if some of these property developers have their way 'England's green and pleasant land' will soon be anything but green, and far from pleasant."

He struck a match, cupped it in his hands until the flame spread, then lit his pipe, his face granite-like. Vanessa found herself watching him, noticing the strength of his long fingers, his broad forehead, the shape of his nose, his mouth, his jaw.

"Freda tells me you play the piano," she said suddenly and rather irrelevantly.

He stared at her. "That's a swift change of subject. Yes, I do, as a matter of fact. Why?"

"I—just thought I'd like to hear you, that's all. I don't know what made me think of it at this moment, but I think it's time we changed the subject, anyway. I shall think about what you've said, of course. I think maybe you're right about what Aunt Maud had in mind."

"Well, that's something," he said. "Shall we make our way back to the house?"

They walked in silence at first. Vanessa savored the smell of earth and peat, letting her gaze soar upward into the leafy canopy above, feeling a peace enter her heart once more and a peculiar oneness with the man at her side.

"Do you—play any kind of a musical instrument yourself?" he asked after a little while.

She smiled and shook her head. "My mother plays the piano. She sings too. Rather well, as a matter of fact, but for some reason or other it was never suggested that I should learn to play—or sing. Perhaps Mother couldn't bear the thought of having to listen to anyone hammering out five-finger exercises. There was always music in the house of some kind, either Mother performing or a record player with whole operas or symphonies."

"So you became a listener rather than a performer. And you never at any time wished you could play an instrument?"

She laughed. "Once when I was still at school I had a go at learning to play the guitar, but I'm afraid I didn't get very far."

"Why the guitar? Did you want to play pop—just chords—or in the classic style?"

"Oh, not pop. At least, not in particular. The classic style, I suppose, or to accompany folk songs."

"Why didn't you persevere?" he asked.

She shrugged. "I don't know. Perhaps it was just a passing phase. The instrument seemed difficult to handle; I couldn't somehow get my hand across the fret or get true notes. It was more difficult to play than I had anticipated. At any rate, I lost interest. I was teaching myself, of course, from a book."

"That's a big mistake. It's always better to have a good teacher."

When they reached the house she asked him if he would play the piano for her.

"All right," he said. "But don't stand over me. Sit in a chair or listen from another room, whichever you like."

She eyed him mischievously. "Is it all right if I hum or tap with my feet?"

He smiled then. "Yes, because then I shall know you're enjoying it and not just listening out of politeness."

She chose a chair near the window where she could see the wide sweep of green lawn and the roses now in full bloom. Ian sat down at the piano and improvised at first—some pleasing sounding chords and arpeggios, then slid into a Chopin waltz followed by a nocturne. His playing was exquisite. Her mother had never played like this. Ian played on. Vanessa felt she could go on listening to him forever.

"Oh, Ian," she sighed when he stopped at last. "Do you think I could ever learn to play like that?"

"You liked it?"

"It was wonderful!"

"It takes practice," he said. "But it's worth it. And many of the classics are quite simple to play really. To love music is the main thing."

"You make me wish I'd learned when I was a child. Do you think I'm too old now?"

"You're never too old," he told her, "but of course the older you get the more difficult it is to learn anything new. Is there a piano in the house?"

"An old upright in the sitting room."

"Well, why not have it tuned and take some lessons? I can recommend a good teacher."

"In town?" He nodded. "Then I'll have to get myself a car."

"That would be a good idea," he said quietly.

There was a silence. Vanessa was remembering the morning when he had put forward the idea of her having a car and a telephone, and how she had rejected both suggestions. Freda had said he would keep a look-out for one for her. She was about to mention this to him when Freda entered with a tray of tea.

"That was very nice, Ian. I would think you could do with a cup of tea now. You too, Vanessa, after your tramp around the estate."

"Thanks," he said absently, and excused himself, saying there was something he wanted from his room.

Freda's gaze followed him for a moment, then she looked at Vanessa with a swift smile.

"You're honored," she said. "Ian doesn't often give a private recital. At least, not until he's known a person for a very long time."

"He plays beautifully," answered Vanessa, wondering about his change of mood when she had said she would have to get a car. Was he still holding her rudeness of that morning against her?

Harry came in followed by Ian, and the talk became general. After tea, Vanessa said she must be going. After all, she had only been invited to lunch, not for the rest of the day, she told herself.

"Oh, but you don't have to run away. Does she, Ian?" Freda said quickly.

"Of course not. She can stay for as long as she likes."

But Vanessa detected a lack of enthusiasm in his voice and felt sure that Freda and Harry would want some time alone together. This might result in Ian and herself being thrown into each other's company, something from which Vanessa found herself shrinking.

"That's kind of you," she said. "But I feel I really must get back. I don't like leaving Nancy alone too much. She's still missing Aunt Maud."

"Yes, of course," murmured Freda.

Vanessa insisted that she could walk back to Puck's Hill by way of the woods and the boundary fence. She was glad that Freda and Harry walked part of the way with her instead of Ian. In spite of the odd moments when they seemed to find a common bond, she felt surer than ever that he disliked her.

But when she arrived home, she sat down at Aunt Maud's old piano. Ian's playing still touched her heart, his strong fingers sometimes caressing the keys, at others commanding them.

The following day her telephone was installed. She called Freda to tell her what the number was. But it was answered by a voice which Vanessa knew at once was not Freda's. It was that of a young woman with a refined accent and a strong hint of haughtiness.

"Freda is not here at the moment," came the voice, in answer to her query.

"Mr. Hamilton? Er—Ian?"

"Mr. Hamilton is busy. Can I take a message?"

Feeling curiously shut out, Vanessa gave her the telephone number and hung up. She wondered who the girl could be, whether a friend of Freda or of Ian. The speculation occupied her mind so much on and off that she completely forgot to call Miles to tell him what her number was. He came to see her about mid-week, however.

"Didn't the telephone company come?" he asked.

Her hand flew to her mouth. "Oh, Miles, I'm terribly sorry. Yes, it's all fixed up. I was going to call you the same evening, but something put me off, and then I forgot."

He waved an admonishing finger at her, then kissed her swiftly.

"I'll forgive you this time. I know you have a lot of things on your mind. I came to ask you if you'd like to go to a dinner and dance. I've got two tickets."

"Oh, yes. Lovely. Thanks very much. What's the occasion?"

"It's the annual 'do' of the Foresters' Club."

Suddenly she felt deflated. Neither Freda nor Ian had phoned to tell her about this.

"Do you belong?" she asked.

"No, but I have a pal who does. He usually wangles invitations for me if I want them. I expect the Hamiltons will be there, but I don't suppose you mind that." He eyed her keenly. "I've never actually asked you. How do you like those two? You had lunch with them on Sunday, didn't you?"

Vanessa led the way into the sitting room before answering. "I like them both quite a bit. Why shouldn't I?"

He shrugged. "As I've told you before, I can't stand Ian at any price. You're not seriously telling me that he's made any kind of hit with you?"

She shook her head swiftly. "I didn't say that. He's not as easy to get along with as Freda, but I think he's a—man of good character and all that. One you could trust."

Miles gave a grunt of derision. "I wouldn't be too sure about that if I were you."

And afterward, Vanessa did not feel quite so sure. Neither Ian nor Freda had told her about the Forestry Club dance. Why? They had not called either, she thought miserably. She hardly expected Ian to do so really, although he had been keen enough for her to get a telephone.

The day after Miles's visit, Freda called. As the weather was still holding well, Vanessa was working outside, digging up more of the hogweed, wondering whether there would ever be an end to it, feeling, on the whole, a little discouraged.

"Poor you," sympathized Freda. "You've set yourself an enormous task."

Vanessa sighed. "I doubt whether I'm going to stick it out."

"You will," encouraged Freda. "But you mustn't try to do too much of it at once." She paused and looked troubled for a moment or two, then added swiftly, "But I came to find out if you've a phone yet. Did the men come on Monday?"

Vanessa frowned. "But I phoned you. I don't know who it was who answered the phone, but you weren't in. Ian was busy. I did leave a message."

"Really? Our daily didn't say anything, and I haven't seen any message on the pad. Anyway, I came to ask if you'd like to come to a dinner and a dance."

Somehow, Vanessa did not think it had been the daily help who had answered the telephone, but she decided not to pursue the matter.

"Is it the Foresters' dinner-dance?" she asked.

"Why, yes. Did I tell you about it?"

Vanessa shook her head. "Miles came yesterday and invited me. He has two tickets."

"But they weren't available until last night at the meeting. He wasn't even there. He isn't a member."

"He has friends."

"Obviously. And did you accep his invitation?"

Vanessa nodded. "I hope you don't mind."

"We—ll, it would have been nice to have you in our party, but never mind. We'll see you there. By the way, we proposed you as a member last night. Meetings are held once a month over the Stag—a lovely old pub just the other side of town. Usually we just talk and have drinks; sometimes we dance. Occasionally we have a speaker. They're good fun, the meetings, I mean, and you meet some interesting people."

"I'm sure. Thank you very much."

Freda eyed her quizzically. "You are pleased? I mean—you did want to join, didn't you? We don't want to force you into anything."

"Of course I'm pleased. It's very kind of you, and I'll look forward to getting to know a few people."

It was difficult to explain, even to herself, this leaden feeling inside her. It was somehow tied up with Ian. It was Freda who was setting the pace, offering friendship, taking the initiative. Without prompting from Freda, he would undoubtedly want very little to do with her. Why the thought should depress her, she didn't know. She told herself how ridiculous and how futile such thoughts were, but she still continued to think about Ian and to be depressed every time she did so.

On the night of the dinner and dance, Vanessa wore a new dress she had bought recently. She and Freda had driven into town together for a day's shopping. Vanessa had bought a sleeveless dress in silvery blue with a matching jacket. But she dressed without enthusiasm and with an odd feeling in the pit of her stomach. Miles called for her. His admiration of her appearance was unmistakable.

"You look terrific," he said spontaneously. "I'll have to keep a tight hold on you, I can see."

She laughed. It was nice to be flattered. She felt she needed it.

The members of the Foresters' Club and their guests were seated at tables for four, six or eight. Doubtless by prearrangement, Vanessa was at a table for six with Miles and two other couples whose surnames were misheard or quickly forgotten in the use of first names. Vanessa did not care much for them. They made a great deal of noise and drank too much. The girls were dressed in what Vanessa considered to be shocking taste. She scanned the tables until she saw where Freda and Ian were sitting. They were at a table for four, with Harry, naturally, and a girl Vanessa had never seen before. In contrast to the two girls at Vanessa's table this girl was dressed with impeccable taste in white. She was also very beautiful.

Between courses there was dancing. Vanessa danced with each of the other two men in turn and hated it. Both held her too closely. Miles and she were sitting at the table alone when Vanessa's attention became riveted on Ian dancing with the beautiful dark girl in white. Suddenly she was in the grip of the fiercest jealousy.

CHAPTER SIX

Miles looked at her face. "What's the matter?"

She started and shifted her gaze back to him. "Nothing."

He gave an amused smile and glanced in the direction of Ian and his party. "If looks could kill, Cecile would have been stretched out on the ground."

"Don't be silly. How do you know I wasn't casting venom at Ian? I've never even met—Cecile, did you say her name was? Who is she, anyway?"

Miles gazed across the room through narrowed lids, still wearing the same smile of amusement. "She is Cecile Harland, daughter of Sir Walter and Lady Harland who live at Kelsley Hall."

Vanessa frowned, trying to think, trying to shake off the effect of that awful feeling of pure jealousy which had choked her momentarily.

"I—thought Lord Kelsley lived there."

He shook his head. "Not now. You're out of date, my love. As a matter of fact she and her parents moved into the area about a month before Hamilton and his sister. They say he followed her here."

"You mean—"

Miles laughed shortly. "Because he wanted to marry her, I suppose. I don't think he's had a lot of luck—so far. But he's nothing if not a trier."

Vanessa supposed vaguely that she ought to hate Miles, but his sneers somehow went over her head. She was looking at the two again; Ian and the beautiful girl, their steps matching perfectly, the rapt expression on Ian's face, the cool detached demeanor of Cecile.

Miles's hand touched Vanessa's. "Come on, let's dance. Sitting looking at those two is giving me the willies."

Vanessa rose, feeling something of the "willies" herself, though she would not have expressed it in quite those terms. She felt like an actress who, for the time being, must keep her own affairs somewhere deep inside in a dark secret place. But what she had felt at the sight of that girl in Ian Hamilton's arms was like a monster which was trying to rear up. *Why did I feel like that? Why? Why?* went around in her brain as Miles swung her on the dance floor. Ian was nothing to her. Nothing.

When the dance was over, Miles led her back to their table, his hand still clasping hers. She made no effort to break free. The other two couples, laughing loudly, also came back to the table, and Vanessa forced herself to join in their laughter.

Glancing to Ian and his party, Vanessa noticed Freda and Ian talking animatedly. They looked as though they were having an argument. Ian shook his head, Freda put her hand on his arm, but Ian shook his head even more vigorously. Then suddenly Freda pushed back her chair.

Vanessa turned to answer something Miles was saying to her, but the next moment Freda was standing beside their table. She spoke briefly to the others, then looked at Vanessa.

"We'd all like you to join us for a drink, if you will—and if Miles doesn't mind."

The meal was now finished. Here and there people were moving from one table to another to greet other friends and mix more generally.

Miles's shoulders lifted. "It's up to Vanessa, of course."

Vanessa glanced across at Ian. Why had he been shaking his head so vigorously? Had she been the cause of their argument?

"I—don't really think I'll come, Freda, thanks," she said.

Freda looked upset. "But, Vanessa, why? Oh, please—"

At this Vanessa wavered. She liked Freda. The last thing she wanted was to be rude or give offence. She stood up. "I don't really think Ian wants me to."

"Nonsense, of course he does. He'd have come to fetch you himself except that he can't stand Miles," Freda said in a low voice. "And but for a mistake you'd probably have been with our party, wouldn't you? In any case, once the dinner is finished everyone moves around and mixes a bit."

It seemed churlish and unfriendly to hold out any longer. Vanessa made her excuses to Miles and the others and went with Freda.

Ian and Harry rose politely. It was Freda who introduced the other girl.

"Vanessa, this is an old friend of ours," she said, confirming something of what Miles had told her. "Cecile Harland. Cecile, Vanessa is a new friend—and our neighbor."

"How do you do," Cecile said in a cool voice.

Vanessa responded in a similar fashion. Ian brought up a chair for her and ordered drinks. There was a little general conversation in which Cecile took no part, smoking a cigarette in a long holder and looking a trifle bored. Freda and Harry did most of the talking. Ian listened and answered when referred to. Vanessa noticed he had replaced his more usual pipe for a cheroot.

After a while Harry asked Cecile if she would care to dance. As they left the table, Ian half rose in politeness and subsided again. There was a moment or two of silence which Vanessa found uncomfortable. Then Ian stubbed out the remains of his cheroot and turned to Vanessa.

"Will you dance?"

She had no option, socially, but to accept. She felt sure he had only asked her out of courtesy. For a minute they danced in a silence which Vanessa sensed was as strained for him as it was for her, then he said, surprisingly,

"You're looking very charming. Are you enjoying yourself?"

Was he being polite again? Well, she could be too. "Thank you. Yes, I'm enjoying myself enormously. I'm with a very lively crowd."

"Yes," he said briefly.

She looked at his face and saw the granite-like expression. "You don't like Miles very much, do you?"

"Do you?" he threw back.

She shrugged and lifted her chin defiantly. "Yes, I do. Why not?"

"No reason at all as long as you don't let your heart rule your head," he answered.

"And what do you mean by that?"

"I mean that if you have any business dealings with him, be sure not to take his word for anything. Have it all in writing."

An unreasonable anger took possession of her. "You're the most disagreeable man I've ever met in my entire life! I'm not likely to have any 'business dealings' with Miles. We're friends because we like each other. I find him courteous, considerate, amiable and—all the things that you are not."

"Thank you," he said icily. "Then I suggest you go back to him."

"With pleasure." She tried to break free, but grim-faced he held her until the music stopped.

"Don't make a fool of yourself into the bargain," he said cuttingly.

Vanessa made her escape to the powder room without answering him. He was hateful, hateful! She didn't want any more to do with him. But it was a struggle to keep the tears away. She had been hateful too. She knew it. She wasn't enjoying the company of Miles's rowdy friends one bit. She would much rather have been with Freda and Ian.

She forced herself to put a stop to her thoughts, to calm herself and return to her party and Miles. He was alone at the table, waiting for her. She blessed him.

"What's up?" he asked. "I saw you dash away looking as though you were seeing red. Friend Ian been his usual pleasant self?"

"You could say that, I suppose. Let's dance, shall we, Miles?"

"Sure."

He rose eagerly and Vanessa could not help but feel warmed toward him. Later in the evening when Ian was dancing with Cecile, Freda beckoned Vanessa over.

"What made you leave us so soon?" she asked.

"Don't ask me, Freda. I told you Ian didn't want my company. We—we just don't get along together, that's all."

Freda shook her head in bewilderment. "I simply can't believe it."

"It's true," Vanessa told her. "Just because I said I liked Miles and was enjoying myself, he suggested I should go back to him."

"Is that all? I mean—is that all that happened?"

Vanessa realized she was not being quite fair to Ian. "Well, I did rather lose my temper."

Freda smiled. "You are a pair of idiots! I knew something was wrong. Ian's been like a bear with a sore head."

Vanessa rose swiftly as the music stopped.

"No, don't go—" Freda said quickly.

"I'm sorry, Freda, I must. Give me a call, or drop in to see me some time."

Vanessa was thankful when, at last, the evening was at an end. Miles drove her home and was all she had told Ian that he was—and more. He was not only charming, he was kind and understanding. When Vanessa thanked him and said she had enjoyed the evening, he put his arm around her shoulder and fondled her ear.

"You've only enjoyed it in patches, though, haven't you, Vanessa? What with Ian Hamilton upsetting you, and the rowdies we were with."

"But they didn't 'upset me'," she protested, beginning to feel like a person who was hard to please.

"I didn't mean they upset you, altogether, but they weren't quite your type. I must admit they got on my nerves at times. We'll have to go there again some-time—on our own." He leaned over and kissed her cheek. "I must say you looked absolutely great. Not only that, you dance like an angel."

She blinked, feeling a ridiculous desire to weep. But she said lightly, "Or do you mean like a fairy?"

"I mean I think you're wonderful. But I mustn't keep you from your beauty sleep—unless of course you had ideas of inviting me in?"

"Not tonight, Miles, if you don't mind. It's very late."

"Of course I don't mind," he said gallantly. "I only mentioned it because I didn't want to pass up a chance of prolonging the evening, if there was any such possibility. Give me your key. I'll unlock the door for you."

She handed it to him. He helped her out of the car, unlocked the door of the house for her, kissed her lightly and said good-night.

"Good-night, Miles. Come and see me soon."

"You bet!"

When he had left, she switched off the lights and went straight upstairs to her room, thinking how sweet he was. How could Ian be so nasty about him?

At the very thought of Ian tears filled her eyes. Suddenly she felt heartbroken. She stood for a moment, her hand over her mouth as if to stem the tide of emotion which threatened to erupt from deep inside her. She took a few deep breaths. This was ridiculous. She was over-tired, that's what it was. She didn't care two hoots about Ian Hamilton. She wasn't really concerned what he thought of her or anyone else. She thoroughly disliked him. He managed to spoil every occasion at which he was present, so far as she was concerned. She was determined not to allow him to upset her.

Unconsciously she lifted her chin and resolutely began preparing for bed. She would not think another word about him. She did not run a bath for fear of waking Nancy, but she washed and splashed tepid water liberally on her face. That was better. A hot drink, a book, and she would be asleep in no time.

But putting him out of her mind did not prove easy. It was not that she thought about him consciously, but his name seemed to be written indelibly across her brain. He was something which had happened to her. He was a part of her. Yet she did not try to analyze any of this. She only knew that, even when she almost dropped off to sleep with her light still on, he was still in her mind.

Following the events of that evening, she plunged herself even more energetically into the work of clearing the grounds of weed and of planning a future business. She talked things over with Nancy.

"You know, I think I'm being too timid for a prospective business woman. I need to be bolder. After all, you have to spend money to make money."

"What had you in mind?" asked Nancy.

"Windows in the barn, for one thing. And electricity for future lighting and heating."

"For the purpose of renting?"

Vanessa shook her head. "I've been thinking. I won't rent the barn after all. I shall want it for plants. If I try to use it for two purposes, I'll have difficulties continually moving things. Besides, once I start renting it, it wouldn't be fair to discontinue. No, I'm going to buy more plants and garden supplies and go into business as soon as possible. Puck's Hill Garden Center. How about that,

Nancy? I can have some posters printed and ask the local stores to display them. In return I could give them a flowering pot plant or fern or something to decorate with."

Nancy thought the whole idea was wonderful. "And why not serve teas in the garden when it's nice? In fact there'll be room in the barn for a few tables in wet weather, as well as the plants. I'm not much of a hand with plants, but I could serve tea and cakes. I think it would make a pleasant afternoon or evening for people—especially on weekends. They could stroll around the garden, have tea, and then buy a plant or so. We hope," she added.

"Nancy, that's it!" Vanessa cried excitedly. "That's exactly what we'll do. You're sure it won't be too much for you? I'm afraid you're doing most of the housework too."

"Of course it won't be too much. It will only be for about a couple of hours in the afternoon. But if anybody comes in the mornings and asks for a coffee—or in the evenings even, well, they can have one. Once we have it all organized, it won't be any trouble at all. As for tables and chairs: I'm sure we'll find plenty of both in the attic and various rooms."

"You're a tonic, Nancy. I'll get in touch with a builder about windows right away. Then the next step will be garden supplies—plant pots, lawn seed—all kinds of things. And some plants already in flower like dwarf chrysanthemums, geraniums and pelargoniums. Foliage plants too. If only I had a car!"

"I thought Ian Hamilton was going to find you one?" queried Nancy.

"He did say so, but—" Vanessa shrugged. "I expect he's waiting for me to ask him."

"Well, why don't you?"

Vanessa's lips tightened and she shook her head. "I'm

not asking any favors of Ian. He doesn't like me, and I don't like him."

Nancy looked at her in astonishment. "But what has happened? I was wondering why he hadn't dropped in lately."

"Nothing's happened," Vanessa told her. "We just rub each other the wrong way, that's all."

"And what about Freda?" asked Nancy quietly.

"Oh, Freda's all right."

That same afternoon Nancy returned from a visit to the stores to say she had seen Freda in the drugstore.

"She told me to tell you that she's going into town in the morning, if there's any shopping you'd like to do."

"That's an odd coincidence," mused Vanessa. "I want to go to the garden center. You didn't tell her I wanted to go, did you—I mean before she asked you to give me the message?"

Nancy shook her head vigorously. "Of course not. She also said she'd been extra busy; that's why she hasn't been around to see you."

It was nearly a week since the Foresters' Club dinner and dance. Miles had dropped in once, but she had neither seen nor heard from Freda or Ian. Nancy supplied an answer to that, so far as Freda was concerned.

"She says she's called a couple of times but could get no reply. I told her I was probably shopping, and you were busy in the garden."

"You seem to have had quite a chat."

"I wouldn't say that. I saw Miles Kendal too, but he didn't deign to speak to me."

"Perhaps he didn't see you," suggested Vanessa.

"Of course he did."

Vanessa said no more. Nancy did not like Miles, but she was as prejudiced in Ian Hamilton's favor as Aunt Maud used to be.

Miles called to see her that evening. Over a cup of coffee, Vanessa told him about her new plans.

"I called a local builder. He can send a man tomorrow to start on the windows for the barn."

He gave her a wry smile. "Determined to make a go of it, aren't you?"

"If I can, yes. I must admit I wavered once or twice, but I'm sure this new plan is the right one."

"And what are you going to do with all the rest of the ground—if you ever get it cleared?" asked Miles.

"What I don't need for growing perennials and other plants, I shall just grass over. I did have the idea of selling part of the grounds, but—"

"You what?" asked Miles in a startled voice.

Vanessa laughed. "Calm down! I decided against it."

"Why? It sounds like a marvelous idea to me, as you're so determined never to sell the house. It would be a jolly good way around the problem."

But Vanessa shook her head firmly. "It was pointed out to me that I'd be compromising on my promise to Aunt Maud, and I saw the truth of it."

Miles frowned. "Who pointed that out, for heaven's sake? Ian Hamilton?"

"As a matter of fact, yes."

"He would. Maybe he thinks you should give it away."

"Hardly. You have given me an idea, though, Miles," she said, her voice quickening. "I could lease a piece of it."

But this idea did not please Miles at all. "Lease it! You mustn't do that," he said agitatedly.

"Why not, for heaven's sake?"

"But why do you want to?" he countered. "You're getting rid of the weed all right, now that you've found out what it is. You've got quite a nice area cleared already."

"I know. But it's so slow and such hard work. It's not that I mind the work, but while I'm spending day after day on that I'm not able to do anything else. The idea with our Garden Center is that people can spend a pleasant half hour or so walking around the grounds if they want to. At the moment it's a case of 'tiptoe through the hogweed'."

Miles frowned thoughtfully. "I admit it's slow going for you. If I'd known you wanted it done in such a hurry, I'd have waded in and helped you."

"I wasn't in any particular hurry for clearing it down at the farthest end, but now I want to speed things up a bit. I thought if I could lease some out to—"

She broke off. The mention of Ian's name to Miles would be as a red rag to a bull; one on which she did not want to dwell herself. Before the evening of the Foresters' Club affair she would have been quite happy for Ian to use part of her land for the planting of seedling trees. He would have been willing to clear the ground himself in that case. But now she was not sure she wanted any more contact with him than she could help.

"Look," Miles said earnestly. "I think your scheme is great. If I were you I'd hang on to every last little bit of your land for your own purpose. Now I know you want it cleared quickly, I can get hold of some men for you. They'll dig more of this hogweed out in a day than you and Joe can in a week. In fact, for a little bit extra, if you're prepared to spend a pound or two, they'd come Saturday and Sunday to have the lot cleared."

"In one weekend?" queried Vanessa doubtfully.

"Yes, in one weekend. You'll see. And I'd throw my little bit of an effort in for good measure. But these fellows I know are used to digging. Then when that little lot is cleared, you could get a local contractor in to level the site, have sod laid—and 'Bob's your uncle', it's all finished."

Vanessa laughed, feeling suddenly as though a heavy load had been taken off her back.

"Oh, Miles, that would be wonderful. You make it all

sound so easy. Can you get your men for this coming weekend, if it's fine?"

"Nothing's easier," he assured her. "They'll be only too glad to earn a few extra pounds. I'm sure the week-end will suit them all right so long as they can toddle off to the local in the evening. In fact, if you can lay on beer and sandwiches for lunch they'll work even better."

Vanessa gave a sigh of relief. "Miles, how can I ever thank you?"

Miles kissed her cheek. "Don't thank me, darling girl. I—would do anything for you, you know that."

At the warmth of her smile, he took her in his arms and kissed her. Something stirred within her. She wondered if she was falling in love with him. Why couldn't Ian be more like this—gentle, loving? she found herself thinking.

Whatever feelings had been stirring up for Miles now began to fade, and she stirred in his arms.

"What's the matter?" he murmured.

"I don't know. Too many things still on my mind to be able to relax properly, I suppose."

He put his hand under her chin. "Can't you 'cast care aside' for a little while? I thought you were just beginning to like me a little."

"I do like you—"

"Well then—"

Again Miles covered her mouth with his, but still the thought of Ian intruded.

"Miles, don't!" she said sharply.

He let her go with a sigh. "Not angry, are you?"

She shook her head. "No. At least, not with you." Even when he was far away Ian could cast a blight.

"Who, then?" queried Miles. "Someone bugged you, and you can't get it out of your mind?"

She nodded. "But I want to. Let's go out somewhere, Miles, if it's only for half an hour."

He agreed readily. "Tell you what. We'll drop in at the

Gainsborough House Country Club. It's a nice drive out and a very pleasant place."

"Are you a member?"

"Well, yes. These places are springing up all over the place, you know. One-time large houses, similar to yours, converted. Belong to one and the membership card admits you to any of them. You don't necessarily have to dine."

It was a pleasant evening. The trees were all in full leaf and still a fresh, unsullied green. Wheat and barley in the fields grew strongly, giving hope of a good harvest. Roses in the gardens of the villages through which they drove, were at the height of their beauty. All the peace-giving, satisfying sights of the countryside, and yet there was a small core within Vanessa which remained unsatisfied, restless.

Miles turned to smile at her. "Feeling more relaxed now? It's a wonderful evening."

"Yes, lovely," she agreed automatically.

Gainsborough House was of the Georgian period, standing white, square and solid in neat, landscaped grounds. A good many smart cars stood in the graveled driveway. Vanessa simply could not see Puck's Hill in the same role, no matter how she stretched her imagination.

Inside, the place was as well carpeted and polished as one would expect. Miles led her into a pleasant room from which, through a wide archway, could be seen part of the restaurant. A concealed loudspeaker plaed light music just loud enough to be heard without intruding on conversation. The room contained chintz-covered love-seats and armchairs. At one end there was even a grand piano.

"Like it?" asked Miles as they chose one of the sofas.

"Very much. It's more like a living room."

"That's the idea. Home away from home, as it were. You could have done the same with your place if you'd had the money. The archway leading into the restaurant is repeated in there—obviously several rooms have been knocked into one."

"Interesting. Does—anyone ever play the piano?" she asked, quite unable to prevent herself thinking of Ian.

"Sometimes. Mind you, although you can relax here, it isn't to everybody's liking. It's too quiet."

She smiled. "Too quiet for you, Miles?"

A waiter brought them their drinks. Vanessa sat back, thinking that the quiet dignity of this room, at any rate, was very much to her taste.

"No—o. Of course, it depends on the mood I'm in or who's with me. There are times when I feel like being lively, but—" he covered her hand with his and turned his head, smiling into her eyes, "when I'm with someone like you, soft lights and sweet music are ideal. The only trouble is, there are too many people in sight. I want to take you in my arms and kiss you."

His face was very close to hers as they leaned their heads back. Vanessa was about to make some light, jesting remark, but the words died in her throat. Through the archway came Ian Hamilton with Cecile Harland. Vanessa's smile faded, then she forced it back again and turned to Miles.

"Do you see who I see—just coming from the restaurant?"

Miles glanced swiftly across the room, then laughed briefly. "Well, well! It's beginning to look as though he's got her hooked again."

Vanessa winced. "I hope they're not going to stay long."

"Darling, we'll leave if they bother you. I can't stand the sight of him myself."

Vanessa would not put her own feelings as strongly as that. All the same— Looking around the room for a suitable place to sit, Ian caught sight of Vanessa and Miles.

He stared for a moment, his eyes flitting from one to the other, then he nodded coolly and led his companion to a corner seat out of Vanessa's direct line of vision.

"There seems no getting away from the man," Miles said, almost echoing her own thoughts. "But let's not bother about him. I want to whisper sweet nothings in your ear. You're very beautiful, do you know that?"

Vanessa laughed briefly. " 'Beauty is in the eye of the beholder', " she quoted.

"That's only partly true," he murmured. "You are beautiful—in every way. But you're especially lovely to me."

She tried not to take him too seriously, not being certain how much in earnest he was. But there was a part of her which wanted very much to feel a man's arms around her. She shook off the feeling by leaning forward and picking up her glass from the table.

"I think you're very nice, too," she told him lightly.

He reached for his own drink. "Well, that's a start. Here's to future progress."

She deliberately avoided looking in the direction of Ian and Cecile Harland, but when Miles suggested another drink, she said she would rather go home. When they were leaving, she discovered the other couple had left without her noticing. At least, they were no longer in the corner.

"They didn't stay very long, did they?" commented Miles. Then he added, "I think those two deserve each other. She's an out-and-out snob, and he'd like to be a gentleman, but isn't. His sister treats him like a tin god because that's what he thinks he is."

Vanessa did not argue with Miles. He was so very nearly right.

Freda drove up to Puck's Hill in her station wagon about half past nine the following morning.

"I thought we might have lunch in town," she said. "What about it?"

Vanessa hesitated, feeling she really ought not to spare the time, but as Freda was being kind enough to run her to the garden center—

"Thanks, that would be nice. I'll just go along to the kitchen to tell Nancy."

As they were driving along, Vanessa thought what a very useful type of vehicle this was.

"I really must look out for a car like this," she said. "That space at the back is ideal for me, especially with the back seat hinged back."

"Er—how would you like to have this?" asked Freda. "I am thinking of selling it, as a matter of fact. I want a smaller one—a car, not a station wagon."

"Are you sure?" Vanessa asked. It sounded too good a coincidence to be true.

"Yes, quite sure," Freda assured her. "We did have a use for it at one time, but not now. I was going to mention it to you. But as it happens, you forestalled me. As far as I'm concerned that space at the back is wasted."

Vanessa asked how much it would be. Freda mentioned what sounded a ridiculously low sum.

"I simply must pay you a fair price for it," she protested.

"And what would you call a fair price?"

"I'm not sure, but—"

"Look, Vanessa, if I let it go in part exchange for another, I shall get very little indeed for it. Much, much less than I'm asking you. I doubt if I'd get a great deal more if I sold it to a local dealer or advertised it. So won't you take it off my hands and stop worrying? If you don't want it, of course, that's a different matter."

Vanessa did want it. "I was just making sure you weren't losing money on it on my account. I'll be glad to have it. As soon as you get your new car let me know, and I'll write you out a check."

At the garden center Freda was staggered at the amount Vanessa bought. Vanessa had a word with the proprietor. He had agreed to let her have all she wanted at special prices. He said her place was far enough away from his not to affect his trade. Later, if her own garden center became successful, she could begin to buy things like tools and other supplies direct from the manufacturers.

"What on earth are you going to do with all this stuff? I thought you were only going to sell plants." Freda asked in a surprised voice.

"I've had a change of plan," Vanessa told her, and enlarged on her idea.

"But isn't it going to eat into your bit of capital?"

"I've decided to take a chance and not be too cautious," Vanessa answered. "I have some men coming to dig out hogweed on the weekend and a builder coming in to put windows in the barn on Monday morning. Perhaps you could give me a good printer in town. I want to have some advertising posters done."

"Oh dear! I do wish you'd talked things over with Ian first. He could have—"

"Why should I talk anything over with Ian?" Vanessa said sharply, then fearing she might have sounded rude, she added, "I'm sorry, Freda, but I prefer to make my own decisions. Then if I make mistakes I have only myself to blame."

Freda was silent for a moment, then she said quietly, "Neither Ian nor I have any desire to tell you what you should do, Vanessa, only to help."

"Yes, I know," Vanessa answered, feeling guilty. "But I want to make my own way as far as possible, and in any case you are helping me."

"Who is it who's coming to tackle the weed?" asked Freda.

"Some men Miles Kendal knows."

"At time and a half?"

"Yes, I think so. But it will be worth it." The other girl gave a shrug of her shoulders. "Look, Freda, I know what you're thinking," Vanessa said raggedly. "You would have liked me to ask Ian. Ian would have had his men come over and put in a couple of days or so, but look what happened the last time when I tried to pay them. I'd rather have it this way, honestly."

They loaded the station wagon with garden sundries and plants, leaving some heavier articles to be delivered. A cup of coffee, a visit to the printer and one or two items of Freda's shopping took them to lunch-time. Freda suggested they eat at the White Horse where Ian had taken Vanessa the day she had visited the lawyer.

"Isn't that rather expensive?" she said.

"It's no more expensive than anywhere else," Freda answered, "and you do get a good meal. Besides—and I hope you won't mind—Ian said he might join us."

Vanessa would have done anything rather than have lunch with Ian, but how could she say so without hurting Freda? And strictly speaking she had no great quarrel with Ian.

"Of course I don't mind. By the way, I saw Ian last night," she added. "Did he tell you?"

"No. No, he didn't," Freda answered thoughtfully. "I knew he was taking Cecile out to dinner. Were you at the same place?"

"Miles called to see me. We drove out there," Vanessa told her briefly.

Evidently Ian hadn't thought seeing her was worth mentioning. He was already in the White Horse restaurant when they entered. He greeted Vanessa formally, invited them to have a glass of sherry and began to ask Freda if she had managed to get various items of shopping for him. Freda chatted brightly—a little too brightly, Vanessa thought, as if she were covering up an awkward situation.

"Wait until you hear Vanessa's plans," she said after a minute or two. "She's decided to launch out right away and not wait until her plants and things are ready for Christmas."

"Oh, really? Well, let's order lunch. You can tell me all about it while we eat."

They went to a table which Ian had reserved for them. When they had ordered, Ian pressed Vanessa for more details. Now and then Freda eyed her brother anxiously as if anticipating his disapproval. Vanessa noticed this vaguely as she talked, and thought it most extraordinary. He listened quietly at first, his face impassive, but his eyes alert. Then when she paused he asked her one or two questions. Vanessa thought fleetingly that she did not care whether he approved or not, yet could not help feeling pleased when he said,

"It all sounds pretty good to me. May I make a suggestion?"

"Of course."

"Don't try to stock absolutely everything at first. Leave yourself a margin of capital. If somebody asks for an item you don't have, just say you can get it—even if it means a special trip into town. That way, you not only find out what the popular demands are and don't waste your money on stocking what there isn't much sale for, but also build up a good reputation for yourself."

"That's a good idea," she said. "Thanks."

He shot her a keen glance as if making sure she wasn't being sarcastic.

"Who are these men who are coming to tackle the hogweed for you on the weekend?" he asked then.

"I—don't know their names," she told him.

He looked puzzled. Before Vanessa could enlarge, which somehow she felt reluctant to do, Freda intervened.

"It's some men Miles Kendal knows," she said quietly,

with again that look as if she feared his reaction. "Vanessa didn't like to ask for our men because last time they wouldn't accept payment."

"I daresay they'd have been willing to come at the usual rate if they'd been approached," he said brusquely. "There are limits to the number of times one can offer help."

There was a heavy silence. An apology hovered on Vanessa's lips. But a look at Ian's granite-like face, and she asked herself what she had to apologize for.

"Miles just happens to be around at the right time," she said with a show of indifference.

"Which seems to be quite often."

At this her lips tightened angrily. She lifted up her chin and sought for the right words with which to answer him. But he spoke first.

"I'm sorry. It's no business of mine who you spend your time with, of course."

But his tone held neither regret nor concern. It had a strong hint of contempt.

"You're so right," she was goaded into replying.

Freda looked frankly horrified. "For goodness' sake, you two, stop snapping at each other!"

"I wasn't aware that I was snapping," Ian answered coolly. "I thought I had just offered an apology—and that for interfering in something which didn't concern me. Namely, the kind of friends Vanessa makes."

"Well, you didn't sound very apologetic," his sister retorted, "what you've just said only makes matters worse."

Ian gave her a long look. "There are several replies I could make to that, but I won't make any at all. Let's just eat."

Vanessa ate without tasting anything; her mind occupied with various permutations of what replies Ian would have made to his sister's remark. But after a minute or two of silence, Freda said brightly:

"Vanessa is going to have the station wagon, Ian, so on the way home will you call at the garage and tell Bill I'll have that little runabout he was showing me the other day."

He gave her another long look. "Oh. Well, I'm very glad about that. You'll find the wagon very useful, Vanessa. It's in good running order, but if you should have any troubles, let me know."

"Thank you." She decided she had better not start talking to him about the price. She would leave it to Freda to work it out with him. She thought she was beginning to understand Ian. He was not only accustomed to having his own way, to being the boss, he was accustomed to women who were more pliant than she was. He liked to organize people. He preferred women of the helpless female type—if they existed these days—rather than one like herself. Above all, it hurt his pride that another man, especially one whom he disliked as he did Miles, was being more helpful than he himself.

He did not stay for coffee. As soon as the dessert course had been served and eaten, he asked them to excuse him, and rose, paying the bill before he left.

"I ought to pay for my own lunch," Vanessa protested.

"Don't be silly," Freda said. "I never knew anyone so independent."

"I don't think I'm abnormally so. Anyhow, isn't it better than being a sponger?"

"Yes, I suppose it is, but both Ian and I want to help you."

"I know, and I appreciate it. But Miles is anxious to be of help too. In fact, people are being extraordinarily kind, but I've been brought up to stand on my own feet as far as possible. I haven't refused help from anyone. It's just that I want to pay my own way."

"Of course you do," Freda said warmly. "That's what I—" She broke off as if she had started to say something she shouldn't. "But never mind. By the way, the Forestry Club meets next Wednesday. You will come won't you?"

Vanessa said she'd love to. She had received a membership card and a program. It looked very interesting. Freda drove back to Barn Hill and helped to unload the station wagon.

"I'll bring the wagon around just as soon as I get the other car," she promised as she was leaving.

By the weekend the barn had four large windows. Vanessa had also made sure the builders had taken away the resultant rubble.

Vanessa eyed the inside walls ruefully. When the barn had had very little light, they had not looked so bad. Now they did not look as good.

"I'm afraid they'll have to be painted," she said to Nancy.

Nancy smiled wickedly. "Why don't you get Miles Kendal to do it? I'm sure he'll be glad to. Emulsion paint is what you want. With a large brush it will go on easily enough. It's too uneven to do with a roller."

Vanessa took up the challenge. "All right, Nancy, I will ask him. Perhaps Mr. Watts will deliver the paint for me. I shall need quite a lot. Meanwhile I'll sweep a few spiders' webs away."

The men came about ten o'clock. Vanessa had to admit they certainly could dig. Miles arrived just in time for coffee, but Vanessa had made a start on the painting herself and was halfway up a stepladder.

"Good lord," he exclaimed. "What in the name of goodness are you doing?"

"What does it look like?"

"It looks like you're doing something you shouldn't."

She hid a smile. "Perhaps you wouldn't mind giving me a hand. I'm not doing all the way up to the roof, just taking a line from floor level to the tops of the windows."

The white-painted bricks were looking most attract-ive, but a second coat was going to be needed for a good clear finish. She popped the brush into a tin containing water and climbed down as Nancy called out that coffee was ready.

Miles gave her a helping hand and gazed all around, a frown on his face.

"It's going to take an age to cover all this. I know a good man who—"

"Sorry, Miles," she cut in. "I simply can't afford to pay for any more labor. If you don't want to help me, I shall just have to do it myself."

"Don't be silly. Of course I want to help you. I don't like to see you doing these jobs, that's all."

She gave his hand a squeeze. "Thank you, Miles," she said mischievously. "I knew you would. Nancy—" she called out as they went out into the open. "Isn't it wonderful? Miles is going to paint the barn for me."

"Very wonderful," agreed Nancy in a tone which said it was too good to be true.

Miles gave a large sigh. "Well, it's not a job I'm too keen on, but for you I'd do practically anything."

Later, when Miles was up the stepladder applying paint to the wall, Vanessa whispered a triumphant "I told you so", in Nancy's ear. But Nancy sniffed.

"He isn't doing it for nothing, you mark my words."

But suddenly the joke was over. "As for that, Nancy, he hasn't any more an ulterior motive for being helpful than, say, Ian Hamilton. They both have their eyes on Puck's Hill—or had. And in actual fact, Miles is being far more helpful in my business enterprise than either Ian or Freda. Don't get me wrong. I like Freda; she's being very friendly and helpful, but both she and Ian have discour-aged me from launching out. If Miles still wanted me to sell Puck's Hill, he wouldn't be at all anxious for me to succeed in business, would he? Quite the reverse."

And having explained everything to her own satisfaction, at least, she found another paintbrush, opened a second can of paint and started on the opposite wall from Miles. This way, using large brushes and not stinting the paint, the whole barn was covered by evening. Vanessa was quite staggered at the amount of weed the two men had dealt with.

They left at five o'clock, promising to come the following day. Vanessa invited Miles to stay for dinner.

"It's absolutely wonderful," she exclaimed enthusiastically, surveying the large area of uprooted weed, after they had eaten. "Miles, you're a genius!"

He grinned. "Of course. Come over here and show me how much you appreciate me."

Lounging on the roomy, old-fashioned sofa, he held out his arm to her. She felt there was little else she could do, in all conscience, except go to him. She sat down beside him, and his arm encircled her shoulders.

"I do appreciate all you've done, Miles," she told him again. "More than I can say. If we can do the same tomorrow, it will all be finished—at least most of it. I shall be able to set out my 'shop'."

At the mention of tomorrow Miles sat up startled. "Did you say the same tomorrow? I'm absolutely worn out after today's effort!"

She couldn't tell whether he was joking or not. She laughed lightly. "Well, the men are coming tomorrow, anyway. And I've made up my mind to a weekend of work. A second coat of paint on the barn won't take long. Of course, I don't expect you to—"

He silenced her effectively by covering her lips with his. "What are you talking about?" he murmured, kissing her again and yet again. "If you want me to help you, of course I will." He grinned sheepishly. "Only trouble is, I'm likely to oversleep on Sundays."

He gave her a long, questioning look, a smile of amusement around his mouth. It was obvious that he was giving her a very strong hint to invite him to stay the night. It seemed to her a very good idea. Why should he go back to an empty apartment to fend for himself when he had worked so hard and would undoubtedly be coming again tomorrow?

"Well, there are plenty of spare bedrooms. After all, I am chaperoned, so why not sleep here? That way, I can make sure you get up in good time in the morning," she finished with a mischievous smile.

"You scheming little so'n'so," he said, pulling her toward him. "But I'll accept your offer with the greatest of pleasure."

It was rather nice having Miles stay the night. Vanessa realized how lonely she had been, in spite of having Nancy living with her. There was something very, very satisfying, she thought, in "having a man about the house."

Oddly enough, considering her hard day's work the previous day, Vanessa awakened fairly early on Sunday morning. At about the time Nancy usually rose, Vanessa took her her breakfast upstairs.

"A Sunday morning treat for you, Nancy," she said. "And one you richly deserve."

Nancy sat up and looked at the clock guiltily. "Oh dear! Thanks, Vanessa. But what got you up so early?"

She smiled. "Got work on my mind, I expect."

"What about your visitor? Not up yet?"

"Not a sound from him so far."

"What are you going to do? Wait until he awakens?"

Vanessa considered for a moment. "I think I'll open his door and take a peep in. Then if he's respectable, go and shake him. If I don't, he's liable to sleep half the day away."

Nancy tut-tutted. "Well, at least you've saved me having to sit down to breakfast with him."

A cup of tea in her hand, Vanessa pounded on Miles's door, but there was no response. She opened it and looked in. Miles was still fast asleep, his head under the bedclothes. She put the cup of tea on the bedtable, gave him a good shake, and removed the sheet from his face.

"Hey, Miles, wake up! It's ten o'clock and the sun's shining fit to burst. I've brought you a cup of tea."

With a great deal of grunting and moaning, he half opened his eyes and looked at her.

"Good lord, is it really you, or am I still dreaming?"

"It's really me. Drink that cup of tea, and then rise and shine. Breakfast will be in ten minutes."

When she went downstairs again, the laborers had already arrived. Vanessa cooked a breakfast of bacon and eggs and toast. She and Miles ate it in the kitchen. They were in the middle of the meal when suddenly Ian Hamilton walked in to stand in the open doorway.

CHAPTER SEVEN

Ian looked at Miles in astonishment.

"You're here early, aren't you?"

Miles eyed him with amusement. "I stayed the night, old boy. Any more questions?"

"No. I'm sorry I asked that one." He turned to Vanessa, his face like stone. "I've brought Freda's wagon around for you. You can settle up with her when it suits you."

He turned and walked out again. Vanessa pushed back her chair and ran to the door.

"Ian—" She caught him and put a detaining hand on his arm. "Ian, thank you."

He gave her a look of contempt and deliberately removed her hand from his arm. What came over her, she didn't know, but it seemed imperative that he should understand.

"Ian, what's the matter? I only asked Miles to stay the night because he—"

But the scorn in his eyes still remained. "You don't owe me any explanations, Vanessa. It's no concern of mine what you do, either now or at any other time."

He strode off. As she stood and watched him, Vanessa's anxiety to be understood and not judged wrongly turned to a consuming anger.

"If it wasn't for hurting Freda's feelings I'd fling the wretched station wagon back at him!" she declared to Miles when she stormed back into the kitchen.

"What's up?" he asked. "Hamilton been his usual charming self?"

"Yes." Vanessa took a deep breath.

"Sit down and I'll pour you another cup of coffee. How much are they asking for the station wagon, anyway?"

Miles poured out the coffee and sweetened it for her. When Vanessa told him the figure Freda had mentioned he grimaced. "Sounds like a bargain, but you can never tell. Anyway, if it's what you want, I should just ignore him—which is all he deserves. Accept it as from his sister. No use cutting off your nose to spite your face."

"I suppose not."

She was tremendously grateful for Miles throughout the whole of that Sunday. Ian's attitude niggled her all day, on and off, but Miles was charming, understanding and helpful. By the time evening came, there was not another piece of hogweed which was not uprooted. The interior walls of the barn had had their second coat of paint. Miles had even helped her to put up trestle tables for plants and other items, and had carried in some of the heavier goods like bags of seeds and potting compost.

"Miles, I'm never going to be able to thank you enough," she told him at the end of the day as they sat side by side on the sofa with their after-dinner coffee.

"Darling girl, don't try," he said softly. He put down his empty coffee cup and relieved her of hers, then took her in his arms. He kissed her, then flicked his gaze over her face, running his finger lightly down her staight nose. "You know, I've learned quite a lot this weekend."

"Really? How to paint a wall in two easy lessons?" she jested.

But he shook his head seriously. "I know now what I've suspected for some time. I'm in love with you."

She caught her breath and something within her contracted sharply. "Miles! Oh—oh, Miles!"

Suddenly he crushed her to him. "Darling girl, I want to marry you."

Vanessa felt tears prick her eyes. "Oh, Miles, I—I don't know what to say."

"Why not just say yes?" He kissed the lobe of her ear and her smooth cheek.

It would be easy, so easy, she thought, in an odd sort of panic. This weekend with Miles in the house, the way they had worked together, had shown her how much she needed the companionship that only a happy marriage could give. And yet she hesitated.

"Miles, I'd rather—think about it for a little while, if you don't mind. You see, I'm—not sure."

"I expect I've rushed you. You're so sweet. Anyway, you haven't said no, have you?"

"No, I haven't."

"Bless you! It means a lot to me. More than you'll ever know."

He kissed her again. "We could be so happy together, you and I. I've never wanted anything so much in my whole life as to spend the rest of my days with you."

Vanessa closed her eyes. The idea sounded wonderful, wonderful; except that, somehow there was the echo of a pain somewhere deep inside her. Later, when Miles had gone, she realized she was still affected by Ian's visit of that morning.

Why did she let him bother her so much? she asked herself as she lay awake in bed. But of course, this must be the influence he had on everyone. This way he had of showing his disapproval, for instance. You wanted to please him, you sought for his approval, and you were worried when you did not have it. Yes, that was it, she decided. The same way he had of wanting to rule everyone's life. It made people defer to him. There was evidence of this in the way Freda looked to him and expected others to also do so. He made you feel you owed him something; that he had certain rights.

Impatient with herself, she turned over and tried to shut him out of her mind. She didn't care if she never saw him again.

Her posters arrived from the printers the following morning. Vanessa drove the station wagon into the village and called at the various stores asking them to display one for her. All promised to do so and wished her well. The butcher went a step farther. As well as nailing one of them on a tree in a very prominent position outside his shop which would catch the eye of passing motorists, he asked for a second one to stick on his delivery van.

In the post office she met Freda, whose manner was noticably cooler, but she managed to smile and say hello.

"Thanks for the wagon—and for transferring the tax and insurance for me," Vanessa said. "It was very kind of you."

"That's all right, though thanks are due to Ian, really. He attended to everything."

Vanessa sighed. "I tried to thank Ian yesterday morning when he brought it around, but he didn't seem to want my thanks—or anything else."

A worried look settled on Freda's face. "Well, it's rather difficult for Ian. You know how he feels about Miles Kendal—and he has good reason. It isn't just uncharitableness. He—didn't expect to find Miles having breakfast with you."

"But there was nothing wrong in that!" Vanessa protested warmly. "Miles was tired. He'd been painting the interior of the barn for me all day and was coming the following day too, so I asked him to stay the night, that's all. I'm afraid I can't choose my friends just to please Ian."

"He doesn't expect you to," Freda answered quietly. "It's just that he's—concerned about you. He knows Miles Kendal far better than you do. Almost certain to."

"But—but why should he be so concerned?" demanded Vanessa exasperately.

Freda looked rather disconcerted. "Well, for one thing, because of knowing your aunt, I suppose. For another, we're neighbors and—I hope—friends. And apart from that, I think Ian would be concerned for any woman he knew under similar circumstances."

Vanessa still thought he had a highly exaggerated sense of responsibility which in effect meant that he liked to dominate. But she liked Freda and did not want to lose her friendship, if it could be avoided. So she said, without a great deal of conviction: "I think I understand, but one can only take people as one finds them, and Miles has been a help."

But the troubled look did not leave Freda's face. "Is it true you're going to marry him, Vanessa?" she asked.

Vanessa looked at her in astonishment. "How could you possibly know anything about that? He only asked me last night."

"Then it's true?"

"I haven't made up my mind yet. But how—"

Freda evaded the unspoken and spoken question. "Look, Vanessa, I must fly. Shall we see you at the Foresters' Club meeting next week?"

"Yes, I think so."

"Good. See you then."

She hurried away. Vanessa looked after her with a sigh. If only she and Ian were not so dead set against Miles. People could be business rivals without disliking each other, surely?

During the ensuing week, Miles called to see her every day. Sometimes, not until late evening, at others during the day. On the Monday evening he brought her flowers. When he took her in his arms, he asked, "Made up your mind yet, darling?"

She shook her head and gave an apologetic smile. "I've been too busy to think about it very much. I'm sorry."

He kissed her. "Not to worry. And I won't keep on badgering you. It isn't 'no', anyway, is it?"

She shook her head.

"Well, that's something."

It wasn't until he had gone that she remembered what Freda had said in the post office. She had intended asking Miles how Ian and Freda knew he had asked her to marry him. But she became so busy with her new business, the matter went out of her head except at the wrong times.

She had a very good response to her posters. Some of the people, she suspected, came more out of curiosity. They strolled around that part of the garden which was already cultivated, had a pot of tea and some of Nancy's homemade cakes, browsed among the plants and other goods, and in the majority of cases ended up by buying either a pot plant or something for the garden. When she was not busy attending to customers, she helped Joe to heap the uprooted giant hogweed in one place for burning. The next step would be to hire a bulldozer to level the ground for the laying of sod.

She saw nothing of Ian Hamilton at all, and when Freda dropped in one evening, she did not even mention his name. Perversely, Vanessa itched to ask about him, but it somehow did not occur to her to ask simply, "How is Ian?"

Miles said he would like to go to the meeting of the Foresters' Club. As members were allowed to take a guest, Vanessa naturally invited him to be hers. He called for her on the night, but before they set out he put his arm about her and produced a small box from his pocket. It contained an engagement ring.

"Like it?" he asked, opening the box to show it to her.

"It's—beautiful, Miles. Really beautiful," she told him rather worriedly, as the big diamond solitaire ring set in platinum winked up at her.

"Are you going to let me put it on for you?"

She shook her head swiftly. "No—please, Miles. Not yet. I—I think I'd rather get this business of mine going before I think of getting married."

He smiled. "Darling girl, I'm not suggesting you should pack it in. You can still carry on with that if you want to. I'd be quite willing to move in here with you. I can soon let my apartment. What do you say?"

She wanted to say yes. Miles had shown her without any shadow of doubt that he loved her, and the warmth of feeling she had for him was equal to anything she had felt for any man. Yet somehow she felt she still wanted more time.

"Miles, I'm reasonably sure. But give me to the end of the week, will you? Come to lunch on Sunday and we'll talk about it then."

"Talk about it? All I want is one word."

"I know. The—the truth is, Miles, I—had one disappointing affair just before I came here. I suppose it's made me cautious. I don't seem to be able to trust my own feelings—or even know what they are. Maybe it's too soon on top of the other."

He hugged her. "All right, darling girl, I understand. Take all the time you want. I'd rather that than rush you into saying no."

She hardly knew what to say. His caring was touching her deeply. She knew that fundamentally, this was what she needed. To be cared for, to be loved, not merely "helped." Her need went deeper than ordinary friendship. She almost said yes to Miles then and there, but she contented herself with putting her arms around his neck and kissing his cheek.

"Hey, that's no use," he said, and covered her lips with his. Then when he released her, "Tell you what, darling girl. Pop the ring into your purse, then when you're sure, just put it on your finger. I'll keep a sharp lookout for it, believe me!"

He dropped the little box into her purse.

They were just going out of the door when the telephone rang. Vanessa turned back.

"I'd better answer it. It might be for me, and I think Nancy's upstairs."

She lifted the receiver to find Freda at the other end. "I was wondering whether we could go to the Club together," she said. "There's no point in taking two cars if one will do, is there?"

"That's—very kind of you, Freda, but Miles is coming as my guest. He has his car, so I shall be going with him."

"Oh. Oh, I see," Freda answered in a flat voice. "All right, Vanessa. See you there."

Obviously having heard her side of the short conversation, Miles's face held the smile of amusement he seemed always to reserve for the mention of Freda or Ian. Vanessa felt suddenly irritated.

"What's funny, Miles?" she asked sharply.

He laughed. "Darling girl, it is funny. Don't you see? He's so accustomed to being top dog. He's been trying to be the great friend and protector; the man to whom everyone—and especially yourself—turns to for help and advice; the man every woman worships and looks up to and so on *ad nauseam*. You have shown him that you want none of it—or of him. And the fact that another man is having some measure of success where he is failing must be burning him up. The more so as *I* happen to be the man. I would think he's gnashing his teeth."

But Vanessa still did not think it was funny, even though Miles's description of Ian fitted in with her own opinion of him. She felt Ian was far too dignified to be "gnashing his teeth", as Miles put it. He might have a strong sense of pride, but she felt sure Ian would never be guilty of petty jealousy.

Miles's attitude to Ian, and Ian's dislike of Miles niggled her all the way to the Foresters' Club room. But Miles was in excellent spirits, not only during the short journey, but in the Club room, so much so that Vanessa found herself becoming increasingly irritated and discomfited. He was not the same person in the company of others. He was more brash, more possessive than she liked, and acting as though he had already proprietorial rights over her. He was constantly putting his arm around her shoulders, calling her "darling", hardly leaving her side for a moment, until at last she managed to escape to speak to Freda.

"Hello, Vanessa," Freda said quietly, giving her a long look. "Miles is creating a certain impression. Does he have grounds?"

Vanessa frowned. "No, not really. I—don't know what's come over him. He's so different when we're alone together."

"The one you're seeing now is the one we know—Ian and I. And I think the same goes for most people."

"Perhaps you don't know him sufficiently well," Vanessa said. "People often behave differently in a crowd. Not everyone's reactions are the same." She glanced around the room. "Is—Ian coming tonight?"

"Later, I hope. Though in a way, it might be better if he stays away."

"Why?" asked Vanessa. She simply could not believe that either Miles's behavior or her own would have all that much influence on him.

But Freda was looking toward the door. "Here comes Ian now anyway."

She waved, and he joined them immediately. As he strode across the room, distinguished-looking in his fine tweeds, Vanessa felt something inside her contract painfully. He nodded to them gravely and said in a quiet voice, "Good evening, Vanessa. Glad you made it. Did you come with Freda?"

Vanessa was about to answer. Why should she be afraid to say she had come with Miles? But Freda intervened swiftly.

"Excuse me, both of you. It's my turn to help with coffee tonight. Ian, why don't you and Vanessa go and sit over there—" she indicated a corner half hidden by a stack of spare chairs. "I'll bring you both a cup of coffee."

Ian looked inquiringly at Vanessa. She nodded, and he put his hand under her elbow and led her between the groups of people standing and talking.

"It's—a long time since we've seen each other, Vanessa," Ian said when they were seated. "How's the business going? I've seen your posters around."

She had the feeling that he was merely being polite and wished Freda had not maneuvered them into this corner together. But she answered that it was going well and warmed up to the subject.

"You haven't seen the barn since I've had windows put in, have you?"

"No, I haven't."

"Oh, then you must," she said, forgetting in her enthusiasm that the last time Ian and herself had met they had almost quarreled. "It looks marvelous. The walls are painted white, making a perfect background for plants. I shall have to think about some heating before the winter comes, of course. It won't be long before I shall need another greenhouse."

His face relaxed into a smile. "You'll soon be needing an assistant too, by the sound of things. Your aunt would have been proud of you. But how are things going financially—if you don't mind my asking."

"Of course I don't mind," she told him warmly, aware of an extraordinary feeling of lightness, their differences forgotten. "I'm not quite at the end of the money Aunt Maud left for me. But I don't think I shall have very much in hand by the time I've paid for the leveling of the ground and the sodding. Still, I hope to start showing a profit in a few weeks' time."

"Have you got much ground clearance to do yet?" he asked.

"No, not a lot," she told him. "The hogweed is nearly all stacked ready for burning, so—"

"Have you contacted a firm to do the leveling?" he queried.

She shook her head. "Not yet. Do you know of one?"

"Better than that. I have a bulldozer you can borrow—or hire, if you insist. Although strictly speaking I ought not to rent it to you as I'm not in the bulldozer hire business. But if you really want to pay something, pay the man who operates it the basic rate for the job."

It was a relief to be able to say yes to his offer. Freda appeared with their coffee and looked swiftly from one to the other.

"Well, you two look happy enough, anyhow. If I were you I'd stay right there."

Vanessa smiled contentedly. She felt as though she could go on sitting here talking to Ian indefinitely. Something odd was hapening to her. She had rarely felt so at peace. As Freda went off again, she caught Ian's eye and smiled, feeling extraordinarily shy.

"Have you done anything about those piano or guitar lessons?" Ian asked her after a moment or two.

"No, I haven't. But I intend to," she told him with sudden decision. "Somehow I haven't felt like it. With my new business and all I—haven't had a minute. But now I shall."

Music seemed suddenly an essential part of her life. She felt so light-hearted she wanted to laugh out loud.

"Do you pick up new things quickly?" he asked.

"I think so. Once I start on anything I usually stick to it and want to reach a certain standard."

"Yes, I can imagine you would." He smiled. "We'll forget about the guitar. There is one difficulty you'll find when you come to learn to play the piano. Your fingers will be stiff for a while. Even those who can play well find the same if they haven't touched the piano for some time. So you'd have to be content with very little more than five-finger exercises for a week or two."

More and more people had entered the Club room since Freda and Vanessa had arrived. Now Vanessa and Ian were hemmed in almost completely. But Ian was leaning slightly to one side and looking across the room. He frowned, then shot an inquiring look at Vanessa.

"Kendal is looking for someone. Could it be you?"

"Possibly."

"Then don't let me keep you."

He half rose from his seat, but Vanessa shook her head quickly.

"No, no, please. I—I'd rather stay here and—and talk to you for a little while longer."

His eyes widened, then his brows contracted in a puzzled frown and his expression became guarded.

"There was a rumor going around that you and he were engaged."

She shook her head slowly. "He asked me, but I—haven't made up my mind yet."

"Why not?"

She stared at him, not knowing quite how to take the query. She would have expected him to show disapproval that she had not turned Miles down completely. Instead his tone hinted that she ought to have accepted him.

She tried to answer Ian, but it was not easy to frame the right words.

"Well, I—I don't think I want to get married yet. I've only just started on my business project, and—"

"Don't 'feelings' come into it?"

"Feelings?" she echoed, as if she had never heard of the word.

"Yes, feelings," he repeated. "Are you in love with the man or aren't you?"

She felt her cheeks warming. "I—don't think you have any right to ask me such personal questions. But if it's of any great interest to you, I—I'm not sure. I don't know whether I trust love, anyway."

The ghost of a smile played around his mouth. "Disillusioned at your age?"

"One can be disillusioned at any age," she retorted.

"True, but one doesn't usually associate disillusion

with love in someone as young and—shall we say as attractive as you."

Her eyes widened at the compliment, but she reminded him, "I didn't say I was disillusioned. That was your word. It just happens that—experience has taught me to be cautious, that's all."

"Experience?" He caught up the word as if to examine and analyze it. Then he said, "I'm sorry. Sorry that you should have had that kind of experience."

She smiled faintly. "It's all a part of life, I suppose."

"Well, you've recovered sufficiently to be able to be philosophical about it, evidently. But it still left you careful."

"Every experience leaves its mark, I suppose. And in the case of—disappointment in love, one tends to mistrust one's emotions," she answered.

He gave her a long look. "If you were really and truly in love, you wouldn't be thinking this way—trying to analyze your feelings."

"You think not? Perhaps one learns to control one's emotions as well as to mistrust them. And maybe I'm not a very emotional or—ardent kind of person."

His eyes narrowed in a calculating look. "I would stake my life on it that you are. If you've never felt really passionately in love, then I would say you've never been in love. No man has been successful in rousing these feelings in you yet, that's all."

She opened her eyes wide. She didn't know whether to laugh or be indignant.

"And what gives you such wonderful insight as to the kind of person I am?" she demanded.

"Well, you're not exactly placid. You've shown that you're capable of a great warmth of affection from the way you came to nurse your aunt. Added to that you're something of a spitfire, aren't you?"

"Am I?"

"You are indeed."

Vanessa could hardly believe that they were talking like this. The jumbled sound of voices in varying tones, bursts of laughter, the chink of glasses or cups and saucers broke over their heads, but they were in a world apart. A man and woman talking, getting close to each other, discussing each other. Vanessa felt a strange sense of unreality, as if she and Ian were standing high on a mountain top, their hands clasped, their fingers entwined. It was important. Treasure this time, hold on to it.

She gave a little smile. "You've been analyzing me. What about you? I've been hearing rumors, as well."

He thought for a moment. "I daresay you have. But tell me what you've heard."

But now Vanessa felt alone on the mountain top. She had asked the wrong question. She had wanted to find out what kind of man he was: how he would treat a woman, whether he would be ardent. Instead, mentioning rumors about him had only served to remind her of Cecile Harland and to talk about her.

"Well, I—heard that you were once in love with Miss Harland, that you—only came to Barn Hill because of her."

He raised his eyebrows. "Is that all?"

"Briefly, yes. It—tells its own story, surely. Is it true?"

"Partly. I did know Cecile before Freda and I moved to this part of the country, but of course there were other reasons why we came here."

Other reasons. So Cecile had been one of them? And was he still in love with her? Naturally it was a question she could not ask him. She would not have wanted to. She asked herself why and knew that it was because she would dread the answer. She did not want him still to be in love with Cecile. She did not want him to be in love with anyone. She stared into her empty coffee cup, aware that it was her turn to speak, yet not knowing quite what to say. There were so many things she wanted to know about him, but it was impossible to ask. She became aware, too, of his scrutiny. When she raised her eyes to look at him, she knew she was in love with him.

"Do you ever wonder," he asked, changing the subject, "what the conditions of your aunt's will are?"

She shook her head dazedly. What did Aunt Maud's will matter? What did anything matter except that she was here? Ian was here, and she loved him?

"No, I—haven't even thought about it," she answered a trifle breathlessly.

"That's very strange. Most people would have tried to hazard a guess or two."

"I've had so many other things on my mind. And if I did try to guess, what good would it do? I would have no idea whether my guesses were right or wrong?"

"No," he agreed. "On the other hand, it might help if you were to give the matter some thought. I believe you said there was a considerable sum of money involved. One of the conditions of inheritance might be that you shouldn't marry. How would you feel about that?"

She stared at him. "Surely Aunt Maud wouldn't make any such condition?"

"She might. She never married herself, and she might not like the idea of a man invading her house and property."

"All she asked," she said after a moment's thought, "was that I shouldn't sell Puck's Hill. The other part of the will only concerns money."

"Which you might not get if you marry."

Vanessa eyed him uncertainly. "You—think I should remain forever single—never marry?"

"That's for you to decide, isn't it?" he countered.

"Decision is not the word I would use," she answered, her eyes flicking over his tanned features, wondering fleetingly how long she had loved him, really. "What is money? When one falls deeply in love, marriage is the natural, the only thing."

His gaze was on her face too. Once more they were together on the mountain top.

"So you would give up everything for the man you loved?"

"Of course."

"You really are worth wooing and pursuing, Vanessa," he said in an oddly quiet voice.

Her heartbeat quickened; the hand holding her cup and saucer trembled. Then someone jogged her elbow and her cup fell sideways, spilling the dregs on her dress. At once there were apologies, people turning to look at them, and someone took the cup from her hand. The magic moments were over. Vanessa opened her purse to find a handkerchief to mop her dress. When she pulled it out, the ring case came with it and dropped on the floor. The lid was evidently not on properly. It flew open at Ian's feet, revealing the ring in all its significant sparkle.

He picked it up and handed it back to her, his face a mask, his eyes cold.

"Yours, I believe," he said icily, and walked away into the crowd.

CHAPTER EIGHT

Miles was at her elbow now. "Darling, so here you are. I've been looking everywhere for you."

Vanessa stood up and looked vaguely around, trying to see where Ian had gone, wanting to hurry after him to explain. He thought she had lied to him, that she was engaged to Miles. How could she make him understand?"

She became aware of Miles's scrutiny. "What's the matter, Vanessa—and how did you come to be pinned in this corner with Hamilton? Has he been annoying you?"

She shook her head swiftly. "No, no, of course not. But I think I'd like to go home, if you don't mind."

"Go home?" he echoed. "But the evening's only half over."

She wished she had brought her own car. It was unfair to drag Miles away really, but she felt she must get away. Miles drew her into the center of the room, his hand under her elbow. There were only two things in Vanessa's mind—Ian, and Miles's ring, once more in her purse. Where was he? Was there someone else who would give her a lift home? She saw Freda collecting coffee cups a worried look on her face. Vanessa caught her eye. Freda carried her tray into the kitchen, then came across the room.

"What happened in the corner there, Vanessa? Ian's gone out looking furious."

Miles put his arm across Vanessa's shoulders. "Your brother looks furious at the drop of a hat. It's my guess that Vanessa is the one who should be looking furious. Like the sweet girl she is, she's probably apportioning all the blame for any—misunderstanding to herself. Come along, Vanessa, I'll take you home."

Vanessa looked apologetically at Freda. "Perhaps we can get together and talk one day. I really must get home. Goodnight, Freda."

She was glad that Miles did not talk much on the way to Barn Hill. When they arrived at the house, he held out his hand.

"Give me your key, Vanessa. I'll unlock the door for you."

Without protest she gave it to him. When he had unlocked the door, he followed her inside. She invited him into the library. There were things she must say to him.

"Would you like some coffee?" she asked, trying to collect her thoughts together.

He shook his had. "I've already had two cups. Come. Sit down and tell me what's upset you. One of these days I'll kill Hamilton."

He took her hand and made her sit down, dropping onto the sofa beside her. She withdrew her hand from his and took out the ring in its case.

"You'd better have this, Miles. I'm sorry—it has to be no, after all."

He looked from the box to her in astonishment.

"But—but, darling girl, I don't understand. Less than a couple of hours ago you said you were reasonably sure, that you were going to tell me by the end of the week. What's happened to change things? I can't think that you've let Ian Hamilton poison your mind against me. Though it would be just like him to try."

"No, no, it's nothing like that. Please, Miles. I—I'm sorry, but I can't marry you. I know it now for certain."

"But—" he took both her hands in his. "But how can you? It's not possible! I'm the same person that I was about an hour and a half ago, you're the same, so—"

She was not the same. She was different. Something had happened to her. She was a woman in love. "Miles, you'll have to take my word for it. Please don't prolong the argument. In fact, I don't want an argument at all. I told you I wasn't sure. Now I am. I'm not in love with you, Miles, that's all."

He drew an angry breath. "What's Hamilton been saying to you? It's got something to do with him, I know."

Vanessa sighed and rose. "Please, Miles, there's no point in discussing it. I'm sorry, truly I am, but liking isn't love. These things often come to one suddenly." She smiled and held out her hand to him. "Goodnight, Miles, and thanks for seeing me home. Thanks for all you've done to help, too."

He eyed her keenly and stood up, ignoring her hand. "All right, Vanessa. But I still think there's more in this than meets the eye. Believe me, Hamilton knows more about your affairs than you think. I wouldn't trust him an inch, if I were you. If you ever did, you'd live to rue it."

He went out, obviously hurt and angry. She could not blame him, but what would have been the use of keeping him in doubt?

Ian. Oh, Ian!

She made her way slowly upstairs, loving him with every breath and with every step; yet wanting to weep at the memory of that cold look in his eyes when he handed Miles's ring back to her. She must see him, make him understand.

Scarcely aware of what she was doing, she made her preparations for bed, even though it was still quite early. Her mind went over and over again everything they had talked about, everything he had said, the way he had looked, the tone of his voice—everything about him. She had loved him for a very long time, of course. That day at his house when she had been sitting on the edge of the pool; the night of the Foresters' dance when he had been dancing with Cecile Harland. She had been in love with him then. Why hadn't she realized it before?

But now the thought of Ian and Cecile Harland filled her mind. Ian had not told her what she most wanted to hear—that though he had once been in love with Cecile, he was no longer.

Trying to sleep, Vanessa tossed around to the accompaniment of her thoughts. Questions and speculations bounced from one side of her brain to the other, but the most important queries were hurled back unanswered.

"You were home early last night," Nancy commented the next morning, giving her a speculative look.

Vanessa nodded. "I—wasn't enjoying the meeting very much, so I had Miles drive me home. I went straight up to bed."

"Was Ian at the meeting?" Nancy asked.

Vanessa sighed. "Yes, he was."

Nancy made no further comment about Ian. She observed, "Miles Kendal didn't stay long, anyway, did he? I heard him drive away again quite soon after you came in."

"That's right—and I don't suppose I shall be seeing so much of him in the future. I gave him back his ring last night."

"I didn't know you'd ever accepted one from him," Nancy said in a surprised voice.

Vanessa explained, "It was silly, really. He dropped it into my purse, and I was to wear it when I decided to be engaged to him."

"What made you make up your mind?" Nancy asked curiously. "Something happen at the meeting?"

"You could say that, I suppose," Vanessa answered briefly.

"Well, I can't say I'm sorry you've sent that young man packing," Nancy said frankly. "I'm sure you're well rid of him."

But Vanessa did not think she was rid of him, as Nancy put it. A few days later he called to see her.

"I came to apologize for my attitude when you

returned my ring," he said. "I'm afraid I never was a very good loser."

"I understand, Miles. I think I would have felt the same in your place. It's hard to accept defeat sometimes—if defeat is the right word."

"It's the right word sure enough. But I came to ask if we could still be friends."

"Why, yes, of course," she said swiftly, anxious to make amends for having hurt him.

He smiled and put his arm across her shoulders. "That's the girl! Well, come and see me off. I can't stay long this time. I'm meeting someone at the Swan."

His arm still across her shoulder, they went outside and stood for a moment beside his car. Vanessa wished he would take his arm away, but it would seem unnecessarily unfriendly to shake it off. He would soon be gone. But as they stood beside his car, another drove up. Vanessa needed only one glance to see that it was Ian. She shrugged her shoulders to remove Miles's arm, but he gripped them more tightly. Ian got out of the car, looked from one to the other quickly, then stepped back in again and drove off without a word.

Miles threw back his head and laughed out loud. Vanessa rounded on him furiously.

"I don't think it's the least little bit funny," she stormed. "You deliberately kept your arm around my shoulder just to make him think the worst!"

"The worst? What on earth is that supposed to be? You care too much what Hamilton thinks." He opened the door of his car. "I understand that you and he were in quite a huddle in that corner the other night. I hope he didn't give you any wrong impressions. He likes to think he's keeping women on tenderhooks. I know quite a few who'd like to know where they stand with him. But they're fools. He's got his eye on the main chance—and that means Cecile."

He smiled and with an imperturbable wave, drove off down the drive.

Her eyes misty with tears, Vanessa felt for a moment as if she hated him. But all he had said about Ian could be the truth. He had talked to her last night as if he were genuinely interested in her as a woman, yet he had carefully evaded telling her what his relationship with Cecile was now. There was no real reason why he should have, of course, except that they had been talking on a personal level.

Between attending to the wants of customers and giving attention to her seedling plants, Vanessa toyed with the idea of calling Ian to find out why he had come. He must have wanted to see her about something. She hoped he would phone her, but he didn't. At last, one evening a few days later, she picked up the telephone and dialled his number. Again, it was Cecile who answered. Vanessa was beginning to wonder whether she was living there.

"May I speak to Ian?" she asked determinedly. "This is Vanessa Woodrow here."

"Ian?" came the cool voice. "Hang on a moment."

Vanessa hung on, her heart beating swiftly, but it was Freda who answered after a minute or two. She did not say whether Ian was at home or not. Vanessa had to conclude, with despair in her heart, that he simply did not want to speak to her.

"Oh, Vanessa," said Freda, "I'm coming along to see you in the morning. Will that be all right?"

"Yes, perfectly. Come and have coffee with me. I'd like to see you. But I wanted to speak to Ian. Is he—"

"I'm sorry, Vanessa," came the answer. "This is a bad line. I'll see you in the morning around 11. 'Bye for now."

Vanessa had no option but to hang up. She replaced the receiver slowly, convinced that Ian had been there but did not want to speak to her. He thought her a person who

lied. He felt a contempt for her because of her association with Miles. But she hadn't lied, and what was wrong
with Miles anyway? She was rapidly coming to the
conclusion afresh that Ian did not really like her and
never had.

"Sorry I haven't been around before," Freda said
brightly when she arrived the following morning, "but I
don't seem to have had time to breathe. How are things
with you? Business flourishing?"

Vanessa said it was and poured out coffee in her study-
cum-library. Freda glanced around at the walls, now
painted in creamy white, the dusty books sold to an
antiquarian book dealer.

"This is marvelous. I haven't been in here since you've
fixed it up," she exclaimed, determined it seemed to
Vanessa, to keep on talking trivialities.

"Ian called a day or so ago," she said at last. "Did he
want to see me about something?"

"Er—yes. That's why I've come really. He asked me
to. It was to tell you that his offer of a bulldozer to level
the land is still good. You're to say what day you'd like
the man to come. He also asked me to give you this." She
took a business card out of her bag and handed it to
Vanessa. "It's a firm of heating engineers—a friend of
ours. Give him a call. He'll come and discuss your greenhouse heating problems. The house too, if you want it.
And if I were you, I would let him do the house. You can
always regulate the amount you use, can't you?"

Vanessa swallowed hard and nodded, but at the
moment the heating of either house or greenhouse, and
the leveling of the land were of little interest to her. It was
Ian she wanted to know about, to talk about.

"Did—Ian say anything after he'd called to see me that
day?"

From Freda's expression it was apparent that he had, but she hesitated before answering.

"Well, he did say that Miles Kendal was with you."

"Is that all?"

"What else should there be?" asked Freda, giving her a steady look.

Vanessa pressed her hands to her face. "I don't know—"

Freda's hand touched her arm. "Vanessa, what's the matter? What hapened between you and Ian the other evening at the club? He won't tell me anything, but he's certainly upset about something."

"He—thinks me a liar, I suppose. We—we were getting along quite well. At least, I thought we were until—"

"I thought you were too. What were you talking about?"

"Oh, all kinds of things. He—asked me if I was engaged to Miles, but I told him I hadn't made up my mind. He even asked me if I was in love with Miles, and I told him I wasn't sure about that either. We talked some more, then I—spilt some coffee onto my dress. I reached in my purse for my handkerchief to mop it up. When I pulled it out, the ring box Miles had given me fell out. The—the top couldn't have been on properly. The ring fell out and—Ian picked it up. He didn't wait for me to explain. He just gave it back to me and walked away."

Freda gave a puzzled frown. "I don't quite understand, either. If you're not engaged to Miles, why did you have his ring in your purse?"

"He brought it with him when he called for me. I hadn't said I would marry him. He—he just brought it. But I still didn't want to accept it. I told him I'd give him a definite answer by the end of the week, so he said—'Well, put it in your purse. When you've made up your mind to say yes, just put it on'. "

"I see. So I suppose Ian jumped to the conclusion you were engaged, seeing you were carrying Miles's ring around. Then he called the other day, and here Miles was again. You can hardly blame him, Vanessa, can you?"

"I suppose not. But why should he think I would lie? Does he think I'm that sort of person?"

Freda sighed. "We all get a bit mixed up at times, Vanessa, and jump to wrong conclusions. And with regard to Miles Kendal, you've had me foxed at times, too. You didn't seem to be his type at all, and yet you've become so friendly with him. He always seems to be around, he's stayed the night here, and you've accepted his help in preference to ours. Even now we don't know whether you're going to marry him or not."

"I'm not," Vanessa told her quietly.

Freda's delight at this news showed in her face. "Oh, Vanessa, I'm so glad. So you've returned his ring?"

Vanessa nodded. "He was a bit annoyed at first. He came the other day to apologize and ask if we could remain friends. I had to say yes, of course. We had no quarrel, and he really has been a good friend. I'm only sorry that Ian happened to call just when he did. I was annoyed with Miles, actually. He stood with his arm around my shoulders and wouldn't move it when Ian drove up."

"Ah, so that was it."

"That was what, exactly?" queried Vanessa.

"Well, it explains why Ian didn't stay and why he thought you and Miles—"

"I suppose so," Vanessa said miserably. "But I called Ian yesterday to try to explain. He wouldn't even speak to me. He was at home, wasn't he, Freda? Because Cecile was there."

Freda sighed worriedly. "This is all very difficult, Vanessa. I hardly know what to say to you. Would you like me to explain things to Ian?"

Vanessa nodded, tears not far away. Explaining to Ian, making him believe that she had not lied to him about Miles would not alter the fact that he did not care for her, nor lessen her love for him. Still less would it make Cecile cease to exist.

Freda eyed her closely. "Why does it matter so much what Ian thinks, Vanessa? What made you decide you didn't want to marry Miles?"

Vanessa's lips trembled. "I can't tell you that, Freda."

"I think I can guess," Freda said softly.

With an effort Vanessa kept back her tears. "If only he didn't dislike me so!"

"But, Vanessa, he doesn't dislike you." She sighed again and stood up. "Look, I must leave. There are a whole heap of things which need clearing up between you and Ian, but I can't very well speak for him. I'll tell him you really aren't engaged to Miles, anyway. I would think he'll be very pleased about that—for your sake. And what shall I tell him about the bulldozer?" she added swiftly.

The bulldozer. As if it mattered! The words which had held he attention were *for your sake*. If only it had been for his sake, too.

"The bulldozer can come any time at all," she answered heavily. "And thank Ian for me, of course."

"I will." Freda looked as though she were about to say something else, but changed her mind and took her leave.

Vanessa had longed to ask her about Cecile, but what would have been the use? she asked herself. She was sure the answer would have only added to the ache already in her heart.

She wondered whether Ian would phone or call to see her after Freda had explained to him about the ring. During the following days her ear was continually tuned to the telephone, her heart leaping every time it rang. But there was nothing from him. The bulldozer arrived and did a wonderful job of leveling the ground where the weed had been dug out. Ian had received her message about that obviously, then surely Freda had given him the other? Vanessa shrank from dialing their number. She did not want to risk Cecile answering it again. Once, in casting a look across the boundary fence she caught a glimpse of both Cecile and Ian through the trees and turned quickly away. On another occasion she saw Ian alone. She hesitated, then waved and would have walked toward the boundary to speak to him, but he turned away. She had no way of knowing whether he had seen her or not. But she had an awful feeling that he had and was deliberately avoiding her. Freda appeared to be avoiding her too. A week passed when Vanessa saw nothing of her. When she did, it was by accident in the village.

"I thought I might have seen you before, Freda," Vanessa said. "Not knowing how I stand with Ian, I didn't feel I could phone you or call at the house. You—did tell Ian about everything?"

"Yes, Vanessa, I did."

"What did he say?"

"He—said he was glad to hear it—that you weren't engaged to Miles."

"Is that all?"

"Well, yes. At least, that's all I can tell you, Vanessa. I don't think he had really believed you capable of telling lies. He said he hadn't known what to think." Then she asked, in a way which Vanessa was sure was aimed deliberately at changing the subject, "Have you been in touch with the heating engineer yet?"

Vanessa said she hadn't. She had had too many other things on her mind.

"Do you intend to?"

"Oh yes, I must—even if it's only for the sake of my plants."

Freda seemed once more in a hurry. "I'll give you a

call, Vanessa. You must come and have a meal with us again."

But Vanessa felt as though she were being let down lightly, that neither Freda nor Ian were anxious to see her again.

On the same day that her sod was delivered the heating engineer called. Asked to by Ian, he said. "Only to advise you. You won't be under any obligation."

"That's very good of you. It's my greenhouse I'm most concerned about, and the barn."

"And what about the house? I understand you haven't any form of central heating there."

"That's true, but I have a financial problem, Mr—"

"Hunt. Geoffrey Hunt. A good many people have financial problems, Miss Woodrow, but I think you'll find that what I have to suggest will be well within your means. But let me take a look around."

She showed him the barn and greenhouse, then took him into the house. As soon as he saw that there was a fireplace in the hall he was delighted.

"Ah, Ian said he thought there was a fireplace. That solves the problem."

"How?"

He explained that he could fix an oil heater there which would heat the entire house.

"No pipes or ducts are needed. Only one small pipe—and that would be to feed in the oil from a tank outside."

"But how can one oil heater keep the whole house warm. Why must it be in the fireplace?"

"It works by ordinary convection currents," he told her. "And it must have a 16-foot-long flue pipe to carry away fumes. That's where the chimney comes in useful. The heat is sent out from the unit with such force that it permeates the whole house, especially if the rooms doors are left open. Those rooms you don't use—and there must be quite a few in a house of this size with only two of you living in it—can be kept closed. That will help to direct the warm currents to where you need them. Bedrooms, bathroom, staircase, hall—everywhere. Besides, I'm sure you'll agree, if the hall is warm the whole house is."

He showed Nancy and herself photographs of the unit. It looked a most pleasing piece of equipment.

"It's the most economical form of heating I know," Geoffrey Hunt told her. "It can be regulated, left on safely all night or when you go out for an evening, and it's absolutely trouble-free."

Both Vanessa and Nancy were won over. As the kitchen was farthest away from the hall, and also had a fireplace, he suggested a small unit in there in addition to the larger one in the hall would make for even greater comfort.

"Don't make up your mind right away. Think it over and give me a call," he told Vanessa. "But don't leave it too long, otherwise we shall get too busy and there might be a long delay."

He said credit could be arranged. It all sounded too good to be true. He advised the same kind of unit for the barn, even though this had no chimney. The pipe in that case could be taken through a hole in the wall and up outside. If Vanessa did not like the appearance, an outside chimney could be built on some time. He suggested electric heating for the greenhouse and promised to send an estimate for the whole operation.

The estimate arrived within a few days. Both Nancy and Vanessa were amazed at the low price. Nancy had insisted that she should pay half the cost, which meant the project would be well within Vanessa's resources.

"It's so cheap, I'm beginning to doubt whether it can be really efficient," she said to Nancy.

"I'm sure it will be. In any case most forms of central heating only give a sort of background warmth. And that's really all that's necessary. The kitchen will be well taken care of. We can still have open fires or additional electric fires in the rooms we use in the evenings—and your study in very cold weather. But if you're in doubt, why not ask Ian Hamilton's advice?"

"Yes, perhaps I will—though he's awfully elusive these days. Every time I call either Cecile Harland answers the phone or Ian isn't in."

"How many times, in actual fact?" Nancy quizzed. "And it could be just a coincidence that Miss Harland happens to have been paying them a visit."

"It isn't a coincidence that he takes her out to dinner," Vanessa answered without thinking.

Nancy eyed her keenly. "And how many times has he taken her out to dinner, to your certain knowledge?"

Vanessa had to admit that it was only once. "But I daresay there have been plenty of other occasions."

"You're only guessing," Nancy told her. "And it's my belief that you're exaggerating, too."

"Maybe."

Several times that day Vanessa reached for the telephone to call Ian, then changed her mind. Perhaps she had exaggerated about the number of occasions Ian had taken Cecile out and was jumping to conclusions altogether about his relationship with her. But there was no doubt about his silence. It was weeks since she had either heard from him or seen him. Not since, in fact, the day he had called and found Miles standing with his arm around her shoulders. Freda's explanation of the engagement ring had made not the slightest difference.

But on a sudden decision the following morning when she went into her study after breakfast, she dialed his number. Cecile surely couldn't be there at this hour unless she had stayed the night, or was indeed living there.

Her heart seemed to leap into her throat as Ian himself answered the phone.

"Oh, Ian, this is Vanessa."

There was a second of silence. Then his voice came cool and impersonal. "Yes, Vanessa? What can I do for you?"

Her courage almost failed her. Apart from his mention of her name, she might have been a complete stranger to him.

"I—wanted to thank you for sending the heating engineer," she said, sure that her trembling voice would give her away.

"That's all right," he answered in the same detached voice. "Did you find his estimate satisfactory?"

"That's what I called you about. It's so cheap I'm not sure it will be any good."

"That's one of the surest attitudes I know of helping to keep prices high," he said in an exasperated tone. "What kind of heating did he suggest?"

Slightly taken aback by his remark, she gave him more details.

"It all sounds very satisfactory to my mind," he said when she had finished. "You can take it from me, Geoff Hunt is an upright and honest business man. That's why I sent him to you. And it so happens that Puck's Hill is the right sort of house for that form of heating. I think you'll find it cheap to run and very efficient. The reason it's so cheap is that installation is so simple. It doesn't entail the whole house being torn apart."

"So you'd advise me to go ahead with it?"

"I certainly would. The only tricky part might be in the lighting of that kind of unit. You mustn't let too much oil get into the bowl at first. Turn it up gradually, otherwise pressure builds up in the flue and you get a terrific noise. It's not dangerous, just alarming. But Geoff Hunt will show you."

"Thanks. Thanks very much, Ian."

"That's all right. Any time," he answered casually.

There was a pause. Vanessa hoped he would say something else, something of a more personal or friendly nature, even if only to ask how the garden business was doing, but he didn't. There was little else she could do except say goodbye and hang up. Calling him had given her no personal satisfaction whatever. She had run away from one hopeless love affair only to become involved in another. But this time she was not ging to recover quite so easily—if ever.

Day after day Vanessa opened up her store for customers, worked in the garden and tended her plants. The heating was installed, and noticeably the hours of daylight grew shorter with the approach of fall. Now and then when the people of the village came to buy some item for their gardens, they stayed to chat and marvel at the progress Vanessa had made in so short a time. Miraculously, it seemed, the giant hogweed, the *Heracleum mantegazzianum*, had gone. In its place, were stretches of green lawn which Joe kept rough-cut with the aid of a rotary mower. Occasionally, Freda breezed in, or Vanessa met her in town for lunch, but Ian continued to hold himself aloof. Occasionally, too, Miles called to see her. Once or twice he asked her out, but she always declined. Whenever he tried to put his arm around her, as he sometimes did, she was invariably firm with him.

One evening when there was a sharp drop in temperature, she and Nancy decided to test out their heating. Very carefully, Vanessa followed the instructions the heating engineer had given her. Soon the whole house was pleasantly warm. Miles called that evening and displayed a great interest in the unit.

"Marvelous idea," he said. "Who told you about it?"

"Ian sent a man called Hunt," she told him.

"Ah, clever Ian," he said sarcastically. "Do you see much of him nowadays?"

"I've been busy—and so has he, I imagine," she answered.

Miles very obviously suppressed a smile. "Well, I'm pleased to know he doesn't always get his way."

Vanessa turned on him. "Miles, if you're going to be unpleasant, I'd rather you leave."

"But, darling girl, I only—"

"And don't call me 'darling girl'!"

He shrugged. "All right, all right." He started to go, then turned, his face serious. "Vanessa, you're not very happy, are you? And I guess it's something to do with Hamilton. I hate to say this, but he's hooked on Cecile, and I think you know that. Why don't you get out of here, sell the place and have yourself enough money to travel or something? Either that or marry me. You could do a lot worse, you know. You might not think you love me enough at the moment, but I'm told by some of my married pals that love often comes after marriage."

Vanessa took a deep breath. What a simple solution it sounded! But she shook her head slowly.

"No, Miles, I can't, but thanks all the same. I know how you feel about me keeping my promise to Aunt Maud, but I feel I must. And I can't marry you feeling as I do about—someone else."

"People are falling in and out of love all the time. It doesn't last for ever, especially when it's one-sided. One of these days you'll fall out of love with him. It might happen sooner than you think. But if you don't want to marry me, how about selling Puck's Hill to me? You'd be better away from here."

"Please don't say any more, Miles. Even if I did leave Puck's Hill I'd never sell it."

He left then, but what he had said had unsettled her. For weeks she had tried not to think about Ian, to keep herself busy, to be so tired night after night that she was falling asleep as she mounted the stairs to bed. But now she was suddenly defenseless. Was it true? Was Ian really "hooked on" Cecile? Vanessa almost groaned aloud. What was she to do? She couldn't go on like this indefinitely. She could not sell Puck's Hill, she thought suddenly, but she had not made any promises about not giving it away. She could give it to Nancy. Surely Aunt Maud would not have minded that? Vanessa didn't think that would be compromising. In fact, she need not actually give it to Nancy. She could simply let her live here, have whomsoever she wished to live with her. Nancy might even be able to find a man to manage the garden business, and so keep that on. It was beginning to pay now and would be even more profitable when her pot plants were coming into flower and ready for sale—which would be fairly soon. Many of them were already potted up. Some people liked to buy them for some weeks before Christmas, and bring them into actual flower themselves.

Yet somehow she knew she did not want to go away. Wherever she went, she would never stop loving Ian. She began to think about him properly; recalling the Sunday she had lunched at the Lodge, the evening at the Foresters' Club before the incident of the ring. Surely he didn't dislike her as much as she imagined? Hadn't he said she was worth wooing and pursuing? It was true that she had been antagonistic toward him at first. This had caused her to be rude often and resent him, so she herself was a fault, if indeed he did dislike her. But Freda had said emphatically that he didn't. He had certainly gone out of his way to help her.

She decided she would not give up without a fight. Freda herself had said there were a whole heap of things which needed clearing up between Ian and Vanessa. The first thing to do was really find out whether there was anything between Ian and Cecile. If there wasn't, she would do all she could to make Ian like her. In any event she simply had to find out the truth.

In the morning she called the Lodge. This time it was Freda who answered.

"Freda, may I come along to see you and Ian this evening?"

"Yes, of course," Freda answered swiftly. "Although Ian has to go out. Would you like to come and have a meal with us or—"

But perhaps it would be better to talk to Freda first, so Vanessa said she would not go for dinner but be there about eight o'clock.

"Nice to see you," Freda greeted her. "Sorry if we appear to have been neglecting you. Is there something special, or did you just want to get out for an hour or so?"

"No, it's a little more than that. I felt I had to come. You see, I'm thinking of going away—probably back home."

The announcement startled Freda. "But why? Just as you're doing so well with your garden center and everything?"

Freda led her into the sitting room where she had some coffee waiting.

"I think, Freda, you must know why," Vanessa said quietly. "But there are one or two things I simply must find out before I make up my mind finally."

"Anything I *can* tell you, Vanessa, I will," Freda told her. "But you must understand I can't tell you anything I know Ian wouldn't want me to."

"Just answer me two questions, Freda, if you can. First, does Cecile Harland really mean anything to Ian? Is he going to marry her? Or would he like to?"

"I don't think so. Ian has been advising her father about his trees—they have quite an estate. We knew the family before we came here to live."

"Miles says he followed her here; that he's—in love with her."

Freda's eyes widened. "How could Miles Kendal possibly know, in any case? He's a thoroughly bad lot, that man. I'm glad you've given him the heave-ho. Anyhow, it simply isn't true that Ian followed her here. It was sheer coincidence. He's only taken her out once—and that was the time you saw them. She's been here once or twice. It's probable that she'd like to see more of Ian, but—"

Vanessa felt she was likely to burst with a sudden feeling of joy and excitement, but she took herself firmly in hand.

"The other thing, Freda, is—what does Ian really think of me?"

Freda passed her a cup of coffee and the sugar. "Now that is a difficult question, Vanessa. I don't think I can answer it."

"Does he hate me?"

"Good heavens, no. What a question!"

"Dislike me, then?"

"No, of course not."

"Then—then why is he avoiding me? Why doesn't he drop in at Puck's Hill like he used to?"

"Vanessa, I can't tell you. How can I? I doubt even if Ian himself would—" She broke off, clearly ill at ease. "Look, Vanessa, I know how you feel, and what a difficult time you must be going through. And believe me, I only wish I could do something about it. But this is something you and Ian will have to work out for your-selves."

"Work out for *ourselves*?" repeated Vanessa in a puzzled voice. "Why do you say that?"

Freda sighed and put her hand to her head. "Vanessa, don't ask me any more questions, please. I told Ian how the engagement ring happened to be in your purse; that you weren't engaged to Miles. He believes that. Now, I've set your mind at rest about Cecile. More than that I can't do. But you must understand, it's very difficult for Ian."

Vanessa could scarcely grasp the significance of what Freda was saying and implying. She felt too utterly bewildered.

"What's—difficult for Ian?" she asked breathlessly,

her voice barely above a whisper. Then, as she received an admonishing look from Freda, "I'm sorry, you said no more questions. But, Freda, I must know—please!"

But Freda shook her head. "My dear, you'll just have to be patient. I only fear one thing—that whatever Ian's feelings are, he might never ask you to marry him."

Vanessa would not have been able to describe her feelings at that moment. Fear, elation and despair screwed themselves into a tight, painful knot inside her.

"But—but why? Why not? What makes you say such a thing?"

But a very determined look settled on Freda's face. "Sorry, I mustn't say any more. I've said more than enough already."

"You—don't think I've been silly or lacking in pride to come and talk to you like this?"

"Good heavens, no. I only hope things will work out—for both of you. I certainly wouldn't be in too much of a hurry to leave, if I were you. How long is it now since you came, by the way? Or rather, since your aunt died?"

Vanessa sighed. She felt drained and could not even think straight. How long it had been since she had left home, or since she had been the owner of Puck's Hill seemed entirely irrelevant and unimportant.

"It must be nearly six months, I suppose."

"I think it is. In which case you might have soon come into the other money your aunt left for you. Have you ever wondered what the conditions might be?"

Vanessa shook her head. "I've no idea. Aunt Maud was a little unpredictable at times."

"Maybe she wanted to see how you'd make out—what you'd do with Puck's Hill. The lawyer did say it was a great deal of money, didn't he? And if the condition *was* anything to do with Puck's Hill—well, there'd be no doubt that you'd qualify. You've done absolute wonders there."

"Ian suggested that it might be a condition that I shouldn't marry."

"Did he? And what did you say to that?"

"What would any girl in her right mind say? Love means a good deal more than money."

Freda's look softened. "Well, I think you have plenty to think over during the next week or so, anyway. Once you can see Ian's point of view, it might be up to you to take the initiative. And don't ask me to explain that," she added quickly. "Just think about it all."

"Think about it all? My mind boggles. I only hope I come up with the right answers."

They had talked longer than either of them realized, so that when they heard Ian's key in the lock they were both startled.

"Heavens, I shouldn't be here," Vanessa said, jumping to her feet. "I meant to be gone before he came back."

"Calm down. It's probably for the best," Freda told her. "But he's certainly home sooner than I expected."

Vanessa met him in the hall. Her heart contracted painfully. She thought how tired and strained he looked.

"Hello, Vanessa," he said. "I thought that was your car outside."

"I'm just going, actually," she told him.

"You don't have to on my account," he said stiffly. "I shall probably go directly upstairs anyway."

With difficulty Vanessa let hurt feelings bounce straight off her.

She reiterated her intention of leaving. "Won't you—see me to my car, Ian?" she found herself saying. "There are one or two things I want to say to you."

He eyed her suspiciously. "What sort of things?"

"Please, Ian."

Freda looked from one to the other uncertainly. Then she said quickly, "I'll put some coffee on, Ian, and make some sandwiches."

She disappeared hurriedly into the kitchen. Silently Vanessa blessed her. She was determined now to use and to take advantage of every possible opportunity to fight for her love. She called goodnight to Freda, then moved toward the door. Ian had little option but to follow her. Outside, he opened her car door and held it open as if very anxious to be rid of her. But for the talk she had had with Freda, Vanessa's pride would have prevailed and her courage wavered. Now, she smiled up at him.

"It's nice to see you again, Ian. I've—missed you dropping in to see me and—sort of bullying me."

He frowned and did not speak for a minute, then he said, "Are you trying to flirt with me, Vanessa?"

She met his gaze. The urge to put her arms around his neck was strong.

"No, Ian, I'm not," she answered. "I'm serious. I've come to my senses at last."

Taking a chance, she reached one hand up to his shoulder and raised her face to his.

His expression alerted. He gripped her arms fiercely. "Vanessa, what are you talking about? What are you trying to say?"

But suddenly the whole sky was lit with a red glow. Startled, they looked in the direction from which it came. Vanessa's eyes dilated as a great tongue of flame seemed to rise from the trees.

"Ian— It's Puck's Hill! It's on fire—and Nancy's in there alone!"

CHAPTER NINE

Without thinking, Vanessa started running in the direction of the boundary fence; her one thought to free Nancy quickly.

"Vanessa—Vanessa, not that way!"

Ian caught her. He grasped hold of her and made her stop.

"Vanessa, it's quicker by car, it really is. I'll get to her. You go inside and call the fire department. They can't have been sent for yet, or we'd have heard the siren."

He gave her a push in the direction of the house, then ran toward his car. Distressed as she was, she realized the truth of what he had said. It *was* quicker by car. As she rushed into the house, she heard Ian's car start up with a roar.

"Freda—"

"What on earth—"

"Freda, quick, let me use the phone. Puck's Hill is on fire!"

She dialled 999 and gave the address in a shaking voice, then clamped the receiver down again.

"Was that Ian's car I heard going down the drive?" queried Freda.

Vanessa nodded and ran to the door. Freda followed her. Together they drove as quickly as possible to the house. As the car turned into the drive the fire siren wailed out on the night air like a monster suddenly released. The next moment the clang of the engine could be heard.

As soon as Vanessa was out of the car she rushed to the front door, but was driven back as the thick smoke billowed out.

Freda ran after her and took hold of her arm. "Vanessa, don't go in. Ian must be there. He'll get Nancy out."

"But—but how?— Unless he got in at the back?"

She ran around to the back door, but that was locked. Through the window she could see fire licking up the legs of the tables and chairs. Vanessa picked up a brick to break open a window and get in that way, but Freda stopped her.

"If you introduce more air, you'll make it worse. The only thing to do is wait for the fire department. They'll know the right thing to do."

As Freda spoke the urgent clanging became louder and louder. In a matter of minutes the fire engine rushed up the drive. But Vanessa's fears were for Ian and Nancy. What was keeping them? Had they been overcome by the heat and smoke? Instinctively, she moved toward the house again, but Freda caught hold of her.

"Vanessa, you mustn't. I know how you feel—Ian is my brother, but he'll be all right, I—I'm sure."

But Vanessa felt her panic rising. To go in after him and Nancy was an urge too strong to be fought down. She shook herself free of Freda's restraining hand and rushed to the door. Again she was choked back by the volume of smoke and the fierce heat, but she braced herself and, head down, rushed blindly into the hall. Flames licked the stairs and banister. It would be impossible to get either up or down. Vanessa made an effort to call Ian's name, but as she opened her mouth and inhaled, she was choked by the thick, billowing smoke. She coughed violently and tears streamed from her eyes. Her senses swam. A feeling of failure hit her forcibly. She made for the stairs again and tried to shout, *Ian—Ian—*

Now her tears were real and not simply caused by the

smoke. She had failed. Ian was somewhere in the burning house, someone was holding her back, trying to stop her from reaching him.

"Ian—Ian—"

Then by some miracle she was in Ian's arms. He was talking to her in a low, urgent, almost incoherent voice. She thought he called her "darling", but couldn't be sure. There was so much noise all around and other voices intruding. Cold night air struck her face. She opened her eyes to find Ian's face within inches of her own.

"Vanessa! Vanessa, are you all right?" he queried anxiously.

She was so relieved to see him, she broke into a sob, repeating his name as she had in what she knew now was a dream of unconsciousness. Still in a half-dream, half-awake state her arms went around his neck.

"Ian! Oh, darling, I'm so glad you're safe!"

She sensed rather than felt him stiffen. Not until she felt her feet touch the ground did she realize that she had been held in his arms. Her brain rapidly clearing, she rubbed her eyes and looked about her.

"Nancy! Where's Nancy? Is she all right?"

Ian took her arm. "Yes, she's all right. Freda is with her in the station wagon. We escaped through a bedroom window in the time-honored fashion of knotting sheets together. I can understand your anxiety, but it was foolish of you to go inside. The best thing you can do now is to come back to our place; both you and Nancy, and stay the night. Freda will go with you. I'll stay here until the fire's out. The firemen will soon have it under control, I think. There's damage, of course, particularly to the stairs and in the kitchen, but the place won't be entirely burned out."

He led her to the station wagon gently, but in a way which clearly expected no argument. Vanessa looked back at the house, reluctant to leave; Ian opened the door on the passenger side and pushed her firmly onto the seat, picking up her legs and planting them inside after her. Then he slammed the door. Nancy was on the rear seat. Freda was already at the wheel. Before Vanessa could begin to argue she had started the engine and was driving away.

Vanessa sighed, realizing the futility of protesting, and admitting to herself that Ian was right as usual.

"Don't worry, Vanessa," Freda said, guessing some of her thoughts. "Ian will see to everything. You can rely on him."

"Yes, I know." Vanessa turned to Nancy and asked if she were all right. Mercifully, she was.

"It was just that I couldn't get down the stairs," she said. "I simply had to pray that sooner or later somebody would see the fire and call the fire department. I knew you weren't far away."

"You'd gone to bed then, when it started?"

"Yes, I read a bit and then fell asleep. I heard a noise and went onto the landing—but already flames were leaping upstairs and the whole place was filled with smoke. I can't think how it started. Everything was all right when I went upstairs."

"What about the heaters? Were they on high? Although, even if they were, I can't see—"

But Nancy said she had turned them both low. It was a mystery and was likely to remain so unless the firemen had any explanations or theory to propose.

When they arrived at the Lodge, Freda insisted on both Vanessa and Nancy going straight upstairs to bed while she made hot drinks for them.

"You must both be in a state of shock, even though you might not realize it," she said. "When Ian comes back I'll let you know how things are, if you're still awake."

Vanessa did not argue. After Nancy, she had a bath to remove the smell of smoke. As she slipped into bed Freda reported from her own bedroom window that the flames from Puck's Hill had died down completely.

But Vanessa had more to keep her awake than the fire. Thoughts of Ian, her conversation with Freda, and everything she had said about Ian occupied her mind. Most of all, his murmured "darling" when he thought she was unconscious. Had she been dreaming or not? Freda had said that Ian would never ask her to marry him. Was it possible, was it remotely probable that Ian loved her, but the question of her inheritance was holding him back? She told herself that this was presuming a terrible lot. Suppose she were wrong? She tried to think back, to search her mind for any signs that Ian might feel the same about her as she did about him. They were only too rare. With few exceptions all she had to go on were Freda's hints. But she decided that whatever the outcome she must make some effort to find out the truth of his regard, or lack of it for her, by subtle or direct means. Her own pride was a matter of no importance now. And Ian's? Perhaps she should at least give him the opportunity of telling her how he felt first.

She was thinking about what she should say to him when she heard his car. A few minutes later, voices were downstairs, his own and Freda's. Vanessa got out of bed quickly and put on a dressing gown she found behind the door. Ian and Freda were talking in the hall and looked up as she appeared.

"It's all right, Vanessa," Ian told her. "It's out now. The firemen made sure of that. And I've locked the doors and windows."

She walked slowly down the stairs. "Thanks for what you did, Ian. Is there much damage?"

"It could have been worse. But I would go back to bed, if I were you. We can talk about it in the morning. I'll go over there with you first thing."

She had reached the bottom stair and stood with her hand on the curved banister rail.

"I'm sorry if I made extra trouble for you by rushing inside," she told him. "I was so worried—not only about Nancy, but about you."

As she spoke she felt her cheeks coloring and her heartbeat quicken, but she stood her ground and waited for his reaction.

He gave her an unsmiling glance. "You—gave us all some anxious moments," he said, "but it's over now. I hope nothing like that ever happens again. Goodnight, Vanessa."

Freda asked her if she'd like another drink, and Ian took the opportunity of disappearing into the kitchen. But with a heavy heart Vanessa went back to bed. It was not going to be easy to talk to Ian.

The house had been quiet for a very long time before she finally drifted off to sleep. As a consequence she slept late. When she went down to breakfast he had already eaten and was outside working. Nancy was having her breakfast in bed.

"She doesn't seem any the worse," Freda said. "What about you?"

Vanessa said she was fine and asked about Ian. Freda smiled.

"He put his coat over his head when he dashed up the stairs to Nancy—and later when he went in after you. So he hasn't suffered any damage. Between ourselves," she added, "he was pretty frantic when he knew you were inside."

"Really?" asked Vanessa eagerly. "It's so difficult to know what Ian is thinking."

"That's because he's doing his best to hide his feelings. You'll have to be very persistent, Vanessa," Freda told her quietly.

After breakfast Ian left his work and drove Vanessa to Puck's Hill. She thought he must be very adept indeed at hiding his feelings. It was difficult to believe that he had been remotely "frantic" for her safety the previous night.

After a brief inquiry as to how she was feeling after her ordeal, he was grim-faced and distant.

Vanessa was appalled at the damage to the staircase. The treads of the stairway were charred, the walls blackened, the banister burnt almost through.

"I'm afraid it won't be safe for you to go upstairs, Vanessa," Ian said. "You'll have to stay with us for the time being. Nancy too, of course."

To Vanessa, the way he put it made her feel she was being a nuisance. Some of her old pride asserted itself.

"There's no 'have to' about it, Ian," she answered. "I can stay somewhere in the village—the Stag, perhaps. Or maybe go home."

"Home?" he echoed sharply. "But what about your business—and Nancy?"

"I can sell the stock and put an end to the business, or maybe get a manager in. And Nancy can have someone to live with her. Don't worry about the house. I shall never sell Puck's Hill," she added swiftly.

He frowned. "You talk as if you intend leaving Barn Hill for good. Hadn't you better wait until you hear from Mr. Oliver, the lawyer?"

There was not the slightest bit of regret in his voice that she might be leaving. She almost groaned aloud. She had not intended saying the kind of things to him that she had. An eternity seemed to pass in which Ian was being drawn farther and farther away from her until he was no more than a distant speck.

"Ian—" she said with swift, sharp urgency.

"Yes?" He looked at her oddly. "Is something wrong?"

She brought herself swiftly from her fantasy. But it was a fantasy which had served as a warning. If she did not take care, she would certainly lose Ian because of her own stupid pride.

"No, no, there's nothing wrong. I—shall be glad to stay with you and Freda for a little while, thank you, if you're sure I won't be an inconvenience. But I'd like to talk to you some time, Ian."

"What about?"

"Not now. Let's go and look at the kitchen."

Here the whole place was black—walls, ceiling, floor, the stove and sink unit. The table was burnt and charred; the curtains completely destroyed. Vanessa sniffed.

"Ian, I can smell paraffin."

He nodded. "So could the firemen last night. And the two heating units were turned up as high as they could be."

"Nancy says she turned them low; that everything was all right when she went to bed."

"In any case—and I've been on the phone to Geoff—no matter how high the units had been they wouldn't have caused fire to break out. And there's no smell of paraffin ever with them."

It was true. "Then how on earth could it have happened?" puzzled Vanessa.

"That's probably what the police will find out."

"The police?"

"Oh yes. They automatically investigate the cause of fires. If a cause can't be found, then arson is suspected—and that's a very serious matter."

"Arson?" Vanessa echoed again. "But who on earth—"

As she spoke there came a knock at the front door. Vanessa opened it to a police sergeant. He asked questions and took a good look around, then asked more questions.

"Who knew you'd had these heating units put in besides yourselves—and, of course, the heating engineer?" he asked.

"I don't know. Very few people, I think," she answered. "Mr. Hamilton and his sister, of course, and—yes, Miles Kendal."

"Miles Kendal, the property developer?" the sergeant asked sharply.

"Why, yes, but—"

"Any of these people might have to be questioned," he said. "But first of all, I must speak to Miss Gould. I understand she was in the house alone at the time."

The whole thing was now emerging as something quite alarming. Vanessa did not like it one bit. If only Nancy had left some clothes airing or something simple like that! But Vanessa knew that she hadn't, nor would she ever. She was far too sensible and conscientious.

Vanessa opened her "store". Ian and the police sergeant went to the Lodge; the sergeant to interview Nancy. Later, Nancy joined her at Puck's Hill and did her best to clean up the stove and sink. The kitchen would need redecorating completely, and the furniture replacing with new. Nancy wanted to pay for these herself, but Vanessa would not hear of it. At present she could not see how she was going to be able to afford either a new kitchen or staircase which would include, also, hall and landing.

The whole affair was depressing beyond measure, particularly as the police decided that the fire was not an accident, but a result of arson. Someone was suspected of forcing open the lock of the front door by means of a picklock, and throwing paraffin over the stair carpet, banister, hall carpet and curtains—the same in the kitchen. Whoever it was had then turned up the heating units to make it appear like an accident—not knowing this would be impossible. Then they left open the front door and set a match to the paraffin. The police also interviewed Joe, the two men who had helped with the weed clearance, and Miles. The greatest suspect was Miles, but he denied being near the house on the night of the fire, as did the other men interviewed.

"I'd rather it were not proved," Vanessa said to Ian that evening. "It's too horrible to think about."

She knew that Ian and Freda, as well as Nancy, thought Miles both capable and guilty. He so badly wanted to buy Puck's Hill and thought to force Vanessa's hand. Vanessa thought it likely too, but she did not want to think about it. Perhaps he hadn't meant to harm Nancy, only to scare her. He must have seen her go out and waited for Nancy's light to go on upstairs. But the important thing to Vanessa was finding out how she stood in Ian's eyes. That evening when Nancy had retired and Freda was upstairs in her room, Vanessa tried to discuss things with him.

"Ian, can we have our little talk now?" she began.

"Of course. What is it?"

She quailed at the cool politeness of his voice, but went on, "First, I want to apologize for all the times when I've seemed—difficult. I'm—not usually so."

His expression was guarded. "There isn't the slightest need for you to apologize about anything, Vanessa. We all have periods when we're not quite at our best, myself included."

"But you were being so kind and helpful. You must have thought me terribly ungrateful."

"Not in the least," he answered.

Vanessa almost despaired. This was getting her absolutely nowhere. She tried another tack.

"Ian, would you be sorry if I left the Barn Hill for good?"

She watched him start, then freeze. "You must do just what you think best, Vanessa. I can only repeat what I said to you this morning. Wait until you've heard from Mr. Oliver."

"Yes, I'll do that," she answered quietly. "But whether I go or stay depends entirely upon you."

He frowned and glanced at her swiftly. "What do you mean? Why does it depend on me?"

"I want to know what you think of me, Ian."

At this he rose swiftly to his feet and stood on the hearth, his back turned toward her.

"Why should you want to know that? And what possible difference can it make?"

"All the difference in the world," she answered softly. She stood up and put her hand on his shoulder. "You see, I—think a very great deal of you."

He swung around and stared at her with wide eyes, his skin stretched taut across his jawbone.

"Vanessa, don't say things like that!"

"But I must. And I must know how it is with you. I—feel about you, Ian, as I've never felt about any man before."

He backed away from her. "Please, Vanessa, don't say any more, I beg of you. It's impossible. I can't. You don't know what you're saying or what you're asking. The best thing you can do is to go back home and forget all about me."

He left, and Vanessa sank into a chair feeling sick at heart. If he'd loved her he would have told her so. It would have been better if she had said nothing. She went out into the hall and heard his footsteps on the front veranda, then the crunch of his feet on the gravel outside. Evidently he was going for a walk through his grounds.

Vanessa went out too. She couldn't possibly stay at the Lodge now. She got in her car and drove back to Puck's Hill. She would sleep on the sofa if the stairs really proved unsafe. When she arrived she telephoned from her study—a room the fire had not reached to tell Freda where she was. Freda protested and argued, but Vanessa was firm. Ian knew how she felt about him now. If he loved her he would seek her out.

She slept little that night, and it was not due in the least to any discomfort of the sofa. She had not bothered to test the stairs, after all. She had felt too utterly miserable.

In the morning a letter was delivered from the lawyer asking her to call and see him in his office in a few days time. She would stay at Puck's Hill until then, she decided, then leave Nancy to do what she liked with the house. She would not sell it or give it away. She would "loan" it to Nancy.

Both Freda and Nancy came to see her to try to persuade her to go back to the Lodge, but when Nancy saw Vanessa was adamant, she insisted on returning too. They discovered that by treading the stairs carefully along the side by the wall, it was possible to go up. Nancy refused to discuss the future at all until Vanessa had seen the lawyer. In vain Vanessa told her that it would make no difference. She still intended to go away.

She did not see Ian at all, but Freda called each day. Though Vanessa felt as though her heart would break, she was beyond tears. All she felt was a coldness, and in her heart a dull ache.

Without much interest she drove into town to the lawyer's office.

"Ah, Miss Woodrow." Mr. Oliver shook hands with her and invited her to sit down. "The six-month period your aunt wanted to pass before you received your inheritance is up today. I've had a good talk with my fellow trustee. We have decided that you have indeed fulfilled all the conditions."

"But what were the conditions? And how can you possibly know whether I've fulfilled them or not? You haven't seen me since the day I came into your office six months ago."

"Ah, but I know all about what you've been doing," he told her mysteriously. "But before we go any further, I think you should meet my fellow trustee. He's in another office. He'll tell you all about it. This way, if you don't mind.

He led her into the corridor and opened a door for her. "There you are, Miss Woodrow."

He allowed her to precede him, or so she thought, but instead he closed the door after her. She was left alone with a man who stood with his back to her, looking out of the window. Vanessa's heart leaped violently.

"Ian!"

He turned. "Yes, I'm the other trustee, Vanessa," he said in answer to the unspoken question in her eyes. "And now perhaps you will understand how impossible it is for me to—take you up on what you were saying the other evening."

She stared at him, trying to fit the pieces of the jigsaw together in her mind, but it was difficult all at once.

"No, I don't think I quite understand," she answered.

He sighed. "It's simple enough. Your aunt has left you a great deal of money and, of course, as a trustee I was well aware how much it was. I also knew the conditions. They were: that you would do something worthwhile with Puck's Hill, that you would not use chemical weed-killer to clear the giant hogweed, and altogether prove yourself worthy of your inheritance. Now do you see?"

"I see your difficulty. How much money is it exactly?"

"Twenty thousand pounds all told."

Vanessa gasped. "Good heavens! I *am* beginning to see."

"I thought you might. But of course, it wasn't much of a gamble on your aunt's part. She knew you well enough. And so there you are. You're a very rich woman, Vanessa. I couldn't possibly take advantage of the fact."

"I'm not asking you to." Vanessa moved toward him. Now she knew what Freda had meant when she said Ian would never ask her to marry him. "All I'm asking is that you answer me truthfully. Do you care for me, Ian? At all?"

He took a deep breath. "Of course I care for you," he shot out. "I would have thought it only too obvious."

"You mean you love me?" she persisted.

He closed his eyes momentarily, then opened them and looked past her.

"Yes, but I'm not going to ask you to marry me."

"Then I'm asking *you*."

"No, Vanessa! Don't you see?"

"No, I don't. But what I do see is a very selfish man. Don't you care that if I can't marry you I shall be the unhappiest woman alive? That I shall remain unhappy for the rest of my life? Is that what you want? Is it, Ian?"

He groaned. "Vanessa, don't. You'll forget me in time, just as I—" He broke off, lines of pains etched deeply across his face.

"Just as you will forget me? Is that what you were going to say? Will you forget me, Ian, 'in time'?"

The next moment she was crushed in his arms, his lips hard on hers.

"Vanessa, forgive me. I love you so much it hurts. I would never forget you, ever. Not for as long as I lived."

Tears misted her eyes. "I'll give the money away if you like, all of it," she murmured, her whole being on fire with the love she had for him.

"Do what you like with it. Do what you like, darling Vanessa, only marry me—please, for I know I simply couldn't live without you."

Locked in his arms, his lips on hers, Vanessa caught a sudden vision of Aunt Maud's face, puckish and mischievous.

"To my dear niece, Ian Hamilton—to have and to hold—"

And suddenly she knew that this was what her aunt had intended from the very beginning.